# Praise for Debra Clopton and her novels

"Debra Clopton's *The Trouble with Lacy Brown* superbly combines humor, romance and action."
—*RT Book Reviews*

"*And Baby Makes Five* is a hilarious story about finding love."
—*RT Book Reviews*

"Debra Clopton writes a terrific story with a great mix of humor and tenderness."
—*RT Book Reviews* on *Dream a Little Dream*

"A wonderfully fast-moving story with many delightfully familiar characters."
—*RT Book Reviews* on *His Cowgirl Bride*

# DEBRA CLOPTON

## The Trouble with Lacy Brown

## And Baby Makes Five

Steeple
Hill®

Published by Steeple Hill Books™

STEEPLE HILL BOOKS

**Steeple Hill®**

Recycling programs
for this product may
not exist in your area.

ISBN-13: 978-0-373-65144-3

THE TROUBLE WITH LACY BROWN AND
AND BABY MAKES FIVE

THE TROUBLE WITH LACY BROWN
Copyright © 2005 by Debra Clopton

AND BABY MAKES FIVE
Copyright © 2006 by Debra Clopton

www.SteepleHill.com

**Printed in U.S.A.**

# CONTENTS

THE TROUBLE WITH LACY BROWN     7

AND BABY MAKES FIVE     233

## Books by Debra Clopton

Love Inspired

*The Trouble with
  Lacy Brown
*And Baby Makes Five
*No Place Like Home
*Dream a Little Dream
*Meeting Her Match
*Operation:
  Married by Christmas
*Next Door Daddy
*Her Baby Dreams

*The Cowboy Takes a Bride
*Texas Ranger Dad
*Small-Town Brides
  "A Mule Hollow Match"
*His Cowgirl Bride
**Her Forever Cowboy
**Cowboy For Keeps
Yukon Cowboy
**Yuletide Cowboy

*Mule Hollow
**Men of Mule Hollow

## *DEBRA CLOPTON*

was a 2004 Golden Heart finalist in the inspirational category, a 2006 Inspirational Readers' Choice Award winner, a 2007 Golden Quill award winner and a finalist for the 2007 American Christian Fiction Writers Book of the Year Award. She praises the Lord each time someone votes for one of her books, and takes it as an affirmation that she is exactly where God wants her to be.

Debra is a hopeless romantic and loves to create stories with lively heroines and the strong heroes who fall in love with them. But most important, she loves showing her characters living their faith, seeking God's will in their lives one day at a time. Her goal is to give her readers an entertaining story that will make them smile, hopefully laugh and always feel God's goodness as they read her books. She has found the perfect home for her stories, writing for the Love Inspired line, and still has to pinch herself just to see if she really is awake and living her dream.

When she isn't writing, she enjoys taking road trips, reading and spending time with her two sons, Chase and Kris. She loves hearing from readers and can be reached through her website, www.debraclopton.com, or by mail at P.O. Box 1125, Madisonville, Texas 77864.

# THE TROUBLE WITH LACY BROWN

Now the end of the commandment is charity
out of a pure heart, and of a good conscience,
and of faith unfeigned.
—*1 Timothy* 1:5

This book is dedicated with all my love to my husband, Wayne, my hero, my best friend, the love of my life, the father of our sons, Chase and Kris. Until I see you again…I'll be missing you.
1955–2003
You are always and forever in my heart and on my mind.

# Prologue

Perched on the door of her topless pink Caddy, Lacy Brown surveyed the sleepy town she'd driven all night and five hundred miles to wake up.

At six in the morning the town looked comatose. It was a pitiful sight, an odd assortment of brick and clapboard buildings staggered down both sides of the deserted street. The place had seen better days. At least Lacy hoped it had; it didn't look as though things could get much worse.

All the buildings were in desperate need of paint. The sidewalks were made from planks, *real planks,* half of which were curled up on the edges or missing. Every aspect of the town screamed for help, but the vacant windows said the most. Smeared with years of grime, they greeted Lacy like eyes lost in absolute despair.

From the pocket of her worn jeans she dug the crumpled newspaper clipping that had changed her life.

"Small Texas town of Mule Hollow—where the cowboys grow tall but the women aren't at all; WIVES NEEDED…."

Lacy had always been drawn to anyone in distress. And goodness, this was an entire town sending out an S.O.S.

So here she was at the break of dawn staring down Mule Hollow's Main Street.

Its appearance tugged at her heart. It was as if the town had seen one too many people drive down this road and keep right on going.

She understood that feeling all too well, but pushing the thought away, she concentrated on her mission. She closed her eyes as the soft whisper of a morning breeze touched her skin and she felt…a heartbeat?

A spark.

That was it! Her eyelids lifted to the warm touch of dawn peeking over the rooftops.

She understood.

Mule Hollow was holding its breath.

Wishing.

Waiting for someone to come along and pump life back into its tired old buildings.

Peace flowed over her.

She'd been right in coming, right in listening to the Lord's call.

*Oh, Father, thank You for leading me here. Thank You, thank You, thank You.*

# Chapter One

"Rise and shine, Sheri, we made it to Mule Hollow."
Lacy Brown leaned over and slapped the pair of pointed,
high-heeled boots propped on the dusty dashboard of
her classic pink Caddy.

The rumpled heap that was her friend and partner
opened one eye. "No, not now," she grumbled. "I just
started dreaming about handsome cowboys fighting over
me."

"Why dream?" Lacy practically sang with enthusiasm. "Open your eyes and look around."

With her hair resembling Rod Stewart's on a bad hair
day, Sheri plopped her feet to the floorboard one at a
time, pushed up to a sitting position and gaped at Mule
Hollow. "You're joking. *Right?*"

"Isn't it wonderful?" Lacy said, flinging her arms
open wide. From her perch on the car's door she felt on
top of the world.

"Wonderful. Lace, are we looking at the same view?
*Look at this place.*"

"No, no, no, don't go all negative on me, Sheri. Look again. Really look." Overflowing with excitement, Lacy jumped to her feet on the Caddy's seat. "Picture all these sad, colorless buildings painted a different shade of the rainbow. Like…like one of those weird ski villages in Colorado—only brighter." She grasped Sheri by the shoulders and met her eye-to-eye. "We prayed about opening our own business. And you know when I read that classified ad, God gave me a vision. I'm telling you, girlfriend, whoever placed that ad is watching the same movie I'm watching. If we open it, they'll come. I know it. I feel it in my heart."

"Girlfriend—" Sheri took a deep breath "—this is no cornfield and you are *not* Kevin Costner."

Lacy dropped back onto the edge of the door. "Nope, I'm not Kevie-baby, but when single women read about all these lonesome, long-legged cowboys pinning away for true love—they're coming. All kinds of man-hunters from all walks of life. Who knows, there may be hundreds."

Sheri rolled her eyes, but grinned.

That's all the encouragement Lacy needed to rattle on. "No joke. Some gals will come to marry, some to play. Either way, when the courtin' starts, where is the first place those gals are gonna head?"

Sheri bit her lip to hide her smile, and then gave in. "Straight to *Heavenly Inspirations,*" she drawled, "Where love is in the air *and* the hair!"

"Yup, yup, yup, that's what I'm saying," Lacy chirped. "With me styling their hair and you sculpting their nails, not only are we going to be independent, self-supporting businesswomen, we are going to get the opportunity to tell each and every one of those ladies what the Lord has done for us." Lacy's eyes twinkled. "There absolutely couldn't be anything better than that!"

Sheri started chuckling and dramatically slapped a hand to her chest. "Okay, Moses, I give up. God told you to come here and far be it from me to get in *His* way. We both know you're the one with the direct line to His office, I'm just along for the ride." She paused rubbed her eyes and stretched her arms heavenward. "But, friend of mine—" she yawned "—we have to take a time-out now and find coffee, I'm dying here."

Sheri was right, it had been a long five-hundred-mile drive through the night. Lacy slid behind the steering wheel, then rammed the gearshift into drive, all in one swift motion. "Coffee it is. I have to say, you do look as though you could use a few cups." She had to dodge a pillow as it was slammed into her shoulder.

Swinging the pink Caddy to the right she aimed it toward a building she'd spied at the end of the street, where a couple of beat-up pickup trucks were parked in front. "The real estate agent said there was a diner of sorts on Main Street. Mmm-hmm, this is it," she mused, swerving into an angled parking space in front of the building. A worn sign proclaimed Sam's Pharmaceuticals And Diner. To the side some small print had been added. Eat At Your Own Peril 6 a.m.-8 p.m.

Lacy stomped hard on the brakes. While her buddy peeled herself off the dashboard, Lacy scrambled over the closed door Dukes of Hazzard-style to survey the dilapidated building up close. She paused when a striped cat hissed at her from its hiding place beneath the plank sidewalk. "What's up, little friend?" Lacy asked, bending down to get a better look at the frightened creature. Obviously not tamed, it backed farther away into the shadows as it continued to emit unearthly noises. "I hope you're not the welcoming committee," she chuckled softly.

From the car, Sheri moaned, "It should be a sin to be so perky. Watching you, no one would believe we drove all night to get here."

Lacy stood and turned toward her friend. "I'm too excited to be tired. Don't you feel it?" She closed her eyes again. The tugging at her heart was stronger now. She felt a whisper of hope. Opening her eyes, she looked straight at Sheri. "This is our future. Our destiny."

Sheri pulled on the door latch. "Only you could read a little ad about a podunk town needing would-be-wives and see your future. *And* hear God's call at the same time."

"*Our* future." Lacy stuck her hand on her hip. "You have a stake in this enterprise also."

"Oh, yeah, my life savings," Sheri retorted. "All three hundred and thirty-four cents' worth."

Ignoring Sheri's teasing, Lacy turned, stepped up on the plank sidewalk and swished across to the weathered building. Lovingly she ran a hand over the rough wood. "You know you're just as excited about bringing this town to life as I am." Ignoring Sheri's complaints was habit. Early on in their lives, Sheri had been the straggler, so shy she could hardly look a person in the eyes. That fact had compelled them into friendship as elementary school kids. Lacy had taken it upon herself to pull Sheri off the sidelines, straight into the action. Because of that, Sheri's confidence had grown over the years and with it her ability to banter.

Tracing a finger along the wood Lacy lifted an eyebrow at her friend, "You know you can't wait to paint this dull, dry heap of wood."

"If this place only knew what you have in store for it, they'd roll up the sidewalks and lock the doors." Shaking her head Sheri strode to the door of Sam's. "I'm getting coffee. *Now.* Before you get us thrown out of town and I have to wait another couple of hours for the next chance."

Lacy watched her not-so-shy-anymore friend stride through the diner's heavy swinging door. Where had that timid little girl gone? Lacy took all the blame for having rubbed off on Sheri, but at least her friend had no fear of new places or new faces. And that was a good thing. With one last glance about, Lacy followed Sheri into the diner. It was definitely coffee time.

Inside the diner, the musty scent of age mingled with smells of pine floors, gumballs from children long grown and strong, fragrant coffee.

"Coffee," Sheri groaned to the older man behind the carved, wooden counter.

He reminded Lacy of a raisin. Small, slightly plump and wrinkled all over, he was so cute she had to fight the impulse to pinch him. Clearly that wouldn't be the right way to start a new relationship. She slid into the booth instead and held up two fingers. "Make that two, please."

She tugged her orange T-shirt from her skin and fanned herself. Riding five hundred miles with the top down made a body slightly sticky and smelly, too. But she loved her convertible and wouldn't take a new car for anything. Clean air blowing through her hair. That was the good life. Who cared about a few bugs here and there, in her teeth, in the eye…?

Tapping her fingers on the table she nodded at the two ancient men hunched over a checkerboard in the corner by the window. So *they* were what early birds looked like.

"Hi," she called.

They nodded in acknowledgment and continued their game of checkers unmoved as Lacy surveyed the room. A jukebox in the corner snagged her attention, drawing her to investigate. Like everything else in the café, it was straight out of a decade before any she'd lived in. The box was covered with bright lights and filled with little records. It was irresistible.

Digging a nickel from her pocket she plopped it into the slot, selected her favorite, "Blue Suede Shoes," then strolled back to her table.

*Thank You, Lord. Everything is perfect.*

The explosive strains of Jerry Lee Lewis singing "Great Balls of Fire" blasted from the jukebox.

"Rattle my brain—Baabaaabie!" Sheri squealed along with the song. "Where's Elvis?"

Lacy shrugged, amazed at how well her friend knew her, even more amazed at how far Sheri's shyness had come since they were kids. "Beats me, that box must have a mind of its own."

"Ain't that the truth," Little Raisin Man said, coming around the counter to set two mugs of steaming coffee on their table. "That there's the only song that thang'll play." He shook his balding head, "I liked the song once, a long, *long* time ago. What can I get you gals to eat?"

Lacy stilled the rat-a-tat-tat of her hot pink fingernails on the scarred pine tabletop. "Nothing for me, but thank you." Offering her hand in greeting, she smiled up at the darling man. "I'm Lacy Brown, and this is Sheri Marsh."

He wiped his hands on his white apron and shook Lacy's hand violently. "Sam's the name. What brings you gals to Mule Hollow?"

"Business. I'm opening the new hair salon."

Sam's expression didn't waver a smidge as his gaze slid to Sheri, and her brunette bird's nest, then volleyed back to rest once more on Lacy.

Glancing at her reflection in the mirror behind the counter, Lacy nearly fell off her chair. Her whipped cream-colored curls licked from beneath her ball cap like curdled milk on a hot day.

Sam, a real trooper, never blinked. "Figures," he said dryly, as if hair like theirs were a common occurrence. "The real estate agent told Adela you'd be here next week."

"I couldn't wait," Lacy explained, tapping her nails again. "Patience is not one of my strong points."

"Craziest thing I ever heard, this plan of the gals. You're the first, you know."

"We figured it," Sheri and Lacy said in unison.

"At least we hoped we were the first," added Lacy.

"By my calculations you might be the only. The women folk put out the ad-verd-is-ment. Not us." He sighed and shook his head as if that told the story in a nutshell.

It was obvious the only one in on this plan other than them was God. Lacy glanced at the checker players, who had abandoned their game to listen intently to their conversation. "By chance, would any of you nice gentlemen know which building out there is mine?"

Sam harrumphed. "Ain't been a building rented out in this town for pert near ten years. Everybody knows your building. It's here on Main Street down across from Pete's Feed-and-Seed. He'd be opening 'bout now. Can't miss it. Only other buildin' with cars out front."

Lacy stood. "Can you catch me later, Sheri? I have to see it."

"Sure, go ahead, check out your destiny. I'm going to sit right here, have another coffee and eat this fine man out of business." Sheri stretched and patted her stomach while grinning at Sam.

"Get ready, Sam, she's not kidding." Already Lacy was pushing through the swinging door, waving goodbye over her shoulder.

Standing on the sidewalk, she tugged the brim of her ball cap lower to shield her eyes against the rising sun's glare. It sat higher in the sky now, and with it a few more cars moved about. Down the street, she spotted a gas station that still boasted a red flying horse sign, clearly ancient. That sign was probably worth a pretty penny at a flea market or auction. But the real jewel of the town could be seen a bit farther down at the end of Main Street—a majestically rambling old house replete with towers, lightning rods and loads of promise. Now that would be worth some exploration, she thought. Then, tugging once more at the bib of her cap, she strode to her Caddy and vaulted over the convertible's door.

The familiar exhilaration filled her when she turned the key and the powerful old engine roared to life. That sound never ceased to thrill her with joy. This morning she was high on life and feeling great. She was pressing the gas pedal when the hissing started—right there between her feet! One minute she had everything under control and then *whamo,* she had a frantic cat clinging to her leg, claws buried in her flesh. Lacy screamed in pain, but managed to stomp the brake, jerking the car to a halt just as the crazy cat sprang at her with teeth bared and claws out!

Clint Matlock needed a shower, a couple of cups of Sam's thick coffee and a noose. It had been another sleepless night, trying to catch a bunch of thieving rustlers. He was mad enough to follow in his great-great-granddaddy's footsteps—hangin' 'em first and asking questions later.

Heading toward Sam's Diner he turned his Jeep onto Main Street and was surprised to see a strange car parked out front.

*"Would ya look at that,"* he whistled, eyeing the ugliest pink convertible he'd ever seen. The ancient sedan was so big it dwarfed the slim woman standing beside

it. A tiny, little thing, she had cotton-white hair that shot out from under a red ball cap in wild curls. Her back was to him as she looked down toward the old Howard estate, but there was no mistaking she was a woman. As he approached, she surprised him when she sprang over the closed door of the car and landed easily in the driver's seat.

Slowing his Jeep behind the vehicular monstrosity, he was swinging into the space beside the piece of junk when its engine roared to life. The next few moments went in slow motion as the pink bombshell blasted toward him, then halted abruptly. Clint reacted by slamming on his brakes, but his empty thermos rocketed into the floorboard, lodged between his boots, the brake and the gas pedal. He was wrestling to get it out of his way when he accidentally hit the gas. Like a torpedo being shot out of a nuclear submarine Clint's Jeep raced toward the other car.

The impact took Lacy by surprise. She had been in midscream, watching the terrified cat fly past her face and out of the Caddy when it happened. The metal-on-metal impact threw her into the steering wheel and she ricocheted back against the seat.

Startled, to say the least, she'd managed to get a glance over her shoulder while being thrashed about and nearly croaked at the sight of the Jeep now connected to her back bumper.

One minute it was a beautiful glorious morning, a morning of bright new beginnings, of wondrous dreams come true. Then her beloved baby's rear end was flattened on the grill of a dusty black Jeep, and her dreams crashed and burned in a flash.

*She didn't have the funds for a mess up like this!*

When the Caddy at last came to a shuddering halt, Lacy had her eyes squeezed tightly shut.

The air was filled with a popping, bubbling sound followed by an ominous hissing and the noxious scent of something burning. *Dear Lord, please don't let anyone be harmed.*

Carefully prying her eyes open, she peeked into the rearview to see who had rammed her. Stormy, dark eyes framed by black smoke filled the mirror. She stared, transfixed by the reflection. The cowboy owning the angry eyes lifted one hand and with his thumb, pushed his beat-up straw Stetson off his forehead. His gaze never wavered from where it held hers in the mirror.

Lacy knew she better start thinking, but she couldn't; that gaze had taken root in her brain.

Rooted to the seat of her Caddy she watched the man in her mirror unfold his long, long legs from the accordion-pleated Jeep. Oh, dear, she forgot everything. Even the cat and the need to figure out the mess she found herself in. The guy was good-looking, the manly take-your-breath-away kind of good-looking. "My, my—oh my…" she gasped. In the mirror she could tell that if he were a specimen of the cowboys this town had to offer, then her vision of success for Mule Hollow was way off base. Woo-hoo! The women of the world were in for such a treat.

He *was* something, all lanky and lean, chiseled in all the right spots, and those eyes…flashing anger, clouded in turmoil— She lost him in the rearview as he made his way toward her.

"Are you all right?" he asked from just over her left shoulder.

His low Texas drawl was slow and gravelly and sent her pulse skittering as she twisted in her seat to face him. Oh, myyy… Swallowing hard, she looked up and up.

"What were you thinking?" he continued, rubbing the bridge of his nose.

*And what a fine nose it was—*

"What were you thinking?" he repeated, holding his voice tightly in control.

Lacy knew that voice. It happened a lot when she was around. "Nothing," she squeaked. She hated squeaking.

"Lady, if you don't know how to drive this piece of junk, then you should keep it off the street."

"Now, wait just a minute," she huffed, forgetting the cat for a moment to take up for her car. "You hit *me*. And watch what you call my Caddy!" Nobody picked on her prized possession. Scooting up, she perched on the top of her seat and glared at the rude cowboy. *That a girl, Lace.* Ohhh…up close, he was better than ever, kind of reminded her of a thirty-something Tom Selleck, minus the mustache. His sandy, brown hair ruffled around the edges of his Stetson. His eyes were deep amber-brown, spiked with charcoal and gold, probably why they were so vivid with anger.

"This happens to be a classic. Why, Elvis drove a car identical to this one," she deadpanned, finding it hard to stay mad at a guy who was going to help her business flourish.

Why, if they'd use him as a poster child for the town, there would be a stampede of women rushing to settle in for the long haul.

Cowboy's scowl deepened. He placed his hands on his hips, squared his shoulders and let out a long, slow breath. With effort, she tore her gaze away to focus on her car and the damage to the rear bumper.

"It…it's true. This is a '58 Caddy," she stammered, vaulting from the car and landing lightly before Handsome Cowboy. Unsettled and nervous, she walked to the rear of her poor car for a better look and a distraction from *him*. The fender was crinkled and the bumper was smushed into a crooked smile. It would have to be fixed at some point, but thankfully her baby was still drivable. Thank goodness for the heavy metal of a '58.

Unfortunately, the same couldn't be said of the Jeep. It had a caved-in front grill, a crumpled fender and more smoke than she liked still hissing from beneath the crinkled hood. It sounded like that horrible cat. "I am so sorry," she sighed.

"Not as sorry as I am. I hope you have insurance," he said dryly.

Lacy swallowed hard. It was the dreaded *I* word. She loved to drive, she spent hours in her car and she'd had only two other accidents *that weren't her fault, either.* But her insurance company didn't care at this point whose fault the accidents were, because of all the people out there to have run into she'd been hit by drivers driving illegally without insurance! "Well, actually—"

"Wonderful."

Lacy's stomach started to churn. She forced her flustered mind to think fast. One more claim against her insurance and she was in a crack without a shovel. Canceled! Hasta la vista, baby. No questions asked.

"Got a problem here, Clint?"

Lacy pivoted around and found she was staring at another very broad chest. This one belonged to an impossibly taller man in uniform. She had to tilt her head back in order to see all of him. Guess that ad wasn't lying about those guys being tall.

"Ma'am," the giant said, tipping his gray Stetson at her. "Seems you've had a little mishap."

"Brady. Irresponsible woman blared out of the parking space and rammed me—"

"I did not," Lacy objected. "Sheriff, it's true I pressed the accelerator because this cat attacked me, but I slammed on the brakes. I was already stopped when he snuck up on me. One minute he wasn't there. The next, wham! Right behind me. I'm sure it has happened to you before—well, maybe not. But anyway, a horn would have been nice!"

"What? Lady, you all but ran me down. Who had time to honk? One minute you were blasting out at me, the next you were stopped. All that starting and stopping caused my thermos to get tangled in the pedals."

"Aha! You *did* run into me."

Handsome Hunk took a step toward her, Lacy puffed her chest out and took a step forward. So there they stood, as eye-to-eye as her height could make it—but she was hanging in there for the count. She even thought her bravado was intimidating him a bit until he looked down his nicely tapered nose with his molten brown eyes, and chuckled.

*Chuckled!* "Why are you laughing?"

"Because this is absurd. Who are you anyway?"

"Lacy Brown," she enunciated very slowly.

"The trouble with you, Lacy Brown, is you don't know when you're whupped."

Lacy bristled. "Cowboy, I've never been whupped in my life. And I certainly don't intend to start now. You don't have a case."

A spattering of laughter broke out from the small crowd that had gathered. Lacy turned her attention to the nice giant standing quietly to the side. "Now, Sheriff—"

"Brady," he drawled.

Lacy smiled and shook his offered hand. "Brady, I'm new in town and don't mean to cause trouble. There must be some settlement we can agree on."

"Lacy," Sheri gasped, walking out of the café. "What's going on?"

"N-nothing. Just meeting the locals." She was squeaking again.

Sheri eyed the damage to both automobiles. "So, I see the ding machine is at it again."

"Ding machine!" echoed Clint the Cowboy.

Lacy glared at Sheri.

"What about a ding machine?" Sheriff Brady asked, crossing his arms over his wide chest.

"What about insurance?" Cowboy Clint asked, cocking his head to one side.

His smoking gaze roamed slowly over her and suddenly her heart started banging against her ribs.

"Well, I don't—"

"Figures," he drawled.

"What's that supposed to mean?" She felt very unsettled by the way he was looking at her. But even more so by the way it was affecting her, even as her heart sank at the thought of how much her insurance company disliked her.

"It means that anyone who would drive a car like that wouldn't have insurance."

"Why, cowboy, you're a snob." He was just assuming that her insurance problems were her fault.

"I certainly am not."

"Yes, you are. You decided that because I drive a car you don't like, that I wouldn't have insurance."

He raised an eyebrow. "You *don't* have insurance."

Lacy tapped her fingers on her thigh and glanced around at the expectant, slightly intrigued expressions watching her. Even Sheriff Brady was scratching his chin and taking in the spectacle she and Cowboy Clint were making. "I never said I didn't have insurance." *You as good as don't have any. You can't use it,* she thought miserably. "You see, the point is—"

"That you caved in the front of my Jeep and you don't have insurance. Therefore you're going to have to pay up. Out of your pocket."

Out of her pocket. Things were not going well for Lacy. True, he had hit her, but the cat was the real culprit here and it was nowhere to be seen. She glanced from Clint to Sheriff Brady, who seemed completely oblivious to his duties, instead, content to enjoy the show. She had a couple of problems. What little money she had was earmarked for the opening of her salon. Without it, all her dreams would go down the tubes. But without her insurance, she couldn't drive. She had to drive. Could her insurance company cancel her policy even if it wasn't her fault?

Licking her lips, she did some fast thinking. After she opened her salon she could fit the repairs into her budget if she had to, and maybe they wouldn't have to make a claim on her Caddy, just the Jeep. If only Clint the Cowboy would have patience and give her the time, which he should since *he* had run into *her*. She didn't mind paying for the damages to her car, because of the cat, but who did this guy think he was trying to railroad her into taking all the blame? This would not do at all. If there was one thing Lacy Brown didn't like, it was a bully.

"Where are my manners?" she asked, thinking it was time to turn the tables. "You know my complete name while I haven't had the honor. It's Clint—?"

Her gram, rest her soul, had always said her smile could melt bricks and buy gold. Holding out her hand, she smiled sweetly and waited for what seemed like forever. *I'm not trying to be deceptive, Lord. Really.*

Finally, after eyeing her hand like it was a rattler, Clint reached out and grasped it in a very firm handshake.

Lacy forgot everything.

"Matlock."

Busy assimilating the reaction to his touch, Lacy

didn't understand the question. "W-what?" Her gaze dropped to their clasped hands, then back to his face.

His eyebrow lifted, his fierce dark eyes shifted dangerously. "My name," he almost growled before dropping her hand like a red-hot branding iron.

Lacy rocked back on her heels. Goodness, where had all the air gone?

"Matlock Clint—I mean Clint Matlock, it's nice to m-meet you," she stammered. Wrapping her hands around her waist she lifted her shoulders, trying to act as if she had not just been poleaxed by his touch. "Now—" she cleared her throat "—do you have insurance?"

"Do *I* have insurance?" he asked, dropping his jaw. "What would I need insurance for?"

"Why, to pay for the damage to my Caddy."

A hoot of laughter rang out in the crowd Lacy had forgotten. Sheriff Brady chuckled. Clint glared at him, then peered down at Lacy.

Regaining her bravado, she smiled again making sure her dimples showed. "Since we're practically neighbors and all, I figured if you don't have insurance—I mean anyone who would drive a dusty old black Jeep—" She couldn't help teasing him. It covered up her nerves. She wagged her finger and clucked her tongue. "Well, you know how those sorts of people are…anyway, I'm certain we can come to an agreement if we just get creative. Besides, we don't want Sheriff Brady having to cuff us and throw us both into jail. Now do we?"

He stared at her, slack-jawed. It was a look Lacy had seen often on people she spoke to. A pin, or was it a needle, dropping into a haystack within a mile radius could have been heard. She waited patiently, enjoying that he was actually taking her seriously.

After a moment, a very long moment, he pulled his hat off his head, dropped his chin to his chest and studied his scuffed boots. Methodically, he slapped his Stetson against his thigh. His thick sandy hair fluttered in the humid breeze.

Lacy studied that mass of hair and waited. She knew she should come clean and confess that she'd only been joking. But he was so cute believing her. She was about to own up to her teasing just as Clint's shoulders shifted upward and a deep throaty laugh escaped him.

Lacy could only stare as Clint lifted his chin off his chest just high enough to cock his head to one side and slant those fabulous eyes her way.

"Are you here to catch a husband?" he asked softly.

"No!" She slapped a hand of denial over her heart so hard she choked. "No, I'm here to help everyone else find husbands."

He lifted his chin higher. He had a lean, square chin. A nice chin.

"And just how are you going to do that?"

"I'm going to style their hair."

"Their hair?" His lips slashed into a quizzical smile. "And that's going to make them fall in love?"

"Oh, yes. *Love is in the hair...*" she sang to the tune of the old *Love Boat* theme. Chortles and more hoots rippled through the crowd.

Clint rolled his eyes and strode to his injured Jeep.

"Clint," Brady called, watching him climb into the

wreck. "What do you want me to do? She *is* new in town."

Clint slammed his hat back on his head before cranking his engine; grudgingly it coughed to life. "Let her go, Brady. I've got rustlers to catch, and if I stand here much longer, trying to figure out little Miss Lacy Brown, I'm afraid I'll get back to the ranch and my entire herd will be gone."

"If that's what you want," Brady said.

Lacy took a step toward the Jeep. Clint dropped the gear into reverse and rammed it into drive. Then settling his hat more snugly on his forehead, he guided the clanking heap in a sad lurching arch northward.

Watching him go, a dangerous sense of anticipation rippled through Lacy.

She did not like the feeling one bit.

# Chapter Two

Standing on the side of the road, Clint peered at his Jeep's radiator. Steam boiled from it, tangling with the smoke curling from the engine. In his haste to get out of Dodge and away from Lacy Brown, he'd just driven off.

That walking tornado had wiped out his good sense. That would explain how he hadn't given a thought to the damage to his vehicle or that it might not make the ten-mile trip back to the ranch. Now, stranded on the side of the road, he had to be content to wait for a ride or walk the last four miles home. He still needed a cup of coffee, but it looked like today wasn't his day for one, or anything else.

He owned a cell phone, but little good that did him out here in the bowels of Texas without reception. It was the luck of the day that this long stretch between Mule Hollow and the ranch was the deader than dead zone.

Outsmarted by a bunch of cattle thieves, then accosted by Lacy Brown, now this—what a combination. Of course, to be fair, he owed Ms. Brown an apology. It was his fault that he'd hit her car. No excuses, all that grief he'd given her about her insurance had been wrong. He shouldn't have carried it so far.

Clint couldn't help thinking that if *she* was what that advertisement Norma Sue and the ladies put out was bringing to town—Mule Hollow was in worse trouble than before the oil wells had dried up.

Rubbing the back of his neck, he walked to the center of the deserted farm-to-market road and stood there, boots planted on both sides of the yellow line. "Nothin' coming down this road anytime soon," he said to the birds gliding high in the blue sky above him.

His ranch and just a few other homes were all that were out this direction from town. This bit of road was as dead as town.

He started walking.

He hated what had happened to the town he'd grown up in. Like all the folks with roots dating back two and three generations, watching the town die had been a hard thing to stomach. Especially when he remembered what a pretty little place it had been before the oil boom busted in the late seventies. He'd only been a kid, but he remembered all the oil rigs that had once dotted the pastures along this countryside. When the wells dried up, the roughnecks took their families and moved on to find work somewhere else. Their departure left Mule Hollow just that—*hollow.*

Nowadays, most all the town had left were herds of cattle and lonesome cowboys.

And man alone didn't build a town.

Mule Hollow needed women in order to build families. But the town had nothing to offer ladies. Ranching was long hard work, which left little time for the men to travel over an hour to the nearest town to find a date. It wasn't happening.

That's when the few older women who were left had a revelation from the Lord Himself, as they put it, and they realized Mule Hollow did have a commodity.

*Mule Hollow had men.*

And that was the start of this harebrained plan and the advertisement for wives. An ad for wives! It sounded like a mail-order bride scheme right out of an old Western. But actually it was straight from Norma Sue Jenkins's family tree. Her great-great-grandma had been a real-life mail-order bride. And a success story to boot.

That didn't mean this would be. And if the women who might respond to that ad were anything like Lacy Brown, then Mule Hollow was probably better off remaining a dried-up hole-in-the-road. The woman really worried him. He'd seen women like her up close, too close. They didn't stay, they didn't stick. And women who didn't stick around when times were rough weren't worth having around in the first place.

Clint paused, took his hat off and wiped his forehead with the back of his hand. He'd reached the mesquite-and-wire fencing of his ranch boundaries. That meant he only had three more miles to go to the ranch house, a shower and that cup of coffee he'd never gotten.

Picking up his pace, his spurs clinking on the pavement, he let his thoughts dwell on the town's predicament rather than his own.

His men were excited about women coming. They were young and he was glad for them. But he himself had no intention of being *bait*. For all he cared, women could flock in by the thousands, but it wouldn't change his mind.

Like he'd said, he, Clint Matlock, had seen up close how fickle women could be, and he would never be one of the men who tried to make this town survive through the sharing of a bunch of useless vows.

Lacy shoved a pile of trash out of the way with the toe of her boot. Sheri had been griping ever since they'd entered the deplorable building. "Use your imagination, Sheri. Everything you see here is purely cosmetic, easily remedied. And *that* will give the salon super atmosphere."

"Yeah, right. Lace, it's a crumbling brick wall for goodness' sake."

Lacy studied the object of Sheri's horror. "It's upscale. Think like a New Yorker."

"In a place named Mule Hollow?" Sheri frowned and arched an eyebrow. "I don't think so."

Standing side by side, they studied the brick wall that ran the full length from store front to back. It was bad, but Lacy had seen worse. After her father had run out on them, Lacy and her mother had moved into their share of run-down apartments in the Dallas Metroplex. Lacy's mom, bless her soul, had never let Lacy know the despair she must have felt. Instead, she'd taught her daughter vision, to look beyond the grime and see the beauty that they could create as a team of two. And oh, what beauty they'd created… Thinking of those apartments, the wonder of a lot of elbow grease, discounted paint and tons of love, made Lacy smile. She and Sheri were each so lost in their observations that they didn't hear the footsteps behind them.

"Lacy is right, Sheri. You have to look past the rubbish and deterioration to see what can be."

Startled, Sheri and Lacy spun around to find three older ladies standing just inside the doorway beaming at them.

"Hello," said the smiling trio.

"Hello," said the young pair clutching their chests, hearts thumping.

These were the ladies of the town, the wise women who had dreamed the dream and followed through with a plan. Lacy was immediately drawn to them. She studied them warmly as introductions were made. There was Esther Mae Wilcox, with her flaming red hair piled high on her head like a triple dip of red velvet ice cream. She had beautiful smooth skin kissed by flecks of freckles. At first glance with the gigantic hair in the way, Esther looked a good ten years older than the early sixties Lacy figured her to be. She knew on sight that Esther Mae would be her first makeover.

Norma Sue Jenkins had the figure of a basketball, but oozed life from every pore of her sun-leathered skin. Her salt-and-pepper hair was as wiry as anything Lacy had seen in all her years behind the chair. That it could use a little conditioner was an understatement. Conditioner and a good cut, Lacy knew a woman in need of a little

TLC when she saw one. And that just happened to be her specialty.

Then there was Adela Ledbetter. It was obvious she'd found a salon somewhere. Her snow-white hair had been cut into a stylish pixie. A wisp of bangs softened the look, highlighting the brightest, most intelligent sapphire eyes Lacy had ever seen. In this woman's eyes, Lacy saw a kindred spirit and the true dream of the town.

"You placed the ad," Lacy said, accepting Adela's proffered hand.

"Yes," she said. Her voice was gentle and cultured. It seemed completely out of place in a town like Mule Hollow.

"Against the wishes of the men," Norma Sue boomed, coming forward to grab both Lacy and Sheri's hands at the same time and pumping them enthusiastically.

"Men! What do they know anyway?" Esther Mae scowled and bobbed her triple-decker.

Lacy chuckled, grateful when Norma Sue let go of her hand. "I couldn't agree more. I gathered from a conversation with Sam that the guys aren't with the program?"

"Well, yes and no." Norma Sue sighed. "Some of them want to be, they really do. But they don't have the eyes to see the big picture. They don't trust the good Lord enough to know that He could work a miracle and keep our town alive."

"So, my good ladies, we have to show them that trust and faithfulness go hand in hand and lead to bountiful gifts," Adela said.

Esther patted her hair, nodding. "The fellas in this town won't know what hit them."

"Boy, is that an understatement," Sheri said. "I have to say, though, that I'm going to enjoy watching all the fireworks this plan ignites. Like earlier with Lacy and Clint. That poor guy didn't know what to do with her."

"He needed that shaking up," said Norma Sue. "The way that boy works, you would think there is no tomorrow. He needs to get back right with God and find out there is more to life than work."

"I'm glad I came," Lacy said. "I think the plan you've hatched will be a great success. And Clint Matlock is the poster boy for this campaign even if he doesn't know it." She strode lightly to the window and stared out across the town. Following her gaze, the ladies moved to stand beside her. She wondered if they could see what she saw. "This is going to be a happening place within the next few weeks. We're going to make people fall in love, get married. Make babies. Y'all, we're going into the matchmaking business, but more, we're going into the business of futures." And I'm going into the business of leading souls to Christ.

All eyes turned to her.

Adela inclined her head to one side, her smile serious. "The first match could be you. Sam said the sparks were really flying between you and Clint. God could have brought you all this way to lead the way."

Sheri choked.

Lacy did likewise and stepped back from the expectant group. "No way! I'm here to run a business. I'll spruce these gals up so the men can't resist them and I'll help you do whatever I can to make this venture a success. But whatever you do, don't try matching me up with anyone."

"But the sparks—" Esther Mae said.

Lacy held up her hand to stop Esther's words. "Sparks or no sparks, I'm not in the market for a hubby."

"Well, for crying out loud, why not?" Norma Sue asked.

At the moment, Lacy didn't want to give her life story on the reasons men weren't at the top of her list. But serious relationships that led to marriage were out of the question for now. "I've got a business to build here. You've got a town to build. By mutual agreement, I think my energies would serve better if I weren't sidetracked by a man hunt of my own. I'm here to concentrate on God and His plan. Not mine."

"Well," Adela said, "I think that's an admirable mission. If we all put God first, just think where we'd be. And you're absolutely right about Clint Matlock. When the women get here and see him strutting down the sidewalk, fireworks are going to strike somebody."

"Which will be good to see." Esther Mae snorted. "The boy's been hard to understand ever since his mama ran off with the circus. He needs some good woman to come along and show him not all women are deserters."

The circus? Now that sounded interesting and sad. Lacy wrestled down her curiosity. There was no doubt sparks would fly any time that cowboy was around. But that was only because Clint Matlock was a big, grumpy ol' lump of coal.

Clint fought his growing frustration as he studied the deep tire ruts crossing the line between pastures on the back section of his ranch. The fence separating the land had been cut and another thirty head of cattle were gone. He'd taken heavy losses over the past three months and was at a standstill on how to catch the thieves. Ranches as expansive as his were hard to protect at all times.

His foreman, Roy Don Jenkins, stood beside him surveying the damage too. Removing his hat, he scratched the top of his gray head. "You thinkin' what I'm thinkin'?" he asked.

Clint curled his fingers around the dangling barbed wire. "That unless someone happens to run up on something they aren't supposed to see or the rustlers make a stupid mistake, we're straight out of luck."

"Yup, 'bout sums it up." Roy Don settled his hat back on his head and spat a long stream of tobacco.

Clint pulled his leather gloves from his back pocket and yanked them on. He had hired hands who could repair the cut fence, but he needed the exertion. He'd been restless since going into town yesterday, and he'd learned early on from his father that work always helped a man through a restless time. Mac Matlock had been a hardworking man. He'd built his life from the land and the cattle that grazed on it. He'd instilled that same sense of commitment into Clint. After Clint's mama left them, Clint had learned from watching his dad that a man could get through anything working out alone on the open range.

Reaching for his tools, Clint prepared to fix the fence. He was preoccupied with finding a way to catch the rustlers at their game.

Roy Don spat another stream of tobacco then grasped a section of wire, as always, ready to help. "Norma Sue can't quit talkin' 'bout the new beauty operator. Says she's a real go-getter."

Clint shook his head. "You saw my Jeep."

Roy Don laughed. "Yup. While I was down at Pete's picking up feed, I heard about all that business yesterday morning. Funny you didn't mention it."

"Well, I'm glad to be the entertainment for the boys at the feed store. Didn't mention it 'cause it wasn't important."

"It sounded like you had your hands full."

Clint lifted his gaze and met the older man's. "You should have seen her, Roy Don. She looked like a feisty hen protecting her chicks, puffing out her chest and standing me off." Thinking about those sparkling, denim-colored eyes flashing at him… *Oh, no, you don't.* The last thing he wanted to do was talk about Lacy Brown.

He wanted to forget her. She had distracted him enough.

Roy Don spat and kept on talking. "Come out here five hundred miles from Dallas. Drove it all in one night. Sam said that friend of hers told him, once Lacy Brown got an idea in her head, there was no stoppin' her. Said

God gave her a vision about Mule Hollow. You think God really speaks out like that nowadays? Gal's got guts, up and moving here like she did."

That, or she was just plain crazy. Why else would she load up and move to a strange town? Clint was of the opinion that anyone who'd drive that awful pink convertible had to be a tad soft in the brains. But he kept his mouth shut and cranked on the wire stretcher in the hopes that his foreman might get the idea and get back to work.

He didn't.

"Norma Sue said she was more excited about this crazy scheme of theirs than they were. Said, she, Adela and Esther had been a bit worried until they talked to Lacy." He paused, thoughtfully twisting the tip of his mustache. "I don't know Clint, but I'm of a mind to think this could get pretty entertaining."

Clint snorted. Finished with the fence he stripped off his gloves and strode toward his truck. "Roy Don," he said, tossing the wire stretcher into the bed of the truck, "things could also get out of hand. Lacy Brown looked like trouble to me. Trouble with a capital *T*."

## Chapter Three

On her third morning in Mule Hollow, Lacy decided to get her routine started right away. The sun was just waking up again and the dew was thick on the grass. Standing on the front porch of the cute frame house Norma Sue had arranged for them to rent, Lacy slowly went through her stretches preparing for her morning jog. The house was in the country down a dirt road all by itself, surrounded by endless green pastures. Birds were twittering and bees were humming around a wonderfully fragrant honeysuckle vine that wove around a post at the corner of the yard. The place was lovely.

Pausing in her stretch, Lacy bowed her head in prayer. *Thank You, Lord, for bringing me to this wonderful town. You know my heart and I pray that You will use me for Your glory. But once more I pray let this be about You and not about me. Teach me patience and meekness…put tape on my mouth if You have to. Let Your will be done. Amen.*

Energy filled Lacy as she jogged down the dirt road.

She'd already started exploring the town last night in her own special way—midnight cruises in her convertible. There was nothing better than a late-night drive. But now, she had this quiet dirt road just outside her door perfect for jogging and meditating.

Looking up, she was filled with more peace as the trees laced their branches into a canopy above her and sunlight filtered through in bright shafts of light leading a pathway along the road. A few more feet and she burst from the trees and into a section where cattle-speckled pasture land was separated from the road by thin wire. A few lifted their heads as she passed them, then returned to breakfast.

She hadn't gone too far when the most pitiful wail she'd ever heard jolted her from her thoughts. She stopped running and scanned the surrounding land for the site of the terrible sound, "Maww". It came again just as she spotted a tiny, white-faced calf struggling in the grass. It was in obvious distress as it fought to get up. The mother cow paced back and forth behind the calf, no less upset. Lacy moved to the fence, unsure how to handle the situation, but knowing she couldn't keep going without doing something. The cow cried out mournfully. It was such hopeless sound. Lacy climbed through the wire fence before she could stop herself.

She didn't have the vaguest idea of what to do, but she was the only person around. She couldn't pass on by.

As she approached, Mama Cow turned fearful eyes toward her. Pushing away her own fear, Lacy eased farther into the pasture, leaving behind the safety of the fence. "Relax, pretty lady. I just want to see what's wrong with your sweet baby. Her crying is making my heart ache."

As if to say hurry, the baby cried louder and its mama grew more agitated, swinging her head from side to side. At close range Lacy was surprised at how tiny the calf was. She didn't know much about cows and things, but this poor baby couldn't be too old, maybe a few days, or even just a few hours old. What she did know was that it was very weak. Its hoof was caught between two small tree stumps and ants were crawling all over it.

"Oh, you poor baby," Lacy gasped. Time was of the essence. Everyone knew that in Texas you didn't mess around with fire ants. They would kill the calf if she didn't act quickly. Keeping one eye on the babe, she yanked her sweatshirt off, thankful she'd worn it and a tank top to jog in today because she needed something to dust the ants off the baby. As she edged toward the calf the mama snorted and lowered her head. Lacy had seen bull riding on television, and if her hunches were right, this was probably a universal stance of war among all cattle breeds.

"Whoa there, girl. I've risked my life with your mama cow over there, the least you can do is give a girl a chance." Lacy prayed Mama wouldn't charge with her baby between them, so she quickly moved behind the crying calf.

Not wasting any time, she swatted the calf. This startled the calf, who bellowed in terror, causing Mama to paw the earth angrily. Lacy did not like the look gleaming in her deceptively calm eyes and dusted harder and faster. Mama stepped forward. Growing anxious Lacy grasped the calf's leg then, trying to be careful, she yanked it free, lost her balance and she and the baby tumbled backward. When she hit the ground she found herself lying with the baby sprawled on top of her.

Not thinking about protection, she gently pushed the babe off of her and stood. "You are a heavy little fella," she said, not liking the pain in the little guy's eyes. Bending forward, she gently rubbed him between his huge brown eyes then ran her hands down his body flicking off the last of the ants.

From behind her she heard a very angry snort.

Lacy's heart slammed into her throat. Spinning around she found herself facing a furious mama cow, who was glaring at her. The mixed up mama was pawing the ground and thrashing her head from side to side. Uneasy, Lacy stepped back, glancing around the pasture, she searched for an escape.

Then, mad-cow-Mama charged!

Clint urged his horse forward as he neared the front pasture. It was a still, quiet morning that promised to be another scorching Texas day in July. Heat simmered about him, causing a thin film of perspiration to bead across his brow. It was his kind of morning.

He respected everything there was about the way God had created summer in Texas. If ridden right you had no problems, ridden wrong you suffered consequences. He'd learned at an early age to work while the day was young, take your time while the sun was high and finish your chores as the sun moved west. This morning he was looking for a missing pregnant heifer due to drop her calf at any time. He wanted to move her closer to the house, so he could help with the delivery if needed. Clint enjoyed the birthing process; it made him smile.

And those didn't come easy to Clint.

Approaching the tree line separating the two pastures, he was alarmed when a shrieking scream filled the calm morning air. By the mere flick of his heel Clint sent his horse galloping through the pine trees just in time to see a tiny woman sprinting across his pasture. An angry cow was right on her tail.

Now, seeing a woman racing about his land wasn't a normal everyday sight. However, when he realized it was Lacy Brown burning rubber in his pasture, he wasn't surprised. Nothing this woman could do would shock Clint.

His horse, always ready for a chase, easily cleared the fence and took up pursuit of the two ladies. Like lightning and thunder, they were close together, striking out toward a lone tree in the center of the clearing.

"Get behind the tree," he yelled, even though he didn't think Lacy Brown in her obvious terror could hear him.

And then, just when he thought she would be trampled, Lacy took a flying leap, grasped a tree limb and swung effortlessly up into the tree branches.

Clint pulled his horse to an abrupt halt, disbelieving what he'd just witnessed. He pushed his hat back on his forehead and scratched his temple. That tree limb looked to be about seven feet off the ground. Her athletic lunge had looked like that of a seasoned acrobat.

"Whew, that was close," she gasped from above, clearly out of breath.

As he stared in bewildered silence, she pushed a branch out of her way and peered out at him.

"Am I glad you showed up," she panted. "I thought I was done for. Can you do anything with that cow?"

Clint pushed his hat back farther. "That depends, Miss Brown, on what *you* are doing here in my pasture at the crack of dawn?"

"Your pasture? I thought this belonged to Norma Sue's boss." Her eyes widened and she shifted on her perch.

"I am Norma Sue's boss."

"Oh, my…" She moved a branch farther out of her way. "Then you're my landlord."

"Your what?"

"Landlord. Norma Sue rented us that small house up by the road."

"You're joking. Right?" Clint felt a severe sinking sensation in his gut. His saddle groaned loudly as he shifted uneasily.

"Nope. Wouldn't joke at a time like this." Her brow furrowed as she looked from him to the heifer, now standing contently to one side of the tree. "Why isn't that cow chasing you?"

"Oh, her, that's Flossy. She wouldn't hurt a fly."

"Ha! She almost killed me."

"All you had to do was turn around and flap your arms at her." Her look of frustration gave Clint an odd sense of satisfaction after the way she'd mouthed off the morning before.

"No way. That cow wanted my blood."

"Nope." He shook his head, loving her distress. "I assure you, you can get down now."

"Not on your life, bud. That cow is crazy."

"Look who's calling the kettle black." Clint dismounted and went to stand beneath her.

"You are saying that with a smile on your face. I hope."

His lips twitched. "A small one, but it's there."

"Well, good. I'd hate to have to fall out of this tree and belt you one."

Clint removed his hat, ran a hand through his hair. "Did your mama ever tell you what a handful you are?"

"All the time. Now about my playing monkey—"

"You don't have to keep hanging around up there. Flossy isn't going to hurt you and I need to go and find her baby."

"Her baby! Ants were attacking the poor thing." She started to drop down and stopped. "You are certain Flossy isn't coming after me again?"

"Certain." Clint sighed, holding out his arms. "Come on down. I'll help you."

"No, thanks. I can handle this."

She slipped from the tree, dropping to her feet in front of him. She had on plain gray athletic pants, and a lime-green top with no sleeves. She had lovely arms, tanned and lean. Even a mess, Lacy Brown was a sight to behold.

Flossy snorted and Lacy sprang up against him. Before he could snag his good sense, he wrapped his arms around her…all for the sake of protection. She fit in his arms like she'd been made to be there. It was a very pleasant feeling. Her wispy hair tickled his nose, tempting him with the inviting scent of lemons. He loved the smell of lemons— "Come on," he growled. Lacy looked up at him and blinked. She had a set of very deceptive eyes. They seemed almost innocent. He had a hard time believing this could be true of such a wildfire of a woman. He dropped his arms and stepped away. "Flossy isn't going to harm you."

"If you say so." She stepped away from him. "But I'll walk on this side of you just in case." She quickly sidestepped around him, placing him beside Flossy.

Clint fought the need to smile.

"The calf is over here," she said, and started trotting.

Clint fell in beside her. The spitfire had a tender heart.

They jogged a few yards before he saw the calf.

"He was crying terribly when I came around the corner. It scared me to death at first. I never knew something so small could make a noise like that. It was heartbreaking. I couldn't stand it if he died."

They reached the tiny babe together and Clint dropped to his knees. Lacy plunked down and gently took the little fella's head into her lap. He hadn't moved and was breathing heavily.

"Tell me he's going to be all right."

He was covered in bites, but Clint had seen worse. Nevertheless, it was obvious that if Lacy hadn't intervened, the ants would have killed the calf. "He'll make it. Thanks to you. I owe you."

Lacy just nodded. When she looked up at him there were tears in her eyes.

*No, not tears—* He lifted the calf in his arms, fighting to ignore the way his heart was thumping. Lacy stood, too, then walked over and picked up a red sweatshirt.

"Is that what you beat the ants off him with?"

She nodded and after inspecting it for more ants, she yanked it over her head then pushed the arms up to her elbows.

"That was quick thinking on your part. Thanks again," he said.

Returning to his side Lacy gently rubbed the curly white forehead of the weak baby. "You're welcome. I couldn't stand the thought of him dying." The wind whipped at her pale hair and Clint had another crazy urge. He wanted suddenly to tuck the feathery strands behind her ear and kiss away the worry lines creased between her eyebrows. *Whoa, Clint...you're one sadistic fool!* What'd he think he'd do with a woman like Lacy Brown? She'd be the kind of woman who'd bring a man to his knees, wild, unpredictable—and then when he couldn't think straight anymore, she'd be the kind to walk away. And never look back.

"The calf will be fine," he snapped, trying to ignore how cute her quizzical expression was.

"Did I say something wrong?"

"Nope."

She dropped her hand and stepped back. "You're sure. You look like you just ate a lemon."

Lemons— "Nothing is wrong, I need to get going is all."

"Can I help?"

"No!"

Her lovely eyebrows shot together. "There is something wrong. The calf is sicker than you're telling me."

She stepped closer. Her bare forearm brushed his and he froze. Sweat popped across his forehead when she lifted her gaze to his. Lacy Brown's eyes were bottomless pools of sapphire. They reminded him of pictures on a brochure he'd seen of the blue waters off the coast of Mexico. The travel brochure had boasted that you could see thirty feet deep in the crystal-clear water. It couldn't compare to the depths of Lacy's eyes.

"Clint, is the baby dying?"

"No—"

"Then I'll come by later to check on him."

"That won't be necessary."

"Yes, it will." She started to move toward the fence then stopped. "Flossy isn't going to trample me, is she?"

"She'll stick with her calf. Go on." Please.

"Well, if you say so." She eyed the cow warily before loping toward the road.

"Sorry about all this," he called stupidly, watching how she moved, liking her fluid movement. Enjoying what he saw way too much.

"No problem," she called over her shoulder. "I'm glad to see all those years of gymnastics finally came in handy." She climbed through the fence then stopped.

"See you later, neighbor." She waved high above her head.

He couldn't move as he watched her disappear around the bend in the road. Only after she was gone did he expel the breath that had stuck in his lungs.

"Not if I see you first," he muttered.

What could provoke those eyes to playfulness? The question hit Lacy like a sledgehammer. *Oh, no, you don't*, she thought, snapping from insane daydreams of Clint Matlock and back to her driving. She and Sheri were headed toward town to work on the salon.

"So he rescued you on his horse."

"No, Sheri."

"How romantic," Sheri sighed, ignoring Lacy's denial.

"There was nothing romantic about it. I almost got trampled by a ballistic cow."

"You know you enjoyed it."

"No, I did not enjoy the mad cow."

"You know perfectly well I'm talking about Clint Matlock with the dreamy dark eyes."

That was it. "Sheri, you know I'm not here to look for a guy."

"And why not?" Sheri turned to face Lacy.

"Because I don't have time. That's not part of the plan."

"That's a cop-out and you know it, Lacy Brown. God has someone out there for you and you can't pick the time and place for His plans to come together."

"Believe me, Sheri, Clint Matlock is not the man God

has waiting for me. Why, we'd never have any peace if that were so. We'd be fighting all the time. And besides, I'm not ready."

Sheri sighed and relaxed into the seat. "When will you be ready? It's been a year since Dillon."

Dillon. Lacy tried not to think about him. Things had gotten better since her and Dillon's breakup, but it still hurt to think about Dillon's deception. She'd broken off their engagement when she'd realized that their life goals and faith were at odds with each other. She'd been determined to seek God's total will in her life even if it meant sacrifice on her part.

Still, Dillon's quick marriage not three months later had shocked and hurt. It stung her ego that he could move on so quickly. "I don't know when I'll be ready, Sheri. I just know I'm not ready right now."

Lacy learned three things immediately: the diner had good food; the jukebox really did only play "Great Balls of Fire" and if plans were to be made, they were thought up over coffee at Sam's Diner.

"Norma Sue, you've got to work on that music box," Esther Mae clucked as she scooted into the booth's bench across the table from Lacy.

Lacy watched Esther's hair and thought for a minute that the thing might topple off her head. She even wondered if the triple-decker might be a wig. But then, after close inspection, she decided the diabolical-do was all Esther Mae's.

"Now, Esther, hold on," Norma snapped. "You know

I can fix small appliances." She nodded toward the juke-box. "Does that there music box look like a toaster?"

"I don't understand why if you can fix my toaster you can't figure out why *only* that one song plays on that machine."

"Esther Mae," Adela interjected calmly, "Norma Sue said she can't fix the jukebox. If she says she can't, then she can't. You'll simply have to learn to tune the music out."

"Tune it out. Goodness gracious!" Esther shrilled along with Jerry Lee. "It's kind of hard to tune out!"

"Sorry, Esther Mae," Lacy laughed. "I couldn't help plugging another nickel into the jukebox. I love it!"

Norma Sue eyed the jukebox like it had issued a personal challenge. "Sam, I'll be back tomorrow to work that thing over. If more new folks come to town, they'll be wanting to play it, too. So it needs to work, or it'll drive us crazy."

Lacy caught the small smile on Adela's lips. The little lady knew exactly what to say to get the job done.

"Thank ya, Norm. I appreciate the help. I got a toaster out back that needs fixing while you're here."

"Yeah, yeah," Norma Sue said, shaking her head.

"What's the deal with the toasters?" Sheri asked, thumping two sugar packets together.

Lacy would have asked, had she not been watching Sam curiously.

Everything paused as he placed a china cup full of creamy coffee in front of Adela and then asked for orders. It was interesting to Lacy that Adela hadn't asked for the coffee and also interesting that instead of the commercial ceramic mug everyone else in the place seemed to drink from, she received a dainty china cup. Also interesting was the plum color Sam turned when Adela smiled up at him in thanks. And although Lacy marked the scene in her memory as a point to ponder, no one else seemed the least bit surprised as they gave Sam their order.

As soon as he moved away, Sheri hunched over the table on her elbows and said, "Tell the tale about the toasters."

Norma sighed. "It's a long boring story. But I'll make it short. I can fix the things and I never get any peace because of it."

"So are you the town handyman?" Sheri asked.

"Woman," Norma corrected with a snort. "Sadly for me, I can fix anything as long as its insides are similar to a toaster."

"Once," Esther Mae piped in, "this fellow wanted to marry her because he thought she could fix his tractors. Norma Sue set him straight right quick. She was so mad she got up under all three of his tractors and messed them up. When she finished, he had parts lying everywhere."

"That-a-way Norma," Lacy said. Taking the soda Sam handed her, she saluted Norma.

Everyone followed by lifting their drinks, too. "Now I know who to call if something breaks in the salon. However, before you dismantle anything, simply tell me whether it's repairable or not. Or if I've angered you in any way that day."

Adela hid her mouth when Sam started laughing.

"Yeah, poor Artie Holboney never did get those tractors working after that. Ended up he had to marry a woman in the junk business."

"Oh, Sam," Adela said, giving him a soft push on the arm. "He did no such thing."

Sam looked at her hand still resting on his arm and beamed like a rooster in a henhouse.

Lacy took in the blush that colored Adela's cheeks when she realized what Sam was looking at. Quickly she folded her hands in her lap. Lacy found the prospect of a blossoming romance between these two lovely people extremely motivating.

"Okay, girls, I think it's time to get down to business," she said. "Let's talk turkey about how to entice women to Mule Hollow. I need you to tell me your plans."

"Well," Esther Mae began, high-pitched and shrill. "There's a bunch of single teachers who teach at the community school we share with a few other small towns."

"Yeah," Norma Sue added. "We bus the few children who live here to a school twenty miles away. The teachers commute farther than that, because most of them live in Ranger, only because it has things to offer them."

Esther Mae nodded vigorously in agreement. Lacy watched her flaming dipper threatening to slide right off her head and do a swan dive off her nose into Norma's coffee.

"Things we don't have," Esther gushed. "Like beauty parlors and dress stores. And *aerodynamic* fitness centers!"

"Aerobic," Norma Sue shot at her. "Aerobic. They're not airplanes, for crying out loud."

"Whatever," Esther Mae quipped. "Anyway, where was I before I was so rudely interrupted? Oh, yes. We're remodeling the old Howard house across the street as a small apartment building. Adela, bless her heart, has the funds and wants to do this for the good of the town. Also, we thought we'd do a fair. You know, a street fair like we used to have years ago."

"Yup, used to have those fairs in our courting days," Norma Sue added. "Met my Roy Don at one. He could stack more hay bales faster than anyone. I kissed him when I gave him his trophy. Boy-hidie, that kiss sparked a lifetime of love so rich I still get teary-eyed thinking about it."

"Norma Sue," Esther Mae sighed, "Hank Wilcox ain't no slouch, either."

"Ladies," Adela added softly, "we aren't here to discuss your sweeties' attributes. Although I'm certain that they are wonderful. We're here to make some plans for the rest of the world to fall in love."

"Of course we are," Esther Mae agreed, smiling at Lacy. "Lacy, do you have any suggestions?"

She had been enjoying herself immensely and now Lacy hunched over the table conspiratorially, ever so ready to share her ideas. "I thought you'd never ask…."

## Chapter Four

"Women! Clint, I just don't know what we're goin-t-do," Roy Don muttered, tugging at his fat gray mustache. He was pacing back and forth across Clint's office, the clink of his spurs punctuating each hard step. "I just don't know."

It had been another long night for Clint, staked out on the back side of the ranch watching for rustlers. Judging by Roy Don's agitated state, the day promised to be even longer. It was midmorning, and another scorcher. The sun had come up fighting mad, bringing Clint home from his stakeout sticky, stinking and wanting nothing more than a cool shower, a fresh cup of coffee and a positive report from his men, who had been camped out at other strategic points of the ranch.

What he'd gotten was Roy Don, pacing anxiously back and forth across his office. "Don't get me wrong," he was saying. "I, for one, couldn't live without my Norma Sue, but, Clint...this scheme of theirs is out of control."

"Relax, Roy Don. You know Norma Sue will settle down after a while. I figure, if any women come at all, it'll just be a few. If more show up..." He shrugged. "Who knows—maybe this *is* the way to revive Mule Hollow." Clint scratched his chest and eased toward the door and the shower.

"But, son, you don't understand. That's what I been tryin' to tell you. You ain't been to town in three days. You ain't seen what I saw this mornin'."

Since finding a trailblazing Lacy in his pasture, it was true Clint hadn't been into town. He'd been busy—with rustlers and all. It had absolutely nothing to do with her. "Roy Don, weren't you telling me just the other day that having her here could be fun?"

The older man's face sagged and he stopped pacing. "That was before. Before she got this all-fired idea of hers."

Clint scrubbed his stubby face; he was tired and he didn't just want that shower, he *needed* it. But his curiosity got the better of him. "What did she do? Tell me."

Roy Don shook his head. "I can't. I can't say the words. But—the town will never...and I mean *ever* be the same."

"Man, what's come over you? Rustlers don't even get under your skin like this."

"All I can say is go to town, Clint. See for yourself. Sam and Pete tried to get Hank Wilcox and me to talk to Esther Mae and Norma Sue. They told us to ask 'em to get *her* to reconsider! But naw, Hank and me figured them crazy women would come to their senses on their own and talk her out of it." He paused to suck in a long breath. He looked as if he'd been to his best friend's funeral. "We were wrong. Dead wrong."

Suddenly Clint was worried. "Roy Don, tell me what that woman's done. Tell me right this minute—"

"Nope. I had to come up on it by surprise—'bout near had a wreck, too. Son, you need the full impact." Slapping his hat against his thigh, he turned and strode toward the door. "It ain't right, Clint," he added tiredly. "It just ain't right."

That was all Clint needed. He snatched his hat from the rack and was in his truck speeding down the road within seconds. Toward what, he didn't know. Roy Don was the mildest-mannered man he'd ever met. It baffled him, wondering what Lacy Brown had done. What could be awful enough to upset the man so much?

A quarter of a mile before Mule Hollow, he nearly drove into the ditch when the town's outline appeared on the horizon. No, way, she wouldn't! Clint cringed, squinting into the distance.

Sure as the day was bright, she was painting her two-story plank building *pink!*

Not just any pink. Hot pink. The fluorescent color used to paint steps. The kind intended to keep people from breaking their necks—ha! Fat chance. He could already see the pileups. The broken bones. The jokes.

Roy Don had been right. This couldn't happen. What had the women been thinking?

Soon as he brought his truck to a screeching halt in front of the atrocious offense, he slammed out of it, asking, "What in thunder do you think you're doing?"

From the rungs of her ten-foot ladder, she stared

down at him. He was ready for war, but he had a sinking feeling when his eyeballs suddenly glued themselves to the sight of her in a pair of bleached-out cutoff blue jeans.

"Pretty in Pink."

Lacy's amused voice broke through the fog. "What?" he managed. Pushing his Stetson back from his forehead with his thumb, his eyes moved up and found her smiling radiantly at him. She was beautiful.

"'Pretty in Pink.' It's the name of the paint. Don't you like it?"

Like it. Clint tried unsuccessfully to focus on her words. Pale as a full moon, her hair spiked out from beneath a bright yellow baseball cap that proclaimed Bad Hair Day across the front. And it wasn't lying, but did that stop him from having the urge to pull off the cap?

"Woman." He bit the word out, angry at himself. "You do like making a spectacle of yourself, don't you?"

"And what does that mean?" She continued to stare down at him.

"The way I figure it, when a woman shows off that much flesh, she's begging to be looked at." What are you doing, Matlock?

She plopped one paintbrush-wielding hand on her hip and a spray of pink paint showered down on him.

"Hey, look out."

"I'll have you know it's a hundred degrees out here. If a man were painting this building, he'd be shirtless.

Like I said the other day, you have some issues with being kind of a chauvinistic snob."

"I most certainly do not," he denied, slapping his hand on the side of the ladder.

"Hey, watch out," she scolded when the ladder shifted. "Far be it from me to ruin your fantasy, if you can't face the truth."

Clint stiffened. "Look who's talking—a woman painting a place of business the color of…of lipstick."

"I'll have you know, a loud color will attract attention."

"What kind of attention? That's all I'm asking. I thought you were here to curl hair. Looks like you're here to curl some fella's toes."

"Clint Matlock. The pink is so everyone will know my salon on sight. Also, it'll get a little talk going. Draw a bit of attention."

"That's what I said." Clint scanned the street. Everyone in town, what few there were at this time of day, either stood on the street corner watching, or peered out a window. Across the street at the feed store, a few of the boys leaned against the porch enjoying the show. He wondered why none of them had offered to help. But then, why interfere? This scheme the ladies had cooked up wouldn't work. Guilt hit Clint. She was, in her weird way, trying to help all these guys.

Softening his tone he asked, "How long have you been at this?"

She'd resumed painting and her hips swayed gently to the rhythm of the brush.

"Since sunup."

"Five hours?"

"Yup." She stretched and painted as high as she could reach and still didn't get the last five feet of the building.

"It's time for a break."

"What?" She straightened, latching her gaze to his.

"I said it's time you climbed down from that stage and moved your body into the shade for a while. You'll have a heatstroke up there."

Big blue innocent eyes blinked down at him. "Look, Clint," she said, as she resumed painting, "I have a building to paint before tomorrow."

"Lacy." Clint slapped a rung of the ladder again to get her attention; she really did need to get out of the sizzling sun before she had a heatstroke. In his exasperation, he slapped the ladder too hard and it shifted.

"Ohhh…" she cried as the thing started sliding. "Ohhh—ohhh—"

Unable to believe what he'd done, Clint scrambled to stop the runaway ladder from falling. He grasped at the rungs, missed and caught Lacy's ankle instead.

Clinging to the ladder, she yelped when it twisted around and put Clint in front of the ladder staring up at a wobbling can of paint! He knew he was in trouble, but he held on to her ankle. He had gotten Lacy into this mess and he would get her out of it. It seemed for a moment that time stopped. One second she was clinging to the ladder, the paint can balanced before her, and then she was dropping into his arms. Unfortunately, the paint landed first.

Her eyes were huge saucers. Her chest heaved and

for the briefest moment her sassy veneer disappeared, making her seem almost vulnerable. Clint felt a surprising and overwhelming compulsion to protect her, as she had protected the helpless calf.

She blinked, her eyes narrowed and the helpless aura vanished. "Is it just me, or do you accost all the new residents of Mule Hollow?"

And he'd just associated her with the word *helpless*. "Who's attacking who?" he asked drolly. "I'm the one with the pink paint dripping off my eyebrows."

Her lip quivered. "And I must say it's a fine color for you. But if you hadn't thrown a hissy and smacked my ladder, I'd still be painting and you'd be your same dry self."

Frowning, he set her away from him, pivoted on his heel and headed toward his truck.

"See what I mean," she called.

He glanced over his shoulder. She stood hipshot and smiling, looking better than he looked at this moment.

"Temper, temper," she clucked.

"Should have dropped you," he muttered then climbed into his truck and hightailed it away from her.

Lacy watched Clint's black truck disappearing into the heat, fumes radiating off the long stretch of pavement. That man really got under her skin. And she meant *really*. Why, she had goose bumps, thinking about how she'd felt being held in his arms. Twice she'd been there and twice she'd liked it. But oh, how she didn't want to.

"You know he makes you all gooey inside," Sheri said, coming to stand beside her.

Lacy quirked an eyebrow and frowned.

Sheri didn't take the hint. "Don't give me that look. You know you're not dead inside that hyperactive skin of yours. You know Clint Matlock is tempting. Admit it."

Lacy couldn't help it. She smiled. "Okay, the guy is… interesting."

"Ha! Interesting. Lacy Brown, you know good and well that if male magnetism could be copied and sold it'd be Clint Matlock they'd be using."

"Really, Sheri, I'd think you have a crush on the man."

"It's not me he can't keep his eyes off."

Lacy whirled away and started toward the alley, where the water hose was connected to the hydrant. Sure, she liked what she saw. She was curious, too. About a lot of things, like why the man was so controlling. Did it have anything to do with his mom running away with the circus? And had he ever overcome the pain rejection like that caused a kid to harbor? And what had that done to his faith?

She pushed aside old feelings of betrayal as they swept over her. She'd had her own feelings to overcome when her father had walked out on her and her mom. Only through the love of her heavenly Father had she been able to forgive her birth father. Still, sometimes the raw ache would slip back in and she questioned why. She was human; abandonment left scars.

"You can't keep bringing this up, Sheri. It's not

time for me to think about this. I don't want to think about it."

Sheri was leaning against the wall watching her. Lacy turned on the water hose and sprayed herself, clothes and all.

"When is a good time?"

"When I say."

"Lacy, Dillon was a jerk. I'd say more but my mom taught me better."

"This isn't about Dillon, or my father, for that matter. How many times must we go through this? This is about me and what I've committed to do for the Lord. I'm here to learn to put Christ first and me second. That goes for relationships, too. Dillon wasn't a Christian." Lacy halted her words when Sheri started shaking her head. Lacy jutted out her chin and frowned. Why did Sheri keep doing this? "I know he misled me—"

"Misled you! Lacy, the guy lied to you. He willingly caused you to believe he was committed to God. He knew what you were looking for in a man, so he faked being what you wanted."

Reluctantly Lacy thought back to the painful memory, then forced it aside. "That's beside the point. God had a plan for me, period. He is in control and this is where I was supposed to come. I'm grateful that things didn't work out between me and Dillon. Really I am." Finishing up with the water Lacy walked over and turned off the faucet. "I believe with all my heart that this is where God intended me to be…building a business. Not, and may I repeat, not finding a man!"

"That's all very good, Lacy. But like I keep telling

you, you can't pick the time, place or who you're going to fall in love with. I just don't think you need to fight this obvious attraction with Clint. He could be the one."

Lacy sighed long and hard and counted to ten. What was she going to do with Sheri? "Okay, let's think about this differently. What, please tell me, has given you that idea? If you think about it, Clint and I haven't spoken more than about six civil sentences. That hardly constitutes the basis for a loving, Christian relationship."

Sheri smiled. "Sometimes people around you can see what you don't want to see. And believe me, I see plenty."

Lacy pulled off her cap and ran a restless hand through her curls. "I don't even know if Clint has a relationship with Christ. Believe me, I'm not making any more mistakes, Sheri. I'll pray long and hard about the next man I fall in love with and I'll make certain to see some fruit from his Christian walk before I say I do."

Sheri nodded. "I guess you're right about that. But I bet Clint is going to pass muster."

"And that would be wonderful if he did. But right now it's back to work. Do you see how much of that building I still have to paint."

Roy Don came out of the office as Clint was stalking stiff-legged toward the house. Since paint was drying in places he didn't care to scrub with a wire brush, Clint didn't stop to explain. Instead he held up a hand. "Don't say anything. Not one word. It's not a pretty story. You can get one of the boys to clean up my truck seat."

A smart man, Roy Don knew when to hide a grin. "It's as good as taken care of."

Clint stamped to the house and yanked open the back door. At long last he was finally getting the shower he'd been dreaming of all night, while hiding in the bushes waiting on rustlers, and he couldn't even enjoy it for all the scrubbing he was going to have to endure.

Twenty minutes later, scrubbed nearly raw, his skin now pinker than any paint Lacy Brown could possibly concoct, Clint stood before the mirror in his bathroom and studied his hair with dismay. He'd already dressed in loose jeans and a navy polo shirt before he'd looked at himself in the mirror and realized that not all the paint had been destroyed.

Lacy Brown had painted his hair pink!

He looked like a lead guitarist for one of those hard-rock bands. Letting out a groan, he planted his palms on either side of the sink and leaned toward the mirror. He was up a creek without a paddle. If just one of his ranch hands saw this, he'd never live down the joking. Texas cowboys delighted in a chance to poke fun at some poor sodbuster. The boss drew the jokes tenfold if he happened to be the one caught in a tender situation. Pink hair! Not in a million years would he have ever thought something like this could happen to him. Of course, since Lacy had come to town, there had been a lot happening to him that he'd never have dreamed of. But this—he'd have to find a way to get rid of the stuff. Pronto.

Lacy would know how.

The thought slipped into his thoughts, but he quickly

put it away; he wasn't about to ask her. Not after the way he'd treated her. *Yeah, how have you treated her?* He stared at himself as he lathered on shaving cream, then wiped his hands on a towel. The woman had come to town to open a business and, in her spastic mind, help the town. She might have her own motives about being here, but essentially, from the little he'd been able to understand from her, she had noble ideas about helping Mule Hollow survive. He ran a hand through his hair and smiled remembering the way she'd suddenly started singing right there in the middle of town after they'd had their little driving mishap. The woman was—he hated to say it—the woman was *sometimes* entertaining and beautiful in a Meg Ryan sort of way. She did have a way of making him smile….

And she was out in that hot sun painting all alone because not a soul had offered to help.

He ignored the pang of guilt; instead he picked up his razor and started to shave his face while trying not to look himself in the eye. So what if it was a hundred degrees outside? Could he help it if the crazed woman didn't know when to quit? He wasn't her keeper—he met his gaze in the mirror. Somebody needed to be!

## Chapter Five

Sweat trickled down Lacy's face so she paused her painting, pulled off her cap and wiped the bucket of perspiration from her forehead with the back of her arm. It was blazing hot. Clint had been right about that. She hated to admit it, but maybe she should get out of the sun and rest. She didn't have time, though. Why she'd only painted a little bit of her building and she wanted a whole lot more accomplished before she stopped. She hadn't even stopped to eat. There was so much to be done. Sheri needed help inside. The walls and wood-work needed painting, wallpaper had to be hung…the list went on and on.

Help would be nice, but Adela and the girls were busy overseeing the remodeling of the old Howard place. They needed some sort of accommodation for the women when they did come, and someone had to take care of that. Lacy understood and agreed that the apartments were a wonderful idea. Besides, it was too hot out here for them.

Dizziness swept over her; she swayed. For support, she grasped the railing that ran the length of the second-story roof. After a moment, the woozy feeling diminished and she placed her brush on the side of the paint bucket. Maybe going in wasn't such a bad idea...just for a minute anyway. She scanned the horizon, took a deep breath of sultry air and started to climb down from her perch on top of the front overhang, when three trucks materialized out of the distant road haze.

Clicking along at a fast pace, they looked like they were on a mission. She wondered who it could be, and then as they drew closer she knew.

"Lord, please give me patience," she muttered, recognizing the large black four-by-four truck in the lead. Clint Matlock had returned.

Tires screeching, he halted his truck in front of her building. The other vehicles followed suit. Clint and six men stepped to the pavement. Why, it looked like the shoot-out at the O.K. Corral. Scuffed boots, snug, work-worn jeans, sweat-soaked Stetsons... These were real cowboys! And they all stood, legs planted slightly apart, fist jammed on hard hips, staring up at her with steely eyes as if she were some kind of bandit. She felt like she should draw her six-shooter or something.

"I told you to get out of this heat." Clint's voice was dangerously low; his spurs clinked ominously as he stepped toward her.

Her pulse skipped about fifty beats—she plunked a hand to her hip and met his deadly glare. "And I told you I had to finish painting today." Goodness, but the man was gorgeous!

"Either you come down off that roof or I'm coming up and hauling you down."

The men looked from Clint to Lacy.

"Two things. One—I'd like to see you try hauling me down from here. And two—what are they doing here?"

"*They* are going to finish this job for you. Now come on down. Or I'm warning you, I'm coming up."

The man was infuriating…and intriguing. He had to be the orneriest man she'd ever met in her entire life. Not many men had ever stood up to her for long. She admired Clint's courage. Plus, at least he'd brought help. She had begun to worry that all the cowpokes were worthless, like the ones that had watched her from across the street off and on all day. They hadn't even offered to help clean up the mess after Clint left. All they'd wanted to know was if Lacy and Sheri wanted to go for a beer when they finished work. The slugs. Automatically Lacy had relegated them to the bottom of her matchmaking list.

"Well, are you coming down or what?" Clint drawled, stepping toward the ladder.

"Don't you dare touch my ladder again. I'm coming down." Thrusting out her chin, she stalked to the ladder. There was no sense letting him know how much she appreciated his coming to her rescue. Or how much she needed rescuing.

Or how cute he was, doing the rescuing!

Watching Lacy descend the ladder, Clint figured he'd been a bit hasty coming back. The woman was dangerous to his mental health. She was trouble all right. He told himself not to get mixed up with her, but…every time he saw her, he liked what he saw. It wasn't only the looks that set her apart, it was her mouth. When she opened it and smarted off—well, he liked it. He kind of enjoyed the banter. But that didn't mean he wanted anything to come of it. Because he didn't.

She'd reached the bottom rung and was mere inches from him. Up close, she was flushed more than he'd first thought. Stubborn woman could be near a heatstroke already.

"Cowboy," she said, cupping her palm against his jaw. He started at the surprise contact. "I can tell you're used to getting your way, people jumping at your every command. I've done it this time—" She dropped her hand and started walking up the steps to her salon. "But—" she paused at the door and looked over her shoulder at him "—I wouldn't get used to it if I were you."

The woman seriously impaired his thinking process. Clint shook his head and forced his gaze from the doorway through which Lacy had just disappeared. To think he'd rushed back to town to show some neighborly goodwill by helping paint her building. All the while telling himself he could handle being near her.

Her touch on his cheek had snagged his attention and set his skin to tingling, but it was the challenge in her words that had him wanting—what? Wanting to crowd her space and see what happened. That's what.

"Clint, you want us to start painting?"

"Yeah, that's what I want," he snapped, turning to his top hand, J.P. He'd walked over while Clint had been drowning in thoughts and now stood beside him staring up at the building in shock. "Get the boys started. I want this building painted by nightfall." Clint secured his hat firmly in place. It wouldn't do for the men to see his pink hair. He'd never get any work out of them for all the bad jokes and rank laughter. He tugged at his waistband and squared his shoulders before turning back toward the doorway. He and Lacy had some business to finish and he needed to make certain she hadn't walked into the cool building and passed out.

"Sir?"

He paused at the door and lifted an eyebrow at the bitter face the younger man was making. "Something bothering you, J.P.?"

"Well—" he shrugged a shoulder toward the building "—pink?"

Clint's sentiments exactly. "Yeah, pink," he said, then stomped into Lacy's flaming flamingo building.

He found her standing beside a small refrigerator downing a glass of water. Instantly his gut twisted at the sight of her, relaxed for the first time. After a moment he forced his gaze away to the safety of surveying the room.

What a mess! Wallpaper peeled away from one wall, another wasn't even drywalled! Instead, naked brick met his gaze. The floor was hardwood and very near ruination. Beat-up with age, it had been swept but would require more than the bristles of a broom to become presentable. The fifteen-foot ceiling wasn't much better with its ancient light fixtures off-kilter, some hanging by mere threads. At best, the place was a regular firetrap. If Lacy were half smart, she'd do herself a favor, toss a match to the place and walk away.

But obviously Lacy and her friend, who was squatted in a corner peeling paper, weren't half-smart. They were slap crazy.

"Don't you love it?"

Love it? He twisted, searching for what Lacy was speaking of, but she was looking at him and he knew, with startling regret, that the adoration in her voice wasn't aimed his direction. "You aren't talking about this place?"

She wiped the last of the perspiration from her forehead with a small white towel and smiled. "Well, what else would I be talking about? You?"

"Of course not," he said, jamming his hands in his pockets, confused as to why that statement bothered him so. He glanced around again at the mess and wondered at the kind of woman who could look past the dirt and grime and see something to love. "My men will finish painting the outside of the building. That way you can start work in here. Why? I don't know."

His sarcasm prompted a chuckle. "You think my place is a wreck?"

"A *wreck*—" he paused dramatically "—would be too kind a word." This statement garnered a dour look from her, and Clint found himself smiling. "You think I'm kidding?"

"Quite the contrary, I know you're dead serious."

He cocked a hip, mocking the way he'd seen her do many times. "Oh, yeah, how's that?"

She fanned herself with her hand. "If there's one thing I know, it's people. You took one look at this place and saw doom and gloom. Same as Sheri."

Clint figured on that point she had him, considering his lack of understanding of how anyone could look at such a dump in any other way.

He was in the process of saying so when her coloring went from flushed to pasty. She swayed, then started crumbling.

One minute Lacy was standing, then she was doubled over in a chair staring at old gum wads stuck to the underside of the seat while Clint Mad-dog Matlock held her head down and commanded her to breathe!

"Do what?" she cried, gasping for air—air that had been forced from her windpipe when he'd crushed her in his big-bear-rescue hug then slammed her into the gum-infested chair.

"Breathe, Lacy. The woozy feeling will pass after a minute."

"I told her to slow down."

That came from Sheri, who Lacy could see out of the corner of her upside-down view, had moved to the sink. From the sound she was wetting something down.

"You'll learn that Lacy does what Lacy wants." She continued. "It's a genetic screwup."

"I love you, too, Sheri," Lacy growled, struggling against Clint's powerful grip.

"Yeah, well, you need to," Sheri snapped, slapping a wet rag across the back of Lacy's neck. "Nobody but me would be fool enough to go along with your nonsense."

Lacy started a comeback, but rivers of water were

running down her neck, up her jawbone and detouring straight into her nose—*I'm drowning here!*

"Haven't you ever heard of heatstroke?" Clint asked.

*Heatstroke? I'm drowning!* The man was completely oblivious to the fact that he was killing her. She managed to turn her head, to take a breath, and was about to do some talking of her own, when she noticed the warmth of Clint's strong fingers and the gentle pulsing movements they were making against her collarbone. She clamped her mouth firmly shut and shifted a tad into the feel of those hands. What nice hands he has….

"In this climate, you work a while and rest awhile."

His voice had shifted to match the soothing rhythm of his hands.

"Especially if you aren't used to it," he continued.

He'd crouched to her level—mere inches from her—and suddenly, just like a moment in the movies she loved, Lacy felt suspended in time, drifting in the moment.

"I—" Clint started, cleared his throat and continued softly "—I work in the heat every day and I still have to call it quits when my body signals it's had enough."

He really had the most beautiful lips, strong lines sloped into a questioning frown. His hands, now still, remained on her collarbone, fanned out wide. Against everything she believed in and wanted, Lacy lifted her hand and touched the corner of his lips with the tip of her finger. And that's when she knew she could be in trouble here.

And that was simply not in her plans.

## *Chapter Six*

Clint took a breath. He felt as if he were having heat-stroke himself looking at Lacy's lovely face. There was no denying that she was appealing.

His heart thudded when her gaze rested on his lips like a gentle butterfly, then flitted upward to meet his gaze.

Of its own accord, his hand lifted and pushed a damp swath of hair from her temple. "I," he started, shifting closer still. "I—"

"I'm sorry," she filled in, straightening suddenly. "I tend to be a bit headstrong. I didn't mean to cause you so much trouble." She was chattering. "And I called you all kinds of silly names—not to mention killing your Jeep. Can you forgive me?"

He swallowed a groan as she leaned in and pressed a kiss to his cheek.

What had he been thinking? He stumbled up and back like he'd been zapped with a cattle prod. "Stay put," he growled, backing toward the door, wanting to run before he did something really stupid like hauling her up and giving her a real kiss. "Don't venture out that door again today."

"But I have to finish. I need to be opened when the women start coming."

He paused at the door, savoring the look of her. "You really think this cockamamie scheme will work?"

"Not think—I *know* it's going to work."

Clint pushed his hat back a tad, feeling frustrated. "You don't say. Are you always so positive?"

A loud laugh rang out from Sheri, who had been silent until now. "If you only knew."

Lacy Brown was going to be the ruination of some poor fella. And it wouldn't be him, he reminded himself.

"Like I said," he said curtly, before Lacy could interrupt, "stay put. My men will take care of painting the outside. You work inside, out of the sun. It's safer that way."

Before she could say anything else—and he was certain she would—Clint spun on his heel and exited the building. He needed to cool off and get his head back on straight. He'd done his duty. He'd acted neighborly, had his men giving a helping hand and now he needed to get back to work. *His* work.

He didn't quite make it. Norma Sue halted him on the sidewalk. "Howdy-doody, Clint," she said, hurtling to a stop beside him. "Roy Don called and told me how neighborly you were being to Lacy. I think that's right nice of you. I thought the girls might like to come on over to the house for grilled burgers and fries later on tonight. Didn't think you'd mind, seeing how accommodating you've been."

Clint scowled. Norma Sue and Roy Don lived in the foreman's house on the ranch. It was just a hop, skip and a jump from his place. Lacy Brown on his territory—he wasn't all too lit up with the idea, but Norma Sue had a right to invite whoever she wanted. "Suit yourself. I'm tracking rustlers again tonight." He started to walk off.

"Now, Clint, hold on a minute. You know those coots will still be there after supper. You come on over and welcome these girls. Wouldn't be right if you didn't."

"Norma Sue—"

"Don't you Norma Sue me! I've changed your diapers and swatted your backside while you were waiting to fill your daddy's boots. He'd have come and so will you. It's the right thing to do."

The right thing to do for who? "I'll be there. But I'm not staying for coffee."

"Fine. I'm sure with a sweet thing like Lacy, I won't have any trouble getting one of your hired hands to come over for polite conversation after supper."

"Polite," Clint scoffed. "Have you met Lacy Brown? The woman wouldn't know polite if she fell in it." Well, that's not completely true.

Norma Sue chuckled. "This is good, Clint. Your feathers haven't been this riled up in…ever. Boy, you ain't had this happen to you before. Have you?"

"If by that you mean, have I ever met a woman made for trouble like that one in there? Then the answer would be no. Never. And I really don't reckon this time has made my day. I've been run over by a pink piece of junk. Had myself painted pink from head to toe by that little filly. Norma Sue—" he paused, shook his head "to be honest—I don't want to think about what comes next."

Trying to relax, Lacy drove toward Clint's ranch. However, she was tired and edgy. She seldom had a problem with energy, hyperactivity being a flaw she'd faced all her life. But tonight her sunburn stung and she felt physically drained. Not to mention that she was disappointed in herself. She had once again not shown a very Christian manner toward Clint Matlock.

"Sheri," she said loudly, talking over the wind whipping around them in the open convertible, "I hate to admit it, but I guess I stayed out in the sun too long."

"Uh-huh. You just now figured that out? Look at you. Our handsome neighbor probably really did save you from heatstroke."

Lacy frowned. She didn't like feeling foolish, but the worst was owing more thanks to Clint Matlock. The bullheaded ox—she could just see his smirk. There you go again.

The man was too domineering for his own good. Too sure of himself. Each time he came near, she felt like she'd just completed a twenty-mile race. *Dear Lord, I know part of the reason I'm reacting toward Clint this way is because I don't want to feel this attraction. So help me to ignore the physical feelings I'm having so that he might see You in me and not me in me.*

Her quick prayer done, she turned into the driveway

of Norma Sue's place and shifted the Caddy into Park. Instantly she knew God had a funny sense of humor because Clint came striding up to the car the minute she turned off the ignition.

"How's the Caddy?" he asked, opening her door.

"Smart move," Sheri said, striding past him toward the porch. "Asking about that car is the way to her heart. That rattletrap has more dimples than my thighs, but Lacy loves it."

Lacy stepped from the car, reminding herself that she had a mission to complete and Clint was not a distraction she needed. "What? No name-calling?"

He shrugged, tipping his hat back a tad with his thumb in that now-familiar way of his. Those disturbing eyes settled on her.

"To each his own," he said dryly. "I figure you also have a picture of Elvis hanging in a prominent place on your wall."

"Doesn't everyone?" she teased, moving toward the porch, intent on getting away.

Clint's chuckle behind her was snuffed out by a burst of laughter from inside the house up ahead. Against her better judgment, Lacy slowed her pace on the pebbled path.

The short path snaked around a huge oak tree flanked by massive rosebushes. She paused beside the oak's twisted trunk. Clint paused beside her, and over the fragrant aroma of roses she caught the fresh, clean scent of soap. A clean soap smell had always been Lacy's favorite.

"So, why the infatuation for Elvis?"

Elvis? Who was Elvis? "It's not really," she said, trying to ignore Clint's nearness and the odd fact that he seemed to want to talk to her after he'd stormed out of her salon like she'd grown horns.

"I—I like his music," she stammered, glancing to the rose beside her, amazed at her trepidation. "He made wonderful music, but his life was a shambles." Looking up, she lifted an eyebrow at Clint. "I've always felt sorry for him. I tend to want to fix…things."

"So, you like to fix people?" He studied her intently.

Lacy lifted a shoulder and smiled. "It's a weakness I have."

"So you came to Mule Hollow to fix things? I hope you learned your lesson out there today. Any more stunts like that one this afternoon, and you'll be the one needing to be fixed."

So much for feeling all warm and fuzzy about the man. Lacy straightened her shoulders and met the infuriating man's gaze straight on. "I thank you very much for having your men finish painting for me this afternoon. However, I did fine before they got there, and I would have finished without them."

"You would have been in bed from that heatstroke I keep warning you about."

"Clint Matlock, you are the most irritating man I have ever met."

"Me? *Ha*." He stepped closer and glared down at her from beneath the brim of his hat.

"Ha." Lacy snapped. Feeling like a prizefighter, she stepped up to Clint. "You are a high-handed domineering bully. If all the men in this town are half as bullheaded as you, then we can all forget this 'revive-the-town plan' right now. And as for you, you can forget about being included. I'm not even going to try and find you a mate. It would be impossible."

"And what makes you think I need *you* to help me find a woman?"

Lacy glanced to her right, then to her left, before locking eyes with him again. "I don't see any around here."

"Well, I'm busy," he grunted. "And I'm not interested in a ball and chain anyway."

"Yeah, right, get original," she added dryly. "That's what they all say."

"What about you? I don't see any men hanging on your arm, lady."

"So—" she paused, still glaring up at him "—I don't need a man hanging on my arm. I'm just fine on my own. I don't need that headache. I'm staying single for now."

"Well, little darlin'," he drawled as he turned away. His last words floated back to Lacy over his shoulder. "That shouldn't be too hard."

Ohhh…she wanted to throw something. She held in a scream and watched him saunter up the steps and into the house. How dare he imply that she couldn't find a husband if she wanted to. She could. She really could. If she wanted. *Couldn't I, Lord?*

"Lacy Brown," Norma Sue yelled, from behind the screen door, "come on in here, girl."

She took a deep breath and sniffed. Of course she

wasn't crying. She never did such a thing. It was tension. Or allergies. "I'm coming, Norma Sue. You sure have some nice roses." She hurried to the porch, up the wooden steps and through the open door. *Dear Lord, please tell me what's going on here.*

"Clint," Norma Sue boomed across the room a few moments later. He leaned against the mantel talking with Sheri and a cowboy who had helped paint the salon earlier. "What were you thinking, leaving Lacy out on the porch all alone? What happened to your manners?"

"Lacy's an independent woman. She didn't want me holding the door open for her."

"Clint—"

"Norma Sue, Clint is right," Lacy broke in. "I'm a big girl. I can take care of myself."

Norma Sue looked skeptically from one to the other. Then her face split open with a wide grin. "I imagine you can. Come on in here and meet Roy Don and J.P. Then we'll head out back to eat on the deck."

Lacy wasn't too sure she liked Norma's smile. Like she knew something Lacy didn't. Well, if she thought the sparks flying tonight were of a romantic nature, then she was wrong. Dead wrong. Clint Matlock could eat his hat.

What kind of fool was she? Lacy asked herself a few hours later. She was stranded on the side of the road with an empty tank of gas and a long, dark way to walk.

Clint had left Norma Sue's shortly after finishing his meal, and then J.P. had given Sheri a ride home. Esther and Adela had arrived before dinner so Lacy stayed and talked about plans for Mule Hollow. Lacy had disclosed her desire to paint all the buildings along Main Street bright colors. She'd been happy when they understood her motivation and had offered to petition the townfolk for the money to buy all the paint. They also assured her that there would be plenty of cowboys who would show up to help with the painting. They had volleyed ideas back and forth until the wee hours of the morning, so excited that they could actually visualize the renewing of Mule Hollow. They also agreed that the ad campaign would need to continue and Adela volunteered to come up with booth ideas at the fair to raise money for the fund.

When they'd all finally headed home, Lacy was keyed up. Far too restless for sleep, she'd taken a drive in the country.

Driving or jogging always relaxed her. As an overactive child, she'd had trouble sleeping. Her mother learned early that a ride in the car lulled her to sleep. Though money had always been scarce, her mother had always managed to keep enough gas in the tank so Lacy could get the rest she needed. Now, driving simply relaxed her and gave her joy. She liked driving with the top down. Feeling the cool breeze on her skin and in her hair prepared her for bed like a gentle massage. She also found that that was when the Lord spoke to her.

He hadn't spoken tonight. He seemed to have abandoned her instead, since she was stranded in the middle of nowhere, flat out of gas. Gas she was sure was there before supper. And the Lord was nowhere in sight.

Nothing was. The moon's earlier light was now

hidden behind a heavy overcast sky. Shadows loomed everywhere.

A strange mournful howl filled the night air. A shiver raced down Lacy's spine. "I'm not scared. I'm not scared," she chanted, rubbing her arms. "Just a coyote looking for love," she mumbled.

Midnight drives down well-lit city streets, she was used to, not dark country roads. Searching uneasily through the darkness, she could barely see the white stripe on the pavement. She prided herself on not being easily frightened; however, it wouldn't hurt if the shadows lifted a bit. Better yet, she wished clicking her heels together three times would get her home and into her warm bed. The chances of that happening or of a car showing up were about even.

She had never felt farther away from the Lord than in that instant. That was a feeling she could not take.

She began to pray. *Oh, Lord, Father, You have my attention. Please forgive me for my many transgressions, especially the ones involving Clint Matlock. I'll try to watch my temper around him and show You through me. I'm sorry I'm having such a hard time doing that. It seems I keep promising You one thing and then turning around and blowing it. I'll do better, but obviously I can't do it on my own. Please help. Now, about me here in the dark, I'm kind of scared and wonder if You could please get me home safely. In Your name and will to be done I pray, amen.*

Stiffening her spine and feeling better, she started walking. She hadn't taken two steps when a loud clap of thunder split the sky open and rain poured down upon her.

"Oh, not now," she sputtered, looking heavenward. She knew Texas weather was unpredictable, but this was ridiculous! She was drenched in a matter of seconds as she hurried back to the Caddy and tried raising the roof. It was stuck, and helplessly she watched as the floorboard started filling with water.

"Great. Just *great*," she yelled. Another blast of thunder rebuked her, roaring through the night. "Okay, Lord," she squeaked. "What are You trying to teach me?" Looking around for some kind of shelter, she found nothing. She couldn't have seen anything anyway if it had been right under her nose, it was so dark.

*Okay, Lord, now what?* She lifted her face to the rain. The plump drops plopped and pounded her skin, rolling over her like cool water from a sprinkler. A mind-jolting crack of thunder rocked Lacy from her thoughts and propelled her to action and she started walking.

Her white sundress slapped about her calves, her sandals flopped against the soles of her feet and her hair turned into a sopping mop that kept sliding over her eyes. She had walked about a mile when a cool breeze blew in and she started shivering uncontrollably.

After the second mile she reached a bridge that only hours before had been over a small gurgling stream. Now, it was covered by a raging flood.

*Lord, Lord, why are You doing this to me?* she questioned, utterly deflated. Her optimism plummeted. What was she going to do? She could try to cross in her sandals, but the water was flowing so rapidly, she couldn't be certain of her footing. If she'd worn her jeans and boots she would have at least had adequate protection against things that might cut her feet beneath the water. But nooo! Not tonight. She had chosen to wear a dress. It really made her mad when she had realized earlier in her stroll that she'd chosen the dress to impress Clint Matlock.

Tales of people drowning while attempting to cross floodwaters passed through her mind, but she knew she had to do something.

"Think positive, Lacy. Think. Someone will come looking for me. Sheri will send someone to find me." Except their phone hadn't been connected yet. She took a shuddering breath, fighting back the tears in her water-logged eyes. Thunder clapped again, causing her to jump before turning and heading back toward her car.

Gloomy images of being found the following morning, bloated and blue, floated before her. She sniffled and swiped at her nose. She'd had such high hopes when she'd come to Mule Hollow. Now look where she was, on a deserted road on foot. Alone. And other than Sheri, not one person would miss her if she didn't make it home.

## Chapter Seven

Clint halted his truck at the far edge of the bridge that stood between him and the road leading home. He'd kept his word and left Norma Sue's early, going to the back pasture in the hope of catching the rustlers in the act of stealing his cattle. The fact that he'd also been escaping from Lacy Brown didn't count. But images had followed him. Images of her in that white dress. Of the way it flowed about her like a gentle caress. Of the way her eyes sparkled in challenge when he'd goaded her. Even before the rain began to fall, he'd lost interest in rustlers.

Now, as usual after a disappointing night, he wanted a fresh cup of coffee and a warm bed. And dreamless sleep. Through his racing windshield wipers he gauged the depth of the rising water, shifted his truck into gear and eased the big four-wheel-drive forward. His vehicle was made to handle rough country, to pass through hazards when most cars and trucks had to turn away. Still, he proceeded with caution. Even though he knew this bridge, knew it was built to withstand these seasonal floods, he understood he was taking a risk. Once on the other side, anxious to get home, he pressed the accelerator. He'd gone about two miles when suddenly out of nowhere a misty shape appeared in the center of the road. He yanked hard on the steering wheel, only to be met by the looming pink form of Lacy Brown's ridiculous Cadillac. Slamming on his brakes, he gave one last powerful pull on the wheel and prayed he didn't hit anything or anybody.

Out of control, the mammoth truck skidded and twisted until it came to a jerking halt deep in a muddy ditch. Unharmed, Clint sprang from the cab and hit the mud running, hoping and still praying that he'd missed the person he'd seen staggering down the center of the lane. It must have been Lacy Brown.

Lightning sizzled across the sky, immediately followed by a thunderous boom that rocked the ground. In the flash of light, he caught sight of the apparition frozen at the side of the road.

"Lacy?" he yelled in disbelief over the howling wind. "Lacy Brown?" What was she doing out in the middle of nowhere?

"C-Clint—"

The strangled sob reached him just as another clap of thunder and bolt of lightning ripped across the night. She flung herself across the ten yards separating them and into his arms. She was freezing and shivering uncontrollably. How long had she been trapped in this flash flood? He didn't stop to ask her questions, but lifted her easily in his arms and hurried back to his truck. He knew he had to get her out of the storm.

"I th-thought I'd killed you," she whispered through chattering teeth.

"Shh," he murmured against her ear, hugging her harder to his chest. "You're safe now."

"S-stupid of m-me," she stuttered, still shivering.

"No, not stupid. The weather out here is unpredictable. There was a chance of rain in the forecast. Not a flash flood."

He made it to the truck without slipping in the mud and managed to get them both into the cab without falling. He'd left the engine running, so he immediately tried to back out of the deep ditch, but his four-wheel drive wasn't engaging. Something seemed to have snapped in the crash.

"I'm not good luck for y-you."

Her voice was a hoarse whisper. A chord inside Clint's chest tightened. Reaching out, he pulled her cold body against him. "We have to get you out of those wet clothes so you'll warm up." He rummaged behind the seat of the truck and pulled out a crumpled denim work shirt. "This thing is a mess but it's pretty clean. It was too hot to work in yesterday, so I worked in my T-shirt instead. You can put it on and then use my sleeping bag to wrap up in. You'll warm up in no time."

A slight nod and a shiver were all she managed as she accepted the shirt. Clint turned on the heater to help get the chill out of the air then reached past her for the sleeping bag he'd brought for the long night he'd expected to spend waiting and watching for rustlers. His thermos of coffee lay next to the bag.

"I'll get out of the truck and give you some privacy while you change out of that dress. Here, I'll unroll the sleeping bag for you, use it for more privacy if you want to. Can you manage all right?" She was shaking so bad it worried him as he shook out the sleeping bag.

As if refuting his concern, she nodded, "I can do it. You're going to get wet, though." Her eyes were as big as the moon.

"I'll be fine." He reached under the seat and pulled out his slicker. "Honk the horn when you're done. I'll come back and we can have some hot coffee." Wrenching his gaze away from her pale face, he pushed open the door and stepped into the rain. He yanked on the slicker and stomped through the mud to stand beside the road, contemplating their situation while the rain washed over him.

It took her about ten minutes to change. When she honked the horn, he was more than ready to climb back into the warm, dry truck.

"I can't believe how cold I am. In the dead of s-summer," she chattered.

Clint could see her arms as she spread her dress on the dash of his truck. "It's your sunburn plus the wind chilling the rain," he said, glad he'd found her before she'd been exposed to the night any longer. He'd only been out in the downpour briefly, but he was feeling the chill, too.

She had his thick shirt buttoned to the neck and he could tell at a glance that it totally swallowed her.

Despite having burrowed into the depths of the sleeping bag, she was still shivering and pale. Exhaustion etched on her usually animated face. The night's ordeal had taken its toll on her, and Clint wanted nothing more in that moment than to see all the energy he'd grown used to seeing bubble out of Lacy return.

At odds with himself, he poured her a cup of coffee. "Drink this," he said gruffly. Her fingers shook, taking the cup from him. Automatically he wrapped his hands around hers and lifted the cup to her lips.

When her lips brushed his fingers as she took a sip of the steaming brew, he froze. There was no way he could deny the chemistry between them. Lacy's gaze met his and he knew without doubt she felt the same.

He didn't want this.

"Thanks," she said quietly, looking away to the rain pounding against the window. "I'm not sure what I would have done if you hadn't—" her voice wobbled "—hadn't shown up."

*Dear Lord*—his quick prayer was stopped by the disarming, vulnerability in her eyes. She looked away, and he sensed she didn't like feeling weak. Couldn't tolerate it.

And that made him want to reach and brush a damp curl from her forehead. He didn't, though, suspecting she wouldn't appreciate that, either. Instead he said, "You would have thought of something." It was true. He'd only known her for a few days, but he knew nothing would hold Lacy Brown down for long. Though she'd had a few mishaps since coming to Mule Hollow, he had no doubt that she could take care of herself. It was obvious she was a strong woman in a small package. Wacky, but strong.

He poured her another cup of coffee and handed it to her. Her hand trembled again as she accepted the cup, but she offered him a weak smile of thanks before taking a sip and looking back into the night. The sound of the storm raging about them, the constant barrage on the windows cocooned them, as if they were standing behind a turbulent waterfall, cut off from the world.

"It seems like you're always saving me," she said softly, nervously.

Clint chuckled uneasily. "All in a day's work, ma'am."

Lacy shifted in the blanket. "So what now?" she asked, taking a long, slow breath.

Clint studied the night. It was safer than looking at Lacy. "We wait for the rain to let up then I'll go for help."

"I'll go with you," she practically sang.

That sounded more like the Lacy he knew. But she wasn't coming. "No way. It's too dangerous, and it'll be a miracle if you don't catch pneumonia as it is." He met her wide gaze and hung on to his guns with everything he had.

Looking into Clint's eyes, Lacy was suddenly aware of the solitude of their situation, of the rain pounding out its rhythmic music on the roof. The stubborn man. His eyes crinkled around the edges as he turned away. She watched him pull his hat low over his eyes, hunch his shoulders over the steering wheel and stare into the night.

Something inside her knotted up. For a moment the intensity of the feeling threatened to start a flow of tears. Confused by the strength of her reaction to Clint, she watched the muscle of his jaw tighten and relax. A tense silence settled around them. She wished for the rain to stop, so they could escape the confines of the truck and she could clear her mind and concentrate on her mission.

After a while Clint cleared his throat. "So, why did you choose Mule Hollow?"

His question was soft; it surprised her. It also gave her a focus other than the man sitting beside her. She latched on to the subject change with everything she had.

"Have you ever wanted something with all your heart?"

Clint didn't answer, just looked at her funny and then nodded. One quick defined nod and then he looked away again.

Lacy swallowed. "Me, too. Only, the whole picture wouldn't snap into place. Like, I knew I wanted to open my own salon. I saved every cent I could for four years, waiting on the right opportunity. There were times when I thought I'd found the right place. But things never worked out and the plans would fall apart."

Clint turned to watch her and Lacy smiled, feeling self-conscious about telling him such personal things. Things only Sheri knew. "And then last year I gave all the baggage of my life over to the Lord, and He set me free from all of it, my past hurts and sins. I began looking for a ministry immediately, and that's when the big picture started to come into focus. It had been there for me all along and I hadn't seen it or been ready for it." Excited at the recollection, she turned toward Clint, beaming. "I had a ministry right in my own backyard as the saying goes, right there under my nose. I could have a wonderful ministry standing behind the chair cutting hair.

"You see, I admire Paul in the Bible so much. His zeal at ministering to people, his obedience is humbling to me. He gave up so much and was so single-minded in his purpose. I wanted that, too, so I started praying fervently for direction…and then I ran across Adela's ad…" She paused, remembering the feeling that had overcome her reading the ad for the first time. "And God spoke to me. And I knew—I knew that Mule Hollow was where He would have me come."

Clint gave her a lopsided smile, and in the shadows of his hat brim thrown by the pale light from the dash, his eyes glinted. Lacy's stomach did a flip-flop.

"Of course Sheri thought I was crazy." She laughed nervously. "But what else is new? You see, I don't know if you noticed, but I'm a bit like Peter instead of Paul. I'm kind of headstrong and I put my foot in my mouth a lot."

Clint chuckled. "No, I hadn't noticed that at all."

"Look, bucko," she said, grinning and feeling weirdly at ease, "laugh all you want, but Mule Hollow will be everything I see in here." She tapped her forehead. "If you could only see what I see when I look down Main Street."

"I'm afraid to see what you see.'

"You just wait," she huffed.

"I already have, thanks to you." He tugged at his hat, securing it to his head. "Believe me, pink is not my color."

Lacy smiled, remembering him doused in pink paint. "No. I guess it isn't."

A comfortable silence stretched between them, and feeling relaxed, Lacy snuggled against the seat. The sound of the rain beating on the window beside her head was hypnotic. She hadn't slept well for days; now the rain, the heat exhaustion she'd felt earlier and her ordeal before Clint rescued her, all overwhelmed her. Of their own will, her eyes closed.

"And a husband? That isn't part of your dream? Your vision?"

His voice echoed as if through a long tunnel. "I don't need a husband," she answered without opening her eyes. "My dad ruined my mom's dreams." She yawned, snuggled deeper into the sleeping bag. "No man is getting the chance to take my dreams—" She yawned. "I want to be single-minded in my quest for God…like Paul." She managed to lift her eyelids briefly and met Clint's brooding, dark stare. Then her lashes drifted down and sleep captured her.

In the darkness, Clint listened to the soft slow rhythm of Lacy's breathing. Sleep had overcome her quickly; her words had slurred and then she was out. It seemed she was an all-or-nothing-type person. She ran on high-octane fuel, and when the tank ran out, the tank ran out. He found the idea touching. He knew that when she woke she'd be her raring-to-go, drive-a-man-crazy-self again…she did drive him crazy.

The thought wasn't at all what he wanted to think. He knew that the less time he spent in the cab of his truck with her, the better off he'd be. Listening to the gentle sounds of her slumber was not easy on his mind. He wanted the rain to stop. He wanted out of his truck, and no matter how many times his mind wondered about how it would feel to kiss Lacy Brown, he wanted to get her home and away from him.

She was everything he didn't want in a woman. Everything…well, maybe not everything. He liked her sense of humor, her love of life, her love of the Lord…. Not many women out there wanted to be like Paul. He smiled. She was like Peter though. In his mind's eye he saw Peter stepping out into that turbulent water, not thinking about anything except getting to Jesus. Clint saw Lacy hopping over the side of the boat in the same manner she hopped over the door of her precious Caddy, intent only on getting to her Savior. The picture brought another smile to his lips.

Here he was, stuck in a ditch in the dead of night, and he was smiling. Since Lacy had blasted into town, he'd smiled more than he'd smiled in years.

He glanced into the darkness and studied the night. Did he want to smile? He rubbed the back of his neck, glancing in Lacy's direction. Thoughts of his mother intruded suddenly. What if Lacy was just a flighty gal, who everyone thought was something she really wasn't? What if everything she'd said was a lie?

Clint knew he needed out of the truck. If she was

the real thing, he needed to protect her from small-town talk. On the other hand, if she was every man's nightmare, he needed to be away from her, because by no choice of his own, he'd been through one nightmare with his mother and all of her lies.

He wasn't ready to volunteer for a second round of heartbreak.

Something woke Lacy. A soft murmur, her own sigh, something. She eased up in the seat, pulling the sleeping bag securely about her. Clint sat rigidly, staring out across the night. Beneath the hat, his expression was stone hard. She followed the direction of his attention to where a faint light bobbed on the midnight horizon.

"What is that?" she asked, rubbing her eyes with her fist. She was embarrassed that she'd fallen asleep instead of waiting out the storm with her eyes open. The least she could do was keep Clint company; it was after all her fault that he was in this situation.

"Rustlers, is what that is."

"What?"

"Cattle thieves. I'd decided they weren't going to move tonight. I guess I was wrong."

"Are they taking your cows?"

"Right now, as we speak."

"And you're just sitting here? Come on, let's go get them."

Clint turned to stare at her in disbelief. "We're stuck and a sleeping bag and a shirt, no matter how huge, is not rustler-hunting attire."

She'd forgotten that her dress was draped over the

dash. "I'll put my dress back on," she said, reaching out and touching the fabric. "It's pretty dry. I'll put it on and we can sneak over there and see where they're going."

"Lacy, that's probably fifteen acres between us, and at least three fences."

"Don't you want to stop these guys?"

"Well, sure—"

"Then look out the window. We're outta here."

Clint shot her a quick glance. Lacy laughed. "Anybody ever tell you that you have absolutely no sense of humor, Clint Matlock?"

"This isn't funny."

"Yes, it is. You just can't see it. Now hold this sleeping bag up."

Obviously not happy Clint took the sleeping bag anyway and held it up. She made quick work of pulling on the damp dress; for added warmth she put his shirt back on over the dress. "Okay. Let's go."

"Lacy, we aren't going after them tonight."

"Why not? The rain stopped. The moon is coming out."

"We aren't going. We're on the backside of my homestead. We'll walk through the back roads. There's a small bridge we can cross and then we can get to my house. I'll take you home from there."

"I don't want to go home." How could he think about going home? She opened the door against his objections and stepped barefoot into the mud, ignoring the icky feel as it pressed into her toes. Since she was already a mess, with her hair plastered to her skull, her dress a dingy bit of ruined cloth, she paid the mud little mind.

After all, muddy feet didn't mean much—she was going to catch rustlers! How cool was that? "Come on, Clint. I want to catch some cow rustlers."

"*Cattle* rustlers," he corrected dryly. "Here," he said a few seconds later, coming up to stand beside her at the fence. He shoved a pair of rubber boots at her, followed by a rag and a pair of socks. "These rubber boots are going to swallow your tiny feet, but they're dry and maybe you can manage to walk in them."

"Where'd all of this come from?"

He lifted one powerful shoulder, "I work in pastures—my feet get messed up a lot. It's always smart to keep a dry pair of socks and rubber boots on hand. If you hadn't been in such a hurry, I would have given them to you before."

"Sorry, but thank you. Thank you very much." Holding on to his arm for support, she wiped off most of the mud with the rag, then after some assistance from Clint, she pulled on the socks, then the boots. Clint didn't say anything, simply stood beside her, assisting in keeping her from falling flat on her face in the mud. Finally she straightened and took a few steps. The boots *were* huge, and at first Lacy feared she wouldn't be able to manage walking in them. But after a few awkward steps, adjusting to the slippy heel-toe/heel-toe clomping, she got the rhythm and did fairly well. Although, the boots weren't only large in foot size, they were also tall, brushing the bottom of her dress with each clumsy step she took. She knew she looked scary, but at least now she could walk, make that *stumble,* through the wet pasture, without mud oozing between her toes.

"Coming," she said, glancing back over her shoulder.

Clint scowled. "All right, but only because I want to catch those bozos so bad. They'll probably be gone before we get there."

He started ahead of her then whirled around. "One thing! You will do as I say, when I say, Lacy Brown or no go."

Lacy slammed her hands on her hips and glared at him. "What's the deal here? Does everyone have to take orders from you?"

"Not everybody. But if this little deal is going down then you'd better listen up. Or I'll have to hog-tie you."

She narrowed her eyes. "I'd like to see you try."

Clint stepped closer. In the moonlight she could see his sharp gaze. "Honey," he drawled, "you don't want to tangle with me."

"Oh, yeah, Clint Matlock," she snapped over the roar of her blood in her ears. "Is that a challenge?"

"No. *This* is a challenge," he said. He startled her by placing his hands on her shoulders, then he kissed her.

Kissed her! Lacy's heart thundered, suddenly she wasn't brave. She wanted to step away, frightened by the emotions raging through her. What had she done, challenging him?

As quickly as the kiss started, it ended. Clint dropped his hands, stepped away from her then strode toward the road. Baffled by what had happened between them, Lacy followed him, as best she could in the Texas-size rubber boots. When she reached him, he was staring at the pavement with his back to her. She studied the tense cords of his back, and shame overcame her. She had practically goaded him into that kiss. How could she have acted that way?

"I'm really sorry, Clint. I acted like a child. Will you forgive me?"

He swung around, and in the moonlight she saw surprise in his eyes. "You don't have anything to be sorry for. I'm the buffoon who grabbed you. There is no excuse for my behavior. None."

His unexpected remorse touched her. "Boy, do you know how to deflate a girl's ego. I'd like to think that I'm irresistible."

He chuckled and her stomach flipped. "Okay, so my irresistibility didn't drive you to kiss me. So let's say it was due to a very stressful night that's never going to end if we don't get going and stop all this jabbering. We have rustlers to catch, remember."

Clint reached for her arm. "Lacy, look. I want to catch the rustlers, but this isn't the night to do it. Wait." He placed two fingers across her lips, silencing her protest. "We have enough ahead of us tonight without chasing down criminals who may not even be out there by the time we make it across the pastures."

Lacy's traitorous heart was skipping around in her chest at the feel of his touch. But it was her mind that surprised her, because she actually agreed with him. Not that she didn't want to hunt rustlers—she did—but she'd put Clint through enough for one day and night. It *was* time to go home. Or at least, time to try to get home before daybreak.

"You're right, Clint Matlock. Lead the way."

The surprise on his face at her compliance was comical, and she couldn't help teasing him. "Okay, you stand there with your mouth open, and I'll lead the way." She clomped away from him, dirty dress swishing.

In one stride, he fell into step beside her. "Lacy Brown, you are the most unpredictable woman I have ever met."

It surprised Lacy that she would have preferred irresistible to unpredictable.

## Chapter Eight

"Do what?"

Lacy stared at the black swirling water that hid a bridge somewhere beneath its surface. Clint didn't blame her skepticism. The waters were treacherous. "I want you to hang on to my waist, my belt actually, and follow me across the bridge."

In the dim light of the moon, that kept appearing intermittently, Clint saw fear flicker across her face before she hid it with serious scrutiny. She'd followed him for the past half hour in silence—amazingly! Now her silence bothered him. "Lacy, it'll be all right. I won't let anything happen to you."

She raised her eyes and Clint thought it would kill him not to kiss her again. She *was* nearly irresistible.

"I know that," she said. "I'm just a bit nervous."

"I'm nervous, too," he admitted. "But if we don't cross, we'll have to spend the night in my truck. And you know that's not right."

She contemplated the idea, studying the water, while nibbling on her lower lip.

Finally, with that quick all-or-nothing manner he'd come to admire in her, she nodded toward the water. "Lead the way. I never was much of a camper."

*That's my Lacy,* he thought. "I'll bet if you wanted to, you could be." When had she become his Lacy?

She smiled. "Do you want to spend the night in your truck?"

He was a Christian, and he knew the temptation and confusion being that close to her caused him. "It might be dangerous. People might talk."

Her smile broadened. "Cowboy, that's exactly why I wanted to cross the bridge. The Lord and I have big plans for Mule Hollow and tangoing with you is not part of them."

"And what Lacy Brown wants—" he murmured, suddenly wanting to hit something, "Lacy Brown gets."

"That's right." Her lip trembled. "At least most of the time, if it's the Lord's will."

Clint tucked a stray wisp of hair behind her ear.

"Now hold on tight, and whatever you do, don't let go. The danger isn't the depth but the swiftness of the floodwater. If it knocks you down, it could sweep you off the bridge—there isn't a railing."

"Believe me, I'll hang on, but I think we need to say a prayer."

"Sure," he agreed. He watched her bow her head and he did the same as she began her prayer.

"Dear Abba, forgive me where I've failed You today and help me to be a better steward in the hours to come.

What a night You've given us. It's been tiring, but exciting, and You know how I like excitement. Thank You for sending Clint to help me, and for bringing us this far safely. I pray that we make it to the other side of this bridge in one piece so that tomorrow we can talk about what a great adventure we had tonight. Thank You for watching over us. I ask these things only if Your will be done. Amen."

"That was an interesting prayer. You talked to God like he was your dad or your friend."

"He is on both counts," she said gently.

Clint prayed, but not like Lacy. His dad had always said more formal prayers, and as a kid growing up he'd learned by that example. Turning toward the rushing waters he quickly said his own prayer and tried Lacy's approach for himself. Peace settled around him, as if he were speaking to friend. A friend above all others.

"Okay, let's do this," Lacy said from behind him. She grasped his leather belt tightly and he heard her inhale deeply.

"Here we go. Hang on." *This is it, Lord. Keep her safe, please,* he thought, then stepped into the water, wishing there were a railing. Lacy followed and he waited, letting her adjust to the feel of the water surging against her legs. Her grasp tightened on his belt and he stepped farther out into the rushing water, adjusting to the strength of the current. One minute Lacy was there and the next she gasped and let go of his belt. Clint spun and in a horrified effort, grabbed for her.

But she was gone, swept out of reach by the swirling currents.

* * *

Like a guppy swimming upstream, Lacy flopped and foundered in the surprisingly strong water, already a foot deep on the bridge. The raging current swept her mercilessly toward the bridge's edge as she tried, clawing and choking, to find something to grab onto.

Suddenly a strong hand wrapped around her wrist and held fast. The next instant she was pulled from the water and into Clint's secure arms. He held her tightly while her heart hammered, and she gagged and sputtered and probably bawled. Her life had just flashed before her eyes with pitiful accuracy, and suddenly all she wanted was to be held by Clint Matlock.

"If you think I'm giving you another chance to save me, you're wrong," she muttered against his neck, absorbing the wondrous feel of his heart, pounding near to hers. Standing in the center of the bridge, his feet planted firmly on the wood, like a solid pillar withstanding the raging waters, he held her securely. It hit her that this was a picture of how life with Clint Matlock would always be.

Wordlessly he began moving toward the bank. His strength evident in his movements through the current. Lacy couldn't have put her feet back in that water if she'd wanted to, but she didn't get the chance. He held her snugly against him and managed the crossing within minutes. When at last they walked onto dry ground, she wanted to kiss him. Who was she kidding! She wanted to marry him and have his children! *Dear Father, what have You done to me?*

"Since I've come to Mule Hollow, I'm not certain who's in the most danger. You or me," she croaked.

He placed his forehead against hers. "I knew the moment I first saw you that you were trouble. I've been saying it at least twice a day ever since." His voice was gruff, his hand gentle as he smoothed her hair. Shifting away from her, he studied her face, then lowered her to the ground. "Can you manage?" he asked, still holding her tight against him.

Her feet barely touched the pavement, and Lacy felt like laughing. She'd read love stories, knew about significant moments when the hero and heroine shared their feelings through eye contact. And she knew she wasn't supposed to laugh.

But this isn't a love story. "You're asking me if I can manage? Me. Klutzola. To be honest, I'm not sure what I can do anymore. Maybe barefooted, I can manage to walk the rest of the way without falling."

"And maybe you can't," he said, and swept her back into his arms and started walking. "I should never have risked you walking across that bridge."

"Clint, put me down," she sputtered. "I can walk."

He didn't stop.

She didn't want him to carry her. She wanted to walk on her own feet. If she weren't careful, she'd forget all about her mission and fall flat out in love with the guy.

Talk, the talk Clint had so sweetly wanted to protect her from, spread like ice melting near an open flame.

By the time Lacy woke the next morning, Norma Sue, Esther Mae and Adela were waiting on her doorstep.

The first thing Lacy saw when she answered the door was Esther Mae's triple-decker doing a shimmy as she shook her head vigorously to something Norma Sue had just said. All three of them clammed up, staring innocently at Lacy the minute she opened the door. Something was up.

"Come in and give me the scoop. What's on the grapevine this morning?" Standing aside, she let the ladies scurry into the living room.

"What scoop?" Norma Sue asked innocently.

Lacy perched on the edge of her flowered couch. Her neon yellow nightshirt blended well with the fluorescent kaleidoscope of colors in the couch's print. "Now, Norma Sue, I know you don't know me very well. Yet, I would hope you realize that I give my opinion and thoughts straight out. I expect the same in return. Now, what's on your minds?"

"Is what Norma Sue says true?" Adela asked.

"Yeah. Did you spend the night with Clint?"

The question startled Lacy, even though she'd half expected it. Their expressions told exactly what they were thinking. Shame on them.

"Oh, come on, girls," Lacy said. "Of course not. My car ran out of gas then the storm blew in and drenched me. Clint *kind of* rescued me."

"Kind of?" Esther Mae asked. Crestfallen, she looked at Adela then Norma Sue. Even her hair seemed to droop. "How do you *kind of* rescue someone?"

Lacy related her story—omitting the kissing. She

wasn't *not* giving the story to them straight, she simply didn't believe certain parts of the evening were everybody's business. Since there were parts of last night that she didn't understand herself, she had no great desire to pass the confusing and private details down the grapevine.

"Well, what happened after y'all made it to his house?" Norma Sue asked.

"He brought me home, then he went home." Again, Lacy didn't think the ladies needed to know how strained the ride home had been.

And they certainly didn't need to know just how disappointed she'd been when he'd turned away and driven off without following through with another kiss.

Just a few short hours after dropping Lacy off at her house, Clint was sitting at his desk whistling as he thumbed through a week's worth of unopened mail. Between rustlers and Lacy Brown, opening mail had been the last thing on his mind. But it had to be done, and after last night's unbelievable events, sitting down at his desk for mail call held even less appeal.

Lacy Brown intrigued him. No matter how much he wanted to deny it, he couldn't. Maybe, just maybe, she wasn't just a flighty, looking-for-fun gal. She really did seem to have real substance. No matter what he told himself, she seemed to be the total package.

*Seemed* being the pivotal word.

He tapped the corner of the envelope on his desktop and wrangled with the desire to forget the pain in his past. Right now all he wanted to do was haul his carcass into town and hold Lacy again.

Even if it went against every good brain cell he had in his head.

Absentmindedly, he glanced down at the letter in his hand. He'd been sorting the many envelopes into piles, as he had to get some work done. Skimming over the return address, he was ready to deposit it into its appropriate stack of bills, personal or ranch correspondence, when the name on the upper left-hand corner jumped out at him. Clint's world tilted as he forced himself to focus on the name in neat script: Amber Matlock. His mother's name stared back at him. She'd used her name as it had been all those years ago, when she'd still been his mother, when she'd still had the right to carry his father's last name. White-hot anger flashed through Clint; she had no right to the Matlock name now, not after the shame she'd brought to it. He dropped the letter, scraped his chair back and away, glaring at the plain white envelope. His heart pounded, and there was a surge in his blood pressure that the three feet between him and the letter did nothing to ease.

How many times as a kid had he wished to see his mother's name on an envelope addressed to him? How many times had he prayed she'd come home?

Rocked to his core, he reached out, picked up the envelope and slowly turned it over in his palm. He was a grown man, and yet he felt transported back in time to that same hurting kid he'd been when his mother had chosen someone else over him. No goodbye, no word…

ever. Until now. His gut ached; emotions he'd fought hard to suppress slammed into him in hard waves.

After years of wondering, years of wishing… His hand trembled with weakness as another wave hit him. What did she want? Was she all right? Fighting back the betraying curiosity, the longing he'd thought he'd overcome, he slowly, very slowly pulled open his desk drawer, dropped the letter inside and slammed it shut with a definite thud.

The silence that echoed through the room held unasked questions. Questions he did not care to give voice to. His mother had torn his childish heart to shreds when she'd left him.

Because of that he'd stopped wishing for anything that had to do with Amber Matlock a long time ago.

And that was how it would remain.

# *Chapter Nine*

Lacy had been working hard in the salon for three days since Clint rescued her from the flash flood. Thanks to his ranch hands, the painting had been done in record time and the windows had been washed and shined. J.P. had helped Sheri hang the light fixtures straight, then Lacy had whitewashed the beat up wood floor. The ragged building now looked like a new place. It had a welcoming ambiance that pleased Lacy. All it needed was a bit of wallpaper, a couple of shampoo bowls hooked up and a mirror hung, and they would be ready for business.

Though he had sent his cowhands to help, Clint hadn't come back into town since that stormy night. It had probably been for the best, because she hadn't been able to get him off her mind. There were quite a few things about that night that she couldn't forget. The kiss, the way he'd held her, the way she'd felt when he'd held her. But the way she'd felt when he'd reached into that surging water and pulled her from danger was the kicker. Everything in her perspective had shifted after that experience. She'd already had trouble getting the picture of him standing in the center of the road the day of their first meeting out of her head, his chin tucked to his chest, his head cocked so that his dark gaze angled upward at her as he asked if she was looking for a husband. Now, that question replayed in her mind like a chant.

She had been in Mule Hollow just shy of two weeks and already her thoughts were straying from her mission. It really bothered her that she could be so fickle. She *so* wanted to stay the course.

Today, as she spread paste on an eight-foot length of wallpaper, her thoughts were churning. She was relieved when the salon door opened behind her.

"Yoo-hoo, Lacy."

"Adela," she called over her shoulder, recognizing the singsong voice. "How's it going?"

"Wonderful. Just wonderful. How lovely it looks in here."

"You think so?" Paper up, Lacy stepped back, plopped her hands on her hips and admired her handiwork. "I've never hung paper before so I was excited to try something new. It's easier than I expected."

"You have the knack."

"I wouldn't say that—but it has been fairly easy."

"Have you done it all yourself?"

"Oh no, no, no. Sheri has helped big-time—she's just gone over to Pete's for more paste. I bought this paper before I left Dallas, and I didn't think about paste. Thank goodness Pete had some, but I think it had been there for a while. I hope it's still good." She spread paste on the next sheet of paper then folded it together, like the instructions said.

"I'm sure it'll be fine. It looks as if it's sticking." Adela ran a hand over the soft pink and white striped paper and nodded.

"What's up?" Lacy picked up the new length of paper and maneuvered her way to the wall.

Adela followed her. "I came to tell you that the apartments are in complete upheaval right now, but the contractor assures me that a couple of them will be ready in time for the fair. The electricians are there now, running wire for the small kitchens, and the contractors have started cutting out openings between rooms that will connect into living and dining spaces. It is amazing what can happen in a matter of days when people are motivated."

"You must have done some mighty powerful motivating." Lacy paused and smiled at Adela. Adela might have been small and serene looking, but behind that exterior, there was a very aggressive go-getter.

"I have a few connections in Ranger, great friends of the family, and they were glad to help out, especially when they'd had another job fall through and needed to keep their men working. God has a way of clearing agendas when the time is right."

"So true, Adela."

"Lacy, I also came to tell you that we had a call a few minutes ago from a young woman who is coming out from Hollywood to see about opening a dress store. Hollywood. Can you imagine?"

Lacy spun toward Adela. "You mean to tell me you didn't come barging in here screaming with excitement about this? You amaze me, Adela! Does anything ruffle your feathers?"

Adela's eyes twinkled. "My feathers are ruffled. I'm extremely excited."

Lacy laughed. "Yeah, I can tell."

"I explained to her that at the moment a dress store might be a bit out of the question." Adela's eyes sparkled more brightly. "However we eventually expected to have a large demand for just that kind of shop."

"And," Lacy prompted when Adela frowned.

"She assured me that she expected a slow beginning. She said part of her business is done on the Internet and it really didn't matter if the foot traffic was slow in town for a little while."

"Excellent. When is she arriving?"

"In two weeks, just in time for the fair. I explained it would be the event of the summer and she would want to attend before going back to the city and making her decision."

"Adela, you are too cool," Lacy said, returning to work. The paste had set on the panel she was working on and it was time to spread the paper on the wall.

"Yes, well, thank you. Are you sure you don't need help?"

"I'm positive."

"Then I'll see you later. I'm off to see Pete about donating supplies to decorate the street. Oh, by the way, I thought the vacant building beside you would be the perfect spot for the dress shop."

"I agree," Lacy called over her shoulder, unable to spare a glance as she started working.

"Tootles, dear."

"Tootles to you, too," Lacy said absently as she smoothed the paper, concentrating on getting all the lines straight. When she finished, she backed away and surveyed her work. "Not bad. Not bad at all."

The door opened behind her.

"What do you think, Sheri? With the other paper up, this is going to look great."

"If you like pink."

Lacy swung around to find Clint Matlock frowning at the wall. She was shocked at the rush of joy that flowed over her. Shocked and dismayed at the same time.

"You don't like pink?" She willed her heart to slow down and her mouth to smother the smile that was trying to erupt from it.

"Nope. Can't say that I do, but it's obvious we disagree on the subject." He looped his thumb though the belt loop of his right hip. "Is everything you touch going to be pink?"

Lacy couldn't help the chuckle that bubbled out of her. "Not everything. I like pink because it's a happy color."

"Not always." Clint lifted his hat from his head and slowly lowered his chin so that the top of his head was exposed. "Like I said the other night, it's not my color."

Lacy gasped. "Clint, you have *pink hair!*"

"As if I didn't know that," he said dryly. "And it doesn't make me happy."

Lacy hurried over to stare at his hair. "I can't believe I didn't see this the night of the storm. But, now that I think about it, you never once removed your hat. As a matter of fact, I remember you yanking on it all night to keep it in place."

"You better believe it. Since this has happened, I've worn my hat everywhere except to bed. Do you know what kind of teasing I'd get if word got out that I have pink hair?"

Lacy laughed. "Oh, my, the world as we know it would end."

Clint relaxed against the door frame. "The question is, can you help me?"

Lacy reached up and touched the stiff patch of hair. Like the crown of a rooster's head it was a three by two section of hair sitting smack on the top of his head. It was quite cute. "You know you could just leave it and start a new trend." Clint lowered his chin and gave her that look she'd come to adore. "Okay, maybe not."

"I tried everything I thought was safe. I've showered more times than I can count. Been through a rainstorm—"

"That doesn't count," Lacy broke in. "You kept the hat on, remember." Giving into the notion, she gave the swatch of hair a gentle tug.

"Hey! Watch out."

Lacy laughed and turned away to move toward the shampoo bowl that was leaning against the back wall.

Clint followed. "I'm getting desperate enough to pour gasoline over my head. Tomorrow is Sunday and I don't usually wear my hat during services."

"I'll get it out for you." She was glad to do something for him. He had, after all, saved her from uncertain disaster. "All I need is my shampoo bowls hooked up and we're in business."

Clint eyed the equipment. "I'm handy with a wrench. I'll install the bowls if you guarantee you can make me look normal again."

Placing her hand on her heart she said somberly, "I promise."

"It's a done deal. I'll go out to my truck and get some tools, then we'll get started."

After carefully placing his Stetson back on his head and giving it a secure tug, Clint strode from the salon. Lacy watched him go, fighting laughter and the strong urge to run up behind him on the street and tip the hat off his head.

*Oh, Lacy, you do have a mean streak in you.*

"What's Clint up to?" Sheri asked as she came in, empty-handed.

"He's going to install my shampoo bowls."

"He's going to help you install shampoo bowls! You who crashed his Jeep, made him run his truck into a ditch, had him trudging all over his pastures in the middle of a flash flood." Her eyes were wide in disbelief.

"Yes. He's being neighborly."

"Yeah, right," Sheri snapped. "The man is interested, Lace." She thumped a fake cigar in punctuation and wiggled her eyebrows.

"Well, Groucho, I'm not." Lacy stuffed some unused wallpaper into the trash bin and ignored the kick her heart gave her ribs.

"Whatever you say, girlfriend, but I think you're crazy as a Betsy bug. Look, Pete has no more paste, so I thought I'd ride to Ranger and pick up some new paste."

"Now? Ranger is sixty miles away."

Sheri tucked her hands into her back pockets. "I know."

"Then what's up?"

"J.P. has a load of cattle to deliver to the auction barn and wanted to know if I'd ride along."

Lacy stared at her friend. "This is getting to be a pretty heavy thing between you two."

"Not too heavy. I'm holding up just fine."

"Sher—"

"Lace, stop. I'm not the one with the hang-up about men. J.P. is a very nice guy. He's fun. And, girl, can he kiss."

"Sheri, this is serious."

"Yes, it is, Lacy. You need to lighten up. That's serious. Now, while I'm gone, instead of worrying over me, why don't you worry about that handsome man who's going to be working beside you for the next hour?" Sheri backed out the door, grinning. "This is a good thing, Lacy. Remember that. A good thing. You didn't like me standing on the sidelines growing up. Well, I don't like you standing there, either. It isn't right. So loosen up and make a new friend."

Lacy watched her jog down the road to where J.P. leaned against the side of his truck. He had one leg braced against the metal fender and he looked happy watching Sheri jog up to meet him. When she came to a halt before him he wrapped an arm around her shoulders and escorted her to the truck, where he opened the door and helped her climb into the cab. A twinge of envy at their carefree attitude swept through Lacy. She turned away, shutting the emotion down. She wasn't ready yet to trust her heart to a man. Not that easily. Not that carefree. Still she envied her friend her ability to do so.

"Okay, that should do it," Clint said about an hour later. Dusting his hands off on his jeans he stood and put his wrench in his back pocket.

"Perfect," Lacy said. "That means I'm practically open for business."

"Me first."

Lacy laughed as he pulled off his hat and exposed his pink hair. "Yes, you are definitely my first client. Everybody else will have to wait until Tuesday morning."

"I have to say, you've done a great job in here. I never thought you could do it in this short time, but the place looks good. You're going to need help with those mirrors, aren't you?" He nodded toward the two large mirrors leaning against the brick wall.

"Yes, they're really heavy," Lacy admitted. She wasn't keen on more help from him. She'd become increasingly agitated working beside him installing the shampoo bowls. More times than she could count, their hands had brushed each other as she passed him tools, or held this or that for him.

"I'll hang them," he offered, interrupting her

thoughts. "After—" He lowered his head and pointed at his hair.

Shrugging off her worries, Lacy smiled then dragged a shampoo chair over in front of the basin. "Sit."

"You don't have to ask me twice."

Lacy bit her lip and met his twinkling gaze, forcing herself to concentrate on getting the right stripping product out of the cabinet. The only problem was as she bent to scrub his mass of hair, he watched her. Their faces were only a few feet away from each other as she bent into the job of scrubbing. To her dismay, it took two different stripping products, and much longer than she'd hoped, to get out the paint. She was overjoyed when at last she was able to declare him paintless. "Praise the Lord, you're a free man," she said, patting his hair down with a towel before letting him stand up.

*And I'm a free woman.*

Her nerves were jittering as she moved quickly away to stand by the front counter. She needed distance between them. She needed perspective on the feelings that were churning around inside her.

He crossed the room, and she watched him lean over and eye himself in the mirror. "Thank you," he said, moving toward her. "I could kiss you for this," he teased.

Lacy tapped her nails on the front counter. "We—we don't need to get carried away."

Clint took another step toward her. "If you knew how important it was to *not* have pink hair…you would understand my pleasure." He took another step toward her, mischief dancing in his eyes.

Lacy tapped her fingers harder.

"I've had you on my mind all week." His voice sombered.

They'd managed to skirt the minor problem of their emotions all afternoon and oh, how she wished he'd kept it that way. Denial was so unlike her, she who met things straight on. But this, this she was not ready to handle.

"You have?" she squeaked. Confused, thrilled.

His eyes twinkled down at her. "I'm only human. It was an eventful night."

"That is an understatement. The rain…nearly drowning, it was all so terrible." Lacy stilled her fingers and crossed her arms across her stomach.

"It wasn't all terrible, Lacy. I enjoyed being with you." He stepped up and cupped her jaw with his hand. "I enjoyed talking with you, spending time with you. You're a neat person to get to know."

Lacy closed her eyes, lost for a moment in his touch. His hand felt so gentle against her skin.

"Lace, I tried to stay away. But I can't get you off my mind."

Lacy swallowed hard and fought to gather her nerve. She couldn't allow herself this distraction. "Clint, I can't do this. I'm here to concentrate on being a witness for Christ. I would be lying if I denied wanting to get to know you better." To kiss you. "But, I can't be distracted right now. My love life is just not in the plan at the moment."

There—she had said it, or at least rattled it out. She'd

been honest and straightforward. She hadn't played games with him. He deserved that much.

He studied her silently for a few moments, before his eyes sobered and his lips slashed upward into that smile of his that had the maddening habit of turning her insides to jelly.

"See you at church tomorrow."

Lacy watched Clint back out the door, then stride to his truck. She sighed. "The trouble with you, Mr. Matlock, is you're simply too cute for *my* good."

## Chapter Ten

The small country church was set in a clearing on the side of town. It was a quaint beauty that had stood its ground for more than fifty years; at least that was the history that Norma had imparted to her the day before. The church was made of plank siding and sported a new metal roof that glistened in the morning sunlight. Immediately Lacy thought of an old song she faintly remembered from her childhood, about a church in the wildwood. The memory caused her heart to swell with a longing she hadn't realized was there. In Dallas, she attended a huge church of brick and stone that had every modern convenience for its members. It even had a bookstore right there inside where she could buy any Christian book she wanted. It was a wonderful church, even if you could get lost in the crowd. But as Lacy sat in her car and took in the peaceful country appearance of Mule Hollow's Church of Faith, she felt a beckoning, an almost overwhelming pull to belong. A smile overcame her as she scrambled from behind the wheel of the

Caddy, refraining, in her haste, from hopping over the door—she was after all at church, and she did have on a dress. Not to mention Sheri watching her like a hawk, making certain she at least tried to act like a lady.

"Hi, Adela," she called, reaching into the back seat to pick up her Bible, waving at the same time. Adela waved back from where she was waiting on the front steps with a man whom Lacy assumed was the pastor, based on the way he was greeting everyone who entered the church. As she hurried up the walk behind Sheri, Lacy's heart hummed with excitement.

Adela hugged them when they stepped up on to the wide front porch. "I'm so happy you both made it this morning. I want to introduce you to the only man in Mule Hollow I don't think you've met. This is Pastor Lewis."

The pastor was a few inches shy of being considered tall, but he had snow-white hair and eyes so apple-green that they popped at Lacy with friendliness…or sheer joy at seeing new blood on the church premises. He took each of their hands in a firm handshake and smiled with gusto.

"You ladies don't know how long I've been praying for you to move here. The good Lord has His own time-table, but I sometimes want to get ahead of Him. But you see, when Adela told me of your coming, I could envision children playing in our playground. Children mean life, especially for church growth."

Sheri met Lacy's gaze and both women's eyes sparked with agreement.

"We're the ones who are glad to be here," Lacy said.

"So far it's been cool watching things unfold." She tried not to think about Clint Matlock and the unfolding of a relationship she was baffled by with every passing day. "This church is charming," she added, pushing thoughts of Clint aside.

"Do many of the cowboys come to church?" Sheri asked, shrugging when the minister raised an eyebrow. "Sorry, I can't help myself."

Pastor Lewis chuckled. "Yes, actually quite a lot of the guys come when their work permits. Sorry to say, but sometimes a cowboy's work does not respect the Lord's Day. Here come a few more of them now. Morning, Clint and J.P. Good to see you, Bob."

Lacy turned and met Clint's gaze. She wasn't pleased at the flush she felt creep up her face. "Hello, Clint, guys." She nodded to the other cowboys that had followed Clint to the steps and now were streaming past, nodding at her and Sheri as they pulled off their hats and entered the church. Clint stood to the side after shaking hands with the pastor and Adela. Lacy heard Adela question the Pastor about the songs he wanted her to play and they excused themselves to prepare for the service. She found herself alone on the steps of the church with Clint. Sheri had eagerly gone inside with J.P. and the others.

"You look nice this morning," Clint said as he took his Stetson off and held it between both his hands. His eyes were steady as they held hers.

Lacy fought down the jitters, something which was becoming habit, and forced her traitorous voice to sound natural. "Thank you. I like your hair." *You would have liked it pink!*

"Why, thank you. Some really nice lady did it for me." Tension pulsed between them for a moment. Then he waved toward the door with his hat as the piano music started up. "After you."

Lacy entered the coolness of the sanctuary and was dismayed when Clint followed her into a pew. She hadn't expected to sit beside him through the service. Hiding her surprise, she reached for the songbook at the same time that he did and their hands touched. He pulled back quickly, letting her have that hymnal while he took the one beside it.

Lacy was about to give herself a good talking-to about focusing on the Lord and not Clint Matlock, when she looked into the choir and nearly bit her lip in surprise. Seeing all those singing cowboys was enough to make many a woman want to join the church, but it wasn't the cowboys that grabbed Lacy's attention. Nor were the clashing floral prints of Norma Sue and Esther Mae's Sunday dresses enough to distract her. The focus of Lacy's attention was a cute young woman. No one had mentioned a young woman in Mule Hollow.

"Who is that?" Lacy whispered to Clint, who was really getting into praising the Lord with his joyful noise.

Not that her noise was any better than his, she was just used to her own.

"Who?" he asked, bending low to hear her whisper.

"That tiny woman in the choir. That tiny *young* woman."

"Oh, that's Lilly Tipps."

"Oh."

Clint heard her confusion in her voice. "She lives on the outer edge of town, near the county line. We don't see her much except on Sundays and occasionally when she comes to town to buy feed."

"Is she married to one of the cowboys?" Lacy knew she should stop whispering in church, but she was so curious she couldn't help herself.

"Lilly. Married. Naa, it was a miracle the first time. It'll never happen a second time." Clint shook his head and resumed his singing.

Though she was still curious, especially since Lilly looked like she was in the midstage of pregnancy, Lacy squelched her questions. Instead she focused on giving praise to Lord, lifting her voice up to clash with Clint's. They sang all four stanzas of "Amazing Grace" then "Standing on the Promises". She and Clint ended grinning at each other while sharing a robust, rather off-key harmony.

When they sat down and Pastor Lewis stepped up to the pulpit, Clint leaned over and whispered, "We might not be Broadway-bound, but God has to be smiling at our effort."

"He's probably rolling with laughter." She chuckled, watching the small group of choir members file down into the congregation. Esther Mae, red hair tilting to one side, winked at them as she passed by on her way to sit with her husband. Lacy watched as Lilly Tipps moved to the far side of the sanctuary, choosing a spot on a vacant row near the side door.

Watching her, Lacy was struck by the memory of sitting beside her mother in a congregation full of people yet feeling all alone in the crowd of smiling faces. She'd always felt that her dislike of seeing people sitting on the sidelines of life stemmed from those times as a child, when she'd felt out of place in God's house. It made her all the more determined as an adult to engage others. Lacy made a mental note that Lilly Tipps would be someone she went out of her way to get to know.

The sermon was taken from 2 Peter 1:5-7. "And beside this, giving all diligence, add to your faith virtue; and to virtue knowledge. And to knowledge temperance; and to temperance patience; and to patience godliness; And to godliness brotherly kindness; and to brotherly kindness charity."

Now Lacy could have believed that the pastor had read her diary, if she kept a diary. The sermon was so close to her heart. It was very thought provoking for her, because if she wanted to work for the Lord she had to learn control…and that was in all aspects of her life.

Beside her, Clint shifted in his seat and drew her attention. Her manner with him was very upsetting to her. He was one of the first people she'd met coming to Mule Hollow, and constantly she lost it with him. He'd very nearly saved her life, and she had treated him terrible half the time. Of course, part of that was because of the maddening attraction she had toward him. God's sense of humor once again. Here she was struggling with issues while new issues kept being thrown her way.

Of course, she *had* always been told never to pray for patience without being prepared for war.

When the service ended, Lacy felt determined, with God's help, to overcome her loose lips. It could be done; she just needed, as Pastor Lewis had pointed out, to rely more fully on His lead rather than her own.

Which was exactly what Lacy was striving to do.

To Lacy's disappointment, Lilly Tipps left quickly though the side door and was nowhere to be seen when Lacy made it outside. Lacy had hoped to meet her and make a new friend.

"Lacy," Sheri said, coming up with J.P. as Lacy made her way to the car, after having said her goodbyes, "I'm going on a picnic with J.P. Want to come?"

The last thing Lacy wanted was to be the third wheel. "No, thanks. All I want is to go home and crash for a while, maybe read a book. But the two of you have fun."

Sheri hugged her, and then headed toward J.P.'s truck as happy as a schoolgirl. The country life was agreeing with Sheri and that was good. Although Lacy had to admit that she missed her friend's company. Since coming to Mule Hollow they really saw less of each other than when they lived in Dallas. It was funny how she felt more alone in this small town than she had in the Metroplex.

"Hey, Lacy, wait up."

Lacy had just reached her car. Turning around, she faced Clint as he came up beside her.

"Are you being stood up for the afternoon?"

"You could say that," she said, and fought to keep her voice from betraying her lonesome mood.

"Are you okay? You sound a little down."

So much for keeping her chin up. "I'm just thinking. That's all."

Clint ducked his chin and searched her eyes thoughtfully. "Well, look, I owe you for saving Flossy's calf the other day and thought maybe I could feed you lunch."

"You don't owe me. You saved me from the storm the other night and you installed my shampoo bowls. Math isn't my strong point, but by my calculations I think we're even on that score."

"I thought you wanted to see Junior?"

He had her on that one. She smiled. "I do want to see the baby. He's doing good, right?" The offer was tempting.

"Getting fatter as we speak. Come on back to the ranch with me, and after I throw a couple of steaks on the pit, we'll go see the little guy. I promise to keep my hands to myself, if that's what's worrying you."

Lacy's heart lifted and she laughed. "In that case, you're on, cowboy."

Clint watched Lacy as she tickled the white curly forehead of the rowdy calf. Her blue eyes sparkled with genuine glee as Junior nudged and prodded her hand with his wet nose.

Clint was leaning against the stall gate and lost his breath when Lacy turned those glittering eyes toward him. Just as their gazes connected, Junior butted her in the ribs and knocked her to the hay-strewn floor.

Most women would have screamed, but Lacy busted out laughing, while he hurried to pull the overzealous calf off her.

"I told you he was feeling good," he said, reaching down and taking her hand while he held the calf back with the other hand.

"You were right," she said breathlessly between chuckles, accepting his outstretched hand. "I'm so glad he's doing well."

The baby nudged Lacy roughly in the hip. "I think he has a crush on you," Clint said, grinning. "Come on, let's get you out of here before you get hurt."

Pulling her through the gate, he closed it quickly so that Junior couldn't follow. The sound of Lacy's laughter washed over Clint like sunshine breaking through cloud-filled sky. He was drawn to her by something he'd never felt before. And though buried in his desk drawer he had a reminder of all the reasons he should walk away from her, he couldn't.

"What did you do to that baby?" she asked. They'd started walking toward the house their arms brushing as they walked. "He's as strong as an ox."

"It's nothing I did. He just knows a pretty lady when he sees one."

"Flattery, Mr. Matlock?" she asked with a sideways glance. Her soft white hair sparkled in the sun and her white teeth flashed at him against her golden skin.

"Hey, I just tell it like it is, Miss Brown. I see your sunburn is turning to a tan. I was afraid you were going to be a peeling mess."

"Me, too. But I usually tan unless I'm foolish and

really overdo it. Thanks to you, I escaped the sun just in time." She stopped walking and placed her hand on his forearm. "Really, thanks for coming to my rescue. Again."

Clint squeezed her hand and then led her along a flagstone pathway around the corner of his ranch house to a private deck that stretched out from the back of the house over a sloping hillside. The view was breathtaking. Clint's land flowed beyond the deck's railing like a patchwork of greens dotted with brown and black cattle and the blues of a stream dissecting the pastures in a lazy arch.

"Oh, Clint. What a treasure," she gasped.

He stepped up onto the deck and pulled out a chair at the patio table for her. He'd worked hard on his home and it was nice to hear someone admire it.

"My dad picked this home site forty years ago." Since his father's death, Clint had done a number of renovations to the place and he appreciated his father's choice of building site even more, now that he'd done so much of the work himself.

Lacy accepted the willow chair he offered.

"This is interesting looking," she said, running her hands over the tabletop. "What kind of wood is this?"

"It's mesquite."

"You mean those awful scrub trees?"

"The same." Clint moved to the huge grill and the steaks he had waiting to cook.

"Who would have ever believed you could make something so beautiful with something so—"

"Useless," Clint finished for her.

"Exactly. Another reminder of how everything God created has beauty. Sometimes it simply takes sanding and polishing to make it gleam."

Clint smiled. That was Lacy, always seeing the big picture. He continued to work at the stone counter.

"Here let me do something," Lacy said, joining him. "I can help. Really."

"Okay, you can go into the kitchen and bring out the salad. It's in the fridge. Can you grab the tray with the cheese and butter for the potatoes too?"

"Sure thing, I'll be right back."

He watched her bound into the house, happy as a lark. He'd had a hard time sitting beside her in church earlier. She couldn't carry a note any better than he could, but they'd praised the Lord with smiles on their faces and joy in their hearts. Sharing that kind of worship had been an unbelievable experience. It was also cause for concern on his part. He'd started seeing Lacy in a better light than he had when she'd first come to town. Still, he had reservations about his feelings for her.

Thoughts of the letter gathering dust in the drawer in his office reminded him that things could change in the blink of an eye. His mother had once seemed to love the Lord, too.

Pushing aside thoughts of the letter from his mother, determined to give Lacy a chance, he forced himself to look at all the good Lacy had done since coming to Mule Hollow.

Despite his reservations, he'd begun to believe that the town might just benefit from her ideas and energy. He'd noticed during the sermon that she'd grown very thoughtful and he wondered if something in the message had bothered her.

"Wow," she said, coming out of the French doors, her arms loaded down. "Your house looks like it came straight off the showcase floor of a building center."

"Thanks. A lot of labor went into those rooms."

"I can tell." She set the salads down and arranged the condiments.

"Lacy, may I ask you something?" He turned to face her. Folding his arms across his chest, he leaned against the rock counter.

"Sure, anything."

"Was something bothering you this morning during the service? I'd like to help."

For a moment her eyes registered uncertainty before she looked away.

"I'm feeling a little confused, is all."

"I'm a good listener."

She took a deep breath and toyed with a napkin, laid it aside then tapped her purple fingernail on the table in her familiar impatient fashion. "Okay, here it is." She strode to the deck railing and looked out over the landscape. The gentle breeze ruffled her hair as she turned to face him. "You know what a mouth I have on me. Not cursing or anything like that, but just a big mouth… I'm sure you haven't noticed that."

Clint laughed at that. "Maybe a little."

She made a funny face at him, then started pacing. Clint enjoyed watching her. She had on a soft dress that, like the dress she wore the night of the flood, swirled around her calves as she moved. Her face was animated as she spun to face him.

"I'm going to be nicer from here on out."

"Does that mean things are going to be boring now?" He was disappointed that she might change. Surprising, but true. He took steaks off the grill, plopped their foil-covered baked potatoes on the plates and took them to the table.

Lacy followed him to her seat at the table. "With me around... Are you kidding?"

"Lacy Brown, I have an idea that it will never be boring anywhere within a two-day drive from where you are."

Lacy laughed. "I hope that's a good thing."

"A very good thing." He couldn't help wonder what he was getting himself into by becoming friends with Lacy.

"But." Lacy grew thoughtful. "Oh, how I would love to tame my mouth."

He concentrated on adding cheese and butter to his potato then paused. "Do you really think your out-spokenness is all that bad?"

Lacy stopped preparing her potato. "Maybe."

"Hold that thought while I say the prayer." They bowed their heads and he thanked God for the food and good company. "So let me get this straight. God Himself doesn't like it?" He took a bite of his steak and watched her contemplate his question. Man, she was cute when she thought really hard. She had reminded him of Meg Ryan the first time he saw her, but when she put her thinking cap on, she really had similar facial expressions. It was entertaining just watching the metamorphosis.

"Not exactly." She pointed her fork at him and smiled. "You sure you want to hear my exhortation on how I don't measure up?"

"Yes, I do." She was serious. The carefree Lacy Brown actually thought she wasn't good enough. The idea slammed into Clint. It wasn't anything like what he expected her to feel. She came across so in tune with herself.

"Well, that list could go on forever. Let's just say that I feel pretty defeated every time my exuberance leads me down the wrong path. Oh, how I wish I could think before I act or speak, more often."

"I have a feeling God likes watching your exuberance. I know I do." He said it and he knew it was true. Who couldn't enjoy watching someone as full of life as Lacy? Who couldn't want to be that way themselves? "You're pretty funny, Lacy Brown."

"You're pretty funny yourself." She grinned as she cut into her steak.

"My dad taught me." Clint cut his steak and let the memories of his dad fill his mind.

"He must have been a wonderful man."

Clint smiled. "The best. A kid couldn't have asked to be loved by a dad any more than I was. Not that we didn't have our differences, but even though—" Clint paused, his heart ached for a moment. He was weirdly emotional today. His feelings seemed to be crowding in on him. "Even though he didn't always tell me he loved me, I knew it."

Lacy put down her fork and laid her small hand over his. "A kid can tell these things. Love is an emotion that doesn't always need words." She squeezed his hand, then pulled back, fiddling with her napkin before picking up her fork again. "I see it all the time in my salon. People, especially men, talking about their kids, and though they don't just blurt out, *'I love my kid'*, it's in the things they say, the way they express themselves. It's in their eyes."

Her eyes held his. Clint could listen to her talk forever.

She leaned her head to the side and smiled. "My mom was different. She told me she loved me almost every hour. I think it had to do with my dad leaving. I think she wanted to reassure me that her love would always be there for me. But she didn't have to worry about that. I knew."

"Where is your mom now?"

"She remarried and moved to Okalahoma. She's very happy. She was excited about me coming to Mule Hollow."

"Really. She wasn't worried about you?"

"Maybe, but if she was, she wouldn't tell me. She got used to my weird ways a long time ago."

Clint thought about that for a moment.

"You make a killer steak." Lacy beamed. "This is really good."

Clint put his fears aside, refusing to dim the wonderful afternoon he was having. "You keep being nice and I might tell you my secret sometime." He was glad to change the subject. He was only human, and he enjoyed her playfulness.

"You tell me your secret and I'll tell you my secret to the best berry cobbler in the world."

Clint leaned back in his chair, folded his arms behind his head and stretched. "Berry cobbler, huh? Let me think about this. You can actually cook. A cobbler?"

"Weird but true."

"You might have to prove that to me before I give you my secrets."

"You've got a deal, cowboy."

## *Chapter Eleven*

Tangled in her daisy-dotted sheets, Lacy plopped over onto her back as the Monday-morning sunshine crept through her bedroom window. It was the first day of a new week. "Good morning, Lord," she said, stretching like a kitten in a sunbeam. Rubbing her eyes with her fist, she sat up. Swinging her legs over the side of the bed, she swung them sideways for a few seconds. She loved mornings. Padding to the bathroom, she brushed her teeth, ran some water through her wild natural waves then picked up her Bible and walked into the kitchen.

Her morning coffee sat waiting and ready for her, thanks to a nifty coffeemaker. After filling her mug she walked out onto the porch and curled up in the swing with God's word.

She'd started sitting in the swing soon after she and Sheri moved into their little cottage. She felt wonderful today. She knew it was because of her afternoon with Clint the day before. "Father, he said he enjoyed my exuberance." She spoke aloud as she thumbed through the Bible. Clint had reminded her before she came home that Peter held a special place in God's heart. In doing so he'd given her something to think about. But this morning she paused in her Bible study, her thoughts fixed on Clint.

She wondered what had happened to his mom after she'd abandoned him. She wondered how he felt toward his mom. Did he ever see her? Had he forgiven her?

It was a huge question Lacy understood completely. She had forgiven her dad for casting her aside for another life. Lacy looked out over the backyard lost in thought. After her dad walked out, she'd never seen him again. It had taken a long time to understand that she needed to forgive her father even if she couldn't see him face-to-face. Even if he hadn't asked to be forgiven. Or cared.

She couldn't help feeling that maybe Clint needed to come to terms with some form of reconciliation with his mother.

She might not have known the love of an earthly dad but she had the all-encompassing love of an awesome heavenly Father.

Lacy and Sheri arrived at Adela's for a planning session and a walk through of Mule Hollow's newly opened apartments-slash-bed-and-breakfast.

The old Howard estate had been built in 1904 by Adela's grandfather on her mother's side. Originally built as a boardinghouse, it thrilled Adela that she was able to bring it full circle. There were six small one-bedroom apartments. There were also two bedrooms that Adela left for bed-and-breakfast rooms for those who were just staying a short time. The house had a huge kitchen and dining room, and though Adela and her husband had raised their three children in the house, the upkeep had been far too much for her after her children moved on and her husband died. She had lived next door in a small cottage for the past ten years. Today there were tears in her eyes when she greeted Lacy and Sheri at the door.

Lacy lost her breath when she and Sheri stepped through the door. The woodwork was gleaming and the dark hardwood floors shone. The staircase that rose three stories was magnificent as it wound upward from the entrance hall.

"Adela, this is fabulous," Sheri actually exclaimed before Lacy could get her breath.

"Oh, Adela," Lacy gasped. "What a treasure this is."

"Come in," Adela invited, breathless with pleasure. "I'm so thrilled with the outcome that I could quite literally burst. My granddaddy would be so pleased that his home was about to be lived in and admired again. You know he did much of the carving himself."

They followed her through the large rooms with its era furniture and crisp white curtains. The home was filled with ornate crushed velvet couches that invited one to sit and read a book. Lacy could envision the place packed with people. The bookcases were even packed with books that had probably been collected over one hundred years. What a treasure.

In the kitchen, Norma Sue and Esther Mae were polishing silverware. Their chatter filled the house, and Lacy laughed as they drew close.

"With all this standing we're going to be doing I bought me some of those Neutralizer shoes to wear," Esther Mae was saying as Lacy stepped into the kitchen. "They are supposed to be real good for your feet if you're standing all day."

Norma Sue paused in her spoon rubbing. "That's *Naturalizers,* Esther Mae."

"Oh, well, either way they are comfortable. My feet feel like they are floating on air. And look, ya'll—" she lifted her hefty leg up "—they're cute, too. Lacy, you need to get you a pair of these for standing on your feet all day in the salon."

"I might try me some. Thanks for the advice." Lacy pulled out a stool and sat down at the bar.

"Just make sure you buy the *Naturalizers* and not the *Neutralizers,*" piped in Norma Sue. "Unless of course you have a bad case of foot odor!"

Everybody got tickled at that, and Esther Mae turned as red as her hair.

While Lacy joined in on the silver polishing, Adela and Sheri fixed a plate of sandwiches and iced tea. When they carried the food to the table, everyone sat down, joined hands and prayed for the food and the town.

"I have a surprise to share," Adela said as they passed the platter around. "Three apartments are spoken for and the two guest rooms are booked for the weekend of the fair."

"Hallelujah!" exclaimed Norma Sue.

"Sheri, I told you they would come." Lacy beamed, reaching out to accept the hug Sheri offered.

"I hoped you would be right," she said, grinning.

Esther Mae patted her updo and expelled a long breath. "Whew, I can hardly wait. When are they coming?"

"Let's see, Ashby Templeton is coming out from California at the end of next week. She's the one interested in opening a dress store. She said she had grown weary of the city and has been looking for a place to open a store. She has a Web site that she sells her clothing on and does a very good business there. So she is a perfect candidate."

Everyone exchanged thrilled smiles, then waited for Adela to continue.

"Two of the apartments are being rented by schoolteachers. We had very good timing with the ad, because a lot of the new teachers coming into the school system hadn't relocated to the area yet, and decided to give us a chance. And then the last room is a columnist and freelance reporter for the *Houston Times*. Her name is Molly Popp. Isn't that a cute name? Reminds me of that old song about lollipops. She said she did a lot of traveling, but was tired and had really been thinking about settling down and writing a book. She is renting a room, but if she feels this is a place she would like to stay, then she is going to rent an apartment. Can you imagine, ladies, she might settle here also?"

Everyone was clapping and she waved them silent. "But it gets better. She's mentioning the fair in her weekly column, and encouraging single women and even families to come out to participate in it. *Then* she's writing an article about the fair's success."

Lacy's heart pounded in her chest as she closed her eyes and thanked God for His faithfulness. Mule Hollow wasn't going to be a sad little town anymore. This was only the beginning.

By Wednesday, Adela had sent out the word that help was needed, and now the entire population of Mule Hollow was standing on Main Street ready to work.

If people were coming, and it sounded like they were, then the ladies wanted them to stay. That meant Mule Hollow had to greet them with more than a sad sigh. It needed to grab their attention and invite them to put down roots from the moment they entered. The ladies and Lacy had decided it was time to put out the call and paint the entire town.

Lacy was impressed. When Adela spoke, people listened. Every rancher and cowboy within twenty miles had to be standing in front of her holding a paintbrush. Why, every parking space along the street had a vehicle in it!

And Clint was one of those who'd shown up.

He'd come bright and early with a trail of black pickups following him. He had helped her organize the tables and cans of paint that Pete had sold them at rock-bottom prices. And now it was time to expose her plan and open the paint.

"Now, all you boys don't get disturbed when I start pulling off these lids." Lacy looked around the crowd, a gleam in her eye then she pried the first lid off a can of canary-yellow paint. All the masculine faces went slack, but she still had them. Then she ripped off the lid of a can of deep raspberry, and they all took a step back.

"Now, don't go anywhere. I promise these colors will be perfect." She could tell they didn't believe her. Clint stood to the side of the group with his Stetson pulled low and his arms crossed over his chest. The hat cast a shadow over his eyes but she could see the half grin of his full lips. Encouraged, she popped the tops off a few more cans.

"Miss Lacy, are we really supposed to paint these buildings those colors?" someone asked.

"Yes, we are." Lacy stood and slowly met each cowboy's gaze, challenging them to believe. "I'm promising you this will work. This is going to be the happiest town in Texas. When people get within nine miles of this place, they're going to see us on the horizon."

"That's for sure," someone else said, igniting laughter. Lacy smiled; she'd expected this.

"Look at my building. I bet when I started painting it everyone didn't think it would look as good as it does now." No one said anything. "Okay," she said, thinking, "in Texas, on a long flat stretch of road between Houston and Huntsville, there's this section of road about nine miles long, and in honor of General Sam Houston, there stands a gigantic statue of him at the entrance of the state park. It has only been there for a few years, and before it was constructed, that long lane of highway was one boring drive.

"For people traveling that stretch of road for the first time it seemed endless, especially if there were kids.

Then someone got the idea of constructing this beautiful tribute there." She had started moving among the guys as she talked. "He's huge." She waved her arms wide. Everyone was listening. "Now, when people come over that hill and hit that long, long stretch they see a white spot at the end of the road before it disappears around a bend. *A white spot.*" She stopped and put her hands on her hips. "I know, I know, what does a white spot change, you ask? Honestly, not much. But there is this *spot* and people are driving and they are squinting and they are saying, What is that? *What is that?* And as they drive, they become so engrossed in wondering what's on the horizon, well, the miles just roll by."

She had come full circle now and was back beside the paint cans. "And as they draw closer, the white spot starts taking shape and soon there he is. General Sam Houston himself, and looking at him is so cool. He even has a wart on his nose. Many people who would have passed on by stop and get out of their cars and look at the monument. Now what does that have to do with us, with Mule Hollow? Everything. What did you used to see when you hit the five-mile mark outside of town?"

"Some ugly brown buildings," Clint said, pushing back his Stetson.

Lacy nodded, beaming. "Yep, yep, yep. Boring brown wood. Now what do you see?"

"Well, it sure ain't nothing white," J.P. said with a grin. "But I kinda like seein' your pink building popping out at me like a big surprise. I've kinda started looking forward to it."

"You do? I mean, *yes.* That's what I mean." Lacy was

ecstatic when all the guys started nodding and voicing agreement with J.P. When Clint caught the edge of his hat and tipped it to her, her heart started thumping harder. "Okay," she said to the group, "so now we paint."

She was busy after that splitting the fellas into groups of two and three, showing them how appealing each colored building would be with the right trim and adornment. The vision God had given her was there and it thrilled her when everyone seemed to warm to it.

Right before they broke into their groups, she was as thrilled as the cowboys, when Sam's niece Amy drove in to town from San Angelo with a carload of girlfriends. College students wanted every opportunity to be around a bunch of hunks, as she put it to Lacy a few minutes after they climbed out of their car.

Clint was heading up the replacement of sidewalk planks and broken windows. And Lacy found herself pausing her painting to watch him in action.

He was quite handy with a saw and a hammer. Norma Sue had suggested he be appointed head of the carpentry duties, after telling Lacy that he had practically renovated his ranch house all by himself.

Lacy had been impressed with the beauty of his home. She wondered why he hadn't told her he'd done the work. She had commented on certain things while she was there, like the massive tiled outdoor kitchen that surrounded the patio where they had eaten lunch. Norma told her that he had just finished that project last winter. It made sense; a cowboy needed something to do after dark on a winter night. He was humble, and though it looked like a talented professional had done the work, Clint had kept that to himself.

Lacy went back to painting, liking the raspberry paint she was applying to the building next to her salon. She kept having to remind herself more and more that she hadn't come to Mule Hollow to think about Clint Matlock. But every so often she would catch him watching her, and when she happened to catch him at it, he would tip his hat at her again, and turn those lips into a slow smile that seemed to light a path right up to her feet.

It was really hard not to think about that, and get lost in her confusion. But she forced herself to have fun like everyone else seemed to be having. It was almost like a fair day without the planning.

Adela and Esther Mae served colas, sandwiches and chicken all through the day, while Norma Sue supplied paint refills to anyone whose paint trays started drying up. Pete, a robust man with a quick smile, stood around and told jokes to anyone who would listen as he watched his old weather-beaten building become a bright grass-green, trimmed in daffodil-yellow. And when it was complete, that's when Lacy got excited. It looked awesome. It looked fantastic! It looked just the way she had envisioned it that first morning when she'd surveyed her new home from the seat of her Caddy.

Best of all, the bright paint brought excitement to the dusty streets of Mule Hollow. The college girls commented on how much fun they were having and how much nicer the painted buildings made the town.

And no one complained about the colors anymore. Everyone had started to see "her vision" as they'd begun to call it. She kept explaining to each person who would listen that it was God's vision.

Clint guided his horse over the dry riverbed and up the bank onto the other side of the ravine. He'd neglected his ranch for three days, while he and his ranch hands had helped paint the town.

Now he was checking back pastures for tire tracks and broken fence line. He'd also come to the more remote area of his ranch to think.

He couldn't deny the enjoyment he'd gotten watching Lacy Brown in action. The woman was something. She had ramrodded the painting of the town with such excitement that every skeptic had begun to believe in what she wanted to accomplish.

The transformation Main Street had gone through in three days was amazing. Once sad and ghostlike, the town was now bright and inviting. She had instructed him to build window boxes for second-story windows, and she'd filled them to overflowing with lively silk flowers. Getting into the swing of things, Clint had taken a few hours, nailed together some planks, and now Sam's Place and Pete's had picnic tables sitting out front. There were even tablecloths and flowers adorning the ones outside of Sam's.

He chuckled, remembering the looks on all the guys' faces when she'd started popping off can tops to expose the colors. For a moment he'd thought everyone was going to turn and run. But Lacy had calmed them down and talked them into going along with her ideas.

One look into those sparkling eyes and he'd been

hooked. Despite his trepidation about her in the beginning, he was starting to think using his mother as a yardstick to judge Lacy by had been wrong. Lacy's sincerity exploded from her with everything she did. Her worries about God wanting her to tame her tongue tickled him. And touched him. For her to be concerned about being the right kind of woman in a world filled with excuses for everything…well, that spoke volumes for her character.

Clint brought his horse to a halt at the edge of a ravine overlooking a huge portion of his ranch. As far as he could see, he owned the land. He was thirty-five years old and tired. Tired of working all day and going home to a silent house. Tired of working on projects for his home when there was no one to share it with. He was tired of having his king-size bed all to himself. What good did everything he owned do him, when there was no one to share it with and no child to leave it to?

His mother had run away with the owner of a small-time circus that had camped out on the outskirts of Mule Hollow for the winter. Clint had only been eight but he'd been old enough to know his mother wasn't happy. There had been a time when she was so high on life that all they did was laugh at home. And then something had changed around the time the town started dying and people moved away.

Many of his mother's friends were forced to leave, and with his dad always working on the ranch, she'd become lonely. He hadn't understood everything then, but over the years the understanding came to him. She'd been lonely, and the owner of the circus had offered a diversion. His dad had tried not to let Clint blame her, by taking on most of the blame himself for having neglected her.

The letter he'd refused to open tugged at his conscience. He pushed the thought away and directed his horse to start the treacherous path down into the valley. His mother's betrayal had devastated his dad, who had thrown himself into his work in order to live through the pain. That had become their way of life.

It had been fifteen years since his dad's death, and Clint had carried on his legacy. Work, work and more work. Until Lacy Brown had blasted into his life, he hadn't known how much he wanted more.

But the more he thought about her, the more he wondered. What if this was simply a phase Lacy was going through? What if she grew bored with Mule Hollow?

What if he fell in love with her before she left?

## Chapter Twelve

"Okay, are you reaaaddddy to rummmbbbble?" Lacy asked Esther Mae as they stared at each other's reflections in the mirror. Lacy held her scissors right above a lock of red hair. Behind them Norma Sue, Adela and Sheri watched expectantly.

Esther Mae squeezed her eyes shut and nodded her head. "It's now or never. Let's do it."

That was all the encouragement Lacy needed. With one quick motion she sliced through the hair and tossed it over her shoulder. "How'd that feel?"

Esther grinned, "Like a relief. More please. I can't wait to see the new me."

"Anything would be an improvement," Norma Sue yelled, from under the dryer, not realizing she was yelling. She was sitting half under the hood with a bag over her head and one ear turned their way so she wouldn't miss any of the conversation.

"Your hair will look wonderful shorter," Adela said

calmly from the manicure table where Sheri was pampering her hands with a paraffin treatment.

The music was playing and Lacy was happily snipping away. The only picture of what Esther Mae was going to look like was in her creative mind's eye. Having fun with it, she continued to toss hair over her shoulder as she cut, thrilled to be open for business and that Esther's red bird's nest was Heavenly Inspirations' first casualty.

Everything was coming together for the fair day, and now that her salon was open for business, she felt great.

"We're almost there, Esther. Just a few more snips and you'll be able to wash and go."

"Am I going to be as good a makeover as Main Street was?"

"*Nothing can compare to Main Street,*" yelled Norma Sue from beneath the hair drier.

"She's going to break our eardrums." Adela chuckled.

"*What?*" Norma Sue barked and, everyone burst out laughing. Norma raised an eyebrow and lifted the hood. "What's so funny?"

"You," Esther snapped. "You're screaming."

"Oh—" Norma laughed "—can you tell I'm not used to this sort of thing?"

"It's not just you, Norma," Lacy said. "A lot of people do the same thing. And now that I'm here, this is going to become like a second home to you. I'm going to pamper you all the time. Okay, Esther, let's blow-dry and we're done."

A few minutes later everyone was speechless.

"Wow," Esther Mae gasped. "Who is that?"

Lacy smiled proudly. Esther's huge hair was gone and in its place was a softly curling short cut that swept away from her face on both sides in a gentle wave. Her cheek bones seemed to lift off her plump face, creating hollows that hadn't been there before. Her eyebrows were just exposed by a soft wisp of a half bang creating an updated and casual new look.

Everyone finally found their voices and let Esther Mae know how wonderful she looked. Lacy felt a satisfaction deep inside, and once again she knew this was a career she could love for a lifetime.

"Okay, so when is it my turn?" asked Norma.

"Right now. Let's rinse out this conditioner, and then we'll get started."

"Do you have any idea what to do with this stuff?"

Lacy started rinsing out the conditioner. "Yes, I do. I've been thinking about how to fix your hair since the first time I saw you."

"Is that so?"

"Yup, that's so. Now come over to the hot seat." Norma hurried over and hopped into the chair. Her kinky hair was all spiked. Lacy started combing.

"While I do this, let's talk about what else we need to do to get this fair day off the ground."

"I'm supposed to take flyers to Ranger tomorrow," Sheri offered. "J.P. is going with me."

"Good. Make sure you put them all over the place," Norma said. "Lacy, are you cutting all my hair off?"

"No, Norma, just half of it. Relax, would you?"

"Clint is going to supply the hay for the seating," Adela said, intent on picking out a nail polish. "Lacy, have any of the men been in for haircuts?"

Lacy shook her head. "They think this is a *beauty parlor.* I'll have to do some convincing to get the guys in here. When you talk to them about coming here, please refer to it as the *salon.*"

"When are some of the boarders coming?" Esther asked as Sheri helped her dip her hands into the paraffin.

Adela looked up from polish picking. "Some will be here Saturday for the fair."

"I certainly hope we have a good turnout," Esther said.

"We will have a great turnout." Lacy spun around and faced everyone. "Think positive."

"Now, we are clear on what games we are going to play, right?" Norma asked, eyeing her vanishing hair with a worried expression.

"Yup." Lacy smiled and kept on cutting. "Horseshoes, washers, watermelon seed spitting, the three-legged race, cow chip toss—"

"Cow *what* toss?" Sheri asked, looking appalled.

"You heard right." Lacy laughed. "With all these dried cow patties, why shouldn't we have a Texas Frisbee-throwing contest?"

"For starters, it's gross!"

"Sheri, you are going to toss one and I'm going to toss two or three. It'll be great fun."

"I'm tossin' one, too," Esther Mae said.

"Okay, Norma Sue," Lacy said, picking up a bottle

of leave-in conditioner. She squirted a little in her palm then rubbed it through Norma's hair. "This is a must-have for your wiry curl. I've textured the curls so that with just a little of the moisturizer you should have an entirely different feeling to your hair. There, what do you think?"

Norma blinked. "How'd you do that? Look, ya'll, my curls are soft. Lacy Brown, I love you."

"Knock, knock." Everyone turned to find Clint peeking in the doorway. "Is this a private party? Or can a cowboy get a haircut?"

"I'd love to give a cowboy a haircut," Lacy said. She was so glad to see Clint. "Come in. I was just finishing with Norma. What do you think?"

Clint placed his hat on the rack next to the door and strode into the room. "Goodness, Norma, you look great."

He circled the beaming Norma, and Lacy enjoyed watching the way she blushed. Lacy knew that Clint and Norma had a close relationship and she enjoyed watching them together.

"You think Roy Don will like it?" she asked, patting her soft curls.

"Like it. Yeah, he's going to like it. Make him take you out on the town. Not our town. Make him take you to a nice restaurant in Ranger. Whoa…" He whistled as he glimpsed Esther Mae. "Lacy, you are good. Esther, you look spiffy. Ya'll better make it a double date."

The ladies laughed and patted their new hairstyles.

Esther spun to look at Norma. "We could go try out

that new steak house in Ranger. You know, the Texas Roadkill, or something like that."

"It's the Texas Road House. They have something named after roadkill on the menu," Norma said. "But I heard it was real good. Come on, let's go snag our boys and head that way. Adela, do you want to come? We could grab Sam. That man probably hasn't been out of the county in decades."

Adela looked thoughtful for a moment. "You know, I bet you're right. It would do Sam good to get out from behind that counter of his."

Lacy and Clint exchanged hidden smiles as Adela stood up and smoothed her dainty dress.

"I think I'll go over and invite Sam to come along."

"Atta girl, Miss Adela," Clint said, holding the door open for the ladies. They strolled out onto the sidewalk shoulders back, heads up. "You all have a good time. And remember your curfews."

"Clint Matlock," Esther Mae said, wagging a finger at him, "you mind your own business. We just might not come home till the rooster crows."

Everybody chuckled then practically bounced down the sidewalk chattering excitedly.

"Lacy—" Sheri sighed "—see what we did. That makes me glad I followed you on this adventure."

"Yep, and I'm glad you came, too, 'cause if I had to paint those nails, they wouldn't be too happy right now."

"That's the awful truth." Sheri laughed, turning to remove her smock.

Clint closed the door and looked from one to the other of them. "What does that mean?"

Sheri turned back and walked toward the door. "Only that Lacy is really good with hair, but she literally can't paint the broad side of a barn, much less a fingernail."

Lacy shrugged. "It's true. I make a mess just thinking about nail polish."

Clint relaxed against the counter, next to the small cash register. "But I thought they taught you those things at school."

"Oh, they try," Lacy said, widening her eyes. "But some things have to come naturally. And just because they teach both at beauty school doesn't mean a person will have talent in both."

Sheri was looking out the window. "That's why we make a great team. We both appreciate what the other does. Oh, there's my ride. Catch ya later."

The room was suddenly silent as the door slammed shut behind Sheri.

"Wow, I can really clean out a joint. Is it something I said?" Clint asked.

"Naa, it wasn't you. They were all just excited. And Sheri had already said she was going with J.P. again to do something." It was obvious to Lacy that everyone wanted her and Clint to be alone together. Who was she kidding? She wanted to be alone with Clint. She had enjoyed their lunch on Sunday. And that had nearly been a week ago. Though she'd seen him every day that they worked on the town, they hadn't had the chance to really talk a lot. His being here in the salon reminded her of the last time he'd been here with his pink hair, and suddenly her mouth went dry.

"Looks like you've been busy."

Lacy looked at all the hair on the floor and reached for the broom. She needed something to distract her. "I have. It felt wonderful. I wanted the gals to be my first clients, so I could pamper them a bit. I've wanted to do that for Norma and Esther from the moment I met them."

Clint was studying her as she dumped the dustpan full of hair into the garbage. He seemed to be evaluating something.

"Is everything okay?" she asked, turning back to him while squelching the jitters that threatened to overcome her.

"Everything's…good."

He ran a hand through his hair, a habit that she'd come to associate with him almost as much as the thumb-to-the-hat trick. However, his eyes were downcast and that was something she didn't associate with him at all. "For some reason, I don't believe you. If…you need a friend to talk to, hairdressers make great listeners."

He smiled that slow smile of his and lifted that lean chin just enough for her to see those eyes. Her heart skipped a few beats. Quickly she turned away and walked to the shampoo bowl hoping to calm her nerves. "Come over here and let me give you a shampooing. You know the routine. Nothing relaxes someone like a great shampoo."

"I kind of like the shampoo part," he said, smiling that killer smile as he sat down and leaned his head back.

Lacy's hands were trembling before she even touched his thick dark hair. Thank goodness he couldn't see them.

"That was nice of you to want to do something special for Norma and Esther. They're good women, and out here in this forsaken backwoods, there isn't anywhere for a woman to be pampered."

He was watching her closely and she paused in her vigorous scalp massage. "That's one of the reasons I'm so glad I'm here. God gave me a vision for witnessing to the women that are going to come to Mule Hollow. But Norma, Esther and Adela who, by the way, only had her nails done today because her hair is already perfect—anyway, I love doing things for them." Lacy found herself staring down at Clint and smiling. Hastily she busied herself with finishing his shampoo then led him to her chair.

He continued to silently watch her in the mirror as she started combing his wet locks. He looked as uncomfortable as she felt. Trying not to be a klutz, she picked up her scissors and began to trim his hair. Touching him was hard enough—her insides kept getting all fluttery feeling, and his watching her so intently didn't help the situation. She wanted to pursue the reason for his somberness but couldn't. If she opened her mouth she might start talking nonstop because of her nervousness. What a hoot! She was afraid of what she might say.

When Clint did speak, it startled her because she was

concentrating so intently on ignoring the feelings that were swirling around inside of her.

"What are you going to do when you move on from Mule Hollow?" His voice was gruff.

She had just folded his ear down to trim the crease hidden there and she paused. "Move on? What do you mean?"

"Lacy, you're ambitious and obviously very talented, judging by what I saw this afternoon. Why would you want to stay in a hole-in-the-road town like Mule Hollow? I mean even if this plan works and we are able to get some life back into the town, it still won't have much to offer you."

The edge in his voice bothered Lacy. She hadn't heard it before and it sent warning signals to her heart. There was more to the question than was being asked.

"Consider Proverbs 27:8, Clint, 'As a bird wandereth from her nest, so is a man that wandereth from his place.'"

Lacy remembered the verse God had led her to that morning in her Bible study. And she understood. God had touched her when she read it.

"I won't be leaving Mule Hollow. I feel as if I've found my place, my nest. I feel like Mule Hollow is the home I've been looking for all of my life." She met his gaze in the mirror. "It isn't a coincidence that God gave me that vision when I read the newspaper that morning and found Adela's ad. God isn't a God of coincidence. He is a God of purpose, not confusion." She resumed cutting, praying she was explaining herself without confusion.

"How do you know God won't change your mind?"

Why was he asking these questions? "The morning I drove into Mule Hollow I felt a special bond. Something reached out and touched me, and until I read that verse this morning, it hadn't fully registered that this was home. I felt a little like the prodigal son or something... not that I've been out eating with the pigs or anything, but you know what I mean."

"No. What do you mean? You are hardly the prodigal son."

Lacy nibbled her lower lip. Clint was pushing her. The question was why? Suddenly out of nowhere she knew it was time for her to bite the bullet. She didn't want to. But God was really thumping her on the head and she couldn't very well ignore Him.

"Clint, I'm fixing to be your friend and stick my nose where maybe it shouldn't be—" She paused when he raised an eyebrow. "Have you forgiven your mother for leaving you when you were a boy?"

Clint's eyes dulled. "Forgive her? Lacy, I know I'm supposed to. I know God forgave me, so as a Christian I'm supposed to forgive her. But honestly, until a few days ago it never crossed my mind that I should forgive my mother for what she did."

Lacy removed the cutting cape from his neck while praying for the words she needed. Heavy in thought, she leaned against the counter and toyed with the telephone cord.

"Forgiveness is weird in many ways," she said quietly. "It took me a while to forgive my dad. But after I forgave him it was I who received the reward. I mean my dad couldn't get the reward—I've never seen him again and I heard a rumor that he died. But I have a peace inside me now that wasn't there before I decided to forgive him and let it go."

"But the other night out in the storm—you were upset about your dad stealing your mother's dreams."

"I still have scars left over from his leaving my mom. And I'm human. Sometimes when I'm really down I'll sulk, and his leaving did change me and form me into the person that I am. I can't forget that. But I forgave him. And inside I know it. But most important, God knows it even when I'm having a pity party."

Clint studied her for a long moment and then he stood and headed toward his hat. "I can't say that I'm made of the same character as you. This just proves once more that you're a special lady, Lacy Brown. A special lady indeed."

With that he laid a twenty on the counter, touched her nose with the tip of his finger, then strode out the door of Heavenly Inspirations.

A lot of inspiring she had done. The man had issues and she hadn't helped him one bit.

## Chapter Thirteen

The black night sky was wide-open, dotted with the sprinkle of stars and a mere thumbnail of a moon. Clint sat in a chair on his back patio staring into the dark heavens.

He didn't believe her. She had good intentions, but she didn't know what this town could do to a woman. She was too talented anyway. There were limitations to her talent here that she wouldn't have in a city. Financially speaking, she could make five times the salary elsewhere. She would see that soon.

He wasn't blaming her or looking down on her choices—it would just happen. He just prayed she left before he was in any deeper than he already was. Every time she spoke, he grew more intrigued by her heart. He had never been around anyone who earnestly sought out God's will like Lacy did.

He was a Christian, but he had to admit that sometimes he felt like he was simply going through the motions. Weeks would go by, and he would realize that he hadn't picked up his Bible except to carry it to church on Sunday morning.

That wasn't so with Lacy. As wacky as she could be, he knew that she walked closely with God. The Bible held the answers, but he knew that many times he didn't pick it up because he just didn't want to. There were days when he'd go all day thinking about needing to read the Bible, and then he would intentionally pick up a ranching magazine or turn on the television. It wasn't something he fully understood.

But he knew it was a rebellious action that stemmed from long ago.

Clint studied the stars. His mother used to study them with him. He saw her laying a blanket on the ground as she'd done when he was young. Then the three of them would lay on their backs, heads touching, and study the stars together. He remembered how once she'd told him that while they were looking up at heaven, God was looking down at them. She said He was smiling because they were looking in the right direction. It was a good memory, and for a moment he toyed with the idea of going to his office and opening the letter he'd received from her.

Lacy would have read the letter the moment it arrived in her mailbox. She had a heart that could expand and embrace…. Closing his eyes, he rubbed the bridge of his nose. Lacy could embrace forgiving her father. But he wasn't as good a person as Lacy. Clint hardened his heart to the good memories of his mother. Though they pounded against its doors, they didn't last long.

His mother left him, cast him off without a backward

glance. And she'd done it the very summer after they'd lain on the blanket and studied the stars.

Funny the difference a year could make.

Clint's heart was aching as he leaned forward in his chair, with his elbows on his knees, and studied the ground. It was rich and fertile for man and cattle, but not for a woman. Lacy didn't understand yet what remote, small-town life could do to a woman. And he couldn't forget.

And his heart couldn't watch someone else he loved walk away again.

And the letter… It could rot in his desk.


"Okay, move those hay bales over there," Lacy directed the two cowboys, Andrew and Bob. They were two great guys who were a part of the many who had been helping all day in the setup for tomorrow. Andrew was a dark-haired man with a funny bone and Bob was a tall, quiet loner who seemed content to help at whatever she asked. He didn't say much, but his presence was that of a giant. The two guys were great friends and Lacy could see why. They complemented each other like missing pieces to a puzzle. She couldn't wait until the right women came along that would fill their hearts just as perfectly. And they were ready, too.

Bob paused beside her now, balancing a square bale on his broad shoulder as if it were a mere brick. "Miss Adela asked me if I'd be in a special booth tomorrow."

"Oh, did she now?" Lacy smiled, leave it to Adela to know exactly the right guys for her *special* booth.

The girls would be lining up for miles to buy lemonade from Bashful Bob. "And what did she tell you about her booth?"

He shifted and a faint tinge of pink crept into his cheeks. "It's a lemonade stand to help raise more advertisement money. I told her I didn't know anything about squeezing lemons, but she assured me the ladies wouldn't mind. Said she thought I was the man for the job, 'cause the ladies would want to watch me learn." His smile beamed and his dimples dug in deep. "I might be shy, but I'm no fool."

Lacy let out a hoot.

"Why, Bob Denton, you sneaky flirt. And I was calling you Bashful Bob."

Andrew sauntered over with a matching hay bale. "Lacy, don't let that shy exterior fool you. Bob is a lady magnet. Why do you think I'm his friend? The only problem is finding the ladies. You're our hero, or I guess I should say our heroine. If you can do for our love lives anything even close to the amazing stuff you've worked on this town, we just might not be lonesome cowboys anymore." He spun around on his boot heels with his empty arm flung wide. "Look at this place."

Watching him, Lacy felt a tug at her heart. These two sweet guys were typical of the men Mule Hollow had to offer: hardworking, good-natured men who would make wonderful husbands and fantastic dads. This plan for Mule Hollow had to work. It just had to.

Bob tipped his hat. "I guess we better get a move on putting this hay where it needs to be. See you later, Lacy."

She watched them stride away, hauling their heavy loads to their designated spots in front of the apple-green building and the periwinkle-blue one beside it. She plopped her hands on her hips and surveyed Main Street. It was looking pretty good. They had the cake-walk set up in front of Sam's so that the cakes could have a cool place to rest while waiting to be given away. The dunkin' booth, where a girl could step up and try and dunk a cowboy was next to the horseshoes, followed by rope tricks, then chip flinging at the end of the road. In the grassy area at the edge of town there was the three-legged race, the three-armed egg relay and a few other contests.

Tomorrow was the big day and time was running out. But everyone had their specific jobs and were busy with the last-minute details. They were all invested in this dream.

Sheri was heading up the talent committee. She and Sherri had discovered that there were quite a few singing cowboys out here on the range and they were putting them to good use at the afternoon picnic.

Norma Sue and Esther Mae were in charge of food preparation. Hank and Roy Don were legends around Mule Hollow for their chili and barbeque, so they were officially declared the cooks for the fair. Besides, it gave Sam the day off.

Adela was the official meet 'em and greet 'em host plus, she was overseeing the lemonade stand. She was also baking more cookies than Lacy had ever believed one woman could bake in a lifetime.

While everyone worked on their duties, Lacy was

busy with hers as the official overseer of everything. She hadn't slept much since Tuesday, and though she had confidence that God was in control, sometimes she had to squelch that voice of worry. This was going to work and Mule Hollow was going to begin the path of reinvention tomorrow. Bob, Andrew and so many more were counting on it—

"Penny for your thoughts." Clint's familiar voice from just behind her jolted her from her brooding with a shiver of excitement.

"I'll take it," she said, spinning around to face the man who had been on her mind every moment she let her guard down. Her spirits lifted at his nearness.

"That cheap? Must be some pretty heavy thoughts to sell out that low." His eyes glittered in the bright sunlight and his unshaven face gave him a dangerous persona. Upon closer inspection, he looked tired.

"My confidence is teetering," she admitted.

"*Your confidence.* I don't believe that for one minute. You are the gal who came blasting in here ready to take on anything." He surprised Lacy when he reached out and draped an arm about her shoulders and hugged her. "You've done a great job, Lacy. Chin up. No one but you could have done remotely what you have in just a few weeks. It's going to happen. I'm so proud of you."

Sighing, she gave in to the temptation to sink into his side and the support he was offering her. He was strong and solid. If she let herself, she knew it wouldn't be hard to stay in his arms forever. How much she'd missed him the past few days slammed into her. She had heard through Norma Sue that he'd been camping out all over his property trying to be in the right place at the right time to catch the rustlers who had struck again the evening she had cut his hair. She wished there was something she could do for him.

"Have you had any luck locating the cattle thieves?" she asked, pulling her feelings off her sleeve and focusing on something safer.

He released her and shook his head, watching as Andrew and Bob walked by with more hay bales on each shoulder. They tipped their hats, "Howdy, Clint. Glad you made it to the fun," Andrew said.

"Lacy sure knows how to give a party," added Bob.

Clint grinned. "Looks that way. You boys are doin' a fine job." He stuffed his hands into his pockets and shifted his weight to one leg before meeting her eyes.

"Haven't had a bit of luck with the cattle rustlers." He continued their conversation after the cowboys moved on. "The night we saw them was the last time I've been near them. I'm beginning to think I'm never going to see them again."

Lacy grinned and poked him in the chest playfully. "You just need me to find them for you. Next time I'm out on one of my midnight rides, I'll keep an eye out for them."

Clint's brow furrowed; his eyes hardened sternly. Not at all the reaction she was aiming for. Lacy squelched her smile. She didn't know what to make of the glint in his eyes.

She wasn't too sure she liked it.

When he spoke she *knew* she didn't like it. Not one bit!

"Lacy, I have some ideas about who might be involved in this, and I don't think it's a good idea for you to be driving that car of yours around late at night. You could get stranded again, and I might not be around to save you."

"Thank you very much, but I can take care of myself, Clint Matlock," she huffed.

"Lacy, I don't want to argue with you but you don't have any business out at night like that."

"Look, Clint." She faced him square and glared at him. And to think she had missed him! "You don't have any reason to be telling me what I can or should be doing." She bit her tongue to hold back on saying more. His demands disturbed her, though deep down she knew what he said had merit.

"Look, Lacy, all I'm saying is be careful. These cattle rustlers are professionals. They worry me, and I don't want you to be the one who comes up on them and catches them by surprise. I don't know what they might do. Brady has been doing some checking, and we have a good idea who they could be. If it is who we suspect, they have records and will not want to be caught again."

Lacy relaxed and forced her pride aside. "Sorry, I know what you're saying makes sense. I'm just so used to my drives that I can't stand not going when I feel like it."

Clint studied her for a long second. Then he reached out and touched a curl of her hair. "Tell you what, I haven't yet ridden in that thing you call a car. So the next time you go, come get me and take me for a spin."

Lacy didn't like the fact that she really liked his idea. But happiness welled within her and poured out in an ear-to-ear grin. "I just might do that, cowboy."

His lips did that slow slide into that crooked smile, Lacy's heart did a giddyap right into her throat. Whoa, Nellie! This was getting ridiculous. And infatuating and dangerous and fun, she was thinking, when a little red sports car whizzed by and came to a halt at Adela's Boardinghouse.

"Wonder who that is?" Clint asked before she had a chance to voice the question.

Lacy started smiling again when a graceful woman, with long brown hair and legs to die for, stepped from the car. Every cowboy standing on Main Street had turned to watch as she straightened and glanced about the town.

Lacy sighed. "That, my friend, is Mule Hollow's future."

"Are you ready?"

Lacy licked her lips, grabbed hold of Clint's waist and nodded. "We can do this," she said, assessing the competition that stood along the starting line of the three-legged race.

Some of their competitors were J.P. and Sheri, Sheriff Brady and the elegant Ashby Templeton, who'd arrived the day before in the red sports car, a cute cowboy named Jake, Molly Popp, who'd also arrived the night before, and six other couples that included the three schoolteachers who were going to board at Adela's. Lacy felt pure joy at the picture they all made tied together, laughing and joking while they waited for Pete to fire the starting gun. This had so far been a glorious day.

There were people everywhere. Women had flocked to Mule Hollow from a radius of a hundred miles. Adela had been taking a poll and the reach of the ads, plus Molly's column had penetrated deep into the heart of Texas and even a few other states. This was proof that all things were possible with the Lord's help.

"On your mark." Pete's booming voice broke into Lacy's thoughts. She tightened her grip on Clint as he pulled her closer.

"Here we go," he said, his eyebrows knitted together in an ominous scowl. He meant business. Lacy giggled, looking up at him.

"Get set, go!"

In a roar of laughter, they were off. Guys were yelling and girls were laughing. Lacy concentrated on trying to keep her shorter stride with Clint's longer one, but they were really mismatched and clumsy. Beside them, Brady and Ashby were much more suited and started taking an early lead.

Clint glared over their way, "Oh, no, they don't," he growled, and nearly started dragging Lacy with him. Lacy started laughing so hard, she wasn't any help. Things went from bad to calamitous. In their haste, their rhythm got off. In the next instant, they were heading toward the ground in a pile of legs and arms.

Clint burst out laughing, too, as they tried to untangle themselves and stand again. They weren't alone on the ground. Half the lineup had taken the same detour and it now looked like a wrestling match rather than a three legged race.

Needless to say, Sheriff Brady and Ashby were victorious and showed no humility. They paraded their blue ribbon around proudly between the losers, goading that maybe everyone else could do better next year.

"What do you think, Lacy?" Clint asked after unraveling their legs and helping her up. "Is this going to happen again next year?"

"Are you kidding? We're going to practice every few weeks so we can make it more than ten feet next year."

Clint laughed and added dryly, "I meant the fair itself."

"Oh, yes, if I have any influence, this fair will become an annual event."

The event so far had been a raging success. Lacy hadn't seen so many happy cowboys in all of her life. The turnout had made believers of the majority of the guys. And the women were having such a great time that many of them had expressed a desire to look into property in the area. Mule Hollow had plenty of cheap real estate. It had been left behind by the families who had been forced to leave for lack of job opportunities.

The real-estate agent from Ranger had come down for the event and she was being bombarded with questions. If this frenzy continued, she'd said she might move to Mule Hollow.

Only time would tell how the town would really benefit from today, but Lacy was very optimistic.

"Are you interested in a glass of Adela's homemade lemonade?" Clint asked as they moved out of the way for the next heat of three-legged racers.

"Sure. But then I want to play Texas Frisbee."

"You really want to throw a cow chip?"

Lacy halted and plunked her hands to her hips. "Well, yeah. I bet I can fling one farther than you. You know," she said, jamming a thumb at herself in jest, "in high school I was district champ at the discus."

Clint shook his head. "You are a jack of all trades. A gymnast and discus star." He pushed his hat off his forehead with his thumb and scratched his temple. "What did you not do?"

Lacy started walking again. "A lot. Let's see, I wanted to play basketball but I was too small. I wanted to run hurdles but I was too small. I wanted to play volleyball but—"

Clint joined in. "You were too small."

"Uh-huh. So when I wanted to throw the discus the coach told me I was too skinny *and* too small. So my mom bought me a discus for my birthday and told me if I really wanted to do it, to do it and not let anyone tell me I couldn't. I practiced all summer and fall. When spring tryouts came, I told coach just to give me a chance to show him what I could do." Lacy slid a crooked eyebrow up and gave Clint a comical glare. "When I stepped up on that platform, everyone was laughing. And I mean laughing out loud, big-time. I didn't weigh eighty pounds wet. But I had worked on my form—you know the discus is really all about form—and mine was perfect. Anyway, I made the team and won district…but got creamed at the next level. I didn't care, I had proven to myself that hard work paid off."

They had reached the refreshment stand and stopped to wait in the lengthy line. Adela's plan had worked. Ladies waited patiently, dollars in hand, to see Andrew's smile and Bob's dimples up close while they passed out the lemonade.

"I bet you wish you'd never asked that question," she said, after they'd settled in for the wait.

Clint shook his head, "Actually I liked finding out what makes you tick."

"Oh, yeah." Lacy wrinkled her nose up and smiled. *Are you flirting with him, Lacy?*

"Oh, yeah," he said, reaching out and tugging at a strand of her hair. "I bet you gave your mama some gray hairs growing up."

"Yes, I can't deny the truth. I couldn't help myself. That was one of the reasons she put me in gymnastics early. She had to scrape the money together each month, but she said it gave my energy a positive release."

"What did you compete in? Wait, let me guess— those two bars that the girls fly from one to the other on."

"The uneven bars."

"That was it, wasn't it? I knew it had to be with the way you practically flew up into that tree the day Flossy was after your hide."

"You got it. I also did some other things, too." She didn't elaborate because they had reached the head of the line and Adela was beaming at them with a mega-watt smile.

"Oh, Lacy, Clint, isn't this the most delightful day." Anticipating what they'd come for, she held out two glasses of lemonade. Each glass had sugar on the rim and a fat red cherry floating among the ice in the cool deep yellow drink.

"What a great drink, Adela! No wonder there has been a line here all day. And, yes, today is fantastic."

"Clint, how are you holding up with all these beautiful women running around?" Adela's direct question had Lacy choking on her lemonade.

Clint was just as surprised. He shifted his weight from one booted foot to the other, then planted his gaze on Lacy before answering.

"I'm holding up pretty good, considering I've had the prettiest gal of all tied to my leg half the day."

Lacy tried hard to keep from letting his good-natured banter plunge through her melting barriers. But the butterflies nose-diving in her stomach were hard to ignore.

Adela handed them both a homemade cookie. "I'm glad to know you are an observant and smart man, Clint Matlock. You two enjoy the cookie and the rest of the day. You should go try out the three-handed egg race."

Lacy couldn't help laughing at the not-so-smooth attempt at matchmaking. "Thanks for the advice, Adela, but there are a couple of big fat cow chips across town with our names on them."

Clint tipped his hat at Adela as they started to leave. "This ought to be good, Adela. Maybe you should come over and watch. I think Lacy has the makings of a champion."

Lacy turned back to Clint and, linking her arm in his, pulled him away. "Come on with me, funny guy. I'm about to make a believer out of you. After all, I'm not just a pretty face."

"*That* is something I figured out a long time ago," he said, and pulled her into the laughing, swirling crowd.

## Chapter Fourteen

"**Y**ou know what we should do," Lacy exclaimed, causing everyone sitting in Sam's to look her way. "We need to come up with a business big enough to employ a lot of women."

Everyone who had been involved in masterminding the fair day was settled into chairs at Sam's place. They were exhausted, tired and *more* exhausted. The day had been an unbelievable success. Adela's place was packed, and if there had been a fifty-room hotel, it would probably have been full. Now it was about midnight, and everyone had gathered at Sam's to discuss the day. They were far too keyed-up to sleep.

Lacy was nearly bouncing off the walls and was afraid she was making everyone nervous. But she knew her idea was good.

"Hey, Lacy girl, that might be a good idea," boomed Esther Mae.

"There's a town not too far from here," added Norma Sue. "It has a huge furniture store that takes up half the old town. They just knocked out walls and connected the buildings. I heard they ship that furniture all over the place."

"Lacy—" Sheri yawned "—you know that town not too far from Dallas that has those baskets…oh, and the one not too far from there that makes those fruitcakes. They ship those things all over the world."

"Yeah, that's what I'm talking about." She started pacing.

"What we need to do," Adela said, "is start thinking of everything that might be a profitable endeavor."

"The way I see it," Lacy said, her mind humming with ideas, "we had a great response from the women from surrounding towns, but they need income in order to move here. I hadn't even thought of that until today. There are more people than just the teachers who might consider moving here if there were jobs for them."

Clint raised his hand and an eyebrow while looking at Lacy for acknowledgment. She smiled broadly at his schoolboy impersonation and pointed at him. "Clint, you may have the floor."

"I was thinking maybe I could hire a truckload of them. I need somebody to patrol for rustlers that I don't seem able to track myself."

Everyone, including Clint, roared with laughter.

Lacy shook her head, enjoying his playful side, and at the same time feeling kind of sorry for him because she knew he really did need to catch the rustlers.

Adela stood and smoothed the front of her cotton paisley dress. It barely had any wrinkles, and one would never have guessed she'd worn it all day and night.

"I guess what we should do is call it a night, and pray that the Lord will lead us in this endeavor. He's done a wonderful job so far by sending us Lacy and Sheri first, and then giving us this great day."

Everyone stood in agreement and, after hugs and good-nights, agreed to pray diligently.

Lacy had enjoyed her day at the fair more than any-thing she'd done in her life. And that was because of Clint. They had spent the entire day together without ever really planning to. It had simply seemed right. For Lacy, the lines between why she had come to Mule Hol-low and why she couldn't fall in love with Clint were blurring.

*Fall in love with Clint*—her thoughts were running away with themselves. She'd meant why she couldn't *date* Clint.

She was about to climb into her Caddy, when the subject of her confusion strode over, dropped his arm over her shoulders and gave her a friendly squeeze.

"I had a great time today."

"Me, too," she said, realizing how much she enjoyed the gesture.

"Sorry I doubted all of this early on. I believe from here on out I'm going to have a lot more faith." He released her and headed toward his truck.

Watching him walk away, Lacy's heart was pounding and her entire wonderful day was replaying before her eyes.

"See you at church in the morning," he called. Looking back at her, he paused while opening his truck door.

*He was gorgeous.* "Oh, yes. Bright and early." She watched him get in the truck then before she climbed into her Caddy she checked the time on her watch. It was one o'clock in the morning. Church started at ten o'clock. Which meant...

Only nine more hours until she could see Clint Matlock again.

"Okay, now you roll the dough like this." Lacy took her rolling pin, dusted it with a little flour and then began rolling out the thick ball of blackberry cobbler dough. Beside her, Clint stood watching as if this were the most important bit of instruction he would ever get. He was making her nervous. She'd been surprised when he'd told her he had something he wanted to bring by her house after church, if she were going to be there. After she had assured him that she would be, he'd come by bearing a bag of frozen blackberries, blackberries he'd obtained from Norma Sue's freezer since the season had ended at the beginning of the summer.

Lacy had been tickled by his presumption that she would drop everything and show him how to make *The Best Cobbler in the World.* Which she did, not that she had anything else to do. She was actually thrilled to be spending another Sunday afternoon with Clint, which she had decided could become habit forming.

And dangerous. Her kitchen was a small space with a low ceiling and the minute Clint had entered it he'd seemed to surround Lacy. Her senses were on overload.

"So now we have it rolled out." She paused and used

the back of her wrist to scratch the top of her nose. "Now we get to cut it in strips."

Clint relaxed against the counter as he watched what she was doing beside him. His arms were crossed over his broad chest; his position had him facing Lacy. She reached for the knife she would use to cut the pastry and paused before cutting.

"You sure you know how to use that thing?" he asked playfully, leaning his shoulder into hers.

Lacy frowned and pointed the tip of the knife at him. "You would be surprised at what I can do, Buster."

"Actually, Lacy, there isn't anything you could do that would surprise me."

Feeling a touch of pride at his words, Lacy started slicing the dough.

"Although, finding out you could cook is a stretch of my imagination." He nodded toward the pastry and the hot berry mixture waiting for the pastry, to finish it off.

Lacy gave him a mock look of disgust. "And just why is that?"

"I don't know." He sobered. "You don't come across as the homemaker type."

Lacy's pride plummeted. Once before he had insinuated that she was like his mother, and now she wondered… "Clint," she ventured. Uncertain how to broach the subject she faltered as she placed the pastry into the bubbling berries. "Do I remind you of your mother?" Well, that was being subtle! Way to go, Lacy.

Beside her he stiffened, then reached out and touched her nose.

"You had a little…uh, flour, um there." Their eyes met and held.

Lacy refused to relinquish her question to his diversion tactic. "Do I?" Please say no.

He shrugged. "Some."

Some. Lacy wanted to cry. Her nose started to burn and her eyes started to sting but she refused to let her lip quiver. She stared at him and fought the insult down with every ounce of self-control that she possessed. Her eyes would not dampen. "I see," she said after she could. "I believe this is ready to go into the oven." She picked up the pan of cobbler and carried it to the oven. Clint followed her. Drat the man.

She had not come to Mule Hollow to fall in love. She had come to prove to the Lord that He was King of her life by giving His vision her total concentration for a while.

But she hadn't been able to do that. She felt like a failure, because before she could be a witness for Christ to even one person in her new salon, she had fallen in love.

And she had fallen in love with a guy whom she reminded of the lowest of the low. A woman who would desert her child.

It was all too much for even Lacy to comprehend. The room had become very quiet. She closed the oven door, then leaned her head against the cabinet. *Dear Lord, help me.*

Clint touched her shoulder. "Lacy." He was standing behind her and his voice was gentle.

*No!* "Clint, I don't feel so good. I think you should go."

"Lace—"

"Really, Clint." She turned to face him, then brushed past him before he could stop her. "I'm tired from yesterday and last night and I want to lie down."

"Lacy, I—"

She cut him off. Spinning around, she glared at him. "Clint, I want to lie down and *you* need to leave. *Now.*"

She didn't want to hear any more. She had been a fool anyway falling in love with the first guy who came along. How fickle was that!

To make things worse, finding out the type of person she came across as proved her greatest fears. It was as if the cock had crowed three times. Her uncontrolled personality, her mouth, caused the world to see a bum package. Her fickle heart caused Lacy to see the same.

"Maybe you're right," Clint said, backing to the door. "Get some rest. I need to get back to work anyway." He tipped his hat, spun on his heel and walked out the door.

Belligerently, Lacy glared after him. She would not cry. She would get back to doing what she came to Mule Hollow for in the first place. She would ask God for forgiveness and she would resume her original plan.

And she would ignore the ripping, wrenching agony exploding in her heart.

His mother wanted his forgiveness.

Clint sat at his desk, the letter, neatly typed and to the

point, lay open before him…an answered prayer gone bad. After days of struggling with how he'd hurt Lacy's feelings, he'd finally set his backbone straight and faced the facts. He needed to open the letter and try and face the past that threatened any future he might have with Lacy.

So he'd opened the letter.

And for the life of him, he didn't know what to do now. He was a man used to making hard, quick decisions. He made them all day long. And now he felt like a lost little kid.

But he wasn't a boy anymore. He was a full-grown man who needed to act like one.

But forgiveness… He stared out the window, across the open range his mother had left behind so easily. She'd walked away from him just as casually as she'd left the land. And she'd never looked back. Until now.

Clint rubbed his temple; the dull throb of a headache was setting in. He was a man. A churchgoing Christian man. A man who took pride in the fact that he'd overcome years of hurt and endless nights of boyhood tears, because God, ever the comforter, had wrapped him in His sheltering arms when he'd hurt the worst.

But forgive her.

Clint pushed away from his desk and stood. The knot in the pit of his stomach wasn't from hunger, and the stinging around his eyes wasn't from allergies. He was a man, all right, a man who hadn't needed God's comfort in a very long time.

Picking up his hat, he strode from the room and headed for the barn and a hard ride on a horse that didn't want to be broken any more than Clint wanted to think about forgiving the woman he'd spent the better part of his life trying to forget.

He knew it would take more than a few nice words to break that colt, and one lousy letter wasn't doing anything for Clint except opening old wounds.

"So what do you think about giving me some highlights?" Molly Popp asked Lacy.

It was Tuesday and they were looking at each other in the mirror. Molly had stayed on for a week while she finished her column about the town and the fair day. Lacy had been pleased when she'd walked in this morning. Clients would be sparse for the first few months, and for a person like herself, sitting was not a virtue she took to with alacrity.

"Highlights would look great on your chestnut hair." She hoped she didn't sound too anxious.

"Then go to it."

Lacy grabbed a tray with all of her foils and went about setting everything up for the color process. She and Molly chatted rapidly about the fair and the ongoing plans to encourage women to establish themselves in Mule Hollow. Lacy was pleased that Molly had such a positive outlook on the idea. She had informed Adela that morning that she would be going back to Houston, closing out her small apartment there, and at the end of the month she would be back. She would then become the third new citizen of Mule Hollow since the newspaper ad had been placed, Lacy and Sheri being first and second.

Molly was a beauty. She had a mane of hair the color of burnt umber that flowed in waves of lively movement every time she talked or turned her head. She was very easy to talk to, which was probably a good thing since she was a reporter. Her eyes were an alert, vivid green. Her hands moved as she spoke and she had a habit of inclining her head to the right when she listened to what you were saying. She was a beautiful, warm and intelligent woman and she didn't know the Lord at all.

"So you came all the way out here because *God* told you to."

Molly's inflection was proof enough that she couldn't know God, or she would have known that what Lacy had done wasn't all that unusual. People listened to God's voice every day. Because she followed His direction, a few hundred miles wasn't a big deal. She hadn't had to sacrifice anything. She was no martyr and certainly no saint. Of course, depending on who you asked, she might be considered crazy. And from the look on Molly's face, this is what Molly thought of Lacy.

"What's the difference in my following Christ out here and you following your heart?"

"Well, hold on. Let me think this out." Molly was different than Lacy in that she tended to think before she spoke. Lacy wondered if she hung out with Molly long enough, some of that habit would rub off on her.

"I guess the big difference is I came here first before committing to it. You on the other hand had already committed yourself, sight unseen. How could you do that?"

"Easy. It's called faith. I trust my heavenly Father and

am willing to go where He leads me. Now, because I did this doesn't mean that I'm a saint or anything. I'm still plugging along, botching things up as I go. But I'm hoping and praying that I'm getting something right as I go."

She had really been wondering about that for the past four days. With Clint, she hadn't gotten anything right. Not so much in what she said but by her actions. And obviously she'd bungled that up hopelessly with her mouth and her heart.

Oh, how she'd missed him. How easily and subtly her heart had betrayed her. After she had thrown him out of her house—his house actually—she realized that she'd admitted that she had fallen in love with him. Her love had clicked into place like a natural fact. It was as if the love had been there since the beginning of time, waiting for Clint and Lacy to walk into it. Or at least Lacy…. Clint was the one who thought she reminded him of his good-for-nothing mother. *Forgive me, Lord. I know I'm not supposed to judge, but I do judge her and I can't seem to stop.*

She had to forget about Clint and place herself in the present, walking Molly through her questions about faith. And while she was at it, she might need to work on putting her own faith back into action.

## Chapter Fifteen

Clint slammed the door to his pickup and yanked his hat from his head. Every cowboy who worked for him was gathered in the stable yard, and he knew by their expressions that they were wary of his fury.

"Four nights and thirty more head gone." At the rate they were going, he might as well get out of the cattle business of his own accord. He'd rather do that than be stolen blind by the bunch of parasites who'd chosen him as their host.

"Tonight I want them stopped. They're coming in at the outer sections of land, and that's where I want you. I want every inch of the outskirts of the ranch under surveillance. Forget about the interior—it's the far sections they keep ripping off."

"But what if they decide to come closer in tonight?" Merle Jansen asked. He was a skinny twenty-something with a gambling habit and a lazy streak that worked on Clint's nerves. But tonight he had just asked the key question Clint had been waiting for. He'd finally figured out that someone was working from the inside, and his hunch had been that it was Merle. His question made Clint all the more positive that his hunch was right.

Clint leveled his gaze at Merle. "They haven't come in yet, and I don't see why they'd start tonight. There-fore—" Clint paused and swept his gaze across the group, including everyone, not wanting to cause Merle to think he suspected anything "—I don't want any man-power wasted within the inner limits. You each know your stakeout positions. Be there. I'm not losing another heifer to these bozos."

With that Clint stalked into the office and slammed the door. His plan was set. He was about to be rid of the thorn in his side, and all he had to do was wait and watch. Brady had been in contact with the Texas dis-trict field inspector and they were on the lookout for his cattle at auctions across Texas and New Mexico. Now all he had to do was catch Merle's cohorts, and if his hunch was right, they were going to come right to him tonight.

Clint's mind was full, he needed closure on the rus-tlers so he could think straight about all the personal issues bearing down on him. Inside information was the only way the rustlers were getting away with their stealing, time after time. It had been an accident that he'd seen them in action the night of the rainstorm. He'd realized finally that he wasn't supposed to be where he was that night. He'd come in from his stakeout early, and Lacy hadn't been in the equation at all. She'd been an accident waiting to happen, with all of her midnight excursions, and the rustlers hadn't figured on her random outings.

Lacy's midnight drives worried him. It was only a matter of time before she ran into the rustlers again. His fear for her was all the more reason for him to want to finish them off tonight.

Tramping into the house, he hung his hat on the rack, removed his boots and his socks, padded into the kitchen. It had been a hard week. And he wasn't talking about rustlers. He was thinking about Lacy.

Rolling his long sleeves up to his elbows, he turned on the water at the sink and washed his hands, lost in thought as he scrubbed. Leaving the sink to yank open the icebox door for something to eat, all he could see was the look on Lacy's face as she'd told him to leave her home.

Other than the letter from his mother, Lacy was all he'd thought about since she'd stopped talking to him Sunday afternoon. He'd dealt with the issue of the rustlers because he had to, but Lacy, sweet Lacy, had been on his mind as he'd wrestled with his plans for their capture.

He hadn't meant to make her mad, to hurt her feelings. But as he was standing there watching her facial expression crumble, all of his feelings and fears rushed into combat in his heart. When he'd let her throw him out, he'd known exactly what he was doing and what he'd become. A coward.

She *was* like his mother. He'd known that from the first moment he'd met her. But she was all the good that his mother possessed, not the bad. And yet he'd still left, letting her believe he thought the worst of her. Because deep inside he was afraid no matter how much she loved the Lord, no matter how much she might love him, if he were lucky...one day she still might leave.

Watching those beautiful Pacific Ocean eyes of hers battle back a tidal wave of hurt, he'd realized how much more it would pain him to see her go.

*God help me, but I couldn't take it.*

Ramming his hands through his hair, he left them there as he leaned his elbow against the refrigerator and let the war inside of him rage. What was he going to do? She couldn't be changed. He wouldn't want her to. It was that fly-by-the-seat-of-her-pants kind of fun spirit that drew him to her. But it was the same spirit that scared him away.

*Dear Lord,* he prayed, standing there with the icy air surrounding him. *I don't know what to do. I need Your guidance. I need to let the hurt from my mother go, but I can't find the forgiveness inside of me. I know that I can't let the pain of yesterday continue to rule me today. And I know if I can't forgive my mother, I can't heal and move forward. I need Your help. I can't do this on my own. I'm praying this as Lacy would pray, not my will but Your will, amen.*

Clint stepped back from the freezer door and allowed it to close. He felt drained and had lost his appetite. His prayer hadn't lifted him up. If anything, it left him feeling even more restless.

Empty.

But he knew where to find his answers.

Turning toward the counter, he stared at the Bible lying there. Waiting.

It had been a long time since he'd picked his Bible up out of want instead of habit. It usually lay on that counter everyday except Sunday mornings when he picked it up on his way out the door to church. Now picking it up, he walked into the den, turned on the lamp beside his chair and sat down.

And then he opened his Bible.

The wind whipped at Lacy's face and hair as she sped down the deserted road. Easing up on the gas pedal, she checked the time on the dash—2:00 a.m. She'd been smokin' the roads for an hour, and still, sleep remained out of reach.

Her life had seemed so focused only a few weeks ago…and now she was lost as to what she should do.

Even the driving experience, the wind in her face and the starry night couldn't cheer her.

Depressed and getting pretty pitiful wallowing in misery, Lacy braked the Caddy to a jolting halt in the center of the road. "Why, Lord? Why did You let me fall in love with Clint Matlock?"

She had spent the week working in her salon in Mule Hollow. The place she had come to, to prove her love for God. The town she'd come to love. The town she'd felt she belonged from that first whisper of hope she'd sensed when she'd closed her eyes that first morning. She'd come to change, to prove to herself that she wasn't a fly-by-night fence rider. And she'd failed. In every way.

A sound in the night broke through Lacy's distress and she lifted her head from where she'd leaned her brow on the steering wheel. As she scanned the darkness, a chill raced up her spine. Given the screams of crickets and the burps of bullfrogs, Lacy wasn't exactly certain there was anything else she could have heard. As she focused on her surroundings and drew away from her weeping heart, she became aware of how alone she was in the remote back roads.

She really wasn't that far from home; as a matter of fact, Clint's home also wasn't too far away. But she was alone, it was after two in the morning and there was definitely something making noise out there in the dark.

There…a flicker of light. The faint murmur of an engine as the light bobbed then angled slightly away and went out.

Rustlers! The rustlers were back.

Lacy turned off her lights hoping they hadn't spotted them yet, and then she guided her Caddy to the side of the road and turned off the ignition.

It was the same as the night she and Clint had encountered each other and the rustlers. The distance might not be as far though, and there was no mud. But she felt sure that just as they'd disappeared quickly that first night, they'd do the same tonight. They'd get away. They would be ghosts once more and it might be weeks before anyone saw them again. Clint would lose more livestock. Her adrenaline started pumping.

She climbed out of the car. "Not tonight, buckos," she whispered to the darkness. She'd learned after the storm to dress for her late-night drives. She wore a soft cotton shirt, blue jeans, boots and socks. She was prepared for anything.

Her adrenaline was surging as she stared into the distance, through a stand of trees looming like a black wall in the darkness. She knew they were out there.

Clint's thieves. Mule Hollow would never be clear to flourish if these rustlers weren't stopped. Why, what single woman would want to settle in the country knowing the hills were alive with hoodlums. Already Molly had found out about the rustlers and was preparing for an article, but the only story Mule Hollow needed about rustlers was about their capture.

Her decision made, Lacy stepped toward the fence. "Dear Lord, help me," she whispered. "I'm about to get into trouble."

She had made it through the pasture, which hadn't been an easy task in the dark. Especially when she started thinking about snakes, rattlesnakes to be exact. She prayed harder than she'd prayed in a long time, for protection from her stupidity. But she had forged on, knowing that Clint's rustlers needed catching.

In the darkness she could hear the bawling of cattle and the soft curses of men. The air was heavy with the scent of pine. As she drew closer to the faint voices, she found a small cluster of pine trees and a gully she hadn't counted on. Half rolling, half walking and crawling, she managed to make the steep embankment in one piece. At the bottom she had to cross a small stream that was barely to her ankles and then climb back up the other side. It was a hard treacherous climb in the dark.

When she finally crawled over the edge she lay sprawled on her back looking up at the heavens. She was breathing hard from the exertion of climbing up the ravine. The sounds of the cattle were much closer now and she had to ignore the first tremors of fear. They rolled over her in a wave.

There was no room for fear out here. This was for Clint. This was for Mule Hollow.

Even if Clint thought so little of her, she knew she had to do whatever she could to help him. She loved him.

That thought was what had kept her from turning back when visions of rattlesnakes threatened to overtake her courage.

She loved him, and even if there might never be a miracle and he could love her, she could do this for him and the town. *Give me strength, Lord.*

Knowing it was time to move again, Lacy sat up, rolled onto her knees then crawled to the trees. She could see lights now. Not big lights but flashlights. They bobbed at the back of a huge trailer into which two men were loading the last of the cattle.

She had made it just in time. They looked as if they were nearly finished, and she knew they would be driving off into the night. This would be the last anyone saw of them for who knew how long.

Her thoughts were rioting with her next move—when suddenly a hand slid over her mouth. Her heart stopped and before she could react, she was yanked hard against a rock-solid frame.

"Don't make a sound," her captor bit out in a gravelly hiss against her ear. "Don't even move."

* * *

What was this woman up to now? Clint held Lacy against his chest and waited for her to stop squirming. She was stronger than she looked and he had to hang on to her mouth harder than he wanted to in order to stop her from crying out.

"Lacy, it's me," he managed to grit out before she bit him. "Clint. Hold still, or they're going to know we're out here."

Lacy stilled in his arms and turned her head to look into his face. She couldn't see him in the shadows of the trees, but she nodded. He removed his hand. Immediately she spun around to face him. He had to bend down a bit to make out her angry whisper.

"You scared the daylights out of me. What are you doing here?"

"I want to know what *you're* doing here."

He was watching the movements of the men who were not more than ten yards away from them. They hadn't heard them yet but Lacy's zealous nature was not on their side.

"I'm trying to catch your rustlers." As if suddenly remembering them, she turned quickly away from him. He moved in close behind her, wishing with all of his soul that she hadn't shown up here. Not when he could smell victory over the cattle thieves.

What would he do now? His plan hadn't included endangering Lacy.

The men loaded the last steer into the trailer and closed it up. Then without a word they went up front to the truck and climbed in.

Clint knew he was about to miss his chance. His hunch about his hired hand, Merle, being in on the rustling from the inside had been right. Clint had staked out here in the hope that they'd come after this particular herd because many of them were pregnant and ready to drop calves any day. What better way to multiply your money than to steal two for one?

"We can't let them go!" Lacy exclaimed as the truck engine purred to life and the trailer's taillights blinked. She made a move as if to follow and Clint grabbed her.

"Whoa, Lacy. You're not going anywhere."

She twisted around, and he knew she was glaring daggers at him, even if he couldn't see her eyes.

"We can't let them go."

Clint mirrored her exasperation. He'd planned to sneak a ride on the trailer as it was pulling away, find out where they were taking the cattle, then report his findings to Brady. But he couldn't risk that with Lacy along. Jumping on trailers and risking his own hide was one thing, putting Lacy in jeopardy wasn't an option he was willing to take. Dropping his hand from her arm, he snatched his hat from his head and raked a hand through his hair, thinking out a new plan of attack.

Unfortunately that was the opening Lacy needed. She shot out of the protection of the trees and after the retreating shape of the cattle trailer.

Sprinting to the trailer, which was picking up speed, Lacy flung herself onto the bumper before she really had a chance to realize what she was doing.

Her impetuousness had taken over once more and she was just going to have to deal with it.

Cows were bellowing, shuffling about, adjusting to the movement of the rough ride. Lacy clung for dear life to the hard steel bars and for a split second she thought about dropping off. Then she found herself staring through the trailer bars at the huge dark eyes of a young heifer crammed inside the trailer. Its face was illuminated slightly by the red glow of the taillights, and as Lacy hung there it jabbed her cheek with its wet, slimy nose, as if asking for help.

"Okay, girl," Lacy groaned, hanging on tighter. "I'm going to get you out of there."

"Lacy Brown, are you crazy?" Clint snapped, swinging onto the trailer beside her, not happy he'd been forced to chase after her. "You're going to get yourself killed." This was not his plan.

"I am not. These guys are cattle thieves. They're not killers."

"You don't know that. Now, drop off while you still can," he demanded. "Lacy, I won't have you in harm's way. Drop off *now*."

"No." She scrambled over the back of the trailer gate and balanced herself inside between the gate and the side railing. Looking down at the dark shapes of the bumping, shuffling animals she felt a bit of fear, at least she saw no horns in this section of the trailer.

That was a good thing.

Clint dropped in beside her, muttering something she couldn't understand, but in the darkness his anger was almost visible.

Well, he could just be angry. She'd started this dance and she planned to finish it. Clutching the rails like a monkey over an alligator pit, Lacy tried to ignore him, but when the truck came to an abrupt halt, she lost her grip and slipped.

Clint shot a hand out and grasped her around the waist and smoothly swung her up against his chest. Obviously he'd had much more skill in the back of a trailer than she had.

After the trailer started moving again, it hit a bump and Clint wrapped his arm tighter around Lacy. He gripped the rail for support with his free hand and fought to keep the shuffling cattle off of her with his body. One wrong move and they could easily be crushed by the huge beasts.

"Don't you know when to control your impulses?" he asked, annoyed that she was here, but glad she hadn't come upon the rustlers alone. He thanked God that He'd put him in her path tonight.

She twisted around to face him in the tight corner where he had her secured. Despite everything, he wanted to kiss her right there. It didn't make any sense; the woman drove him crazy with her spontaneity. She was uncontrollable.

But he loved her.

He had admitted this to himself that afternoon while he read his Bible.

He had no claim on her. She'd made that clear over and over. And after this little stunt, he was beginning to question his sanity in wanting to call her his... "Forgetting those things which are behind, and reaching forth unto those things which are before."

The words in Philippians 3:13 echoed through his heart. God had led him to that verse as he'd read His word. Clint knew it hadn't been a coincidence that this was the scripture God had sent to him. His mother's rejection was behind him and Lacy's love, if he could hope, was before him. God was letting him know that he needed to move forward.

The terrifying question plaguing Clint was how could he live never knowing what she would do next? A little crazy driving, a cute, hot temper, mixed with a soft heart and a bewildering amount of determination to achieve her goals—these things, surprisingly enough, drew him to her. But this reckless willingness to endanger herself…he wasn't sure he could handle.

Even with God's assurances.

# Chapter Sixteen

Lacy stared between the cattle trailer's iron bars into the dark night speeding past. Clint's nearness was making her senses wobble more than the trailer ride. She had to keep reminding herself how little he thought of her and that she had goals to achieve that had nothing to do with loving him.

She stole a thoughtful glance at Clint. He was on his cell phone talking to Sheriff Brady. Clint had been trying for the past fifteen minutes to get a call through to him, which was no easy task in these parts. Now that he'd connected, he was giving Brady as much information on their steadily moving location as he could, just in case they couldn't get a connection again. Staring back into the darkness she fought to ignore his presence beside her.

Life had its little jokes.

Could she change Clint's opinion of her? Could she prove she was worthy of his love, that she wouldn't abandon him or their children if she were so lucky? It was something she'd pursue if she hadn't gotten them into a situation they couldn't get out of...

"Brady's on his way," Clint said, breaking into her thoughts. "Or at least on his way to this area. He's going to call Ranger's sheriff department for backup."

"Do you know where we are?" Lacy asked, hoping.

"Not exactly. It's hard to know in the dark, the last road mark I was able to give them was before we got on this dirt road. Hopefully this is the only gravel road off of a farm-to-market road near a power tower."

Lacy tried not to worry. But she knew that she had gotten them into this by her impulsive lack of thinking.

After what seemed like forever, the trailer slowed. Clint placed a protective hand on her shoulder as the cattle shifted and bumped them around. The trailer passed over a cattle guard and Clint leaned close.

"We need to be ready to hop off this thing before they get to the corral," he said near her ear.

Nodding, Lacy ignored the tingling sensation his breath sent skittering over her skin, and she started climbing out of the trailer.

"Be careful," he said, holding her arm for support as she shimmied over the rail.

Lacy concentrated on keeping her footing. Once she had her feet securely planted on the bumper, she scooted out of Clint's way. "Your turn," she said, then watched him climb easily out beside her.

The trailer bounced over a rough spot but he maneuvered out onto the bumper with ease.

Holding her gaze, he suddenly leaned in and kissed her. "You are a beautiful woman, Lacy Brown. A handful of trouble, but beautiful."

There he went, confusing her again!

"Come on," he whispered, as if nothing had just passed between them. "Let's get into the shadows of that barn."

Feeling off balance, she waved a hand at him. "Lead the way."

He grabbed her hand and they hopped from the trailer together. Fading into the night, they circled out of the way of the headlights.

"Where do you think we are?" she asked, once they were safely flattened against the wall of the barn. This was no time to figure out what was going on between them. That would have to wait, even though her heart was racing and it had nothing to do with rustlers.

Echoing moos and the heavy thud of hooves signaled the cattle were being unloaded. Clint snuck a peek and didn't answer her. Lacy bent around him and snatched a look of her own. In the beam of a spotlight, two cowboys moved the cattle into an empty roping pen.

"Do you recognize either of them?" she asked softly.

"Get back, Lacy. I don't want you getting hurt," he said without answering her question.

Lacy straightened. "I'm not going to get hurt. Clint Matlock, you're the most maddening man."

"Not now, Lacy," he sighed, grasping her arms and

holding her still. Leaning forward he rested his forehead against hers.

The rising protest congealed in her throat. Seconds passed and she could only stand there, wondering at the thoughts passing through his mind.

At last, keeping his forehead against hers he said, "My plan was to find this place and wait for backup, it wasn't to get caught standing here having this conversation. This isn't your fight and I don't want you taking any more chances. I want you to stay here while I get a closer look. Is that too much to ask?"

"It *is* my fight," she whispered, glancing about, fearing Clint was right and they would be discovered because of her runaway mouth. "These men are threatening the good reputation of Mule Hollow. As a business owner and a citizen, that makes everything they do my concern." She squared her shoulders. "I've already told you not to worry about me. I'm not *your* concern. Besides, I can take care of myself. And after all, I got us into this. Remember."

Briskly he slid his hands up and down her arms, as if fighting his own conflicting emotions, then he pulled her gently against him.

A shaking, she could have handled. A hug, caught her off guard, more so than the earlier kiss had and her heart swelled.

Breaking away, she stomped toward the far end of the barn away from the light. Away from Clint and the things he made churn inside her. One minute he was comparing her to his *mother* and the next he was kissing her, hugging her, playing with her heart. No! Do not allow this.

"Where are you going?"

"I'm going to find out where we are, and figure a way to catch these guys." As she spoke, she concentrated on not falling over an old tire.

"I don't want them knowing we're here, Lace—"

His voice sounded funny all of a sudden and Lacy looked up to see why he'd quit griping.

The shotgun stopped her dead in her tracks.

"Too late," said a voice from the darkness. "Looks like I already know you're here."

This is not good. Lacy stared at the barrel of the gun as the man behind the voice stepped from the end of the barn. He was tall, shrouded in black, with a cigarette hanging from the corner of his mouth. The red tip bounced with each word he spoke.

"Stay calm, Lacy," Clint urged, touching the small of her back with his hand.

Too late, Lacy's adrenaline was up, plopping her hands on her hips, she glared at the cigarette-smoking bandit. "*He* better stay calm."

Clint jabbed her.

"Me?" Cigarette-butt chuckled wickedly. "I think you've got this little situation confused. I'm the one with the gun. Now move it."

The cold metal against her shoulder brought a little sanity to Lacy's insane behavior. He pushed her shoulder with the double-barreled shotgun and she decided maybe now was the time to do as he instructed.

"Don't hurt the lady," Clint said, a menacing edge to his voice that exceeded their captor's.

"I'll do what I want. And now I want you to move. If you don't, I'll shoot her."

"Do as he says, Lacy." Clint turned and Lacy followed him toward the sound of the cattle being unloaded.

Lacy decided she didn't like the gun jabbing her in the back at all. "You'll never get away with this," she snapped.

"Lacy, be quiet."

Even though fear was screaming inside of her, Lacy ignored it. "I will not be silent, Clint Matlock!"

"So that's who you are," said gun-toting Cigarette-butt. "Get tired of us ripping you off?"

"You're right about that, bucko," Lacy answered for Clint. "He's tired of you jerks."

"Lacy, for crying out loud—" Clint muttered in exasperation. "Would you cut it out? I'm trying to save you here. Or hadn't you noticed the man has a gun pointed at you?"

They'd reached the front of the barn and stepped into the view of the other rustlers.

"Looky what I found draggin' around the back of the barn," Cigarette-butt called to his friends. Turning, they stared into the spotlight hanging on the barn behind Lacy and Clint, then sauntered over.

Lacy cringed. They looked like the big, the bad and definitely the *ugly*. Up close she could see that one even had a patch over his eye.

"Well, look what we have here," One-eye said, leering at them.

"Knock it off, Austin," Clint drawled.

Lacy shot a glare at Clint. "How'd you know his name?"

"The patch. Brady gave me some descriptions he'd come up with from the Cattle Raisers Association field inspectors. There aren't too many rustlers with one eye. It seems Austin and his boys pull these scams off all over the country. The One-eyed Rustler is wanted in five states. We had a hunch it was them. The patterns matched their previous jobs."

"Why didn't you tell me?" Lacy asked, stung by the fact that he hadn't confided in her.

"Because it was my problem."

She stared at him to no effect. He hadn't taken his eyes off of the one-eyed Austin. "You could have told me." She knew she was being childish…. They were standing in the middle of a bunch of could-be cutthroats and she was hurt because Clint hadn't told her he knew who the thieves were.

"Yeah, Clint, you could have told her," Austin mimicked, stepping up close to Lacy. When she moved to back away, he wrapped an arm around her waist and yanked her against him. "This could be a fun night."

In his arms, Lacy felt the first real fear that she had ever felt. Austin leaned his head in close to her; she twisted, averting her face from his hot breath. Her gaze met Clint's and her heart stopped. His expression had turned murderous, his eyes, hard as stone.

When Austin ran a hand holding a pistol along her jaw, Clint lunged. "Keep your hands off her—" He never saw the butt of the shotgun as it slammed into his shoulder, barely missing his skull.

Lacy screamed as she watched Clint go down on one knee, saw the sick grin that played across Cigarette-butt's face. She tried to bend down next to Clint but Austin held her firmly away. "Clint," she cried as Austin placed the barrel of his pistol against Clint's temple. She went very still.

*Dear, Lord, please don't let anything happen to Clint. And deliver us from this mess I've gotten us into.* She prayed like she'd never prayed before.

"Lacy," Clint said, breaking into her prayer with a voice as hard as concrete. "Do exactly as they tell you. Austin, as far as I know, you don't have killing on your record. I wouldn't start now."

Austin pressed the barrel more snugly against Clint's skull. "I've never been in this situation before. If I had, I might have made my first kill a long time ago."

His chuckle sent shivers down Lacy's spine.

"We have backup coming," she blurted out, hoping to distract Austin. She had to do something to get that gun barrel away from Clint's head.

"Oh, do ya now? Did Clint here get through on a cell phone?"

"Yes, he did, and there will be cops swarming all over this place within the next few minutes." Her voice held more mettle than she felt.

"Boss, maybe we better get out of here," the third slug chimed in.

Austin shook his head and jabbed Clint in the shoulder with the pistol. "He's bluffing. His odds of getting through on a phone line way out here are slim to none. Why do you think I leased this place?"

"But maybe he got lucky. Maybe that sheriff is on his way. They know who we are—"

"They won't be telling anybody."

Lacy saw the gleam in Austin's eye and her heart stilled again. She couldn't lose Clint—she had to draw the gun away. She had to do something to distract Austin. His hand gripped the gun more tightly and her attention flew down to Clint who was looking up at her, watching her with steady eyes—probably willing her to control herself.

*Or watching for the right opportunity to strike back.* She knew he needed her to distract them…. If she drew the gun, they had a chance.

Clint's eyes hardened; steam practically started rolling from his ears and he shook his head oh so slightly. "No," he mouthed, but she'd already started screaming…and she knew he was reading her thoughts. She knew she could distract them. She yanked hard against Austin and continued screaming. Her adrenaline spiked, she saw Cigarette-butt looking panicked. Felt Austin shift against her and she screamed louder and squirmed violently.

Austin's hands were full, holding her in one arm and holding a gun on Clint. Though she was screaming she registered that he was a control freak or he'd have let Cigarette-butt hold the gun on Clint.

*"Woman!"* Austin exclaimed, rewarding her screams by pointing his pistol straight at her. "Be still or you'll get the first bullet."

"Lacy, be still." Clint's voice was soft, drawing her gaze, quieting her screams.

The gun was at her temple, she could feel tremors racing through Austin's body, knew he was near breaking but felt no fear. She felt only love looking at Clint.

For a moment she'd succeeded and drawn the gun away from Clint. Only to see the now-alert Cigarette-butt level his gun on him.

"Austin," Clint said, his words tight, clipped, "take the truck and go before the sheriff gets here. You can still get away and you won't have harmed anyone. You do not want to harm Lacy."

"Why? I'd be doing the world a favor getting rid of this magpie."

Clint frowned. "No. You wouldn't." He slowly started to stand.

"Hold it right there, buster." Cigarette-butt snapped, jamming his shotgun into Clint's shoulder. "Nobody told you to move. Shoot her, boss, and let's get out of here. Carl, load up," he snarled at the man Lacy had decided didn't have a brain of his own. Carl practically ran to the truck and hopped inside.

Angered, Austin pressed the cold metal harder against her temple and she could see the fury building in Clint. Her pulse screamed at high speed, fearing he was about to get himself shot. Shifting toward Austin, she focused on the control freak in him.

"Who's the boss here?" she asked, cutting her eyes at him. "You or Smokin' Joe over there?"

Austin grimaced. "Shut up. Dawson, we aren't going anywhere until I say so."

Dawson. He finally had a name.

"Look, we got plenty of cattle sold," Dawson snapped. "I ain't hanging around here so some officer can waltz up and handcuff me. I ain't goin' back to no prison 'cause you won't admit it's time to call it quits."

"Yeah, boss," Simple Simon chimed in from the cab. "Daw has a point."

"I give the orders here!" Austin yelled. The air rang with fury as he pushed Lacy forward so he could step toward Dawson. Lacy lost her footing and stumbled, catching Austin off guard. He yanked her back but it was too late. Losing his footing, they both tumbled forward.

Clint rammed his elbow into Dawson's gut, then lunged for Austin. She was knocked to the side as Clint locked on to Austin's arm, one hand on the gun, one hand around his neck, pushing him back as they wrestled for control of the gun. Lacy started to get up to help, but Dawson shoved her from behind and sent her sprawling toward the side of the trailer.

She caught herself before running into it, spinning around just in time to witness Dawson slamming the butt of his shotgun into the back of Clint's skull. The sound reverberated with a sickening thud and Lacy's whole world tilted as Clint's knees started buckling and his hands fell limp and lifeless to his side. "Clint," she cried out, reaching for him. In that terrifying instant, watching him fall forward, her life flashed before her eyes.

*What if I never have the chance to tell Clint I love him?* What if Clint died because of her stupidity? *Oh, dear Lord, what have I done?*

What if he were already dead?

Clint fought back the darkness overcoming him as he hit the ground. Searing pain ripped through his skull.

"No!" he heard Lacy scream, and he forced his head upward. It felt heavy and the effort was daunting. Blood ran like a river into his eyes as he tried to focus on Lacy. He found Austin standing above him, gun leveled down. He saw Dawson turning toward Lacy's voice, then to his horror, he saw Lacy evade Dawson's reach and throw herself at Austin.

Like a wildcat, tears streaming down her cheeks, she clawed at his face. *Dear Lord, she was beautiful, and faithful.* He knew she would fight till death if she had to.

Clint struggled to regain his senses; he had to help her. Austin shoved her back. Yet, tough as nails, she belted him in the nose with her elbow. Staggered by the force of the blow and bleeding profusely, he tottered away from her, his gun dangling dangerously in his hand.

Clint focused on the gun aimed at the woman he loved. Determined, he willed his limbs to move, tried to shake the blackness swallowing him. Then Dawson stepped into view, now with two guns aimed at Lacy.

"Lacy," Clint called and, with all the strength he possessed, forced himself up. He propelled himself toward her, trying to draw the fire from the thugs as the darkness engulfed him.

The gunshot was the last thing Clint remembered.

# Chapter Seventeen

Clint awoke with a start. Lacy.

Where was she? His surroundings came into focus and he realized he was in a hospital. Ranger's hospital.

A nurse stood at the foot of his bed studying a chart. His head throbbed like a jackhammer, but he struggled to sit up. He had to find Lacy. Had to know if she was alive—

"Hold on, big guy," the nurse said. Coming to his side, she gently pushed him back onto the pillow.

"Lacy," he whispered, his voice gravelly. His head was spinning.

"She's in the waiting room. The doctor has gone to tell her you are going to be okay. We stitched up your wound and the scan showed no other damage to your skull. You were very lucky, though you could have some short-term memory loss. But that's yet to be seen. You'll hurt like thunder, but you'll be fine in a few days."

She was alive. She wasn't harmed. "Thank you," he

managed. Drained, but thanking God that Lacy hadn't been shot, he relaxed against the pillows.

A few minutes later the door opened and Lacy stepped inside. He drank her in, wanting nothing more than to see her safe. She was pale, her eyes were huge and he could see her body tremble.

"Clint," she whispered, moving to his side. "I'm sorry. So sorry."

"For what," he rasped. "You saved me."

She started to cry. "No, Brady saved us. He got there right after you passed out. He shot Austin in the hip." Silent tears streamed down her beautiful face. "I nearly got you killed. If I hadn't jumped on the back of that trailer…then I— I couldn't keep my mouth shut." She hiccupped and rubbed at the wetness on her face with the back of her hand.

Clint forced himself up on an elbow, wanting so much to hold her. "You were only trying to help." He reached for her and she came into his embrace willingly. Her tears wet his shoulder until the nurse returned and berated him for sitting up.

Reluctantly he leaned back against his pillows and watched Lacy attempt to dry her eyes with a tissue the nurse handed her. Reaching out, he clasped a wobbly hand over hers.

"I'm going to marry you," he said, more certain of the prediction than he'd ever been about anything in his life.

Lacy gaped at him, disbelief etched upon her face. "You said…I—" she gasped through her hot tears

"—remind you of your mother, and I almost got you killed." Abruptly she turned and started to walk away.

Clint stopped her, holding tightly to her hand. "You do, sugar," he said, gently tugging her back to his side. "I didn't know what I was doing that day in your kitchen. My insides were going crazy and my heart was tripping out on me. You scared me." He paused, fighting back the emotions welling within him.

"But I've figured some things out since then," he continued. "I had planned on coming over today or yesterday—I've lost track of time. I'd planned on making everything up to you, but I got a little sidetracked."

Lacy lifted her head. The hope in her eyes melted any reserves he may have held. This was his woman. His gift from God.

And he was going to keep her.

"No." She pulled her hand away and took a step back. "No, I can't."

"Lacy. What's wrong? What do you mean no?" He didn't like the look in her eyes.

"This will never work." Lacy spun toward the door and he would have lost her had he not held firmly to her hand, determined to never let her go.

"You don't need to love m-me Clint." She sniffled and tried to compose herself. "You're right. With the way my personality is, there is no telling what I'm going to wake up and do tomorrow. I tried to come here and carry out a promise I made to God and I couldn't stay faithful to even Him."

"Now, hold on there." Clint tugged her to sit beside

him on the hospital bed. "What do you pray every time you end your prayers?"

Lacy didn't understand what he meant.

"You pray for God's will to be done and not yours. I've heard you pray many times, and you pray that every time. Don't you?"

"Yes." Lacy stopped crying. "I wanted my coming to Mule Hollow to be about God and not about me."

Clint lifted his hand and gently rubbed strands of hair off of her damp cheek. "This isn't about you, Lacy. Not in the way you think. I've watched you, and I've seen your heart, and you've changed me. I had shut God out of my life and hadn't even realized it until I saw your relationship with Him.

"This was about me…and everybody else that has watched you in action. You might get a little carried away at times, times I've come to love observing, but your heart is true. You may not want your personality compared to the apostle Peter's, but, Lacy, just like God knew Peter's heart, He knows yours. He knows how true and faithful your heart is. And so do I."

Lacy shook her head and buried her face against his chest again. His words reached deep inside of her. Had her pride and her desire to let God use her in the way she saw fit overshadowed the *real* reason for His leading her to Mule Hollow? Could it really be true?

"Lacy," Clint murmured in her ear, "you are my answer to prayer. I've needed you for so long. I love you, Lacy. And if you'll marry me, I promise that we'll work together to fulfill the vision God gave you for Mule Hollow."

Every thought Lacy had deserted her when Clint said he loved her. She looked up and met his smoldering brown gaze. Slowly she touched his cheek with her trembling fingertips.

Light seeped into her veins, flooded her heart and a smile burst to her lips.

"Could you really love me, even after all I put you through last night?"

In answer, Clint leaned in and kissed her. The kiss was slow, strong and steadfast and chased away any doubts she might have had. When he lifted his head, his eyes were twinkling.

"Like I said before, the trouble with you, Lacy Brown, is you don't know when you're whupped. Will you marry me?"

In that moment she knew Clint had been right. They had been wrought for each other by the mighty hands of God to balance out their different personalities into a perfect union.

"Oh, Clint, I love you, too. But look where I got you with my stupid, impulsive actions. Why, I couldn't even keep my smart mouth closed when I had a gun stuck to my back. Clint…I could have gotten you killed!" Overcome with uncertainty, she buried her face against his chest and wept.

"Yeah, you could have." His voice was gentle as he smoothed her hair with his hand. "I have to tell you, Lace. I've never seen anyone braver than you. All the while, knowing you would make yourself the target of their frustrations, you stood up to those guys. They didn't know what hit them when you started screaming. *I* didn't at first." He pushed her away from him and lifted her chin so she had to look at him. "I wouldn't ever try to hold you back, Lace. I just want you on my team."

Lacy melted at his words; hope and pure joy surged through her. "Oh, Clint," she sighed. "I thought God brought me here to be the matchmaker. And He was pulling the strings all along."

Clint loosened his hold on her and cocked his head to the side. "Imagine that."

Clint nestled her against him and in the sweet silence filled with awe at their decision, Clint's heart changed.

"Lacy," he said, "Will you come to New Orleans with me?"

"I'd go anywhere," Lacy sighed against his cheek. "Any special reason?"

Clint thought of the letter he'd stuffed into his jeans pocket earlier that afternoon. "I need to see a lady who lives there. I need to invite her to a wedding."

# *Epilogue*

Lacy stood with a small crowd on the corner of Main Street. Her heart was thumping with wild anticipation as she watched the moving trucks pulling around the corner. Glancing up, she smiled at Clint. He immediately drew her near, under the shelter of his arm.

"Look, Lace, it's what you envisioned," he said, bending close to her ear. "They're coming."

Lacy thrilled to the warmth of his breath against her skin. It delighted her soul to look around the small crowd waiting to help the three schoolteachers move into their new apartments.

Molly Popp, now a Mule Hollow resident for three weeks, had attended church faithfully every Sunday since moving to town. That told Lacy that she'd been right in coming.

Lilly Tipps also stood on the edge of the crowd beside Norma Sue. Lilly had been hurt by her ex-husband when he abandoned her upon learning she was pregnant, but Lacy felt an irrepressible spirit in Lilly. Looking down

Main Street, it hit Lacy that she'd felt that same spirit in Mule Hollow when she'd first sat in her pink Caddy and felt that whisper of hope calling to her. It was a feeling of being down and out, but of not giving up. Lacy had a feeling that Lilly would never give up. And she knew just the ladies to give her support.

Scanning the rest of the crowd of familiar faces she had come to love, Lacy wanted to shout aloud for the hope she felt surging all around her.

*You are so good, Lord. You are an awesome God!*

"Can you believe it?" Esther Mae said, clapping her hands together. She hugged her husband, Hank. "I told you this plan was going to work. I told you."

Hank raised an eyebrow. "You were right. And I'm glad of it. You ladies did a mighty fine job of reviving the town. Looks like this just might work."

"Well, sure, it'll work," Norma Sue said. "You men had the doubts, we women knew the Lord had it under control all the time."

Laughter burst around Lacy, and she couldn't help it—she spun out onto the street with her arms open wide. "Come on, let's go welcome the newest residents of Mule Hollow."

Clint grabbed her hand, and together they walked down the center of the street toward Adela's apartments.

She and Clint had traveled to New Orleans and he had started a new relationship with his mother. She would be attending their wedding in March. Wedding.

"What's with the dreamy expression?" Clint asked, tugging on her hand.

"I was thinking about God's sense of humor. Just think about us—we came from standing on this street clashing heads together, to preparing to walk down the aisle together in marriage."

"I like God's sense of humor." Clint stopped walking and pulled Lacy into his arms. "I can't wait until you are Mrs. Clint Matlock." And then he kissed her.

"All right, that's enough of that, you two," Norma Sue said. "We've got things to do and there's no time for dawdling."

"Hey, Lacy," Bob called from where he'd taken the lead, "What's next on our plan for Mule Hollow?"

"Oh, now it's *our* plan," Esther Mae harrumphed, then she smiled. "That's just like a bunch of men to join in after the fact."

"Well, I was thinking," Lacy said, glancing at the colorful buildings lining the street. "We've got the ads out and women are coming, but so is winter. We might just need to be patient. We can't expect Mule Hollow to turn into a metropolis overnight." Suddenly an idea started to bloom. "However, I bet we could do a Christmas or Epiphany pageant of some sort."

"You mean acting?" Andrew asked, frowning.

"Cowboys acting in a play," Lilly added. "I'd have to see that to believe it."

"I was thinking that you could be in it also."

"Me." Lilly stopped and stared openmouthed at Lacy. It was that look Lacy knew so well. "Do you know how large I'll be in a few months? Why, I'm getting round so fast that my shirts are going to be screaming mercy soon."

"Yup, I know. You'll be just right."

"I don't think so—"

Clint tapped Lilly on the shoulder. "You might as well give up. What Lacy wants, Lacy gets."

"I told Clint that," Sheri added. "So you might as well get ready. If Lacy wants you in the play you'll be in the play. Baby and all."

They had reached the vans and the teachers were stepping down from the cabs. Immediately, the cowboys went over and offered their help. There was a lot of promise in the air.

It made Lacy want to sing.

So she did.

"Love is in the air…Mule Hollow, where all your dreams come true…"

\* \* \* \* \*

Dear Reader,

I'm so glad you decided to join me on this wild and wacky ride with Lacy Brown! From the moment Lacy popped into my head, driving that pink Caddy and talking my ear off, I knew I was in trouble. A good kind of trouble. Her zeal for God made me want to draw closer to the Lord in my daily walk and to seek His will with all my heart. She made me want to let my hair down, too, and have some fun. She made me laugh—and that was a very good thing for me at a time when I really needed to smile. I pray you had as much fun as I did and that God blessed you in a special way as you read Lacy's story.

Lacy so wanted to please God—I believe ministry is the way to do that. I hope if you aren't involved in some type of ministry in your church or community that you get involved with one. You'll be blessed through your involvement and be a blessing to someone at the same time.

Until next time…keep smiling, seeking God with all your heart and reaching out to those around you.

Blessings,

Debra Clopton

# AND BABY MAKES FIVE

Teach me to do Your will, for You are my God; may Your good Spirit lead me on level ground.

—*Psalms* 143:10

This book is dedicated to my sons:
Chase and Kris.
I love you.
May you always have as much joy in
your lives as you've brought to mine.
Dream big, guys.
You can do all things through
Christ who strengthens you.

# Chapter One

Samantha, bless her weird, little, mischievous soul, was up to no good.

Lilly Tipps knew this. She knew it all the way down to the tips of her water-retaining, swollen big toes. Trouble was brewing, and Samantha was the cause of it.

Again!

Scanning the icy darkness, Lilly scrunched her brow and absently massaged her tight stomach as another Braxton-Hicks contraction started building in its intensity. The false labor pains had been hitting her off and on for the past two weeks, but tonight…oohhh! Lilly took a deep breath, then exhaled slowly. Tonight they were stronger than usual and it was all because of Samantha.

In an effort to ignore the pain, Lilly pulled her coat closed over her rotund tummy, flipped her collar up about her ears, then settled her red wool cap over her corkscrew curls. She concentrated on the task at hand as the pain, more of a nuisance than anything, peaked.

"I must admit, sweet baby…" she said aloud—she'd taken up chatting or singing to her baby early in the pregnancy. She knew it was a good thing to let her child learn her voice, and also, it was nice to have someone to talk to other than Samantha. "I'd trade my whole cache of banana Laffy Taffy and half my chocolate-covered peanut stash for a man to help search for Samantha." She inhaled deeply and let it out slowly. "I'm so not wanting to wander around in this freezing weather looking for an ornery old donkey."

It was a little odd. Not everyone had a donkey cohabiting with them, and Lilly was finding that keeping the old girl home was a major job, especially for a single gal eight months pregnant and growing by the second.

*Buck up, Lilly. You volunteered to take her on.*

"Yes, I did," she said into the wind as stinging prickles of ice misted across her bare face. It was obvious that Samantha had decided to take her aging little body up the road to her old homestead. It was also obvious that the only one to fetch her back was Lilly. Pregnant or not. False contractions or not.

So be it. Surrendering to her decision, Lilly waddled from the protection of the barn into the icy wind toward her truck. She sympathized with Samantha, she really did. Being forced to give up your home and move would be hard, even if it was only down the road. Lilly had been born and raised in Mule Hollow and couldn't imagine living anywhere else. Samantha needed to learn Lilly's home was now her home. Containing the donkey was an almost impossible task, since she was like the great Houdini, escaping constantly.

Lilly bit her lip in concentration. She had to find a way to keep her little friend home. It was for Samantha's own good. If half of what Lilly had heard circulating in Mule Hollow about the new owner of Samantha's homestead were true, then trespassing on her former stomping grounds could very possibly get Samantha shot.

Lilly at last reached her truck without mishap. The pangs had disappeared for the moment, thank goodness. Why couldn't these fake labor pains hit during the day while she was in her warm house designing her cattle sales catalogs? At least then she could stop and relax until they passed. But the pains had to start in the middle of the night, just like Samantha misbehaving. Lilly sighed, glad the contractions had given her a reprieve. She wrestled open the door of her ancient truck, then hoisted herself into the high seat, which was no easy feat with her small, roly-poly stature. Once up there, she had to rest for a second before she could proceed. After a few moments she caught her breath, twisted the key and, to her dismay, listened as the engine rumbled to life.

"Why, thank You, Lord, for Your steadfastness," she muttered. "I guess this is a sign that I truly do have to go on down there and get myself shot." Looking heavenward, she smiled. God knew her. They'd been building a solid relationship for the past few months and she realized she wasn't hiding anything from Him. He already understood the truck's reliability hadn't been priority this evening.

She was more afraid that if Cort Wells caught

Samantha, he might tan not only her wrinkled hide, but Lilly's, too.

However, she wasn't about to let rumors color her views of the man. A person couldn't escape the gossip in Mule Hollow—where some towns had a grapevine, Mule Hollow had an entire vineyard. Mr. Wells was being discussed in the feed store and at the gas pump, especially the gas pump. Just yesterday, minding her own business pumping unleaded into her truck, Applegate Thornton and Stanley Orr stood not three feet from her, openly debating what would cause a man to have such a scowl etched between his eyebrows. That scowl was legendary, and though she'd never witnessed it, evidently it hadn't wavered during any of his dealings with the locals in the short time since he'd moved to town.

Why, even the ladies at Heavenly Inspirations Hair Salon had mentioned it. If they noticed it then it must be something, because Lacy Brown, the owner, didn't like gossip at all and certainly didn't put up with it. Apparently she had said to the group that they all needed to pray about what kind of problem would make a man want to walk around glaring at people like that.

Lilly started praying. She prayed that Samantha would behave and they could sneak away without meeting the man. Of course, that wasn't very Christian. It was more of an all-out rebellion against her duty as one of His. She sighed. Hermit or no hermit, she still had to be neighborly. It seemed she was always failing at that particular portion of her renewed walk with the Lord.

Then again, the grannies had taught her well the

many reasons to excuse bad behavior when it came to interacting with men. Two generations of grannies, plus her mother, who'd all had their hearts trampled by the men they'd loved, had no sympathy where a man's feelings were concerned.

Great-Granny Shu-Shu literally hated men. Granny Gab would have strung a man up by his toes and never shown him any type of common courtesy. There was a time when the men of Mule Hollow practically walked across the street when her grannies went in for supplies. Over the years, because of the intervention of sweet-hearted Granny Bunches, who was really her great-aunt, they'd come to tolerate each other in order to live in the same small community. But still, all her life Lilly had been taught to believe the worst about men.

Old habits that ingrained were hard to break.

But since her change of heart, her upbringing was no excuse to show bad behavior to her new neighbor.

Having let the engine warm sufficiently, Lilly rammed the heater lever to the on position, but made no move to engage the gears.

Of course… She paused, an idea blooming in her mind. It was late and Cort Wells would be sleeping like a normal person, unlike herself. She'd simply creep in, grab Samantha and scoot right back home.

The man need never know they'd been around.

Surely he was snoring in a warm bed, totally ignorant of the world around him.

*Okay. Okay, Lord.* Sucking in a breath, Lilly squared her shoulders. No one could be all that bad. The man was a horse trainer, for goodness' sake, not an ax murderer.

Why, as she kept saying, she should already have popped over there and introduced herself. He was after all her closest neighbor within ten miles.

If she'd been able to afford Leroy's place, then Cort Wells wouldn't have been her neighbor. She'd have been all the way out there, forgotten and blissfully alone, just the way she liked it. *But you weren't able to afford the ranch,* she thought, *and now you have a new neighbor, and so be it, tonight or in the next few days, you are going to have to make his acquaintance one way or another.* God would have her stretch past her own desire and reach for His purpose. That's what she'd been learning—that's what she was striving to do.

With that said, and before she chickened out, Lilly stomped hard on the gas pedal, grimacing when the truck lurched forward.

Again Lilly frowned, thinking about the ax-murderer portion of her imaginings about her ill-tempered, large, glowering grinch of a neighbor.

She was heading to his house in the dark of night. Truth was Cort Wells wasn't an ax murderer—thus far. But he hadn't met hairy old meddling Samantha.

Yet.

Cort Wells figured his frozen ears were about as hard as a block of ice and ten times colder than ears had any right to be. His fingers were numb. His nose was colder than his dog's after a dip in the fishpond behind the barn. After three hours of hiding inside the horse stables, Cort also figured that when he tried to remove his boots, his toes would be stuck to them and he'd be too hypothermic to care.

He hated cold weather.

Texas wasn't supposed to have winters ten degrees below freezing, which was one of the main reasons he'd chosen to relocate here rather than somewhere in his home state of Oklahoma. That and the fact that Mule Hollow was next to nothing in population made it the perfect place for a guy like him.

Or at least it would be right after he caught the prankster who'd been vandalizing his new home for the past few days. Caught him, taught him and maybe even quartered him.

Flexing his numb fingers, Cort rewrapped them around the slender rope he'd been holding and continued his vigil. Watching, waiting and anticipating. Anticipation had all but been lost to him since the month after he'd contracted the mumps and Ramona, bags in hand, had informed him he was no longer capable of fulfilling her emotional needs or her wants in life. With the blow delivered, she had promptly marched out the door, not looking back.

The mumps. Kids had the mumps. Even now, a year later, he found it hard to believe how profoundly what was supposed to be a childhood illness had altered his life.

One day he'd had everything a man could want: a place to call his own, more than enough business to go around and a beautiful wife sharing and building a future filled with love, laughter and eventually children. Lots of children.

Then he'd contracted the mumps.

It had been a long road to acceptance, shaking the very foundation of his faith. He hadn't yet figured out what the Lord was doing, but Cort had finally managed to set what life he had left on a shaky path toward a future he hadn't planned or wanted or could ever envision being happy about.

Determined to take back some kind of control, he'd bought this secluded ranch and seven days ago he'd moved in. Here he hoped to create some semblance of a future for himself and his dog, Loser. Here he wanted to forget the anger he'd been struggling with and come to some kind of understanding about the situation forced upon him.

However, after six nights of being repeatedly vandalized, Cort found he was looking for an avenue through which to vent the fury eating away inside him.

Tonight was the night for some poor yahoo to discover exactly how humorless Cort Wells found life.

Anybody getting their jollies from unlatching stall gates and releasing thousands of dollars' worth of prize studs to tango with the mares was looking for trouble. He'd upped his stakes by ransacking Cort's feed room and tearing up his hay stash. The clown wasn't only pitiful, he was childish, because there wasn't anything any more important than alfalfa cubes inside Cort's feed room. Vandalism—pure, simple vandalism—that's what this was.

And it had Cort madder than a bull in a rodeo chute.

Trouble had seriously come knockin' at the right door.

The crunch of footsteps on gravel alerted him that he was about to entertain a visitor. He jerked to attention and welcomed the flow of warm anticipation as it surged through his chilled body. With the gentle flick of his wrist he whipped the rope in his hand to life just as the wooden door creaked, signaling his guest of honor's entrée into the barn. He heard the soft nicker of a horse and the rustle of a curious colt.

From his hiding place, Cort could hear his intruder as he shuffled over the concrete alley that ran down the center of the horse stalls. One. Two. Three steps and the clown—the chubby little clown—stepped into the circle of light from the wash bay's bug zapper. Cort hesitated, a bit surprised at the short, bulky stature of the intruder. Flicking his wrist, he heard the soft whisper as the rope sailed through the air. With an expertly tempered yank, he tightened the lasso—and had himself a culprit!

Leaping from the shadows before the first muffled cry rang out, Cort felt immediate justification when the man fell to the ground with a thud and a grunt.

That is, until *he* flopped over and turned into a *she! A very pregnant she!*

"Whoa!" Cort jumped back, shook his head and gaped like a fool. She didn't disappear. She didn't get any less pregnant.

Instead, frozen in the circle of light. she stared up at him with wide, warm eyes of golden fire. "Well, now, *that* was entirely uncalled for," she drawled, huffing a bit as she lay on the floor carefully touching her protruding stomach. "Do you do this sort of thing often?"

Cort was trying to scrape his lip off his boots and had absolutely no inkling of a reply. Like a buffoon, he could only stare.

She wrinkled her nose. "I know, I know. I look like a blimp floating across a full moon, but I'm not. I'm your neighbor, from down the road."

Her voice was snappy, fire and ice swirled together—and appealing as all get-out. He pictured her clowning around with small children with that voice, or whispering sweet nothings in the ear of a lonesome cowboy.

"Neighbors?" he managed at last, feeling like a stooge. Certain he looked like one.

Slowly, as if speaking to one of those toddlers he'd imagined her playing with, she nodded her red-capped head and repeated, "Neighbors. So you see, the rope really isn't necessary. As a matter of fact, you could let me go and I promise not to harm you."

That kicked Cort into gear. Things hopped out of slow motion and started to focus. He'd steer-dogged a pregnant woman! Thrown her on the ground, baby and all, and left her there.

Left her there rocking back and forth on her back, waving her arms in the air like a derailed turtle straining to flip from her back to her feet. In this case to sit up. Spurred to life, Cort grabbed her arm and started tugging.

"Thanks," she grunted. She was looking up at him with eyes full of laughing regret. "Once I'm down I'm pretty much out for the count. You know, 'help I've fallen and I can't get up.'" She chuckled at her own wit.

Cort did not. "Woman! Have you lost your mind? This is *not* a laughing matter. You could be hurt. You hit that ground like a concrete block."

"And I thank you s-o-o-o much for bringing that picture to mind," she replied. "Actually, I'm sure I look more like a beached whale doing snow angels."

Cort bit back his agreement and tugged her into a sitting position—or at least a kind of sitting position, a ninety-degree angle being a physical impossibility with her small stature and protruding stomach. The awkward position forced her to lean back into the support of his arm and compelled him to lean down over her. She was breathing hard from the exertion, and little white puffs of her warm breath mingled with his as she smiled up at him. She had a cute little pixie face dominated by sparkling eyes and dark lashes. Intelligent eyes.

"Grace in motion, aren't I?" she continued, crinkling her nose again.

Cort frowned. "Mind telling me what your name is? And what would possess you to risk your child on a night like this?"

"Lilly Tipps. And I'm padded enough that the fall didn't hurt."

*Didn't hurt?* This was too much for Cort. "What kind of fool is your Mr. Tipps that he lets his pregnant wife roam the countryside?"

"There is no, and has never been a Mr. Tipps."

Cort's gaze dropped to her protruding tummy and the rope resting drunkenly over it. It hit him again that he'd really lassoed a pregnant woman! His dismay must have shown, because she patted his arm in a comforting way.

"Don't look so serious," she urged. "I was trespassing on your land. You had every right to hog-tie me. It's better than being shot."

"True," he agreed with a scowl. "But we'll talk about that later. Right now we have to get you up and make certain everything is okay. Make certain that baby isn't harmed." He slipped his hands beneath his strange intruder's arms and hefted her to a standing position. Why she would be outside, heavy with child, tore at him, and the way she was leaning against him now, breathing hard, sent alarms clanging through him.

"Are you hurt?" he snapped, dropping his gaze to the top of her head where it met his chin. Her little red cap tickled his nose as she rolled her head from side to side against his chest. "What's wrong?"

"I'm all right." Her voice was muffled against his heart. "Just need to catch my breath."

Despite the intelligence he'd glimpsed in her gaze, he thought something important was missing upstairs when a pregnant woman thought nothing strange about tramping around in the middle of the night. Alone. In a storm. Unprotected.

Where was the baby's father?

Having gained her breath at last, she stepped away from the protection of his arms, and to his horror, he had to fight to let her go and drop his hands to his hips.

He watched as she adjusted her bulky coat over her

bulkier body. Her face was bright, her eyes twinkling. "Thank you."

Cort couldn't tear his gaze away from her.

"I don't get much breath in here," she was saying as she ran a hand lovingly over her tummy. "That'll change in about three weeks. Although the doctor says I'll probably go past my due date."

Cort didn't see how. She looked ready to give birth any day. *Great with child* had never been a more perfect description.

"That is," she continued, "if Samantha doesn't get me killed before the end of this pregnancy. When I get my hands on her, I'm going to hog-tie *her*."

"Who's Samantha?" Cort snapped. Multiple avenues of this scenario were rubbing his already waning good humor raw.

"Oh, I'm sorry. Sam—"

A nerve-jolting screech broke through the night air. Cort nearly jumped out of his jeans.

Half-asleep horses came alive with startled nickers and whinnies, and from inside the house he could hear his dog barking. Loser never barked. "What in the world—" Cort bit out the words, striding toward the barn door.

Lilly's laugh stopped him. "*That* is Samantha."

On one heel Cort spun toward her.

Lilly hid a smile behind her hand. "She'll be quite ornery if you changed the lock on the hay barn. Tell me it isn't so."

"Well, yes—today, as a matter of fact. The old

one was broken. Some jerk keeps tearing up my hay bales."

"Samantha," Lilly mouthed softly. "She doesn't like locks on her barn." Lilly chuckled more. "She's gonna be mad."

*She's* gonna be mad? "Who is this Samantha person?" Cort exploded, stomping toward the door intent on finding out on his own who could make the noises coming from outside the barn.

"Watch out," she called in warning. "The hay barn was her domain."

Having reached the closed door, Cort pivoted to glare at the exasperating woman. "What? Who is Samantha?"

The words were barely out of his mouth when the barn door flew open, walloped him in the backside and sent him flying to his knees.

Lilly gasped. Cort ate dust and shot a glare over his shoulder. And there framed in the doorway stood the fattest little donkey he'd ever seen.

"Cort Wells, meet Samantha." Lilly presented her with a wave.

Cort could only stare, too startled to move. Samantha had to be the ugliest, most unassuming bag of whiskers— "A donkey!"

Lilly chuckled again and waddled to stand beside him.

"You're telling me *that* has been vandalizing my place?"

"Well, yes. Samantha used to live here and hasn't given in to nesting at my place yet."

As if to show she reigned in this domain, Samantha lifted her nose haughtily, swished her tail twice, then sashayed past them into the barn. From his stunned, all-fours position Cort had a perfect view as she swept past. He was not impressed. To say the least, Samantha was a sight—short, putty colored and instead of a smooth fat stomach she had rippling, bulging saddle bags that stretched from shoulder to rump in one roll after another. She beat all Cort had ever seen.

As he watched from his position in the dust, Samantha pranced, albeit heavily, to the feed room's closed door, wrapped her slobbery pink lips around the oval door handle, gave a twist, backed up and pulled the door open. This achieved, she stuck her nose in the air and clomped lightly inside with her tail swinging proudly.

"Well, I'll be." Cort stood, dusting off his jeans, and scratched his temple. "I'd never have believed it if I hadn't just seen it."

"Leroy, the prior owner of this ranch, raised her from a baby, bottle-fed and all. She's lived her entire twenty years here on the ranch. By the way, she thinks she's a human, or a dog at least. When she was smaller, they say she even ate bread out of her own bread box in the kitchen."

"That must be where those strange scrapes came from on that big drawer."

"Teething. She also likes you to rock her in the cedar swing next to the barn."

"Rock her. Swing? You've got to be kidding."

Samantha, on her tippy-toes, trotted out of the feed

room, a green alfalfa cube sticking out of her poochy lips.

Cort jogged to the opening and groaned at the mess.

Lilly ambled over to his side. "Whew! What a nightmare. Leroy always kept her a tub of cubes open. That way she didn't make a mess, but still thought she was being sneaky."

"Just what I need. A sneaky jack—'

"Burro. Samantha prefers the less critical term to the biblically correct one. It's less demeaning to her character, if you know what I mean. And besides, she's a jenny."

Cort frowned, expressing to Lilly exactly what he thought of her terminology correction. "And *she* told you this?"

The lady had a screw loose, but at this point he'd believe anything.

"Not exactly," she said, crinkling her nose.

"Thank goodness—you had me going there."

Lilly chuckled, and he smiled at the infectious sound. Maybe she wasn't too crazy.

"She told Leroy and he told me."

Lilly's new neighbor thought she'd lost her mind. She could tell. It was written all over his face. "You really aren't as bad as everyone said." It popped out, and she could have just kicked herself for saying it. Then again, she'd never been one for holding back.

"And just what have they been saying about me?" he drawled, staring with stone-hard disapproval.

It was a shame, too, that disapproval—all those carved lines messing up his face. Boy, could he stop traffi—

The sudden tightening of her stomach broke into Lilly's runaway thoughts. Gently she rubbed the hard knot. Her back ached and suddenly the excursion took its toll. Like a glass of water being drained, she felt exhaustion overcome her. That would explain her unlikely infatuation with the new neighbor. She had learned her lesson up close and personal seven and a half months ago. All the I-told-you-so's from six generations of Tipps women would be ringing in her ears for the rest of her life for the bad choice she'd made. Yep, it was time to gather Samantha and head home to her bed before she fell over right here in the middle of Cort Wells's freezing horse barn.

However, she couldn't take that sour look one more instant. He needed to lighten up. Playing the part to perfection, she shook her head somberly. "The gossips down at Pete's Feed and Seed have been saying mean, nasty things about you. Why, you wouldn't believe what's been circulating."

His lips compressed into a thin line. "I see. And these things. You believed them?"

Lilly nodded gravely. "I was afraid to come over here tonight. Shaking in my boots. Literally." Nearly, but not exactly.

He studied her, his mouth a hardened line. The tension radiated just below the surface of his cobalt-blue eyes, and Lilly knew the moment he realized she was teasing, because his eyes mellowed ever so slightly.

"Shaking in your boots," he drawled. Arching an

eyebrow, he dropped his gaze to her boots, then her stomach, then settled once again on her face. "You don't shake in your boots," he stated flatly.

Lilly laughed. "No, Cort Wells, neighbor extraordinaire, I do not shake in my boots. Nor do I listen to idle gossip with eager anticipation. The only thing I believed was that you didn't smile much and had an unfortunate habit of losing patience a little too easily." Not exactly true, but kind of.

"Which is why you stole down here to rescue Samantha from your ogre neighbor before he shot her, or worse, made glue out of her."

"Exactly," Lilly said, meeting his gaze.

For a long moment he studied her. Then, making an all-out liar of her and all the gossips, he smiled.

And Lilly, well, she shook in her boots.

# Chapter Two

Standing in the center of his freezing barn, Cort stared at his kooky neighbor and felt the first smile he'd smiled in over a year spread across his face. It was an odd feeling—not unpleasant, but totally unexpected. It assured him that he needed a good, hard, swift kick in the head.

At thirty-six he was picking up speed on the down slide toward forty. His wife had left him, he couldn't father children and now he was attracted to a woman too young for him.

This was not good. Everything he'd believed in growing up he'd failed at thus far—mainly his belief that a man could be measured by his success as a good father and husband. But despite his failures, nothing altered his number one belief that a child deserved two parents.

Lilly had informed him there was no Mr. Tipps, as if it was the most natural thing in the world for a single woman to be pregnant. Obviously her view on the matter differed from his. She might be cute, but for all Cort knew, she didn't even know the name of her baby's father.

It didn't matter how good this smile cracking across his face felt—the best thing he could do for himself was get Lilly off his property. And her misbehaving donkey with her.

However, before he could do that he had to make certain she was all right. Because, despite her cheerfulness, she looked a little as if she might be hurting some in her back.

"Look," he said, blowing air into his fists to warm them. "I know you must be freezing, so why don't you come into the house, and I'll make us a pot of coffee to warm up. I'll introduce you to Loser, my dog, and then we'll get you and Samantha home." It was pure and simply an offer to warm up, nothing more.

Her eyes brightened. "Coffee," she said. "You know, I'd do fifty toe touches for a stiff cup of hot coffee—that is, *if* I could touch my toes. But I really need to get Samantha home before this storm finishes us off. The sneak, she doesn't realize what a toll her adventures play on a mammoth like me."

Cort grimaced at yet another pregnant wisecrack. To be fair, given the size of her burden, he'd bet his stash of banana Laffy Taffy that her twisted sense of humor was a cover-up. She might not care about the father of her baby, but she seemed to care deeply about her unborn child, even if she'd acted foolishly in coming out on a night like this.

As if reading his thoughts, she dropped her gaze

# GET 2 BOOKS

IF YOU ENJOY A ROMANTIC STORY that reflects solid, traditional values, then you'll like *Love Inspired*® novels. These are heartwarming inspirational romances that explore timeless themes of forgiveness and redemption, sacrifice and spiritual fulfillment.

We'd like to send you two *Love Inspired* novels absolutely free. Accepting them puts you under no obligation to purchase any more books.

## HOW TO GET YOUR
## 2 FREE BOOKS AND 2 FREE GIFTS

1. Return the reply card today, and we'll send you two *Love Inspired* novels, absolutely free! We'll even pay the postage!

2. Accepting free books places you under no obligation to buy anything, ever. The two books have combined cover prices of at least $11.00 in the U.S. and at least $13.00 in Canada, but they're yours to keep, free!

3. We hope that after receiving your free books you'll want to remain a subscriber, but the choice is yours— to continue or cancel, any time at all!

### EXTRA BONUS
**You'll also get two free mystery gifts!**
**(worth about $10)**

# FREE!

**The Reader Service— Here's how it works:**

Accepting your 2 free books and 2 free gifts (gifts valued at approximately $10.00) places you under no obligation to buy anything. You may keep the books and gifts and return the shipping statement marked "cancel." If you do not cancel, about a month later we'll send you 6 additional books and bill you just $4.24 each for the regular-print edition or $4.74 each for the larger-print edition in the U.S. or $4.74 each for the regular-print edition or $5.24 each for the larger-print edition in Canada. That is a savings of at least 23% off the cover price. It's quite a bargain! Shipping and handling is just 50¢ per book in the U.S. and 75¢ per book in Canada.* You may cancel at any time, but if you choose to continue, every month we'll send you 6 more books, which you may either purchase at the discount price or return to us and cancel your subscription.

*Terms and prices subject to change without notice. Prices do not include applicable taxes. Sales tax applicable in N.Y. Canadian residents will be charged applicable taxes. Offer not valid in Quebec. All orders subject to credit approval. Credit or debit balances in a customer's account(s) may be offset by any other outstanding balance owed by or to the customer. Books received may not be as shown. Please allow 4 to 6 weeks for delivery. Offer valid while quantities last.

▼ If offer card is missing write to: The Reader Service, P.O. Box 1867, Buffalo, NY 14240-1867 or visit www.ReaderService.com ▼

**BUSINESS REPLY MAIL**

FIRST-CLASS MAIL    PERMIT NO. 717    BUFFALO, NY

POSTAGE WILL BE PAID BY ADDRESSEE

THE READER SERVICE
PO BOX 1867
BUFFALO NY 14240-9952

NO POSTAGE
NECESSARY
IF MAILED
IN THE
UNITED STATES

to her stomach and placed a palm protectively on the mound where her child nestled. Cort found himself wanting to put his hand there, too, to feel life beneath his palm. A sudden violent wave of regret shook him. He'd never touch his own child that way.

He didn't like being reminded of the experiences of fatherhood that he would never have. He had come to Texas to forget them. He'd prayed that God would release him from this need, that he wouldn't be tortured forever.

Lilly moved toward the door, one hand remaining on her stomach, the other on her back, offsetting the unequal proportions.

She had moved only a couple of steps away from him when she gasped. He was beside her in a stride. "You're hurt."

Shaking her head, she paused again, exhaling slowly. "Relax. Please. I have these Braxton-Hicks all the time. You know, false labor contractions." She took another sharp breath. "My doctor assures me there isn't anything to worry about."

"Your doctor didn't know you were going to be used for roping practice when he told you not to worry."

"Forget the roping. You had every right to believe I was a thief." She gave him a quick smile. "By the way I'd like to learn that trick someday. Knowing how to use a rope like that might come in handy. Might need to catch baby Tipps. Or Samantha," she said with a wink. "Anyway, I'm just glad you didn't greet me with a gun. With an aim like yours I'd be singing praises to the good Lord right now."

Cort started to speak, but she laid one hand on his arm and touched his lips with a finger from her other hand. "There isn't anything wrong with me that my warm bed and a bit of sleep won't cure."

Cort forgot what he was about to say. She'd touched him. Big deal. She was tired and she was rambling, which he found endearing, despite himself. "How far a walk did that donkey put you through?"

She stepped away from him and started ambling along. "Oh, I parked at the end of your drive. It's not far, especially when you consider that I walk two miles every day for exercise. Poor Samantha—she doesn't mean to be so much trouble."

What had she been thinking? She'd come out in the stormy night in her condition, searching for an animal! And here he'd been thinking about how much she cared for her child. "I hope you don't make strolling around past midnight a habit," he snapped, irritated at himself as well as her.

"Scared of boogeymen, Mr. Wells?"

"Boogeymen! We're talking about being out on deserted roads alone. You're a woman. A mother-to-be, who doesn't have any business being out this late, much less alone in weather like this. You might be young, but you should have better sense."

She raised her eyebrows to where they nearly touched the edge of her red knit cap, and plunked her fists on her rounded hips. "I don't think I like your attitude."

"My attitude? My attitude! Lady, no wonder your Mr. Tipps didn't hang around." He was sputtering. He never sputtered! And he couldn't stop himself. "Anybody knows women shouldn't walk around past midnight when a storm is brewing, especially looking for a short, fat, hairy beast. And most especially when they could give birth any moment!" Cort halted his harangue to catch his breath, only to feel another tirade building as long-pent-up anger fought for release. Snatching his hat from his head, he rammed a hand through his hair and held his tongue, biting it to keep quiet.

She studied him, then shook her head slowly. "My, my, Mr. Wells. Dare I say the gossips were correct? You are positively livid. And pink all over."

The woman was making him crazy. He'd known her all of thirty minutes and she was making him crazy. This wasn't like him.

"Samantha," she called.

Cort found himself staring as she straightened her funny red cap and lifted her chin in defiance.

Cold sobering sleet belted him in the face from the open doorway. Bewildered by his reaction, he paused to gather his wits and went to survey the dangerous conditions outside his barn.

Barely hesitating, Lilly tottered past him into the fierce night.

Unbelievable! What did she think this was? An eighty-degree, midsummer night? "Hey, do you need a keeper or what?" he yelled. He never yelled. "You can't walk in this carrying that…that baby."

Catching up to her, he grasped her arm, saving her, he was certain, from an icy catastrophe.

Ungrateful woman that she was, she promptly rewarded him with a couple of wimpy slaps on the hand. Then, yanking away from his protecting hold, she fried him with a glare.

"Would you mind? Leave me alone," she snapped above a burst of whistling wind.

In the faint glow of the light mounted above the riding pen her eyes flashed like the dancing flame of a match. It struck Cort like a burn that she sure looked cute when she was angry. She was spunky. And despite himself, he found he liked the life surrounding the little woman. He wondered at the heart behind that spunk.

"I am not an idiot, Mr. Wells," she continued, snapping him back to reality. "The icy rain has just begun to fall. You should know it hasn't had time to freeze the ground. So would you mind dropping the 'Me Tarzan, You Jane' routine? And by the way, this is my child. Mine alone. And there never was a Mr. Tipps—and won't be if I have anything to do with it!"

Cort stared. Puffs of white-hot air wafted about Lilly like steam off the steamroller that had just flattened him.

"And thank you very much for once again proving my grannies right on all counts."

"Oh, yeah?" he managed weakly, suddenly uncentered and feeling, well…feeling alive! Lilly might be pregnant. She might be outspoken, hard to handle—the list seemed to go on and on—but after a year of walking around in a stupor, he realized Lilly Tipps had brought him back to life.

Whether he was ready or not.

"Well," she said, cutting into his spinning thoughts. Her voice was soft, deliberate. "In the words of my great-granny Shu-Shu, other than assisting in the conception of a baby, men are pert' near useless. And otherwise too bossy to worry about."

Later, watching the taillights of Lilly's truck disappearing slowly in the drizzle, Cort reminded himself that it was better this way. For a minute there he'd nearly lost his head. She'd brought him back to reality with a bang. Now he realized he didn't like her going home alone in this storm, but it wasn't his business. She was her own woman.

It didn't matter if that bit about men being useless rubbed him the wrong way. Did he care what she thought of men?

But she was something. *Something else.*

She'd tied that crazy donkey to the back of her truck and headed out at a crawl on the two-mile trip to where her home sat at the end of the lonesome road. The real estate agent had mentioned Lilly, and how she lived a fairly solitary life. They were basically secluded and cut off from everything. Except for each other. Cort had assumed she was older, and at the time he'd been happy to know his only neighbor for miles wouldn't bother him.

The real estate agent hadn't mentioned anything about her being pregnant. Or, well…kooky.

He probably hadn't wanted to scare Cort off.

Smart man. Cort would have to remember him if

he ever decided to sell. Not everyone would be sharp enough to recognize a selling disadvantage in Lilly and her sidekick.

He studied the swirling sky. The full force of the storm would strike by the time she made it home. Ice pelted his face like needles. On the other hand, at the pace they were traveling the storm might have passed before they got there.

He grimaced. This was no joking matter. The weather would be a record breaker for this part of the state, for this time of year. Turning back, stiff with fatigue, nearly chilled to the bone, he headed down the drive toward the warmth of his house and the bed he'd forgotten to think about. All the while he continued to tell himself that Lilly wasn't his responsibility, a fact she'd made clear to him. Perfectly clear.

Still, as he opened the door and strode tiredly into his kitchen, he couldn't stop thinking of her. What if her truck broke? It didn't look to be in great shape. What if she slipped and fell on her way into her home? Who would help her? Samantha?

That thought spurred him to turn to the window. Loser appeared from the other room, sauntered over and with a sigh dropped his shaggy head onto the windowsill.

A perpetual sigher, Loser sighed again, drawing Cort to look down at his pitiful dog. It had been a weak moment of loneliness outside the supermarket that had been Cort's undoing. That and the cutest little brown-eyed girl trying to find a good home for the ugliest baby mutt he'd ever seen. A sap for kids, Cort had taken the pup and on a melancholy note christened the forlorn dog Loser. He shouldn't have. It hadn't been the poor pup's fault Ramona had divorced Cort and left him feeling like a loser.

Reaching down, Cort scratched him between the ears with his frozen fingers. They tingled as blood started flowing and warmth seeped back into them. Loser grunted—which was more response than Cort usually got. It was Cort's own fault. He hadn't given the dog much to aspire to by labeling him with such a lousy name. He really should change it.

But it was a name he lived up to with pride. He enjoyed hot meals, warm beds and cool breezes on sunny afternoons. He didn't like cold weather, loud noises or hairbrushes anywhere near his matted body. When he wasn't sleeping, he moped around stumbling over his own ears and looking at people's toes from beneath droopy eyelids and bushy eyebrows. The poor dog had mountains to overcome if he were ever to drag himself out of the pit of self-pity shrouding him. A state of being not unlike Cort's own.

In part, this move to west Texas had been Cort's step in the right direction. At least he was moving on with life by realizing what he couldn't have and making a new start with what he had. And most important, he had God's grace. Cort knew God's grace was sufficient to overcome the grief consuming him. But to have lost his wife and any children he'd hoped to father… He rammed a hand through his hair. He needed time to come to terms with such an incomprehensible loss. He loved the Lord, had walked every mile for the past fifteen years with a strong unfailing faith. But this wasn't something he could just move on from and pretend never happened. Lately, even trusting the Lord was a struggle. He felt as if part of him was lost forever. The Bible said there was a time to mourn and a time to dance. He wasn't ready to dance. Didn't know if he ever would be.

And he for certain didn't need a neighbor who represented everything he couldn't have. Everything he'd lost.

"We've got problems, old boy," he said to Loser. "I heard you barking. I had to think twice to realize it was you, but you knew I was in trouble up to my eyebrows. Didn't you?" Loser shifted his chin's position on the windowsill and his tail flopped halfheartedly. This, too, was more than usual. Cort reached to scratch behind Loser's ear.

"You're feeling kinda spry, aren't you? I see that tail a-wagging. You keep this perky attitude and I might have to change your name." Loser's shoulders heaved with another sigh as he returned his gaze to the storm. Cort's gaze followed the animal's and his thoughts returned to Lilly.

"I don't know why I'm worried, Loser. She wasn't. She acted as if men have leprosy or something." He glanced back at the dog. "Said we weren't worth anything if we couldn't father a child—" Loser raised his eyebrows just enough to look pityingly up at Cort. Cort frowned at the reflection he saw of himself in the dog's eyes. The reflection of the fool he'd almost been again.

"Yeah, yeah, I know," he said wearily, scrubbing his eyes and turning toward his bedroom.

"It sounded like she'd been talking to Ramona."

## Chapter Three

Lilly's eyes popped open and she stared up at the ceiling. Sunlight danced across the pale yellow paint. All was quiet. No sounds of ice! Thank goodness there was no sleet this morning.

Slowly she rolled to her side. "Ohhh!" she yelped, then used her arms to rise to a sitting position, or at least a semi-sitting position. The last stages of pregnancy were a real bug-a-boo. To catch her breath she had to prop her hands on the mattress behind her just to hold herself upright because of her growing-by-the-second tummy.

She ached all over.

The run-in with her new neighbor and his little lasso had caused more soreness than she'd expected.

At least, to her great relief, the Braxton-Hicks contractions had stopped. She hadn't wanted to admit it out loud, but for a little while she'd feared she really was in labor, and she couldn't be. Not yet anyway. She had things to do. Tonight was the very first production of the

Mule Hollow Cowboy Dinner Theater. And even though she had protested until she was blue in the face, she was now looking forward to being in the production.

"What a night, kiddo," she said, yawning and rubbing her tummy. "I hope you aren't sore." Talking to her baby brought a big smile to her lips. When he responded with a good hard kick to the belly button she laughed. Oh, how she loved having her little boy to talk to.

A boy. The doctor had informed her she was expecting a boy and she still couldn't believe it. A baby boy Tipps! After all these years. Wow. The grannies would most definitely be surprised.

Lilly rubbed her eyes and focused on her day. She needed to find some way to keep Samantha at home, but she didn't have the time. She had to be in town by noon. Everyone wanted her to take it easy, but she wanted to help with the last preparations for the show.

Still, she knew she couldn't be foolish again by taking chances like last night.

The weather report had predicted that the icy weather would come and go for the next week. Cort had been right about her not needing to jeopardize her baby by being out in such weather, lost burro or not. It had been only by the Lord's grace that she hadn't been harmed last night. She was determined that after the show tonight she would slow down and start acting more like how a pregnant woman ought to act.

Of course, she had to get through the show tonight. She and Samantha. They had a very important role.

Pushing herself off the bed, she padded to the bathroom and turned on the water. She had gained only thirty pounds with her pregnancy, but with her height she felt as if she was as wide as she was tall. Not that she really cared—she was having a baby!

For that wonderful cause she wouldn't care if she were, as Granny Gab would have said, as big as the broad side of a barn. *She was having a baby!*

And that was as wonderful as life could get.

Nothing else mattered. Lilly would again gladly go through everything that had led up to her pregnancy. She felt blessed.

She was blessed.

Reaching into the shower, she tested the water with her fingertip and thought about the dinner theater. Hopefully the bad weather wasn't going to hinder the program. Ever since the older ladies in the town had hatched a campaign to bring women to Mule Hollow, the town hadn't been the same. It had all started with an advertisement about lonesome cowboys looking for wives. Of course, Lilly wasn't interested in finding a husband. Everyone knew that she'd taken a chance against everything her grannies had taught her and married Jeff Turner.

And everyone knew she had no interest whatsoever in going down that road again. She had learned her lesson and learned it well.

She'd thought she could change the luck of the Tipps women. Lilly's mother, God rest her soul, had thought the same thing in her life.

Wrong.

Her mother had wound up picking the lowest of the

low. And Lilly hadn't done any better. But that was water under the bridge and she had moved on.

There was only one good thing that had come of her marriage, and it was this baby she was carrying. Neither she nor her mother had been able to stop the legacy of bad choices, but as her good friend Lacy Brown had recently pointed out to her, she had another choice to make. She could either wallow in the past or move on.

And now she was making choices for two. Another life was counting on her.

Lilly showered quickly. Normally she could hang out in the hot spray until her toes shriveled, but today she had things to do and places to be. She had to get to town and help finish decorating. Who knew a newspaper ad about lonesome cowboys needing wives would have had such an impact on her small town? Lilly combed her curly hair and chuckled at the memory of Lacy whizzing into Mule Hollow. As the first respondent, she'd been so determined in her mission. She was convinced God had called her to come to the dusty, dying town of Mule Hollow to open a hair salon, where she could witness to people as she cut their hair.

For a town left with just a handful of old-timers and a host of lonesome cowboys, the thought of families—or even of women at all—seemed an unreachable goal. But in the late 1970s after most of the town's financial support had dried up along with the oil well, many families had had to move away. Their departure had left a shell of a town that had slowly deteriorated over the decades. But now there was hope in the town. Because of the faith of three older ladies and Lacy Brown, Mule Hollow had a new spring in its step.

Lilly admired Lacy's faith. She admired her desire to follow God's plan for her life by believing He would bring women here and she would get to spruce them up to fall in love and lead them to the Lord in her hair salon, Heavenly Inspirations. In an ironic twist, it had been Lacy who'd fallen in love and was soon to marry Clint Matlock. Theirs would be the first marriage in Mule Hollow in ten or more years.

Lilly didn't count her own marriage.

The wedding had taken place at the courthouse in the nearby town of Ranger, and the marriage had lasted just over a month. She was such a hermit that most people in Mule Hollow hadn't even known she was dating, much less gotten married! But everyone was so understanding when she explained how she'd made such a horrible mistake. And they were absolutely thrilled when they found out she would be having the first baby born in Mule Hollow in the past ten years. It was the start the town needed. And hopefully tonight's show would continue bringing new life to Mule Hollow.

Norma Sue Jenkins, Esther Mae Wilcox and Adela Ledbetter were the three ladies who'd hatched the original plan and put the ad in the papers. Tonight was the culmination of another of their ideas. Lilly would never have believed she would be participating in this cowboy dinner theater. But she was.

All because Lacy had seen her singing in the church choir.

Lilly had always loved to sing. And after Jeff left her

she'd continued to go to church and sing in the choir. It was strange—even though she was hurting inside and wanted only to be alone, there was just something about being in the church singing praises to the Lord that ministered to her spirit. It didn't mean for one minute that it changed her mind about men. God was going to have to do a mighty work on her heart for her to ever look at a man as a potential husband.

Her grannies had hated men and taught her from an early age that they were useless, worthless liars, one and all. And with good reason, since they had each experienced the worst that men had to offer. And after her experience with her own loser, she'd decided to believe them. True, in the four months she'd known Lacy she'd softened to at least being able to kid around with some of the lonely cowboys who lived in Mule Hollow. Lacy had helped her see that as a Christian she needed to have a forgiving heart and not judge all men as completely useless. And by being in this presentation tonight she'd even come to like some of the guys as friends.

Friends. As Granny Gab would say, untangling grapevines took more than an hour. It wasn't until recently that Lilly had realized Gabby was talking about regaining trust. She *was* making progress, but there would never be anything more between her and another man except friendship. Her heart couldn't take it. She imagined that she was going to be like Paul in the Bible and stay single for her lifetime.

Yep, it would be just her and her baby. That was something she could trust wholeheartedly.

She finally finished getting dressed, gathered up

everything she would need for the afternoon, then went to load Samantha into the trailer.

When Lacy had first approached her about letting Samantha be in the program, Lilly had been uncertain. But after a while she'd been worn down by Lacy's enthusiasm and had consented. Then, because she loved to sing, she had finally agreed to be in it also. Especially after hearing what their part would be. She couldn't resist.

She just hoped that everything went as planned. She didn't need any false labor pains tonight.

Singing while sitting on Samantha's back was going to be challenge enough.

"What do you think?" asked Molly Popp.

Lilly surveyed the room. "It looks great. Did you ever think when you moved here a few months ago that we'd be having so much fun trying to get more women to move to town?"

Molly laughed. "Honestly, I came because the entire story of what the ladies were trying to accomplish intrigued me. But I never really thought about being in on the adventure myself. This has been incredible. All these weeks of practice and planning have been great."

Lilly smiled and gently rubbed her stomach. Molly was a journalist who had a column in the Houston paper each week. After coming to the old-time fair that the town had hosted to draw women in, Molly had chosen to move right out to Mule Hollow to chronicle its progress while she started writing a book she'd been dreaming of writing.

She'd dated a few of the guys, but so far, Mr. Right hadn't come along. Unlike Lilly, Molly was still looking.

The old buildings had been transformed into part of a rustic theater. In the past few months the town had drawn together and torn out walls between two buildings, built a stage and installed woodstoves to keep the place warm for the program while still giving it the ambience of the good old days. It was a great idea.

Tonight would be the first gathering in Mule Hollow's new community center/theater.

"Lilly!" Lacy called, jogging into the room. Her short white-blond hair looked as if it had gotten caught in a blender, bouncing Meg Ryan-fashion in all different directions as she came to a jolting halt beside Lilly and Molly.

"What's up?" Lilly asked.

"I just wanted to check and see how you're doing. You feeling all right, not having any pains? Not too tired?"

"Slow down, Lacy. I'm feeling fine."

"When I asked you to do this, I wasn't thinking about how cold it was going to be. Are you sure you are up to doing your part of the show outside by the campfire?"

"My costume includes a blanket draped across my shoulders. I'll be warm enough. I love the idea of the campfire. I was over there looking at it earlier while the guys were setting up all the hay bales. It looks fantastic. Lacy, don't worry. I'll be okay. Leroy taught me to ride

Samantha, and believe me, she hasn't near the energy she had way back then. The fire will give a lot of heat, and there's no drizzle on the forecast until late tonight, so I'm good to go."

Lacy grabbed her and Molly in a big hug. "Our program is going to be great tonight. I can just feel it." Lacy's face beamed with anticipation. "Yep, yep, yep, this is going to be good."

Lilly had come a long way in the past three months. She was still a loner, but she was taking steps to overcome her past.

Lacy had given her the encouragement she needed to start letting people into her life. They didn't crowd her. They recognized that she needed her space, and they gave it to her.

"Okay, it's time to get dressed," Lacy said. "I see Adela and Esther Mae coming up the street, so they'll be ready to start taking tickets as the ladies arrive."

Lilly and Molly followed Lacy into the back, where their costumes were hanging. Lilly's part wasn't until after the dinner, so she would help with waiting tables during the play, something they'd all tried to stop her from doing, but she'd insisted. Lilly had always pushed herself and always would.

She didn't know any other way.


Cort stepped into the brightly lit building full of chatter and laughter and was met by Adela Ledbetter. She was a nice lady with a gentle elegance. Her bright blue eyes set against stark white hair sparkled with welcome.

"Hello again," she said as he removed his hat and looked warily around the crowded room. "I'm so glad you decided to join us. When I invited you the other day in town I wasn't sure you would accept the invitation."

"To tell you the truth, ma'am, I didn't know I was coming until an hour ago." Cort stroked the rim of his hat and glanced around the full room again. There were women everywhere—which had him backtracking on his decision to come. What had he been thinking?

Ms. Ledbetter placed a hand on his arm and smiled up at him. "God inspired you to come, because He knew you needed to be a part of this. You're going to get a blessing."

Cort looked down, about to deny that God had anything to do with his decision, but she was looking at him with such certainty and wisdom it made him keep silent.

"Well, well, well…what do we have here?" Norma Sue Jenkins said, coming to a halt in front of him like a steamroller hitting a brick wall. She had on a pair of overalls stuffed into rubber boots and a straw hat on her head with a red bandanna wrapped around it as a hatband.

Cort had run into Norma Sue a couple of times at the feed store in the few days since his arrival in town. Both times she'd tried to start up a conversation with him, but he'd been blunt and unresponsive to her friendly overtures. Now he felt about as low as the dirt on the bottom of his boots. She beamed up at him with a genuine smile of welcome that split across her round face from ear to ear.

"Glad you could make it, son. We need all the draw we can get."

"Draw?" Cort asked.

"You know, reasons for making some of these women want to move to our town."

"Now, Norma," Ms. Ledbetter said calmly. "Cort is new in town and he doesn't fully understand the importance of our endeavor."

"Well, that will soon change. Every cowboy needs a wife. You follow me and I'll put you in a good spot between two nice ladies."

"Ms. Led—" he started to say, but she patted him on the back.

"It's Adela to my friends. Don't let Norma scare you."

"Ma'am, I just came to see the show. To see what the town has been up to." He looked around the room skeptically. "Couldn't you sit me somewhere out of the way?"

Norma Sue hooted with laughter, then grabbed his arm and practically dragged him to a table full of women. Grudgingly, Cort found himself sitting between two women who immediately started firing questions at him that he didn't want to answer. He was trying to figure a way to get up and go home when his eye caught his neighbor walking out from a room at the back of the building.

In keeping with the hillbilly theme, she also had on overalls, and her hair was split down the middle and tied into two bushy tails on each side of her head.

She was cute.

In her hand she carried a large pitcher of tea. He couldn't believe it—the woman was waiting tables! Didn't she know she was pregnant?

What else would she do to endanger her baby? The woman was obviously a glutton for punishment. Weren't women as far along as she was in their pregnancy supposed to be sitting down most of the day with their feet propped up? And here she was walking around as if everything was normal.

He watched her move among the crowd. She seemed more reserved than she'd been when he'd accosted her in his barn. She smiled and nodded and poured tea. But she wasn't sassy and talkative as she'd been in his barn. He wondered if she was tired.

She'd almost made it to his table before she saw him. When she did, she plunked a hand to her hip. At first he thought she was going to turn and walk away. He had gotten a bit overbearing the night before. But with good reason.

"I see you made it through the night," he said, deciding he'd start the conversation if she wouldn't. He hoped she was feeling better.

Her features softened. "Yes, we made it. I should say thank you—"

"Not necessarily. I'm the one who threw you on the ground. Remember?"

"What?" the two women beside him both gasped.

"Threw her on the ground!" one exclaimed.

"No, the lasso was a good idea," Lilly said hastily, her eyes skittering to the ladies then back to him. "Like

I said last night, you might need to teach me to use one. You never know when one might come in handy."

She smiled then, and Cort remembered why he'd thought of her all day. That smile was the prettiest he'd ever seen, but it was something about her eyes that drew him, something in them that said back off. As if she was used to being alone, as if she expected the very worst from people…or men.

The lights dimmed, cutting off his thoughts as a group of people moved out onto the stage. Lilly quickly filled tea glasses and moved out of the way. Cort decided it was just as well. He hadn't come here tonight to think about the things he liked about his neighbor or the things about her that made him curious about her. He'd come to…well, he wasn't certain why he'd come tonight. He'd just felt compelled to check it out.

## Chapter Four

Lilly sat on Samantha's back and waited in the shadows. The dinner had been a big success. The cowboys had served up hot bowls of spicy chili and she'd watched the show from the back of the room. Everyone was laughing and having a good time. Lacy had a great cast. She had cowboys who'd never stood in front of a crowd before, singing songs and reciting cowboy poetry as if they'd been doing it all their lives.

There were comical hillbilly skits, featuring Lacy, Esther Mae and her husband, Hank. They had people nearly crying they were laughing so hard. Esther wore a moth-eaten, pea-green housecoat that looked a hundred years old, her hair was half in, half out of pink curlers and she was carrying a flyswatter that she would swat Hank with every so often during his droll portrayal as a couch-potato husband. Lilly laughed thinking about Esther grinning at the audience every time she wanted a laugh. She had blacked out one of her front teeth, and she'd give this big grin that exposed the gap, then she'd swat Hank for an added laugh.

Lacy got hoots of laughter on her own playing their less-than-intelligent, husband-hunting daughter. They worked well together—they were having as much fun doing the skit as everyone was having watching them.

Then there was Clint, Lacy's real-life fiancé, who also played her newfound love in the skit. It almost gave Lilly hope watching them singing love songs together—they couldn't carry a tune in a bucket, but that made it all the more humorous.

"You're next, Lilly. Hang on, now."

Lilly was roused from her thoughts and looked down from where she sat on Samantha's back. Bob Jacobs smiled up at her. Since starting the play, they had become good friends. He had the cutest dimples and a friendly but shy way about him. He would make someone—not her—a great husband. Maybe tonight's show could help out with that.

"We don't want anything happening to you tonight," he added, checking the saddle to make certain it was tight. "Okay, hold on. I'll take care of you." He winked up at her.

Lilly smiled and settled herself securely on the side-saddle, thankful that it helped her proportions angle more comfortably into the ride. She was a great rider; she'd been taught by the best. Leroy, the only man she'd ever been around much during her life, had taught her and she had no fear of a mishap. Everybody else was a bit apprehensive, but she'd be okay. Samantha would never intentionally do anything to harm her. Goodness, if Lilly hadn't been pregnant she'd have been riding bareback.

"Lead the way, Bob. Good luck—I mean break a leg." He grinned at her traditional theater jargon, pulled his costume hood over his head and took on the role of Joseph leading Mary toward Bethlehem.

The production inside had been in fun, but around the campfire were cameos of different Bible stories. Hers was a retelling of Jesus' birth.

"Let's go, Samantha," she said, patting the little burro on the neck as she started taking slow cautious steps. She knew it was Sam's nature to prance, but with Lilly on her back, the little dear was doing her bit to protect Lilly. It seemed to Lilly that Samantha understood the serious part they were playing in the drama. Samantha perked her long ears up and slapped her tail as if to say here we go, and then she followed Bob into the circle of light made by the large campfire.

In the crowd Lilly could see the faces of women and some children. Cowboys were interspersed in the gathering also. Friends had been made tonight by many of the singles, and Lilly was glad for them. The more social things that the town could host, the more likely it would grow. She was glad to be a part in helping with that goal.

Whether she believed there was any love out there for her or not.

Cort was standing to the side of the campfire. Roy Don, one of the few men Cort had met at the feed store and had actually let himself converse with, was playing the part of an old cowboy telling stories from the Bible. With each story he told someone dressed as that character stepped up and sang a song. It was entertaining and creative. Cort had to give them credit—the town had talent. Everyone gathered around the campfire seemed to really enjoy it. It was a nice touch of old-time authenticity to it and a great ending to a great night.

Despite his misgivings, he'd enjoyed the evening. He'd laughed so hard his gut was sore.

He surveyed the setup. They'd placed about forty hay bales around the camp for seating and had more stacked around with cowboy decorations hanging off them. He'd never seen so many lassos, lanterns, hay bales and hitching posts.

Someone had put in many hours of decorating for this night. When they decided to do something, they went all out.

Leaning against a porch post, Cort surveyed the crowd. He hadn't seen his neighbor for a little while. To his relief she hadn't done anything else after pouring the tea. The cowboys who weren't in the play did all the serving of the food. Cort had relaxed. He didn't know why he worried so much about the little sable-haired mother-to-be, but he did. Maybe the foolishness of the night before hadn't been out of negligence toward her baby, but out of misguided loyalty toward her donkey.

When he saw her being led out into the circle of light balanced on Samantha's back, he took back every nice thing he'd just been thinking.

The woman was due anytime, and she was sitting high up on a donkey. He hung his head in disgust.

It was all he could do not to stomp up there and lift her off her precarious perch. The fool woman ought to have her head examined. But when she started singing, he froze.

Her voice carried out across the crowd with a haunting melody. Cort took a step off the porch, drawn toward the sweet music.

It was a beautiful song. A beautiful voice.

It was a gentle whispery sound that floated over the audience in a poignant melody that pulled Cort to attention and took him on a journey of wonder. She sang of a mother, unsure of her future, uncertain of what God had in store for the child she carried, afraid of not raising him right, but believing that God had a plan and knowing she had two choices—trust God or turn Him away.

The song reminded Cort of how vulnerable Mary must have been back then. A mother-to-be with an unbelievable story. It amazed him how Lilly was able to incorporate all the angst and hope into one song. And all the while she sang, Samantha stood still, doing her part as the donkey that carried the special burden of God's Son and His mother into Bethlehem to bring hope to all people.

It was a stirring cameo. Of all the wonderful things Cort had seen during the evening, this was the most important and most touching. This one scene brought the essence of life into perspective.

He now understood the significance of the scene to Lilly. Why she might have thought it vital enough to sit on the burro's back as near term as she was. She did look at ease sitting there, even if she had to accommodate the roundness of her middle by leaning back. And Samantha had been perfect.

He was about to eat crow and relax when out of the corner of his eye he saw a kid toss something black into the fire.

*Bang! Bang, bang!*

Yells and screams broke out within seconds of the eruption of the firecrackers. When the explosions burst suddenly in rapid succession Samantha whirled and backed into the campfire flame, even with the grip Bob had on the lead rope.

Cort had already started forward to help Lilly when the fringe on Samantha's tail caught fire.

The old girl yanked her head up in panic, kicked her hind legs out and bolted. Terror filled her wide eyes.

Cort snatched the nearest lasso off a hitching post and jumped into the path of the frenzied animal. Lilly was hanging on to the sidesaddle, but had nothing with which to control Samantha. Cort could almost imagine the panic she must be feeling. Bob had been knocked down in the fray and was trailing them, but losing ground.

The flames on Samantha's tail were blazing. Cort knew he had to stop her before the fire reached her flesh and real pain began.

With a flick of his wrist Cort had the lasso spinning. He took a firm stance and let it fly just as Samantha whirled toward the alley and open range. Cort prayed his aim was true, and was rewarded when the cord settled over her head. He held on as the rope tightened.

Someone reached Samantha and threw a blanket over

her tail to smother the fire just as Cort drew the rope taut. Lilly, miraculously, had managed to hold on during the fiasco.

Everything had happened within a few short moments, and now everyone was in motion, putting out the fire and trying to get Lilly off the donkey. Cort wrestled through the throng, reached up and lifted her from the burro's back.

"Are you okay?"

Lilly laughed.

*Laughed!*

Her eyes were sparkling, dancing. "You are really good with that rope. Wow! Samantha? How's Samantha? Man, that was some ride."

What? Did the woman have no sense? No shame? Once more she'd endangered her child. Her defenseless little baby who might, and then again might not, be born into this world.

"That donkey is fine," he growled. "You're the one who needs her head examined. The fire only singed her tail. What were you thinking?"

Everyone around them went silent. The only sound was the cold wind whistling around the edge of the buildings. Cort didn't care. Why, all of them were foolish if they saw nothing wrong with Lilly riding that stinkin' donkey.

"I was thinking I had it under control. I was thinking that I knew how to ride—"

"Well, that was a wrong assumption."

"Now, wait just a minute," Bob interjected from where he was again holding Samantha's lead rope. This time he had it wrapped around his hand tightly. "I'm the one to blame here. I was supposed to control Samantha. If you're going to tear someone up, then tear into me."

He looked remorseful standing there. And he should. He'd made a grave mistake. Cort scanned the group of men and couldn't figure out why none of them had kept Lilly from getting on that donkey's back.

"Lilly, I'm sorry," Bob continued. "That song does it to me every time. I just forget about everything when you sing it, and I wasn't holding on securely."

"Bob, I'm a big girl." She patted his arm. "And I can take care of myself on a donkey or a horse's back. So relax." She lifted her chin and locked eyes with Cort.

Cort seriously doubted that the statement had merit. "Control? You were barely hanging on to Samantha's saddle horn. You could be on your way to the hospital right now. You're about the most thickheaded woman I've ever met."

Lilly rammed a hand through her ringlets and took a step toward him. Steam practically spewed from her ears. Good, Cort thought with satisfaction, she was mad. Someone needed to get through to her. Needed to make her realize that what she was carrying in her womb was precious cargo. That not everyone was so lucky.

"Thickheaded? Cort Wells, you are the most high-handed, overbearing man I have ever met. Have I, in any of our bizarre encounters, given you the slightest notion that I was in need of your guidance? I don't think so."

Cort watched anger play across her beautiful pale skin…. *Oh, no, you don't!* He yanked his thoughts away from admiring her and back to the problem at hand. "You might not think it, but that doesn't change anything."

"Ohhh!" She glared at him and stomped her tiny foot. "This was such a good night, and now it has morphed into a bad dream. And you are—"

Lacy Brown stepped up beside Lilly, placing her hand on her arm to stop her from speaking. "Y'all 'bout ready to finish the play?"

Cort frowned and Lilly glowered at him, her flashing eyes alive with fiery indignation as Lacy proceeded to call everyone back to the campfire.

Cort figured she had a point. There was no sense in his continuing to make a scene in front of the entire town and its guests. There was, after all, no reason for him to make a scene period.

Lilly meant nothing to him.

He didn't even know the woman. Why he'd gotten it into his lame brain that he had a right to tell her what she should and shouldn't do was completely beyond him. As everyone else moved back to the campfire, he headed to his truck. He'd never been big on crowds and had had about as much fun as one man could stand in a single evening.

He needed to be out in the country where he could be alone.

Cort hadn't been sure why he'd come to town, but Adela had been way off the mark when she'd said he was going to get a blessing from it.

Blessing? Cort couldn't remember the last time God had granted him one of those.

## Chapter Five

Lilly needed a shower. She needed to feel the hot water pelting the fog from her brain and the soreness from her muscles. She hurt everywhere. Okay, she'd been foolish and reckless and was paying for it. Thankfully, her baby wasn't. He seemed fine, kicking and moving and generally having a grand time this morning.

A rap on her back door startled her. Company? At this hour? Her fingers froze in shock on the top button of her flannel pajama top. When was the last time she'd had someone rapping on her door?

Forever.

The knocking grew to a pounding, so she turned the shower off and waddled as fast as her short legs would carry her down the long hallway lined with pictures of her many generations of Tipps women.

"Hey, Grannies, someone is knocking at my door." Company was a very abnormal occurrence—still, Lilly wasn't sure that made her talking to photos any less pathetic. Maybe she should get out more. She reminded herself that she had been helping out with the play a couple of nights a week for the past month. But now that the play was over, she had nowhere to go.

That was okay. She obviously had no people skills. She'd behaved shoddily last night. It had been such a wonderful night, and then she'd allowed Satan a hold over her and run her neighbor off with her sharp tongue.

All night she hadn't been able to get the memory of Cort stomping away in anger out of her mind. She'd driven him away, and he'd just been trying to help her.

True, he was bossy, and had a bad way with words. But so did she, and she hadn't had control of Samantha. Her adrenaline had simply been pumping from the excitement, and she'd said some pretty silly things. She needed to apologize to Cort. They were neighbors, for crying out loud. Why couldn't they get along? They were the only ones around for miles.

A quick look in the mirror by the door had her slapping a hand over her mouth.

"Eeks!" It was a bad, bad thing to wake up looking like Shirley Temple gone wrong. *Way wrong.* She really needed that shower.

"I hope whoever is on the other side of this door has a good heart," she muttered, then straightened her back and lifted her chin. Who cares what I look like, anyway? she thought.

Cort, standing on her porch, immediately made a mockery of that thought. She ran a hesitant hand through her tangled hair, but the moment his stone-cold gaze met hers she knew it was hopeless. His eyes flickered to her curls, registered alarm or hysteria—two very close expressions—then flicked back to her face. To his credit he controlled his laughter.

That is, if the man had any laughter. Just as he'd looked last night, he looked about as friendly as a porcupine. Granny Gab would say he looked as if he'd swallowed a pickle with a hook in it.

"I believe I have something that belongs to you," he drawled, none too happily holding up the end of a lead rope. A lead rope attached to—

"Samantha!" Lilly exclaimed, stepping onto the porch. "You didn't? Not again."

"What's new?" Exasperation edged his voice, and Lilly couldn't blame him.

"I found her stuffing her face in the alfalfa bin when I went out to ride this morning. Don't you feed this animal?"

"I am so sorr—*yes,* I feed the little pig. Leroy spoiled her so much that I don't know what I'm going to do with her." Lilly wrapped her arms about her tummy and shivered in the icy morning air. After the show ended last night, the sleet had rolled in again. The sun had come out for the morning, but the wind was still bitter.

Despite his obvious irritation and dislike for her, Cort motioned toward the doorway and remained true to his bad habit of telling her what to do. "You'd better get back inside. I'll tend to Samantha. You tend to your baby."

If she hadn't been feeling guilty about her own bad behavior, and if she hadn't been so cold, she might have rebuked him. Instead she backed toward the door. The last thing she wanted was the irritating man having to take care of her business, but she was too chilled to protest. And he was right. She didn't need to risk falling.

"Her stall is the second one in the barn. Surely she has to be exhausted from all her scavenging. I think she'll stay put for at least a little while."

Cort didn't look as if he agreed. He stomped off the porch and strode toward the barn with long, determined steps.

He hadn't gotten far when he slipped on a patch of ice. His legs went flying from beneath him and he splattered right at Samantha's feet.

"Oh!" Lilly gasped, starting toward him.

"Stay right where you are!" Cort's harsh shout stopped her with one foot hovering between the inside and the outside. "Don't even think about coming off that porch." Slowly sitting up, he rubbed the back of his head and glared at Samantha.

His hat had flown off and his dark hair fell across his forehead in a thick, shiny swath. It wasn't exactly the time to notice, but he had really nice hair, despite his grumpy disposition.

"This little beast is going to get one of us killed. The sun's made all this ice very slick, so stay put."

Nice hair or not, he really didn't need to repeat himself. Lilly had already complied with his demands— only because she was afraid she would end up on the ground beside him if she didn't. Her bones were aching from the last two nights' escapades. She didn't need any more strenuous activity.

She watched him straighten his six-foot bossy frame. Cort was an extremely attractive man. Even if he was difficult.

The grannies would not have been pleased to know she continued to notice such a thing. Lilly nibbled on her lip. Of course, it hadn't helped that she'd thought about his smile off and on for two days. But most of all she'd thought about his frown.

What would make a man frown so much? It was a question she was really curious about. There was a part of her that wanted to make him smile.

Poor guy—meetings with her had certainly not given him anything whatsoever to smile about. Except that once.

"You do know that it's a proven fact that if you were having a bad day, a laugh or even just a smile would improve your disposition." Now, why in the world had she said that? He replied with the same question when he nailed her with a glare. She wasn't doing his disposition any good. Things had gone quickly from bad to worse.

And it didn't improve when in the next instant, to Lilly's horror, Samantha picked Cort's hat up off the icy ground and started chewing!

Lilly closed her eyes and groaned, "Oh, Samantha, how could you?"

When it came to being around his new neighbor, Cort had endured about as much humiliation as one man could stand. Had it not been for Samantha nosing around his barn, this would have been the last place he'd have come this morning.

After last night, he hadn't cared if he ever saw Lilly again. She and her donkey had become thorns in his side.

Forget feeling alive again. He wasn't sure he liked the cost.

Right now he was cold and wet, and his attitude toward Lilly or Samantha wasn't improving. Both seemed to have a distaste for him. His hat, on the other hand, was an altogether different story.

The hairy bag of bones was staring down at him with doe-brown eyes while mutilating his favorite Stetson with her slobbery mouth.

Something about this picture just wasn't right.

Carefully he stood up. Not wanting to sprawl on the ground again, he hid his pride, made like a little old man and took his time.

"Gimme that," he growled once he was on his feet. He snatched at the hat—or attempted to snatch it—but the cantankerous donkey bit down on the brim and held on as if she had lockjaw.

That did it. Cort's patience snapped. Grasping the brim of the hat, he yanked hard, but Samantha, the little prankster, was having none of it. She wagged her head from side to side and started backing up in a tug-of-war.

"Hey, you little beast! Let go of that."

"Samantha." Lilly whooped with laughter from the doorway.

Cort shot her a sharp look. So much for his pride. It was on the line and she was laughing.

"Samantha needs obedience school," he snapped. "What is up with this donk—" He nearly fell over when Sam let go of the hat abruptly and trotted off, fried tail swishing to and fro in a singed frizzy ball.

Cort grunted, slammed his hat onto his head and carefully followed Samantha to where she stood looking at him like an expectant puppy. In all his years dealing with horses, he'd never come across anything quite like Samantha. She was almost human.

"Cort, leave her there and come in. You're cold and wet and I'm so sorry about all of this. Please." She hesitated, replacing the edge in her voice with sincerity. "Please let me make you some coffee. Believe me, Samantha isn't going anywhere right now. And I think we need to start over. What do you say?"

Thawing to the invitation, Cort turned toward Lilly and raised an eyebrow. "How do you know she isn't going anywhere?"

Lilly laughed. "She's like Curious George. She'll have her nose plastered to the window the minute you enter this house. The busybody wants to be in the know about everything."

Coffee did sound good. And the donkey was home. And Lilly was smiling, offering coffee…and they were neighbors. They needed to be able to get along. So why was he standing out in the cold when he could be inside with a cup of hot java?

Looking into the laughing eyes of his neighbor, he could think of a lot of reasons.

But at the moment he didn't want to list them.

# Chapter Six

Lilly held the door open wide to allow Cort entry. He stepped onto the linoleum, moving just far enough inside for her to close the door, as if he wasn't certain he wanted to be there. She didn't blame him. She wasn't positive she wanted him, either, but she'd had to invite him in. It was the neighborly thing to do.

In the small space of the entry hall his stature was magnified, making her lack of height all the more obvious. Standing there, he looked uncomfortable, with his rumpled hat in hand, wet jeans and heavy work jacket.

"Oh, here!" Lilly said quickly, reaching for his hat. "Let me take that. Oh, your poor hat. I'm so sorry about the chewing. Why don't you take off your coat and I'll throw it in the dryer while we have that coffee I mentioned."

Boy, could she use it, too. She really didn't know what had gotten into her. Men didn't usually make her nervous. But then, she hadn't ever been as rude to a man as she'd been to Cort.

Of course, no man had ever made her as mad as he had, either.

But none of that explained why her heart was pounding so erratically or why her brain had gone west. Or south—? Ugh! She needed some coffee. And some taffy wouldn't hurt, either.

"You really don't have to dry my jacket," he said, stripping off the damp coat. "It's waterproof. It looks wet on the outside, but I'm dry except for my jeans."

Lilly took the jacket from him and studied it. Sure enough, it was dry inside. Cort's spicy scent rose from the coat and tickled her senses…. *Nope, none of that.* "I'll just hang it up here, then," she said, hooking the coat and hat on the rack beside the door. She caught a glimpse of herself in the mirror as she did, and cringed. She could just hear Granny Gab exclaiming, "Child-a-mine, you look like something the cat dragged in."

Yeah, well, so be it. Pushing aside her pride, Lilly moved through the doorway into the kitchen. "Come on in," she called over her shoulder.

She pressed the button on the coffeepot. She always prepared the pot the night before so that it was a quick thing to have her morning caffeine fix. She'd tried the decaf and had high hopes that it would grow on her, but so far it was a no-go. Therefore for the baby's sake she allowed herself only one cup of regular coffee in the morning.

"Why don't you stand over there?" She waved a hand toward the wall heater and avoided eye contact with Cort as she popped the top off the canister next to the icebox and grabbed a couple of pieces of taffy—the way she was feeling, she held back from tucking the whole can under her arm and running away to scarf it down. "You can dry out those jeans while I go do something about this monster on my head." Not waiting to hear him agree or disagree, she hurried out of the room and down the hallway.

At least, she tried to hurry. Waddling gave a person little room for speed no matter what the emergency. There was no way she could appear pleasant knowing she looked the way she did. Man or no man, no one should have to endure what she'd seen in the mirror.

Cort watched as Lilly disappeared down the hall. She was a cute little thing, with her hair all crazy. Those curls looked alive the way they stood out all over her head. He'd noticed immediately that they bounced with her every step. He'd also noticed the way they curled around her pixie face and how the darkness of the curls contrasted with her pale skin and caused her golden eyes to warm like honey in the morning sunlight. But there was something more than the way she looked that had him following her with his eyes. There was a wariness about her. She was a paradox. At times he glimpsed a take-charge kind of bravado and at other times he glimpsed something almost sad hidden in her eyes—it seemed that she, too, had a past. A past that—like his—had left scars. He wondered how deep hers ran.

*What was he thinking?*

He didn't like the effect his neighbor had on him. He was here to get his life back on track. And that had nothing to do with a kooky gal about to have a baby. Walking over to the wall heater, he waited for Lilly to return while he warmed his back and closed down his newfound need for companionship.

Companionship that could go nowhere for a man like him.

Feeling like a bear in a trap, he took in his surroundings. Lilly's home reminded him of his grandmother's house. The kitchen was large and open with white painted cabinets and green Formica countertops. The green-and-white-checked curtains in the window had red roosters lined up across the bottom. In the corner of the kitchen beside the gas stove there was a large whitewashed cupboard with chicken wire insets in front of a mass of brightly colored dishes. In the center of the room was a long wide island, and Cort imagined many meals having been prepared there. It was a farmhouse kitchen—warm, useful and inviting.

A noise at the window beside the breakfast table drew his attention. Samantha stood just outside the pane with her damp nose plastered to the glass, two huge circles of fog highlighting each nostril as she breathed hot and heavy against the glass. That was truly one strange little burro. As he watched, Samantha turned her head sideways and plastered one eyeball against the glass, as if trying to see at a better angle. Her eyelashes made stripes in the fog as she batted them against the glass.

"She's a nosy girl," Lilly said, startling him.

He turned at her comment. In a matter of seconds it seemed she had tamed her hair with something that smelled good. She had changed into a pair of overalls and a bright pink top. She looked—what did it matter how she looked? Cort tore his gaze away from Lilly and focused on the hairy girl in the window.

"Nosy. You can say that again," he agreed. "I don't think I've ever seen anything quite like your Samantha."

Lilly grabbed two mugs from the cabinet and poured coffee into them.

Cort was in need of the rich-smelling brew. His brain was fogged up more than all the steam streaming out of Samantha's nose onto the windowpane.

"Cream or sugar?" Lilly asked with a bright smile. It was obvious that she was trying to be pleasant to him. He needed to do the same.

"Just black, thank you."

She pushed one cup toward him, then counted out three heaping teaspoons of sugar into the other cup. Walking over, Cort picked up his cup and watched as she proceeded to dump just as much if not more creamer into hers, then pick up her spoon and begin to stir.

And stir.

And stir.

She grinned. "I stir exactly twenty-seven times. Granny Bunches always said that twenty-six was too little and twenty-eight was too much. Twenty-seven was the magic number that caused the coffee's flavor to bloom to its full potential."

Cort lifted an eyebrow and watched Lilly place the cup to her mouth, close her eyes and sip.

"Mmm, mmm, good. Granny Bunches sure told the truth."

The woman could sell coffee to millions if she were on TV. Watching her savor the aroma before she took a sip had Cort wanting to trade his cup in and have what she was having. Normally he never added cream or sugar to his coffee. His only weakness was for taffy, but that was it on the sweet stuff. He could never say no to taffy.

She laughed, popping her eyes open and winking at him. "My granny was full of weird little top secret things like that. She shared them with me throughout my childhood." She rattled off a few more things about her grannies, tilting her head to the side and chuckling as she recalled them. There was a softness in her voice and a twinkle in her eye at the remembrance. Then she frowned. "Of course, not all they taught me was cute or funny. Granny Shu-Shu would be madder than a wet hen if she knew your kind was standing in her kitchen."

Cort took a sip of his hot coffee and tried not to choke on the steaming liquid when Lilly lifted her eyes to meet his and winked at him again. He could almost hear Granny Shu-Shu telling him he was worthless.

"Are you okay?" she asked, shuffling over and peering up at him.

"Fine. I'm fine." He bit out the words while the hot liquid burned a layer out of his stomach before fizzling out.

"Granny Gab would say take smaller sips." She was beaming and wagging a finger at him playfully. The flicker of a frown was gone, replaced by the lighthearted girl who seemed almost determined to show him that she wasn't hard to get along with.

Cort scowled down at the little pixie smiling up at him. She had a way about her. "You always like this?"

She backed away, one hand resting beneath her tummy as if supporting it. "Like what?" Picking up her cup, she ambled over and sat at the table next to the batting eyeball of Samantha. She thumped the windowpane with her fingers, making Samantha turn her damp nose and smudge the glass.

"Perky." The word jumped out of him. Yeah, *perky,* that was the word to describe Lilly Tipps. Waddling or not, the woman was perky personified.

He watched her lift her feet one at a time and place them with a thud on the chair she'd scooted out in front of her. She had on striped socks that looked like gloves for the toes.

"I wouldn't call this perky. I feel like I'm gonna blow any moment now." Sighing, she took another sip and wiggled her toes. "These legs of mine feel about as heavy as—oh, never mind. Yes, I usually have a lot of energy. But that's enough about me. I truly am sorry for all the trouble Samantha is causing you. And about my rude behavior last night. I didn't have everything under control. I just get excited about weird things sometimes. I am so grateful you caught Samantha before the fire reached her skin. Thank you."

Cort studied Lilly. "You're welcome," he said,

noticing how she looked tired around the eyes. He couldn't help wondering about those false labor pains she'd been having that first night in his barn. He might have come to Mule Hollow seeking solitude, but there was no way he could ignore the fact that his neighbor looked as if she needed a little bit of help.

Even if all those grannies she was so fond of quoting had filled her mind with a bunch of hogwash about men. He also kept reminding himself that everything she did was her business. It didn't matter if he agreed or disagreed.

"Don't worry about Samantha. It looks like she's been wandering for a long time. I'll figure something out," he said. Being alone and pregnant, the poor woman had enough to worry about without having to fret over Samantha bothering him. "Her visiting me isn't that big of a deal. If it weren't for my show stock it wouldn't matter at all."

"I understand completely," she said with a sigh. "I know I could lock her in. And I should."

She rubbed an earring between her thumb and forefinger, worry in her eyes. Again it hit Cort that she had a lot on her plate. Where was her husband? The question had bothered him ever since she'd told him there was no Mr. Tipps. And never would be. So if there never was, then what had happened to her? With her distaste for men in general he didn't know what to think.

*What does it matter? It's none of your business,* he thought.

Yeah, but Samantha was one thing he could help her with.

Setting his cup on the counter, he reached for his jacket. "Leave her be and I'll figure out something over on my end—that is, if you don't go out looking for her in the middle of the night again." He pinned hard eyes on Lilly, hoping she'd heed his warning for the sake of her baby.

She looked almost as if she had a jaunty reply ready for him, but then surprised him with one of those smiles that socked him in the gut despite his need to dodge the blow.

"I can do that," she said. "I guess you need to get home?"

"I've got horses to exercise and stalls to clean, and daylight's burning," he grunted, forcing himself not to ask for another cup of coffee. "The sun's not going to last long, you know. That ice is going to start laying down again after lunch. You need anything?" He had to ask. His conscience would allow nothing less of him.

She shook her head. "Nope, thanks. I'm fine."

Nodding, he stepped out the door. The blast of cold had him wishing for the warmth of Lilly's kitchen, but his better sense told him to go home and stay there.

Lilly might not think highly of men, but that didn't keep him from wondering just why exactly that was. What could have happened to turn all the Tipps women against men?

Lilly watched Cort walk carefully out to his big truck and drive away. The man was not a grinch…not exactly. She'd caught that hard look he'd given her when he'd asked if she could hold herself back from going out in the night in search of Samantha. Her first reaction had been to tell him that it wasn't any of his business what she did, but something had passed across his tough expression, something in his eyes, in the softening of his voice—longing, regret…something. Whatever it was, it had touched Lilly. It had reached in deep and wound around a dark place in her heart that she had locked away and was determined to keep locked…and yet she'd responded to it by keeping her mouth shut.

The grannies wouldn't have liked it, but what was done was done. Instead she'd smiled, nodded and told him she could refrain from wandering around at night taking care of Samantha, for her baby's sake.

Lilly was all her baby had. Her grannies were gone. One at a time they'd passed on into eternity, leaving her alone with a bunch of heartfelt advice. And memories. So many memories. When she thought of Granny Shu-Shu and Granny Gab she pictured vinegar mixed with sugar. So much hurt and bitterness filled their lives. Both had been hurt by the men they'd loved. Their pain also ran through Lilly's veins, put there like poison. Granny Bunches had tried to turn aside the bitterness, to show Lilly that there were other opinions in the world. But after Lilly experienced her own rejection, her heart had hardened. She was working on expelling the past, on moving forward. Some days were good. Some days weren't.

Cort Wells confused her. He seemed to have his own pain, or memories to fight. Maybe that was why she felt this odd connection with him.

Lilly pushed herself out of the chair. She needed to do her chores for the day and then do some work on the catalog. There was always a fence that needed fixing. But the weather was too bad for that. Tomorrow she'd check the fence down by the creek that connected to Cort's place. She didn't want Tiny, her bull, getting over on his property. Cort had enough problems with Samantha trotting over there whenever she pleased. Lilly decided to catch up on her laundry first—anything to get rid of the disturbing internal need she kept feeling to see that smile return to her neighbor's lips.

## Chapter Seven

Lilly stretched. She was glad she'd decided to remain indoors. She'd plenty to do to fill up her day. Running a small cattle operation needed supplemental income. Lilly had been configuring a cattle sales catalog for a cattle company out of Ranger for the past five years. She scanned the pictures into the computer and made certain all the pertinent information on each animal was correct, then sent it to the printer for her client. It was a good business and it helped her continue living on the ranch by providing the extra income she needed to survive on the land that had been in her family for generations.

It also meant endless hours sitting at her computer staring at the screen long after most people had the good sense to go to bed. But the job had to be done.

Glancing around the house, Lilly sighed. It was quitting time. She wouldn't get any more done tonight. It had been a long day and was way past time for bed. Her steps were heavy as she padded into the rear entrance hall to lock the door. She paused to rub her throbbing back. Whew, maybe heat would help. Forgetting to lock the door, she decided to grab the heating pad from the pantry.

Her back was throbbing like a jackhammer.

Five hours sitting in front of the computer screen was entirely too much. But she had a deadline and it couldn't be helped. Commitment was something she took very seriously. And she needed the money. She had a baby coming she needed to support. Alone.

Jeff Turner intruded upon her weary mind. She tried not ever to think about her ex-husband. His lack of commitment to anything, especially her and their baby, always stabbed her with regret. It ripped at her determination to move forward and forget about the things she couldn't change.

Regret. Lilly forced it from her mind and heart. It wasn't always an easy task.

There had been a few very hard weeks in a marriage that fell apart as quickly as it had begun. A marriage that hadn't really been a marriage, but more of a rebellion.

Funny, optimistic Lacy Brown had helped Lilly gain perspective on trying to allow God's timing and His will to take precedence over her past. Lacy had impressed Lilly with her brute determination to do God's will. The joy that animated Lacy was contagious, and Lilly was trying to learn to renew her mind by replacing negative thoughts with positive. "For as he thinketh in his heart, so is he." Lacy had asked her to memorize the verse from Proverbs. She found herself quoting it often.

She'd been raised by a band of grannies who had

many takes on how life should be lived. Many of those ideas she was trying to rethink. It wasn't always easy, but she was determined to be a positive-thinking, active, Christian mother to her child.

Speaking of which, she remembered telling Cort that there had never been a Mr. Tipps. There hadn't been a Mr. Tipps. She'd been Mrs. Turner before returning to her maiden name, but despite the legalities of the wording, she had misled Cort. She'd have to remedy that. He needed to know that she valued family. She'd just let her mouth get carried away while she was angry—her mouth did that quite often. One of the negative things about being raised by her outspoken grannies was that two of them believed it was okay to say whatever was on their mind.

No matter whom it hurt.

Mind renewing was hard work! But with the Lord's help Lilly was determined to rid herself of some very odd ideas from a very odd upbringing.

Suddenly realizing she was standing by the icebox lost in thoughts of her past, she focused. Did she need heat for her aching back or something cold? Granny Gab was the one who'd taught her to use a bag of frozen vegetables as an ice pack. Black-eyed peas happened to be her veggie of choice.

Heat. She needed heat tonight.

A noise at the window made Lilly close the icebox and walk over to peer into the darkness. An ice-encrusted Samantha stood staring back at her.

"Samantha!"

The little mischievous dear, whose neck she often

wanted to wring, would be ill if this continued. But what was she to do? Cort had been right. She couldn't keep going out in this weather.

Samantha knew where her stall was. She knew there was fresh feed and dry straw in the barn, as well as plenty of protection from all this sleet.

"Please go to bed. I can't take a chance leading you over to the barn." With a heavy heart Lilly grabbed the heating pad from the pantry, turned off the light and trudged down the hallway to her room. There was nothing she could do for Samantha right now. No amount of worrying was going to change that tonight. Her baby came first.

She was pulling the covers over her and about to turn out her lamp and settle down with the heating pad when the electricity blinked and went out.

This was not good.

Worse, Lilly thought, sitting up on the edge of the bed, pain radiated all through her lower spine and down the backs of her legs. She'd definitely worked too long today. After a few moments the lights remained off and a chill started to creep into the room.

Samantha had walked around the house and was now staring at Lilly through the lace of her curtains. Lilly felt truly sorry for the obstinate old girl. The heater was off and a touch of the coldness Samantha was enduring was settling into the house.

Lilly rose. Despite the pain, she knew she needed to start a fire. Loading her comforter into her arms and grabbing her pillow, she headed down the hall into the living room. There was already a significant feeling of ice in the air inside the house. It didn't take her long to build a roaring fire in the large fireplace.

"Thank you, Lord, for giving me a fireplace." Pulling the fireplace guard closed, she was turning to crawl onto Granny Shu-Shu's overstuffed couch when she was engulfed by pain. Red-hot explosions of agony ripped through her back, around to her abdomen and buckled her knees. She caught herself with her hands on the edge of the couch and fought to stand.

*This* was not Braxton-Hicks.

There was nothing false about what was happening to her.

It was time.

As Lilly concentrated through the contraction, a groan escaped her clenched lips. She held her abdomen and eased toward the phone in the kitchen. Who would she call? She wasn't ready. She was supposed to have a month to prepare.

Gasping when the pain hit full force, she made it to the kitchen and grabbed the phone.

This was too soon. Not the way it was supposed to be.

Lilly dialed 911 and put the phone to her sweaty cheek. It took a moment for the silence on the line to register.

She was in labor, in the middle of nowhere, and the phone was dead.

Zip, nada, nothing…dead.

Cort woke with a start in the faint light of the full moon that wrestled through the gray clouds to illuminate his curtainless room. Wind and hail pelted against the panes, jolting him from a comatose state of bad dreams to the tickling sensation of Loser's mangy paw crammed up his nose.

Snorting and gagging, he slapped at Loser's stinky toes and instead hit himself in the eye. Yelping in pain, he managed to push the sleeping mutt from his pillow, only to sneeze violently when fuzz and who knew what else fluttered about him. It was a terrible thing for a man to wake up to—the sight of Loser's ugly mug drooling across his pillow.

Glaring at the loose-lipped grin plastered across Loser's hairy face, Cort felt real pity for himself. It was a feeling he despised. When a foul smell pervaded the room he bolted from the bed.

"That does it," he grumbled, pushing at the rank dog. "Off the bed. No more sharing my pillow. No more drool on my covers. No—"

A scraping noise interrupted his ranting. His kitchen door was opening. Cort whirled around and for the first time realized the storm hadn't wakened him.

Someone was breaking in to his house.

Loser heard the sound, too. He snapped to attention. His propeller-sized ears stood out—as much as ears that size could stand out—and a mighty war cry, such as Cort had never heard, nor wanted to hear again, erupted from his shaggy depths.

Stunned by the unlikely actions of his otherwise lethargic dog, Cort jumped out of the way when, amazingly, the dog came to life. Yowling zealously, Loser zipped from the bed, toenails sliding on the wooden floor, his legs moving in triple time as he skidded out and around the door with a roar of wild fervor.

Cort's head was swimming, his adrenaline pumping. He'd managed to make it to the door when Loser howled like a cat caught in a fan and streaked back into the room, colliding with Cort's feet and sending both of them flying.

The next thing Cort knew, he'd landed with a thud, flat on his back with Loser's worst half draped over his face, and a rear paw rammed in each of his ears.

It was closer than Cort ever wanted to be to a dog again.

Spitting hair, he shoved the trembling mop of fur off his face.

"Loser! Dog! What's come over you?" Heavy clopping on his hardwood floors drew his attention and, looking up, he nearly screamed himself.

Samantha—or he thought it was Samantha—stood in the doorway. Her whiskered face was shrouded with fine powdered ice. Icicles hung from her ears like sparkling earrings.

It was the strangest sight he'd ever seen. Cort thought for a moment that the hairy beast was even carrying a purse!

Samantha the donkey in earrings and a purse. It was as close to a nightmare as Cort had come in a long time.

That was until she snorted, sending a spray of melting ice all over him. "Awh—now! Why'd you go and do that?" he groaned, wiping his face, and glared at the beast—and the lady's purse hanging from her neck.

\* \* \*

Lilly couldn't believe she'd hung her purse around Samantha's neck, couldn't believe she hoped the burro would take the note stuffed inside the purse to Cort. She couldn't believe her contractions were real. But they were, and her only hope of help was a whiskered little sweetheart with an impossible mission.

It was all true.

God sure had a sense of humor.

Thank goodness Samantha had been hanging around the house. The little darling had practically knocked the door down to help Lilly. The inspiration about the purse had just come to her as she was standing in the doorway, knowing there was no way, with the pain she was in, that she could get to her truck and drive to the hospital. The purse hanging on the coatrack had been a blessing.

After she'd accomplished sending Samantha for help, Lilly had managed to make it back to the living room. She'd pulled her quilt off the couch and spread it on the floor in front of the fire. Her contractions had eased for a while, then started back hard, grabbing her with the force of a sledgehammer. After each subsided she lay there, as she was now, exhausted and panting, delirious with worry.

Poor baby! This would be the most unfortunate child on God's green earth!

What child would want a mother who hadn't the sense to prepare for emergencies? A mother forced to resort to slinging her purse over a donkey's neck and sending her to find help?

At least Samantha was smarter than Lilly, and hopefully she'd made it to Cort's. Hopefully he was on his way this very minute. Hopefully, she thought as another contraction slammed into her, she'd make it through this.

Gripping the blanket, she tried desperately to relax, to focus on a spot on the wall as the Lamaze books taught. With her eyes clamped shut she couldn't even see the blooming wall!

How was she supposed to hang on and have this poor child when she couldn't complete the first steps?

How was she supposed to have this baby alone?

Her life was a shambles, and did God care?

Hardly!

Panicking wasn't Lilly's style. She'd never been a crybaby, but with each pain building, intensifying, she couldn't help herself. She wished for something, someone, anyone to lash out at, to latch onto. She wished she could get her hands around the neck of the jerk who'd said natural childbirth was the way to go!

Transition.

The contraction eased, the worst wave subsided. She felt a bit of relief knowing the anger mingling with her fear had a name. Transition. She'd heard about it, seen comical movies where, because of it, the nice mother-to-be turned into an evil witch making the moviegoers laugh when the recipients of her wrath were thrown into hilarious upheaval.

But this wasn't funny.

As Lilly lay on the blanket before the slowly dwindling fire, things about her life started coming into focus—sharper, clearer.

She wished someone was there to calm her fear. To share the change the pain caused in her. Someone to stand by and hold the hand she didn't feel like giving, to mop the brow she didn't feel like having mopped. Someone beside her to love her through the good and the bad. To share the pride when all was done and they held the prize.

Lilly had no one.

No flesh and bone, no one to fill this want that had always been there inside her heart.

She was so tired. Exhaustion claimed her and she closed her eyes as the contraction ended. Her mind was too numb to feel any fear, any anger. She could only acknowledge her situation with a dull sense of wonder. Had the grannies passed through this same valley of doubt? Had they ever wished for things to be different, for someone to stand by them?

Were men really the way they believed them to be?

Lilly had always secretly wished they were wrong. She wanted to believe in heroes.

Were there any heroes out there?

# Chapter Eight

Cort stared through the windshield at the tree blocking his path. He'd made it only halfway to Lilly's house, and it had taken him nearly thirty minutes. The note in the purse had been scribbled hurriedly and simply said, "Baby coming—help."

"Some cavalry we make," he growled at Loser, who cocked his head and barked once. "I guess we walk from here on in." It was Loser who growled at that. He didn't like the idea at all and showed it by scrambling to the far side of the truck. Squinting his hairy eyes, he glowered at Cort.

"Don't look at me like that. I had to bring you." Not certain when he'd make it back home, he'd snatched up Loser and hurried to the truck.

Now, reaching for the dog again, he wasn't pleased when Loser crouched against the door to avoid being snagged and drawn into the cold. His toenails scratched the seat as he tried to cling, and had Cort not been so worried about his neighbor he might have laughed.

Instead he stretched, clasped Loser about the middle and lifted him from the stranded vehicle.

He'd just started creeping down the slippery road, wondering how he would ever be able to help Lilly, when out of the darkness came Samantha, hauling her little fat body as fast as Cort had ever seen a burro move.

And she wasn't happy to see him standing there.

Cort couldn't blame her. He'd left Samantha at his place, not taking the time to lead her back home after he found the phone lines were dead and the electricity was off. However, he hadn't counted on the storm having toppled trees over the roads. And he'd never dreamed the burro would make better progress than he would. Poor Lilly. If she needed help fast, she was in trouble.

Samantha must have come to the same conclusion, because she took one look at Cort, stuck her nose in the air and clomped past him and Loser. The dog yelped, snapped at her heel and was promptly rewarded with a bump on the snout from Samantha's leg as she stopped suddenly to study the fallen tree.

Cort headed toward the ditch just as Samantha stuck her nose down and plowed past him into the lead. Cort continued on, following her, with Loser snarling all the way.

This was the burro's territory, and the best way to help Lilly was to get there by the fastest route. If that meant tailgating a burro—a very smart burro—then he'd do it.

In the next five minutes Cort slipped and slid on the ice more times than he cared to count. The night was so thick with billowing sleet and snow flurries that he couldn't see four feet in front of him. Finally for Lilly's sake he gave in, threw his leg over Samantha's back and settled in for the rest of the trip. It wasn't a pretty sight, and he thought that if any of his buddies from the show circuit saw him riding this hairy bag of lard his reputation as a serious breeder and trainer was history.

And that was before Loser got excited and nipped Samantha on the rump.

Lilly lifted her eyelids and screamed.

Not only did it feel as if she was giving birth to Attila the Hun, ice monsters were invading her home! She must be hallucinating, she thought, from the pain or too much oxygen hitting her brain from the useless breathing exercises she'd been attempting to master for the past hour and a half.

"Lilly, don't scream. It's me, Cort. I've come to help."

Lilly stared as another contraction grabbed her. "What happened to you?" she gasped, then started he-he-he-ing and puff-puff-puffing. She felt like a Saint Bernard panting on a sizzling day without any shade. She was so tired, but had caught a slight second wind somewhere along the way of total delusion and despair.

Cort wiped his ice-encrusted face, ran a hand through his mussed hair and frowned. "Samantha happened to me. The question is what's happened to you? Don't you know better than to have this baby out here in the middle of nowhere?"

The contraction peaked and held. Exhausted, but

relieved that she wasn't alone anymore, Lilly squeezed her eyes shut. She clawed at the blanket and nearly wept when Cort's steady hand wrapped around hers and held on. Lilly had never been so happy to see a man in her life.

A calm, take-charge kind of man.

The type of man who would have the grannies rolling over in their graves if they knew she'd been lying here praying for Cort Wells's intervention in the birthing of her baby. It was true—she'd been trying to practice walking by faith, and somewhere along the way it hit her that she had to trust that God was going to get her through this. That no matter what happened He was in control, that for some reason Cort was just down the road at the time when she needed him and that with God's hand guiding her, Samantha was going to accomplish the task that Lilly had sent her on.

Faith.

Lilly breathed a sigh and relaxed.

Cort didn't like what was happening. For Lilly's sake he forced himself to seem calm. Truth was, he wanted to turn tail, hop on Samantha's back and ride right on out of there.

He couldn't deliver this baby!

Sure, all he'd ever wanted was a family to call his own, but that was as far as his interest went. He couldn't deliver a baby. He had never been able to watch his own horses deliver because of the way he sometimes fainted at the sight of blood.

Babies couldn't be born without a little blood being shed.

He looked at Lilly. She was sweating in obvious deep pain, but bravely managing to maintain her composure. She was squeezing the blood out of his hand and her eyes were weak with fatigue, but she had spirit. He'd known that in his barn, the moment she first spoke to him. She was as independent as they came and now she was looking at him for help. As if he was a hero.

He swallowed his fear. This was his fault. He was the one who'd lassoed her and thrown her on the ground. He'd probably caused the early labor. He would never forgive himself for that.

"How far apart are your contractions?" he asked, astounded at the calmness in his voice. It brought boundless gratitude to Lilly's expression, which kicked his courage up a notch.

"I'm not sure. All I know is I'm not enjoying this." Her brow furrowed and she grimaced.

"Where are the keys to your truck?" He denied the urge to smooth the wrinkle from her forehead.

"In the truck," she said through gritted teeth.

"Are you up for a ride?" he asked. When she nodded he continued. "I need to get you to the hospital." Quickly he said a prayer that God would help him get her there before the baby decided to join them. But he had a bad feeling the hospital would be too little too late. "I'll be right back." He almost ran from the house. Knowing there was no time to waste, he grabbed Loser on his way out the door.

"Sorry, buddy, but it's back to the truck." Outside

the wind was howling and the ice was thicker, causing every step to be treacherous. It took some effort to make it to the barn, trying to hold an unhappy dog and not fall flat on his face at the same time. It also took a lot of concentration and prayer, especially since lately it seemed the ground was the place he always ended up. He would have put Loser down, but he didn't want wet dog all over the cab of Lilly's truck. The going was rough, and he was thankful once more when Samantha came hurtling around the barn door just as he yanked it open.

He felt sorry for the old girl. She was covered in ice, but he knew she would follow the truck as she had before, and maybe when they went to pick up his truck she would go into his barn to avoid the storm—and eat the rest of his alfalfa cubes. If she didn't follow them, then Cort would have to lead her there and padlock the stall for her own good.

"It'll all work out, Samantha. You just follow us. I promise I'll take care of her." Reaching out, he scratched between Samantha's eyes. *I'm talking to a donkey.* Shaking his head at the uncharacteristic act, he climbed into the cab, turned over the ignition and praised the Lord when the ancient truck sputtered to life.

He backed out from the protection of the barn and Loser drew close. He watched Samantha as they passed her, then turned and watched her trotting next to the rear fender. Cort maneuvered the truck close to the porch before hopping out and heading inside to get Lilly.

He wished for a cell phone. His last one had been stomped by a horse the week before when it fell out of his pocket during a training session. The town of Ranger was so far away that he hadn't had time to go all the way there and pick up a new one. But it might not have done him any good anyway. Spots in Mule Hollow were dead zones when it came to signals. Still, if he had a phone he could at least have tried to call for help.

Lilly met him at the door. She was standing in the kitchen, a coat thrown over her shoulders and a little suitcase at her feet. Her face was pale and her eyes were as big as peaches, but she had a smile plastered on her face even though he could tell by the white knuckles gripping the counter that she was hurting through and through.

"I'm ready, but we better hurry, 'cause the contractions are closer." Her face contorted with pain at that moment and she would have fallen had Cort not reached her in time.

He scooped her up in his arms, grabbed the bag, glanced at the fire that still burned in the fireplace and knew he'd have to come back later to put it out and lock things up.

"Hang in there, Lilly. We're going to get you and your baby to the hospital. I promise." He'd never meant anything as much as he meant that promise. He would get her to a safe place. As long as the Lord was willing.

When Cort opened the door of the truck and gently placed her on the seat, pain was pounding through Lilly's abdomen like a jackhammer manned by the Energizer Bunny. She was hurting so much she was about to embarrass herself by screaming when the bushy-browed dog sitting in the center of the seat caught her attention. Focusing on the curious animal, she closed off some of her discomfort and forced herself to concentrate on him. He studied her with a forlorn kind of quizzical anxiety, trembling all over. His appearance actually made Lilly smile. He was such a pathetic little creature, making her want to stop everything, scoop him into her arms and love him until he wiggled with excitement instead of fright.

Reaching out, she was about to touch him when Cort yanked open the driver's door and climbed in.

"Whew, what a night." He put the truck in gear and pressed the gas pedal in one fluid motion.

*What a night is the understatement of the year!* she thought, bracing her hands on the dash as the truck jerked forward. She was startled when Cort shot a hand out and grabbed her elbow.

"Are you all right? This ice is making everything trickier."

"I'm fine. Go as fast as you think you can and still get us there in one piece."

Cort was already concentrating on the road, skillfully maneuvering the truck along the gravel road. Lilly was studying him, trying not to think about how close the contractions were getting, when a new one hit her.

"Ohhh!" she gasped. The dog and Cort both swung their heads to stare at her with wide eyes. "Ohhh, ohhh, I think I need to lie down—"

"Move, Loser. Down, boy!" Cort boomed, and the

poor dog hopped to the floorboard, then turned and stuck his wet nose in Lilly's face.

It registered with Lilly as she fell over in the seat that Loser was a bad name for a dog. Really bad. And her pain was really bad. *Really, really bad.*

*Please, Lord, don't let my child be born here in this truck!* It was a fervent prayer. She was still praying when Cort stopped. He came around to her side and quickly tugged her into his arms, then stepped out into the bitter cold.

"What are you doing?" she asked, clinging to him. Trusty, surefooted Samantha came trotting up beside him.

"I'm changing trucks. I'm sorry about this, but I've got to get us past this fallen tree. My truck is on the other side. There is no time to be careful. Thank goodness Samantha can walk in all of this."

It registered to Lilly through the pain that Samantha was leading them around a huge fallen tree. Loser was following them with a disgruntled scowl. Lilly couldn't help it—her tears turned to laughter and she started giggling.

What a sight they made. A fat, bumpy donkey, a grumpy dog and she and Cort—it struck her that she was the bumpy and he was the grumpy of the two of them… or actually right now she could be both the bumpy and grumpy.

Cort shot her a glare as her giggles grew.

"Poor guy." Lilly hiccupped through the pain and the silly laughter. "Probably wondering what you got into by moving all the way out here." She rested her head on his shoulder and clutched him tighter. "I think you're a gift from God."

Beneath her, she felt him tense.

"I don't know about that, but I'm glad I was here to help," he said gruffly. They reached his big four-door truck and he carefully placed her in the back seat. Then he and Loser climbed into the front. Samantha was watching Lilly through the window as Cort started backing the truck down the road toward town. Loser stood on his back legs eyeing her curiously. His chin rested on the back of the seat and his floppy ears bebopped with every bounce of the truck.

Cort swung the big vehicle around in his driveway and then they were heading down the road again. Lilly concentrated on Loser after she lost sight of Samantha trotting behind the truck as fast as her short legs would carry her. Keeping up with the truck this far had been a losing battle and Lilly lost her in the distance. She knew she'd be safe at Cort's place, but her heart twisted when she heard Samantha's forlorn cry at being left behind. She loved that little donkey….

Weary with both fear and pain, Lilly closed her eyes and prayed. She didn't want to have this baby on the side of the road, but she knew they'd never make it to Ranger.

"How you doing back there?"

Cort's question was tense, clipped. Lilly wanted to cry, she wanted to scream, she wanted to say that nothing was right. That her whole life wasn't right. But she didn't. How could she tell a complete stranger something that she'd tried her entire life to keep suppressed deep inside herself? You couldn't.

*Renew your mind with faith.*

"Not so good, but we're hanging on." She gritted out the words between clamped teeth. She'd be positive even if it killed her. She would force the darkness away and look to the light.

God was in control.

"God's in control, Lilly." Cort echoed her thoughts, slightly scaring her that he could read her so well.

His reassurance washed over her. Like words spoken straight from God, they calmed her. She smiled a thank-you into the darkness toward God and sighed with relief that He was out there. He really was, because He'd sent her three of the most awesome guardians that anyone could ever have.

A darling donkey, a delightful dog and a dashing grinch—who wasn't such a grinch after all.

## Chapter Nine

Cort concentrated on getting Lilly to the nearest help. She grew quiet in the backseat. He knew she was fighting pain like a warrior. She had guts and then some. And she was depending on him. His mind was racing as he went over his options. He could try for Ranger.

Too far.

He didn't know much about the baby business, but he knew they would never make seventy miles to Ranger, even if the roads weren't ice covered.

His best bet was Mule Hollow.

Of the few women there were in Mule Hollow, most lived at Adela's apartments. Before he'd bought the ranch he'd been surprised to discover just how few ladies resided in the little town.

With the sour view of women he'd had after his wife walked out on him, the lack of females had actually been a selling point on his choosing the town as home.

What irony. For a guy who hadn't wanted even to

see a woman for a year, now he was praying for God to open up the heavens and rain them down on him.

Loser's tail slapped him on the neck and Cort glanced at the mutt. He stood with his paws on the seat back staring at Lilly, and he'd started whining and wiggling like a nervous father. He moved in closer when Lilly groaned, and his shaggy tail smacked Cort in the face like an out-of-control windshield wiper. Lilly moaned again and sucked in a sharp breath. This caused the dog to jump, yelp in Cort's ear, slap his sharp paws on Cort's shoulder and start tap-dancing. Cort could almost hear him yelling, "Do something! Anything!"

*Yeah, Cort, do something!*

"Lilly, breathe," he coaxed, glancing over his shoulder. In the dim light he could see her eyes wide with alarm and pain. "You know, he-he-he. I think that's the way they do it."

To his immense relief he heard her copy him. "That's it, atta girl. Keep it up. We're coming up to the crossroads. Town is not far away. Help is there."

"Thank you…I need…to push—"

"No!" Cort's heart socked him in the chest. "No pushing. No way. Town is just a bit farther. Breathe. Breathe. Suck that air in, but whatever you do, don't push!"

Panic rose like hot lava within him and he stomped the pedal as hard as he dared in the sleet. The truck fishtailed. He let off the gas, turned the wheel, then gassed it again when he felt the tires catch and hold on the road. "No pushing," he said again. "We're going to make it."

*Lord, I cannot deliver a baby in the middle of the road! Do not do this to me. Town is just two miles away.*

Someone would know what to do. Adela Ledbetter had struck him as a very wise woman. Surely she'd been around many babies being born.

She would be able to help Lilly.

*Lord, whatever You do, let Adela be the one to answer that door when we get there.*

Glancing over his shoulder again, Cort's heart nearly broke when he met Lilly's scared eyes. They looked so frightened. She didn't want to have her baby in a truck, either. It was bad enough knowing she was going to give birth in a house out in the middle of nowhere without any benefit of state-of-the-art medical equipment in case of emergency. The least he could do was get her to where there would be the comfort of someone who'd know what to do.

Shrugging off Loser's clinging paws, he reached over the seat and took her hand from where she clung to her stomach. It was damp and trembling, and felt fragile within his large palm. Gently he squeezed it, feeling her fingers tighten around his—in a vise grip! The little lady had some strength.

"It's going to be all right, Lilly," he said. If she needed to squeeze the feeling out of his hand in order to ease her pain, then so be it. "God's here. He's watching over you."

He glanced back at her, not daring to take his eyes off the road for too long. She was drenched in perspiration and in the grip of a contraction, but she managed a nod and a feeble smile that cut Cort to the core.

"My…grannies are…probably giving…Him…grief." The words came out between clenched teeth.

They'd reached Main Street. Letting Lilly keep his hand as pain relief, Cort turned the corner with one hand on the wheel. The tires slid, then grabbed on the ice. Loser flipped onto his back, his legs churning as he slid across the seat into the door, then tumbled headfirst onto the floorboard.

"Sorry, Buddy," Cort apologized, grinning—despite his anxiousness—at the astonished look on Loser's doggy face. "Keep breathing, Lilly—he-he-he…" he added for good measure.

"The he-he-ing isn't working!"

The huge old house that seemed to be the cornerstone of the old town sprang into view through the dark night. It reminded Cort of a hotel rather than a house, and he could see how easily it had been turned into apartments.

It was the prettiest sight he'd ever seen. Relief washed over him like cold water on a sizzling day.

In the darkness his headlights illuminated the front porch as he whipped into the circle drive and skidded to a stop. Thankfully there were lights in the front window. They had electricity.

His truck lights came to rest on an old pink Cadillac sitting out front, and his frenzied mind registered that it was an odd car, one he'd seen parked in town the few times he'd come in for feed.

Who would drive such a car? he wondered for a split second before he slammed the truck into Park and wrenched his door open. "We're here. No pushing yet!"

With no time to waste, he jumped from the truck. Loser followed him to the door, as ready as Cort to exit the truck.

His whiskered eyebrows shot up when Cort slammed the door, leaving him trapped inside the cab with Lilly. She was he-he-ing and huff-huffing like the little engine that could.

Cort banged on the large carved door. After just a few moments it flew open, but it wasn't Adela who stood in the lighted doorway. Instead it was Lacy Brown who greeted him with her wild white-blond hair, a bright orange-and-yellow T-shirt, hot-pink pajama bottoms and lime-green fuzzy slippers.

She *was not* the Florence Nightingale he'd envisioned.

"I need to push!" Lilly shrieked as Cort's strong arms swept her through the doorway and into Adela's home.

"We're almost there, babe. Where's Ms. Adela?" he asked, striding toward the room Lacy pointed out for him at the front of the house.

"She left earlier to visit her sister in New Mexico for a week and I'm house-sitting," Lacy chirped, winking at Lilly. "And now I get to help deliver the first baby in Mule Hollow in ages and ages. Wow! Lay her right here, Cort. Lilly, this is gonna be exciting. God's good, isn't He?"

Cort shot her a startled look and Lilly, despite her pain, laughed. Leave it to Lacy to look at what was happening as a blessing. Lilly wanted that kind of faith… that kind of joy. Lacy had used that same joy helping in Mule Hollow's transformation, as well as when she helped track down a band of cattle rustlers. But that was a story for another time. Lilly needed to concentrate on the baby. Her pure love of the Lord was infectious and Lilly was glad to see her. She was one more blessing that God had sent Lilly's way. Delivering a baby would be a piece of cake for Lacy. With the Lord's help. Lilly needed all His help she could get.

Lacy asked Cort to knock on the doors of the apartments and wake up all the ladies to help.

Cort hesitated, and Lilly realized she was gripping his hand like a vise. But when she released the pressure he continued to hold her hand as if it were a delicate flower. He looked from her to Lacy. He didn't want to leave her. He made her feel so special. Dampness gathered at the corners of her eyes. He was the special one.

He was wonderful. His heart was huge. Though he'd tried for some reason to hide it, she knew the truth.

Lacy slapped him on the shoulder. The sound crackled through Lilly's thoughts and jolted her from her wistful reverie.

"Hop to it, Cort. Let's get this show on the road. I'll call the ambulance, but the baby is coming fast. I need the other women."

But he didn't move.

Only when Lacy patted him on the shoulder and assured him she would take good care of Lilly did he make a move. Running a hand over her hair, he cupped her face. "You can do this, Lilly," he encouraged her, then strode from the room.

Cort was knocking on the first door he'd come to when he heard Lilly scream. He barely registered the wild-eyed woman who answered the door. She glared at him through the crack left by the bolt chain. "Baby. B-baby's coming." He knew he was stammering, but all he could think about was getting back to Lilly. Did she need him? "Please, wake up the other women and come help Lacy deliver Lilly's baby."

"Baby?"

"Yes. Help," he added over his shoulder, already racing back through the doorway leading into the main part of the house. Behind him he could hear the sleepy woman fumble with the chain, then pad down the hall banging on doors.

Cort took the elaborately carved stairs of the old mansion three at a time. Hot water and towels. Weren't those things needed when delivering a baby? He'd reached the main floor when Lacy stuck her head around the door frame.

"Towels. They're in the bathroom." She pointed across the hall, then disappeared back into the room. In two strides he was in the bathroom yanking open doors. Bingo! He snatched a towel, then grabbed the entire stack just as he heard Lacy yell his name.

As he rushed back into the hall he registered three things: first, a mass of women stampeding down the stairs, second, Lacy rushing toward him with a huge grin plastered on her face and third, the tiny infant cradled in her arms.

The tiny, blood-covered newborn…

"Uh-oh."

Cort woke to the freezing chill of cold water splashing across his face. He coughed, sputtered, fought the rivulets filling his nostrils and then coughed some more. Wiping the water out of his eyes, he realized he was surrounded by women.

One stood above him with a grin on her face and an empty pan in her hand. She was the one who'd thrown water on him! If she'd been a man he'd have belted him a good one. He gagged again, wiped more water out of his eyes and looked around at the women hovering over him. There was a woman patting him on the cheek and another fanning cold air on his chilled face. One woman stuffed a pillow under his aching head and another one threw a blanket over him and started tucking it in around him as if it was a straitjacket.

He felt like a drowned rat. From his supine position

on the floor, Cort could see through the doorway into the room where Lilly was, and he caught sight of Loser cowering under the bed, leery of the whirlwind of activity. Cort didn't blame him—he wanted to hide, too. Fighting off the blanket, he started to sit up, only to be pushed back by a set of determined hands.

"Not so fast, cowboy."

Cort shot a glare at the newspaper reporter, Molly Popp, and sat up anyway. He regretted it instantly—the rudeness and the sitting up—but he didn't let it show. The other women backed away as he pushed himself off the floor, staggered then straightened.

His world tilted again when one of the ladies opened the door wider and he spied Lilly sitting up holding her baby.

She looked exhausted, but radiantly happy. She smiled at him and held out her hand toward him.

She was beaming, sitting there holding her child.

A knot formed in Cort's stomach. An ache welled within him and it was all he could do to move toward them through the doorway. He was mesmerized.

"Cort, you scared me to death. Are you okay?" She wiggled her fingers at him when he made no move to take the hand she held out to him.

He'd held her hand all through the contractions, but now, looking at her slender fingers, he was petrified as he reached out and closed his large fingers about hers.

"I'm fine," he said, his voice gruff. He pushed aside the feelings threatening to overwhelm him. "I don't seem to be able to handle the sight of blood. How are you?" he asked, changing the subject, but genuinely interested in her well-being and that of the baby nestled in her arms. They made a perfect picture of peace.

They made his heart ache.

"Worn out but ready to fly," she was saying, and he had to concentrate on her words. But his carefully constructed fortress was cracking up around him.

"Have you ever, ever in your whole life seen anything quite so beautiful?"

"Never," he said, and knew he meant it. They were a vision, mother and child. The little boy had dark hair, and a full head of it.

His children would have had dark hair.

Shards of regret flew at him, ripping at his heart, the anguish of what he'd lost fighting to be free for all to see. He tried to swallow, but his throat was dry, as if he'd just eaten a spoonful of flour.

"Okay, ambulance is on the way," Lacy said, entering the room in a flurry of color and movement.

She slapped him on the back, then hugged him, and he turned his attention back to reality and focused on her words, not his what ifs.

"You did a great job getting her here," she said. "Though I'm certain you want us all to forget about the little fainting episode, I have to tell you it was really cute."

She stepped over to Lilly and the baby and looked at him with a huge grin. "God works in weird ways sometimes. We've been trying to get Lilly to move to town. Trying to get her away from that lonely place way off out in the middle of nowhere. But she seems to like hiding out in the country all alone. Wouldn't it have been horrible had you not moved in when you did? You, Cort Wells, are a gift from God."

He was no gift, of that he was certain. But the way he saw it, God used whoever was around when the need arose. And he didn't want to think about what could have happened to Lilly if he hadn't been there. Why would she endanger her life and her baby's by stubbornly remaining alone out in the sticks with only Samantha?

But, he reminded himself, it was none of his business. It was a hard reminder. They were tied by this event, by this great adventure…by this life changing bond, but it was still none of his business.

And why did he keep thinking it was?

"Lacy, the baby came early," Lilly said, weariness weighing her words. "I was going to go stay in Ranger, near the hospital, as soon as my doctor thought the baby was ready to come."

"Yes, I know that. But you have friends here. You could have come and stayed with me and Sherri. We would have taken care of you."

Lilly blushed and looked down at her baby. "I know," she said softly.

Cort got the feeling she understood she could count on Lacy, but didn't want to count on anyone. He knew the feeling well. He didn't ever want to count on anyone again in his life.

He needed a cup of coffee. He needed to stop wondering what made his neighbor tick. He needed to pull back, step away from all the goodwill going on around him.

"You need anything?" he asked Lilly, fighting the need to take her in his arms as he had that first night in the barn. She'd felt so right.

He pushed back the sentimental yearning. Too many things about Lilly rubbed him raw, and because of that he knew nothing had changed since that first night. He still needed a good, hard, swift kick in the head.

She smiled up at him. "No," she said, reminding Cort that he'd asked her if she needed anything. "I've got everything I need right here in my arms." She kissed the top of her baby's head. "You should go get some rest, though. Because of us, you didn't get any sleep."

The picture of him lassoing her and yanking her to the floor in his horse barn flashed through his mind's eye again. "This is my fault," he said. In the distance he could hear the sound of a siren. The sound brought the full impact of the night into reality. His stomach rolled.

"How did they get here so fast?" Cort asked.

"They're not stationed in Ranger," Lacy explained. "They use the school as their central location to the surrounding areas. That way they can get to an emergency easier. But the baby came so fast I didn't have time to call until after he was born."

"Knock, knock. Can anybody join this party?"

"Clint!" Lacy exclaimed. "I'm so glad you made it before I went with Lilly to the hospital."

Cort watched her almost fly into the arms of her fiancé.

"Looks like there's been some excitement here," he said, kissing the top of Lacy's tousled hair and reaching out a hand to Cort at the same time.

They'd met at the town celebration the night before. Cort shook his hand, glad to see a male face in a sea of females.

"Excitement is a mild word for what's been going on tonight. I thought this was a quiet little town," Cort said just as he heard the ambulance whip into the drive.

When everyone's attention turned to the ambulance Cort turned back to Lilly. He was relieved she was about to get the help she needed. "You're going to be all right now," he assured her, reaching out to touch her soft cheek. "You were amazing tonight, Lilly."

The smile she gave him was tired, but her eyes were bright when she reached up and grasped his hand. "Thank you, Cort. What would I have done without you?" She said it so softly he had to lean down to hear her.

The kiss she planted on his cheek surprised him.

It was quick and neat and innocent—and had his mind reeling and his skin tingling. He wanted to take her in his arms.

"Could I ask you one more favor?"

"Anything you want," he managed to get out above the turmoil the kiss had raised in him.

"Could you look after Samantha while I'm at the hospital? It probably won't be but for today, maybe tonight."

The emergency team entered the room in a flurry.

"I'll take care of everything. Don't you worry about anything but this little boy. I'm going to get out of their way now, but you take care. Okay?" He started to reach out and touch the baby's soft cheek, but stopped himself. Looking into the sleeping face of Lilly's son, he felt a band of anguish tighten around his heart. He fought the lump forming in his throat and the burning behind his eyes.

No use. Regrets belted him in the gut. Slammed into him so hard he wrenched away, hoping his pain wasn't written on his face.

It was time to go home.

It was time to get back to reality.

He'd come to Mule Hollow to make peace with God and a future he despised letting go of. And instead he'd run headlong into a wide-screen viewing of what he'd lost. Of what he'd never have.

He glanced back before he reached the door, and it took every ounce of willpower he possessed to keep going.

There was too much sitting on that bed that he'd always wanted.

God was pushing buttons he didn't need pushed.

It hit Cort as it had for the past year that sometimes God asked too much of a man.

He chanced one more look over his shoulder and watched them load Lilly onto the stretcher, then he strode from the room and out into the freezing night.

The frigid air wrapped around him like the clamp that gripped his heart.

Sometimes it wasn't easy hanging on to God. Especially when it felt as if God had turned His back on him, trashed his life and expected him to sit up and be happy about it.

# *Chapter Ten*

Lilly was home. At least, she thought it was her home. It had been overrun with people. Good, caring people. Loving people. Esther Mae and Norma Sue had made themselves at home when Lacy and Clint brought her and her newborn, Joshua, home from the hospital.

For two days they'd taken care of her and entertained her. They were like Ethel and Lucy. Esther Mae had flaming red hair that just a few months earlier had been piled high on her head like the…well, Lilly couldn't exactly come up with an analogy of what it had looked like, but it was really bad. Then Lacy came to town, cut it off and now Esther Mae looked like a million bucks.

Most of the time.

Like Lucy, Esther Mae was loud and sometimes said the most goofball things. Things that made Lilly laugh out loud.

Norma Sue was round, had kinky gray hair, a smile

that could stretch from one end of Texas to the other, and a heart just as big.

They were in the kitchen while Lilly rocked Joshua in the rocking chair in the corner of the living room. She paused in the lullaby she was singing and listened to them. They were such dears to come and take care of her. Her grannies would have appreciated their care of her.

"So, I was telling Hank just the other day that we needed to go down there and get to know this Cort Wells," Esther Mae said.

Lilly could see them through the doorway as they cooked supper for her. She'd insisted that she was able to do for herself but they refused to listen, said they could do it for at least one more night. Lilly let them at last.

"Roy Don said he talked to him a few days after he moved in and he thought Mr. Wells was just a loner. He said he didn't get the feeling that the man was a grouch like the rumors that some of those old geezers started down at the feed store. And that was the opinion I got at the pageant when I met him."

Esther Mae sniffed. "Those old coots at the feed store need a life. Why, the man is a saint in my book. What would Applegate and Stanley know about that? The old meddlers."

"Now, Esther Mae, there you go letting things get to you. God loves those fools, too."

"No, the Bible says God has no pleasure in fools. Believe me, I looked it up. It's just like a fool to start rumors about a poor fellow before he's had a chance to take off his hat and put his feet up in a new town."

Lilly couldn't help smiling. Esther Mae always did have a way with words. Of course, the best times were when she got her words mixed up, said one thing and meant another. Everyone still picked on her about having the stinkiest feet in Mule Hollow because she told everyone she wore Neutralizer shoes, rather than Naturalizers, because her feet were so bad. Norma Sue said Esther Mae was the only woman she knew who could take a perfectly serious sentence, change a word or two and turn it into a hilarious situation. Lilly understood, since she, too, had her own problems with words when she got tired.

"Lilly, what do you think?"

Lilly looked up from watching Joshua drift to sleep to find both women standing in the doorway.

"About?"

"About Cort Wells." Esther Mae came into the room and sat on the sofa before the fire. "Is he as grumpy as App and Stan said?"

"Does he frown all the time and snap your head off when you ask him a question about his past?" Norma Sue came to sit in the chair beside Lilly. "I mean I met him the other night, but that was just for a few minutes. A person doesn't always show all of his cards in the first game. So I was wondering what you've seen of the man. What do you think?"

"Well, I…" How to answer such questions? She hadn't exactly been around Cort *that* much. Yes, he had saved

her life. Who knew what might have happened if he
hadn't had the good sense to follow Samantha through
the freezing sleet to her house? He was her hero. So her
thoughts of him during the delivery were fond, even
confusing, deep down inside.

Yes, he'd been kind of snippy in the barn after he'd
thrown her to the ground. But that could simply have
been due to the shock of realizing he had just roped a
pregnant woman. It was a situation that seemed to highly
agitate the poor man, and why not? It was pretty careless
on her part to be out on such a night.

And yes, he was bossy and he got on her every nerve
when he accused her of being neglectful of her pregnant
state. But from where he was standing looking in, it
could very easily appear that she *was* being careless. If
she admitted it to herself, maybe she had been, without
really realizing it. But who else was going to take care
of things around here?

Despite it all, he had a way about him. A way of
making her feel safe. Of making her want to be around
him more.

And she couldn't explain the need that kept plaguing
her to find out what had happened in his past to account
for the sorrow she saw in his eyes. The man tugged
at her heart as nothing ever had, despite the fact that
he made her angry at nearly every meeting. Every one
prior to the night he'd rescued her and helped deliver
her precious baby.

She cleared her throat and smiled at the ladies. She
decided it was better if no one knew the turmoil Cort

caused her. She schooled her emotions so that they didn't play across her expression.

"Honestly I can only say that in such a highly stressful situation as I placed him, Cort Wells was the man for the job. He was amazing."

"My," Esther Mae said, relaxing against the cushions of Lilly's great-great-granny's couch. "That was well said. Norma Sue, don't you think that was well said?"

Norma Sue was studying Lilly with an odd expression on her face. She looked over at Esther and they held eyes for a minute. Lilly got the distinct impression that she was missing something. Something important.

"How old a man would you say this Cort Wells is?" Norma Sue's attention was back on Lilly.

Age? Age was something Lilly hadn't thought about. She'd been raised by a band of grandmas. Age was never a factor. You were either older or you were younger. Hmm…Cort was older than her twenty-six years…but not much. "Maybe thirtysomething."

"Cute, too?" Norma raised her eyebrows and Lilly got a twinge in her gut.

"Maybe. He has a hard edge to his looks. Like a stone wall. So *cute* isn't exactly the word I would use to describe Cort. Handsome, yes."

"Then how would you describe him, Lilly?" Esther scooted forward on the couch, her elbows on her knees, fist under her chin.

Lilly glanced down at Joshua, peaceful and blissfully content, and a sense of meaning surrounded her. This child, this darling boy was actually hers. She fought away the lump that threatened a rush of tears. God had truly blessed her. Then her thoughts turned to the man who had been sent to assure her baby's safe birth, the man who had made Joshua's contentment possible, and her heart got a weird heaviness around it. "Cort's good-looking, there's no denying it. But it's the sadness in his eyes that makes him seem angry. I do wonder about that." Had she said that out loud? He'd been so wonderful to her and to Samantha, and now she was blabbing about his personal business.

Norma Sue nodded and Esther Mae smiled. Seeing them looking at her, Lilly was overtaken by a sense of dread. What was going through their minds? *Oh, no!* No...no. *"No!"*

"No what, dear?" Esther Mae cooed.

Lilly zeroed in on Esther and caught Norma with her peripheral vision. "Do not even begin to think that there is the prospect of a romance brewing here." Lilly started rocking Joshua. "My grannies, bless their souls, were telling the truth when they said the Tipps women had no luck with men. Why, you saw what happened to me. You saw what happened one after the other to my mom and grannies. Men do not—and I repeat—men do not stick around." Lilly didn't want to think about this. She had overcome it. She was a Tipps. She had reconciled herself to a life alone. She and Joshua...the first boy in a long line of girls. The first boy who would naturally carry on the Tipps name. Why, she had even gotten back her sense of humor as her pregnancy had progressed.

This wasn't a good thing, this idea of Norma and Esther's. Yes, she still daydreamed about finding the man God had made for her...but that was all it was. A daydream. And yes, Cort Wells caused her to wonder, caused her heart to skitter and lunge, but…

"I know the two of you, and Adela and Lacy, have this thing about bringing women to Mule Hollow. And I know that all the women heading this way will eventually keep y'all busy. So you can just set your sights on them and leave me out of this matchmaking plan." She was rattling. Rambling. Fumbling. "I stuck my neck out on Joshua's dad, and that landed me flat on my face in his tracks eating his dust. Nope." She rocked harder just thinking about the humiliation, the confusion. "Nada. No way. Not on your lives."

Esther smiled. "Now, hold on to your belt loops, Lilly. Do you think that Norma and I would do anything that would upset you? We know that baby doesn't need to have you all agitated. We were simply trying to get a feel for what you thought about the man. Remember, there were a few ladies there the other night when he brought you to Adela's place. We're just trying to get your opinion. Right, Norma?"

"Right, Esther. Lilly, when you said that about the sadness in his eyes, well, *naturally* we got to thinking that maybe falling in love would put a spark in the place of the sadness. God, after all, does say that it isn't good for man to be alone. Maybe Cort needs a wife. Maybe that's why God brought him to us. You do have to admit that Mule Hollow is a bit off the beaten track."

Lilly hated it, but found herself pondering the thought.

"Yeah," Esther agreed. "If it wasn't an act of God,

then what in the world would have brought the man here to Mule Hollow?"

Lilly had kind of wondered the same thing. What had led the man here? When she was in pain she had thanked God for sending him here. But other than being her hero, what had caused him to move to the remote ranch?

Cort led Ringo back to his stall, then headed toward the house. The bad weather had eased up and the sun was shining bright and clear. The unpredictability of Texas weather, especially west Texas, was a factor that Cort appreciated. As the old saying went, if you didn't like the weather you were having today all you had to do was wait a day and it would change. It made winters tolerable.

The distant rumble of a truck had him pausing in the drive. For the past four days he'd watched one truck or car after another pass by as the town of Mule Hollow embraced their newest resident. He'd wondered how Lilly and Joshua were doing. He'd even tossed around the idea of checking in on them. But they'd had plenty of visitors making sure everything was all right. They didn't need him nosing around.

Besides, there was nothing for him next door except another broken heart.

Slapping his hat on his thigh, he walked the rest of the way to the house. It wasn't neighborly not to go. But then, who said he was neighborly? He hadn't seen any Mule Hollow citizens beating down his door to welcome him to town.

And that was just the way he'd planned it. They'd leave him alone and he'd leave them alone. He was the one who'd started the talk about how mean he was when he'd chosen to be so cold to everyone.

Maybe he'd made a mistake. Maybe it wouldn't hurt for him to find friends in Mule Hollow. Maybe his self-imposed solitude was off base.

Thoughts of Lilly and her baby had been repeatedly on his mind. After he'd watched them being whisked away in the ambulance four nights ago he'd driven to her house, put out the fire in her fireplace and closed the place up until her return. Then he'd gone to find Samantha.

The little donkey was nowhere to be found and he'd spent hours searching for her in the icy weather. He'd retraced his steps and found her slowly making her way toward Mule Hollow along the road at the edge of the trees. She was cold, tired and hungry, but in pursuit of Lilly. There was a loyalty in that donkey that Cort envied. He had been forced to leave her there on the side of the road, return home and get his small horse trailer. By the time he'd returned, loaded her and taken her home, the sunlight was bright in the morning sky.

Loading the obstinate animal had been an adventure of its own. Samantha wanted Lilly, and she wasn't taking no for an answer. Cort had had to use every ounce of his experience as a horseman to get the little animal into the trailer.

She had pranced and danced away from him like a lumpy ballerina on ice. Cort had finally resorted to talking to the old girl, cajoling her with sweet talk and promises of carrots, apples and sweet feed.

Suddenly he was hit with a wave of guilt. He hadn't come through on those promises.

He paused. He should take care of that. It wouldn't hurt for him to go check on Samantha. With Lilly caring for her son, Samantha had more than likely not gotten the attention she was used to. She could probably use a little company. He sure could. Besides, if there was one thing Cort appreciated it was a sense of loyalty. Yep, he needed to make sure that Samantha's loyalty was rewarded.

Lilly wouldn't even have to know that he was out there in her barn. He'd just quietly drive over there and not disturb mom and child. Yep, they were probably holed up inside the house nice and toasty, sitting in front of a warm fire—that is, if they had enough firewood. He might check on that, too, while he was saying hi to Samantha. They would need firewood, and all those people may not have thought to check on her supply, thinking someone else had done it. He'd noticed her large stash of wood was a pretty good way from the house. Lilly shouldn't have to be lugging firewood all that distance. She wouldn't want to leave her baby alone all that time…. That's what he'd do. He'd sneak right over there and check on things. Repay Samantha for her loyalty and make sure mother and child had everything they needed.

They didn't have to know he'd even been there.

## Chapter Eleven

The air was crispy cool as Lilly walked the length of her small stables. She felt more like herself with each new morning, and when she'd seen the sun peek through her curtains at sunrise she'd known it was time to try to get some chores done.

Samantha needed new straw, and that meant shoveling out the old. Lilly was actually looking forward to a little physical activity. She'd been housebound for the past few days, and the thought of using her muscles again thrilled her. There was more than enough neglected work to get her back in shape.

There was firewood to carry up closer to the house, a fence to fix—pronto—not to mention a leaky faucet that she'd been too large to get to before. Crawling under sinks when you were heavy with child was not a good thing to attempt. She knew, because she'd tried it.

She laughed, remembering squatting, or trying to squat, then maneuvering around to try to reach up and under the sink in the small space. In the end she'd lain flat on her back, arms and legs flared, as she let a cramp ease out of her side. She almost hadn't gotten up from that little debacle.

But that was while pregnant. Normally she was handy with a hammer, a wrench and almost anything else that came her way. The grannies had taught her self-sufficiency. This little ranch had been supporting itself for the past fifty or so years.

Lilly paused in her climb up the ladder and listened to the baby monitor that sat on the work bench below her. The gentle rustle of her baby wafted to her. It was a fantastic sound.

The sound of her baby.

*And* the sound of her baby sleeping.

She was starting to realize that not all babies slept through the night. Joshua had odd hours. Thirty minutes here, two hours there. Never, never more than two hours at a stretch. Joshua also wanted to eat all the time. Why, she had more bottles fixed and ready just to be able to keep up. Lilly had to adjust everything accordingly.

Life was not anywhere near what it had been—not that she was griping, because she wasn't. She was simply still trying to figure things out.

Norma Sue had told her to sleep when Joshua slept in order to keep herself from getting worn out. But Lilly hadn't quite figured that out yet. There were the tons of things that needed doing, and they weren't going to get done if she was sleeping or rocking Joshua.

And since she loved rocking Joshua, she'd decided to give up the sleeping. So far she was making it okay.

She didn't need an abundance of sleep anyway. Things would be fine.

The fresh smell of hay filled her nostrils as she stepped gingerly off the ladder onto the wood loft. She was hurting just a little as she walked to the stacks of square hay bales. It didn't take much to prove she'd lost a little strength in the past nine months. Instead of carrying the bale of hay, she dragged it to the opening above Samantha's stall. With her pocketknife she sliced the twine, then reached for her pitchfork with her gloved hand.

Her movements were sure and easy. She'd been taught early to care for the horses that used to roam this land before Granny Gab sold them all. That had been a sad day for the Tipps household. Especially for Lilly. At ten years old she hadn't understood why suddenly Granny Gab didn't want to raise horses. Lilly shook off the hard memory and dug the fork into the sweet-smelling hay, broke it up, then tossed it down into the rack below her.

While she'd been pregnant she'd used the hay stored below in the extra stalls. But now that she could climb, she was trying to get things back to normal. The exertion felt good.

Oh, sure, she'd pay for it tomorrow, but it was worth it.

She'd worked up a good sweat in the cold shadow of the loft by the time she'd finally tossed enough hay below into the rack.

Where was Samantha anyway? The little munchkin had trotted off a little while ago, which was unusual.

Normally when Lilly was outside Samantha stuck right by her side, snooping around, seeing what was going on.

Lilly walked over to the loft door and slid it back. The cold wind whipped through the opening, stinging her cheeks and making her eyes water. Whew, it was getting colder. Again.

Glancing out across the land, she could just make out the top of Cort Wells's house. His place was only about a mile from her home. Using the dirt road it was more like two. As a kid she'd taken the road less traveled. She knew every nook and cranny between her place and Leroy's old place. She'd been welcomed there then. She wondered about now, now that it was Cort's home.

Poor man. He was probably glad to be rid of her. She hadn't heard or seen anything from him since the night of Joshua's birth. She wasn't exactly sure how she felt about that.

Lilly wondered if he thought of that night. Of the way he'd held her hand. Of the gentle words of encouragement he'd said to her. She just wondered. That was all.

He'd been her dream. Her hero.

Dragging her eyes away from Cort's home, she scanned the acres around her house looking for Samantha.

Where was that long-eared little troublemaker? Leaning out the opening, Lilly held on to the door frame so she could see around the side of the barn to the house. A-hah! There she was, trotting out to the pasture, toward the firewood.

Toward the man stacking logs in his arms.

Cort—Cort Wells was here.

Lilly pulled back into the loft and scrambled for the ladder. A warm glow surged through her and a smile burst to her lips. Cort was here.

It was a good day.

Cort stacked the last pieces of wood into his arms and started for the house. The pile was too high, almost above his head, but he wanted to finish quickly. He'd stopped the truck at the edge of Lilly's drive and left it there, not wanting to disturb Lilly and her baby.

All looked quiet at the house, so maybe mother and child were taking a nap. In the daylight Lilly's house looked as if it hadn't been changed in fifty years. The old farmhouse was whitewashed, with pale yellow shutters. There was a long porch running the length of the back of the house, with many chairs fashioned from tree branches. Colorful cushions made Cort think about sitting down and having a conversation with Lilly. Maybe watching the little boy playing nearby as he grew—

*In your dreams, Wells. You came to check on Samantha and carry firewood. Remember.*

Forcing the ill-gotten thoughts away, he stalked toward the house. This was his third trip, because she had indeed been low in her stash next to the house. That wouldn't do in case there was another storm and the electricity went out again. She'd need the wood to stay warm.

He had gotten halfway to the house when Samantha

trotted up to him. Not a stranger anymore, she nudged him with her nose until she found the pocket that held the carrots.

"Hey, Samantha. How's it going, ole girl?" Cort would have scratched her between the ears, but his hands were full. The wood had shifted as he walked across the pasture, so he concentrated on his balancing act trying to keep the short logs from tumbling out of his arms and onto the ground.

Samantha wasn't shy. She was, however, persistent. She nudged his pocket, then started nibbling at the edge of the carrot stalks that dangled from the slash pocket of his coat.

"Back off, Samantha. Mind your manners."

He tried to twist around so she couldn't get her bulging lips on the tempting treats, but she was too fast. She swished around, grasping a green stalk, then tugged. As Cort fanned his elbow out attempting to distract her, the logs tilted. He stopped, leaned to one side, bent one knee, righted, then bent the other when the wood shifted again. Samantha had no pity. She didn't care that he was wrestling with his burden. Instead she maneuvered her mouth around until she got a good grasp of the carrot and coat at the same time. Cort glanced down. "No, Samantha!" he called again just as a ragged piece of wood toppled from the stack and whacked him on the forehead, bounced off his shoulder, then hit the ground, taking his hat with it.

He staggered, and a second log would have followed if a slender gloved hand hadn't reached over his shoulder and caught it.

"My, my, my, don't you live dangerously, Mr. Wells."

His head was throbbing, but his heart was smiling. His lips were, too, because the sound of Lilly's voice just did that to him.

He'd missed her. A fact he didn't really want to admit.

He felt the carrot finally slip from his pocket and saw the plump rump of Samantha as she passed by him, trotting away with her newfound treasure sticking from her whiskered jaws. Her singed ball of a tail swung to and fro as she made her great escape. He started to shake his head then caught himself, not wanting another block of wood to fall. He needed to concentrate on keeping the pile steady.

Lilly laughed, reached down and scooped his hat off the ground. "First rule of Samantha survival—never have your hands full if you have food in your pockets. It's a no-win situation."

Cort laughed, too, watching her carefully dust off his hat, then handle it gently with her gloved fingers as though not to harm it. She must have forgotten it was beyond help since Samantha had tried to eat it days ago.

"I'm beginning to understand that about Samantha," he said. "We spent an interesting night together after you were carried away in the ambulance."

"Oh, I hope she didn't cause you too much trouble."

Cort thought about the hours spent in the cold sleet coaxing the donkey into the trailer. "It wasn't any trouble. I enjoyed getting to know the little beast. I think she's human."

Lilly's eyes sparkled in the sunlight and her curls bounced beneath her red cap as she nodded agreement. He liked her red cap. It went with her cute red nose and cheeks. And her spunky personality.

"Not think. Samantha knows she's human. She just hasn't been able to convince God to give her a girlish figure so she can convince everyone else of her true identity. Here, let me straighten these up, or carry some of them." With her free hand she reached to move the disorderly wood into place and started to take some off the top.

"I've got it," Cort said, straightening and heading toward the house again. Lilly moved to walk beside him. He noticed she was nearly skipping to keep up with his long stride, so he eased up.

She smelled of hay and—what was that…baby powder? A unique combination.

"Thanks for rescuing me," he said, grinning like a fool, liking the way her eyes twinkled in acknowledgment of the smile. Also really liking the scent of her.

"It was the least I could do. Anytime you need me, just call and I'll be there to rescue you from here to eternity. And it would never be enough to pay you back for rescuing me. What are you doing here anyway?"

They had reached the house. Cort stooped and dropped the wood to the ground. Lilly's snappy lilt tugged at him. He'd come to recognize it as uniquely hers. He'd know her voice if he was blindfolded standing in a crowd of a hundred women. She sounded as if she was smiling and couldn't help it. It was nice.

Now that his hands were free, he raked one through his hair in an attempt to get it off his throbbing forehead. His fingers grazed a raw knot forming above his left eye. "I decided it was past time for me to help my neighbor. It's supposed to get really cold again and I'd noticed when I brought Samantha home that your wood was getting low."

"Oh, Cort, you're hurt."

Lilly was staring at his forehead with wide eyes. "Here, hold your hat so I can get a better look at this."

He took the hat she shoved at him, then she yanked off her leather gloves. Letting them drop to the ground, she pushed the hair back off his forehead. Her hand was warm against his cold skin.

"It's nothing," he said, making no move to get away from her gentle touch. Her eyes shifted with concern as she studied the wound. This close he could see a slight darkness beneath her eyes, a tiredness lurking underneath the spark.

Removing her hands, she stepped away. "Follow me. I need to clean that out. You have a couple of splinters in there. And I need to check on Joshua." She tucked her hands into her coat pockets.

The memory of her cozy house topped with the thought of seeing her with her son—it was a tempting picture better left alone. "I really need to get back home—"

"Men! You need my help and you're going to get it.

I'm not taking no for an answer." With that she grabbed his arm and towed him toward the back door.

"You make men sound like a dirty word," he said, offering no resistance as she opened the back door and led the way into the warm house. He knew he might regret this, but she seemed so intent on taking care of him that he couldn't say no. It had been a long time since he'd felt the gentle touch of a woman. And he liked Lilly's touch.

"You have to understand my upbringing."

Cort helped Lilly remove her coat before shrugging out of his and hanging it on the rack beside hers. In her jeans and turtleneck sweater she was a charming picture with her girl-next-door beauty.

The girl next door to him.

# Chapter Twelve

"Please have a seat at the table. Help yourself to some coffee if you like. It's fresh. I need to check on Joshua, and then I'll grab my tweezers and peroxide." She smiled at him before turning and heading down the hallway.

Instead of sitting, Cort stayed in the hall studying the array of pictures lining the long wall. It didn't take but a few seconds to realize there were no men in any of the photos.

In the back of the house he could hear Lilly cooing and chatting with her baby. From the things she was saying he guessed she was changing a diaper. He continued to look at one picture after another of what looked to be six or seven women in various stages of their life. There were a few of Lilly growing up, and in some of them Samantha was standing beside her. No wonder their bond was so tight. They had a past together.

"Here we are," Lilly called, stepping into the hallway.

Mother and child. Cort's throat went dry watching them move toward him.

She had Joshua in her arms. He had on a cute little blue fuzzy thing that covered him from neck to toes. There was a blue dog appliquéd on his chest. A sharp stab of regret ripped through Cort's heart and he forced it away.

"You've got a lot of pictures here." His voice sounded gruff even to his ears as he nodded toward the wall. The only picture he was interested in was the real one standing in front of him. But that was a reality he'd never know.

Why had he come here? This was slow torture.

"Yes, I have mountains of photos and I talk to them way too much. Follow me into the kitchen and I'll talk your head off while I yank those splinters out of your forehead."

Cort laughed, and despite his trepidation followed her into the kitchen. "I'm not too certain if I should take you up on such a tempting offer. You sound as if you like inflicting pain a little too much. Did I do anything to make you mad?"

She laughed. "Aw, pour yourself a cup of coffee and sit back and relax." She winked at him over her shoulder before placing Joshua in a swinglike bassinet sitting in the corner, near enough to the heater to be warm. She was a gentle mother—clucking her tongue when he started to get fussy, then smiling when he settled down. She pushed a button and the swing started to rock.

"That's a neat contraption you've got there." Cort had been guilty of walking down rows of baby items once or twice, intrigued by the items available for bringing up babies nowadays. That was before his life had fallen apart and he realized he'd never have any use for such things. That didn't stop him from admiring cool inventions.

"It was waiting for me when we came home from the hospital. Adela gave it to us. And you don't know how many times it has saved my life. Some nights he just won't sleep and I can put him in there and it rocks him to sleep immediately."

Cort took a cup from the rack next to the coffeepot and filled it with the rich-smelling brew. "Would you like a cup?" he asked.

"Yes, please," she said as she started to heat a bottle for Joshua.

"I'll pour it, but you'll have to fix it. I don't think I can get all the additives and stirring right."

She chuckled and removed the lid of the sugar bowl.

A few minutes later, warmed by the coffee and the heater, Cort settled back and watched Lilly prepare to work on the bump on his head.

"My grannies would have had to adjust their view of men if they'd met you."

Her words startled him as much as her first touch.

"Is that so?"

"Mmm-hmm."

She was biting her lip as she gently prodded his forehead with the point of the tweezers.

She was so close. Cort studied the way her dark lashes curled. Dark and long, they fluttered as she studied the wound intently. She had a sprinkling of freckles across her nose and a tiny scar at the corner of her right eye.

"So tell me more about these grannies," he said, needing a distraction from her. He was also curious about her unusual upbringing. "It sounds and looks, from the photos in there, like they really didn't have much use for men."

Her fingers paused and she grew very still. "Well," she said, looking down at him, "let's just say all of them had sour experiences with men…then decided to do without them. They never knew a hero like you. It's sad, actually. I never knew one until you, either."

She blushed, then averted her eyes and studied his forehead again. Her breath feathered down around him, engulfing him.

"Ow!" he exclaimed. Thinking about what she'd said, he'd forgotten to brace himself against the tug of the tweezers.

"Sorry," she said, holding up a splinter a quarter of an inch long. "Wow, I told you…just look at this splinter! Look at the size of that bad boy."

"Is part of my brain attached to the end of it?"

Lilly laughed. "That bad, huh? I'll warn you before I yank the next one out. It doesn't look as large."

When she finally stepped away from him with not just two but three splinters, Cort was struggling. He could fight the longings that Lilly evoked in him from a distance. But with her standing so close to him, knowing all he had to do was reach out and wrap his arms around her—it was agony. At one point her lips were mere inches from his while she tried to get a good view of the last splinter.

He'd wanted nothing more than to lean into her and kiss her.

What would she think about that? he wondered. No doubt her grannies wouldn't have liked it. He knew that for a fact. No matter how much she thought their opinion would have changed if they'd gotten to know him.

"Refill?" she asked, holding the coffeepot out to him.

"I really should be going."

"Please, please stay for a few minutes. I have to feed Joshua. Please, we could light a fire and visit awhile."

Cort needed to go. He needed to get out of there. But three pleases in a row tugged at him.

"I—I don't usually get many visitors, and like you said, we are neighbors...but I understand."

She placed the pot back on its pad. Torn by feelings he didn't want to fight with, he watched her lift Joshua from the swing, then reach for the bottle she'd warmed in the microwave.

"I could stay for a few minutes." The words surprised him and filled him with anticipation. There it was again.

Anticipation had become a common feeling that wrapped around him with every thought of Lilly.

And Joshua.

Lilly beamed. "Wonderful," she quipped, and led the way into the cozy country living room. He moved to the fireplace, focusing on getting a fire going as Lilly settled into the rocker next to the window.

Cort chuckled when a big black nose flattened against the pane next to her.

Donkeys were natural guard animals. Many people used them to protect herds of cattle, sheep or goats from predators like coyotes. Cort wondered about Samantha. She seemed to have appointed herself as Lilly and Joshua's protector. Though she was a bit small for a true protector.

"Was Samantha ever used as a guard animal?" Cort asked, moving to sit on the couch, watching Lilly cradle Joshua in her arms as he greedily sucked on the bottle of formula.

"No, she was too small. That's why Leroy got her in the first place. She was smaller than most, and the breeder he bought her from had no use for her. So Leroy brought her home to help him break his bulls."

"I can see that. The first time I saw a burro breaking a foal I was intrigued. I've never done it personally, but I know it works with cattle or colts."

Lilly laughed, tapping her fingers on the pane, drawing Samantha's eyeball to replace her nose. "The first time I saw it, it was hilarious. Docile old Samantha was harnessed to this brawny buck of a young bull and he didn't want anything to do with learning manners. He'd head to water and Samantha would just stand there with that halter stretched as taut as could be. She'd look patiently at that bull and stand her ground. She had to drop-kick him a few times when he got overzealous. In the end he was the best-mannered bull Leroy had."

"That explains a lot about her. She's a good animal."

"Nosy, spoiled and lovable. She and I have been together through so much."

Cort couldn't help but wonder what some of those things might have been.

"What happened to your husband? I know it's none of my business, but for two people who've been thrown together so much over the past few weeks, we really don't know a whole lot about each other." And he wanted to know everything about Lilly.

For a moment she continued to study Joshua's face, as if she hadn't heard him. But he could tell she was simply trying to decide whether to tell or decline. One thing he'd learned about Lilly was she did only what she wanted to do.

"He left," she said at last, looking up at the last moment to meet his gaze straight on. She gave a brief smile. A sad smile. "It wasn't meant to be. It was just one of those things in life you wish so hard for…that when the chance comes your way, even though the odds are against you, you take a risk."

Something in her voice had him wondering if he shouldn't have started the conversation. But he couldn't put his finger on what that was exactly. What did he say when he didn't have anything positive to build someone up with?

"It really wasn't all Jeff's fault. A woman should ask the man she's marrying if he wants children. I assumed way too much going into my marriage. The biggest assumption being what kind of man I was marrying."

Cort had assumed too much going into his marriage, also.

"What about you, Cort? What brought you to Mule

Hollow? And if I may be so bold, why are you not married with a houseful of kids?"

Her question slammed into him, surprised him. Stalling, he let out a soft breath. "Payback time. Okay, fair is fair," he said. What did he care? "I came to Mule Hollow after my wife left me. I'm struggling to embrace the way my life has played out."

Lilly studied him for a moment, compassion in her eyes. "That happens to the best of us. I'm having a hard time dealing with the hand I've been played, also. Of course, I've got Joshua and that makes me happier about everything. Being raised by my grannies way out here in the country with no kids my age made me into a lonely recluse. At one point I dreamed of having a houseful of children someday because of my loneliness." She smiled and shrugged one shoulder. "But that was before—oh well, that's not important. I have Joshua now. That's all that counts, that I have a son. I've been blessed."

A silence stretched between them. Cort tried to think of any blessings.

"Ramona left because I couldn't give her children." There, he'd said it. He'd spoken the words out loud for the first time.

Her eyes registered understanding. "That must have been hard. I'm sorry."

He'd never told anyone reasons for the failure of his marriage. What had he expected Lilly to say? What would anyone say to something like that?

"Do you miss her?"

Did he? Still? "Yes, sometimes. I loved my wife. But..." Opening up to Lilly was alien territory for him.

Normally a private person, he didn't tell people his business. But Lilly was different. They were neighbors trying to become friends. He cleared his throat and started over. "I loved my wife. Like you, she'd always wanted a houseful of children." What could he say—that he didn't blame her? But he did. He would have stayed with Ramona no matter what. "I can't blame her totally for leaving. But I thought she was made of stronger stuff. I thought she meant her vows when she said for better or worse."

"Her betrayal still hurts."

Cort stared out the window behind Lilly. "Yeah, it hurts. I was angry, still am. But I came to Mule Hollow to come to terms with everything. Maybe there was more to the marriage's failure, more I could've done. God and I are struggling at the moment. I'm not certain what He wants from me. I'm not real excited about my life as it stands. But I'm here biding my time. Waiting."

"Ramona wanted children. What about you?" Lilly asked.

Lilly believed in shooting straight. "Yes." Regret knotted his chest. He rubbed the back of his neck and met Lilly's eyes. She looked so tired, more so with every passing minute, but there was compassion in her gaze. "I wanted kids with all my heart." What choice would Lilly have made if she'd been in Ramona's shoes? "We have to take what God lays out there for us. He knows the future, like you said. He has the plan. And obviously children aren't in my future."

"And why not?"

"I'm not planning on marrying again, for one. For two, what do I have to offer a woman? I can't give her children."

"You could adopt. Or maybe the woman will already have children. Who knows?" The encouraging lilt was back in Lilly's voice.

It wasn't as easy as she thought it was. He needed to change the subject.

"Okay, what about you? Do you plan on challenging this luck of the Tipps women? Are you going to remarry and give Joshua a daddy?"

She bit her lip. "I just had a baby. I don't want to think about anything except Joshua right now. But…I'd have said a flat no if you'd asked me before he was born. Now, looking at him…every baby deserves a daddy." She paused, studying Joshua. "I chose a real loser last time. Maybe that's what's wrong with the Tipps women. We're terrible judges of character." She looked at him and gave a halfhearted smile. "Anyway, like I said, I've just given birth and that's all I want to think about right now. God's going to have to change my mind, if it's to be."

Cort felt better about opening up. There was a comfort in knowing that they both were trying to wait on God. To trust Him. Cort had come a long way in the few weeks he'd been at Mule Hollow. He gave much of that credit to the stubborn woman sitting across from him. She'd kept him busy. He certainly hadn't envisioned anything like what had happened to him since moving down the road from Lilly. A smile spread across his face. It felt good to smile. It was getting easier. It seemed to be becoming habit around her.

"Here." Lilly startled him, popping up from the rocker and crossing to stand before him. "Hold Joshua."

"What! No, that's okay." His protest went unheard. Lilly placed the baby in his hands, then walked away so he couldn't just give Joshua back. Despite all his attempts to avoid the infant, Cort found himself holding Joshua. What if he dropped him? He only weighed something like ten pounds. And he was staring up at him with bright eyes. Man, he was a cute little thing. Cort watched, dumbstruck, as Joshua held up a fist and jerked it around a few times.

"Hey, little buddy, don't hit yourself with that thing." The words came out before he could stop them. Joshua smiled and cooed.

Cort felt stiff and awkward, but Lilly had stepped into the kitchen and was rummaging around where he couldn't see her. Cort decided he should rock, so he rocked the baby the way he'd seen Lilly doing, but it didn't feel right. It didn't look right, either. It had looked natural when she swayed back and forth. Maybe he should move to the rocking chair. But if he tripped walking over there… He'd better stay right where he was on the couch. That way no disaster could strike. He wouldn't trip over his big feet while crossing the room.

Lilly was a good mother—at least, he'd thought so before she'd decided he was a safe bet to hold her baby. He tilted Joshua a little closer to his chest so that they were actually touching. Lilly had acted as if he wouldn't break the boy. He figured she might be right.

He was getting the hang of this.

And Joshua acted as if he liked him okay.

Looking up, he found Lilly watching him from the doorway of the kitchen with a sad little smile. When she met his gaze she blinked, then the smile bloomed.

"I think he likes you, Cort."

# Chapter Thirteen

Lilly followed Cort outside. She'd finally rescued him from Joshua right after her son had fallen fast asleep snuggled up against Cort's heart.

She pushed the tugging of her own heart away and concentrated on being a good neighbor. And a friend. They'd both been through a hard time—it was a bond that made her determined to befriend him.

He'd looked so cute not knowing how to hold Joshua. His look of bewilderment had sent a jolt of joy and compassion surging through her. And it had started a small idea forming at the back of her mind. It was something she'd have to think about, that she couldn't make a mistake about. It was something she'd have to spend a lot of time in prayer about. But she had a feeling she already knew what God was going to tell her.

"He went right to sleep, didn't he?" Cort's voice broke into her thoughts.

There was wonder in his words. She smiled up at him as they walked down her driveway toward his truck.

The crazy guy had parked it near the road so that he wouldn't wake them up if they'd been napping. He was so sweet.

"Yes, he did go right to sleep," she agreed. "You got really good at cradling him next to you. That is after you stopped holding him out like he was going to kick you or upchuck on you." She laughed again, remembering the scene…and the ache that it had caused in her heart.

They reached the truck, and Lilly stuck her hands into her back pockets and rolled a rock with the toe of her boot. The wind had picked up and the temperature was dropping quickly. The smell of moisture rode on the cold air, of damp earth and cedar. But it was Cort's scent, spicy and masculine, that lingered in her senses, and the sweet memory of him holding her son.

"Lilly, I'd like to help you with anything I can around here. I'll come back tomorrow and finish bringing up firewood and take care of anything else you need to have done."

"I can take care of it. There's no reason for you to take time away from your horses. Really, you've done way too much for me already."

"Lilly, we're neighbors, and we've been through a lot together. I'd like to do this for you."

Lilly's first inclination was to say no again. But they *had* been through so much together. And really, she could use a little help. She just wasn't used to asking for it. "Okay, but only if you have time."

"I've come a long way since our first meeting. I'm not the nasty old ogre anymore. I hope."

"Yes. Yes, you have come a long way. I don't even

recognize you." She took a step backward, yanking a thumb in the direction of the house. "I have to go inside and check on Joshua. But I'll see you tomorrow. Neighbor."

Cort watched Lilly trek up the driveway. Her hair was bouncing loose just above her collar as she tugged her coat tighter about her. "See you later," he said softly to himself. Regret settled over him. He'd come there intending to get in and out without seeing her. Now that he'd seen her he didn't want to leave. There was such a beauty that flowed from her. There was far more to Lilly than a pretty face. She had an inner beauty that glowed. That worried him.

Watching her stride away, purpose in her steps, he realized his heart was telling him, despite his efforts to convince himself otherwise, that Lilly was more than a neighbor.

Pushing the thought into the shadows, he was getting into his truck when Lilly whirled around.

"Thank you again, Cort," she called.

Cort shut down feelings tugging at his heart. "Anytime."

Her smile broadened, then she turned on her heel and hurried toward the house. She could actually move pretty fast when she wasn't waddling. He frowned. Waddling or not, Lilly made him want things. But she was too young to be saddled with a man who could never give her a family.

Joshua was going to need siblings.

A picture of Lilly and all those children he'd envisioned her with on their first meeting popped into his head.

Scowling, he turned back toward his truck and climbed in.

Who was he kidding? This attraction had him scared to death.

Lilly sat in the booth at Sam's Diner and smiled at the chaos going on around her. The jukebox, which seemed to have a mind of its own, was blasting out the strains of its latest choice, "All I Want for Christmas Is My Two Front Teeth." It had been stuck for months on Jerry Lee Lewis burning up the piano with "Great Balls of Fire," with everyone exclaiming *Goodness gracious!* every time the jukebox played. But now even the mention of wanting two front teeth for Christmas got a bad reaction.

Norma Sue had been able to at least change out the forty-five so that Sam could get some relief from the same song playing 24/7, but then she hadn't been able to get the silly Christmas tune unstuck from the holding mechanism. It never failed that someone coming into the diner stuck a nickel in the slot just to ruffle everyone's feathers.

Today Sherri and Lacy had invited her to bring Joshua to town for a hamburger. She hadn't realized they were actually throwing her a surprise baby shower. The little country diner and pharmacy was packed.

Why, there were more frilly packages stacked on the counter than Lilly had ever seen before. Birthdays at the Tipps household had always been fun, but because there-had never been an abundance of people at the gatherings, or money, the gifts had been slim, but always filled with love. From the look of things here, Joshua might not need a change of clothes for years.

Frogs seemed to be the theme. Frogs and cowboys. Joshua was going to be a frog-loving cowboy. He had shirts with frogs and sleepers with frogs. He had diapers with frogs. He had red bandannas, plaid shirts and little tiny blue jeans with cowboy hats and lassos appliquéd all over them. He even had a tiny Stetson for his little head. He was going to be a lassoing cowboy who *Fully Relied On God.* Thus the F.R.O.G. theme. Lacy had come up with the idea. Lilly loved it.

"Lilly," Lacy called as she grabbed the next package in line for Lilly to open. "We tried to invite Cort to this party, but he wasn't home when I stopped by."

Lilly looked around the room full of women and wondered why they would want to invite Cort to her baby shower. Not that she wouldn't like seeing him. She would. As promised, he'd come and brought plenty of wood up to the house for easy access for her, but he hadn't stayed to talk. Instead he'd insisted he had work to do at home. Lilly tried not to let it bother her. But it did.

She'd decided the man could just stay home, for all she cared. She didn't want him coming over just because he thought she couldn't take care of her own stuff. She could. She'd agreed to let him help only because he'd acted as if he really wanted to.

Keeping her feelings to herself, Lilly offered Lacy

a bright smile. "I'm sure he has things to do. Anyway, there aren't any other guys here."

"Beggin' your pardon, but I'm here," said Sam, the owner, coming out of the back carrying a cake. Samantha had been named after Sam back when he and Leroy were best friends growing up. "I ain't decided if that's a good thing or a bad thing. Thar's a lot of you gals in here. Then again, *that's* a good thing."

Lacy set a couple of presents on the table in front of Lilly. "You're right about that, Sam. I just thought since Cort helped get Joshua delivered, he might like to come. That's all. Oh Sam, that cake looks yummy. What kind is it?"

"It's an Italian cream cake," he said, carefully placing it on the table, where a bowl of punch and cookies were already waiting.

"My favorite," Sherri crooned, scooting out of the booth and going over to get a better look. When she reached a finger out and scooped a dab of icing off the plate Sam swatted her hand.

"Not yet, young lady."

"Sam, you know how I like to eat."

"Yep, that I do. But for this you have to wait till Lilly gets them presents opened, and by the looks of it, that won't be for another hour or two."

Lilly laughed. "I'd better hurry," she said, scanning the room. Molly snapped a picture of her, startling Joshua from sleep. He started to scream, immediately triggering maternal feelings from a host of ladies.

"Oh, now," Adela cooed. Being closest to him, she

beat the others and competently scooped him out of his carrier.

Adela was such an elegant woman with her stylish white hair and her lean carriage. Her incisive blue eyes lit up as she cradled Joshua.

"You are such a sweet dear," she crooned, and to Lilly's surprise Joshua stopped crying, instead opting for watching her beaming face as she talked gently to him.

"Times a-wastin', Lilly," Norma Sue said. "Better get goin' on the presents or by the looks of things we might be here tomorrow."

To make them happy Lilly ripped open the brightly colored present. "I think I need some help. My arms are getting tired." They were all grinning at her and it made her heart swell with warmth. It felt good to be out. To be in this circle of friends. "It's a good thing I live alone, or else there might not be any place to put all this wonderful stuff."

Sherri slid into the seat, grabbed a present and started tearing it open. "I bet you could squeeze a man into the house even with all of this. Oh, and I'm helping 'cause I want a piece of that cake. Tonight! I've got to wait too long for Lacy's wedding cake."

Lacy set a few more presents on the table, then tapped her hot pink fingernails on the surface. "February fourteenth can't get here soon enough for me either, Sherri. But it has nothing whatsoever to do with cake."

Lilly fought off a twinge of sadness. That wedding was going to be something. The whole town was getting excited. She was so happy for Lacy. It was good Lacy had found such a wonderful man to love—not that there weren't some other great guys in Mule Hollow, because she'd learned that there were.

Despite what her grannies had taught her.

It was late in the afternoon when they loaded her truck with all the gifts and she headed the vehicle toward home. Joshua was awake as she pulled away from the diner. Every time she looked at the transformation the town had made in the months since Lacy Brown had come to town, she was amazed. The buildings that had once been just dead, weathered wood were now bright as a box of crayons with paint. The hot pink two-story building that belonged to Lacy always made her smile, remembering the day Lacy had started rolling on the vibrant paint. Boy, it had put the men in such a dither. Especially Clint Matlock. That was the day the townsfolk believe he fell in love with Lacy. Right in the middle of fighting with her over what she was doing to the town.

"Joshua, you see that building right there?" Lilly nodded toward Heavenly Inspirations. "Well, that building can be seen from all the way back at the cross-roads. One day you're going to point your little finger and ask, 'What's that, Momma?'" Lilly reached over and wiggled his toe. "You are…yes, you are—that is, unless you're color-blind."

He smiled at her as she turned and headed out of town. Well, at least she was going to call what he did a smile. Everyone said three-week-old babies didn't smile, but until she got home and found proof in his diaper that he'd been up to something else, she was going to say that little Joshua smiled at the thought of seeing a bright pink building out in the middle of nowhere.

Lilly was dreaming of sleep by the time she arrived home. It had been a long day. She was now trying to heed Norma Sue's advice and sleep as much as she could when Joshua slept. But bills had to be paid, and uploading pictures and information for the catalog didn't get done while she slept.

The sun had lingered for a few days, but ice was in the forecast again. She didn't care. She and Joshua would hole up in their house and spend time together. She would work fast, get some sleep and, who knew, she might even cook. Other people had babies and took care of things at the same time. She could, too. She wasn't a superhero or anything, but she could do this.

She'd bought a small turkey before the cold weather crept in, and hadn't felt like cooking it. She might just give it a try. Yes, get the Sunday dinner tradition started again. She needed practice, because the last time she'd attempted cooking turkey and dressing had been with Granny Bunches, and that had been years ago. Sadly, with all her grannies gone, Lilly had let all traditions falter.

Things were different now. She had Joshua to think about. She had memories to make for him. That settled, she started singing a lullaby to Joshua, just as Granny Bunches had sung to her. When she finally turned her old truck onto her dirt road, she was feeling positive that she would cook that turkey. She'd practice up for next year. If she started now, by the time Thanksgiving and Christmas came around, she'd be a pro. She might even be good enough to invite people from town.

Maybe Cort would like to come? The idea struck her as she was passing his place. Yes, dinner would be a gesture of appreciation for all he'd done for her. Maybe that would help get them back to where they'd been the day he'd held Joshua.

It still bugged her. What had happened to make him seem so distant?

Though his place sat off the road a good way, she could see the entrance of his barn. She was looking that direction when a huge black horse charged out of the barn. He was flying like the wind when he actually jumped the fence and galloped out into the pasture.

Lilly didn't have to wonder but a moment about what had happened to the big horse. Samantha trotted out of the barn and stopped beside the cedar swing, threw her head back and let out a loud *Eee-haw*.

"Oh, no! I should have known you'd be up to no good," Lilly groaned, swinging her truck into the drive and heading toward her impossible ward before she let the entire stable loose. Sometimes she wished Leroy had taken the donkey with him.

Then again, what would she do if she couldn't see Samantha? She did love the little minx.

Cort knew the moment he saw Lilly's old truck that something was amiss. It took only one guess what *Miss* that might be when he opened the door of his truck and Loser bounded off the seat and scurried off around the far corner of the barn, barking. Loser barked at only one thing. Samantha.

What had the donkey done now?

He found Lilly standing with one hand on her hip, the other wrapped around a rake, and by the look on her face, he could tell she was ready for him to jump down her throat. And he might have a few weeks earlier. Sucking in a breath, he surveyed the damage and willed his temper down. Lilly obviously thought this was her fault, and she looked so contrite and cute at the same time he wanted to take her in his arms and soothe her feelings.

He was always wanting to take her in his arms…and that wasn't going to happen. He had to get a grip. He had to get out of this trap his heart was setting for him, or he was a doomed man heading for more heartbreak.

When he spied the baby carrier sitting on the bench next to the wash bay, his heart slipped another notch into the snare. He didn't want to look at Joshua. Ever since he'd held the boy, Cort hadn't been able to think straight. He'd continued to see that sad smile on Lilly's lips. He could think of nothing other than that she wanted a houseful of children—and he could never give her what she wanted.

This attraction he felt for her didn't make sense. There was no way that he could feel, this quickly, the things his heart was trying to tell him he was feeling.

No way.

But he was drawn to the baby just as he was drawn to Lilly. And his heart ached, knowing he was no good for them, knowing they were right down the road from him, but feeling they were as far away as the moon. It had been all he could do to stay away. But he had. Now here they were, on his turf, tempting him with their wholesome lure.

Lilly stepped beside him and they quietly watched Joshua sleep for a moment. He was all bundled up, his little face barely visible. Cort's heart swelled with longing for a family of his own. The nearness of Lilly, the scent of baby powder, reminded him even more of what he didn't have.

"I like watching him sleep," he said, fighting the feelings. It wasn't bad enough that he wanted to wrap his arms around Lilly—he also wanted to reach out and touch the top of the baby's head. To see if it still felt as soft as the muzzle of a horse, as he remembered. But he didn't. Touching mother or child was going to do nothing but amplify the things he couldn't allow himself to feel. Turning away, he strode to the pile of feed that littered the floor.

"Samantha did this, didn't she?" The accusation came out harsher than he'd meant.

"I'm sorry. I saw her coming out as I was passing by."

"I guess I'm gonna have to get the whip after the ole girl." He tried to joke, to relieve the tension eating at him. It didn't work. Lilly whirled toward him, eyes blazing fire.

"You wouldn't dare! True, she's being a pest, but don't even think about hurting her. I promise this isn't like her. She has never, never been this destructive."

Her words cut him to the core. "After all we've been

through, you think I'd really hurt Samantha?" At least she had the decency to look confused. "Lilly, I was just joking. I wouldn't harm Samantha. I don't know what's going on with her, but after what she did for you the night Joshua was born, I wouldn't be much of a man if I hurt her. But I'm not saying I haven't been tempted to tie her to a tree." He smiled.

"Oh," she said in a breathy expulsion of air.

He reached for the rake she still held. When she didn't let go, he raised an eyebrow at her.

"You can let go now. It looks like I came home in the nick of time."

Lilly relinquished the rake, dropping her hands to fidget with the seams of her jeans. She was tired—he could see it in her eyes and in the set of her shoulders. Not that she would admit it. That would mean she was in need of help. He was quickly recognizing that she didn't like to admit she needed anything.

"You don't have any business out here trying to clean up a mess like this. Take Joshua and go on home." His words were callous, but the need to protect her was overwhelming. The sooner she went home the better.

When she didn't make a move to leave he dared to look more closely at her. Something more was wrong. The dark circles under her eyes told the story. She was more than tired. She was worn out. Maybe the baby wasn't sleeping. He should have put his foolish feelings aside and gone back down there to help her out as he'd said he would. What kind of neighbor was he anyway? What kind of man was he?

She swallowed hard and shifted from one foot to the other.

"Samantha let one of your horses out."

## Chapter Fourteen

Cort's expression changed faster than she could blink. It was exactly what she'd feared. Why couldn't he have come home an hour or so later? By then she would have located the horse, had everything cleaned up and been home resting with Joshua.

Cort swung around and spotted the empty stall. "Ringo! You know it had to be him," he growled, stalking out of the stable, his expression dark. "Let me guess—he jumped the fence."

Lilly trailed him, nearly running to keep up with him. When he got outside he halted abruptly and she promptly smacked into him.

"Sorry," she said, backing away. "I was going to go after him as soon as I cleaned everything up."

Samantha chose that moment to trot around the corner. She came to a skidding stop, slapped her big ears back against her head, lifted her upper lip, exposing her teeth, and grinned like a chimpanzee.

That was not the thing to do.

Cort snorted and walked past her, but Samantha followed right behind him. Loser trailed after the donkey, snapping at what was left of her tail. Those two were just begging for trouble. Shaking her head, Lilly backtracked to retrieve Joshua so they could tag along, too.

She shouldn't have cleaned up Samantha's mess first. She should have gone after the expensive horse. What if something happened to it? What would she do?

*Please, Lord, let Ringo be okay.*

But what could happen to the horse? He was just out joy running….

He'd already jumped one fence.

Oh, no! What if he was out jumping every fence he encountered? What if they couldn't find him? It wasn't normal for a horse to just jump fences. Did Ringo do this often or had he done it because of being spooked by Samantha? Oh, this wasn't good.

"You don't think he'd jump more fences, do you?" she asked, lifting a hesitant eyebrow when Cort stopped to look back at her.

"All the barbed wire in that section hasn't been changed to pipe, and there are mares on the other side that he might try to get to. If he wants over there bad enough, then he might paw into the wire or run at it and harm himself. Ringo is pretty dense for a horse. If he got too anxious, yes, he might jump again." He disappeared into the tack room, then reappeared a few seconds later with a halter and a rope. With Samantha still trailing him, he headed for his truck.

"Wait for me," Lilly called, hurrying to catch up,

struggling to lug the baby and carrier across the gravel drive.

"No! You go home," Cort snapped, and pointed a long, blunt-nailed finger at Samantha. "And take this bag of trouble with you. It's starting to look like a three-ring circus around here."

Lilly bristled. "Do not tell me what to do, Cort Wells."

Holding open the driver's door, he stopped with one foot in the truck. Loser sailed past him onto the seat, rushing back and forth from him to the passenger's door watching Lilly wrench open the rear door and lift Joshua into the truck.

"At least someone is glad to see us," she muttered, reaching for the seat belt.

Cort stomped around the truck, and Lilly whirled to meet him. Slamming her hands on her hips, she glared up at him. Too tired to care whether he wanted her along or not, she wasn't prepared for the way his nearness supercharged her pulse rate.

"Lilly, this is crazy. You need to take Joshua home and get him out of this weather. It's getting colder and he's probably hungry. If he isn't now, then he will be before we get back."

Now he was trying the bad-mother routine on her! "Wait right here and I'll get his bag."

"Lilly! Take the boy home."

He was so irritating! What was the big deal about them going along? Did he dislike her company that much? Had she imagined that day she walked him to his truck that they were becoming friends? She fought the urge to concede and go home. But he needed her. Whether he thought so or not.

"Cort, what if Ringo gets cut? What if there's blood?"

His eyes stilled, studying hers. His shoulders relaxed a bit as what she was saying sank in. Lilly could feel the tension that continued to radiate from him, but her words had hit their mark and he nodded.

"Get your diaper bag." He took a step back, allowing her room to scoot past him. When her arm touched his, her mouth went dry. Her senses were getting crazy with fatigue.

Trying not to think too much about the sensations assaulting her, she snatched the diaper bag from her truck. Butterflies churned in the pit of her stomach as she made her way back to Cort. He waited beside her door, one hand resting on the top corner as he held it open for her. His other hand was stuck in his back pocket, one booted foot slightly out front, leaving his weight on the back leg. Lilly had seen a hundred other men stand the exact same way and none of them made her pulse skip. Only Cort could do that to her. He was just a man, she told herself. But no other man had ever caused her insides to melt.

She was tired.

That's all it was.

When he reached and took her elbow, she nearly jumped into the seat from the sheer shock of his touch.

Tired. Tired. Tired. The man had touched her before. But this time she'd felt…something. She was tired.

"If I can't beat you I guess I'll have to let you join me." His words slapped her in the face.

What was she kidding herself about? Obviously he got nothing out of touching her. "I reckon that's right." It took all she had to grit the words out as she stared straight ahead. What had she been thinking?

Electricity! Phooey! She was so tired she was just flat-out nutty. And that was all there was to it!

Cort drove through the pasture, figuring Ringo had headed straight toward the west boundary, where he knew he could get into some tomfoolery. He'd done this all the other times that Samantha had let him out, and thankfully, he had yet to get hurt acting silly over a bunch of females. What worried Cort the most was the show he had coming up next week. The last thing he needed were war scars on Ringo from another stallion or barbed-wire tears on his sides or his forelegs.

He should have already taken care of the fence.

Guilt swamped him.

*You shouldn't have been angry at Lilly.*

"Look, Lilly, I shouldn't have gotten angry like that. At you. I'm sorry."

She was sitting rigidly in the seat beside him. Her chin was up as she scanned the pasture in the waning light. Cort's insides were trembling just being near her.

"Fine," she said with a faint nod of her head. "I'll accept your apology if you'll accept mine. I should have taken care of Samantha long ago."

"I told you I'd fix it. And I didn't."

"No matter. Samantha is my responsibility, and I should never have told you I'd let you handle my problem."

The woman had to be the most exasperating female he'd ever met. Stubborn, uncooperative—

"There's Ringo!" Lilly exclaimed, pointing out across the pasture. "Oh, my! Cort, don't look…."

Fainting wasn't macho.

Not that he'd ever worried about that too much. But it was hard on a guy's ego.

Since he'd known Lilly, it seemed that he'd spent more time on the ground than at any time in his life.

Thank goodness he hadn't fainted this time. Only because it was twilight and Ringo's coat was as dark as blood, and Lilly's warning had given him time to say a prayer. God had been faithful.

Ringo's injury turned out to be merely a deep scratch on his nose that bled profusely. Lilly might be stubborn and uncooperative, but she had a beautiful heart. Warm and caring were the two adjectives he'd left off earlier. She'd felt terrible for Ringo.

Her compassion for the horse touched him. She'd been persistent, insisting that she help care for the wound.

She'd driven him mad with her nearness. The more he was around her, the more he liked her. The more he liked her, the more certain he was she needed lots of children. She had a heart for loving.

It was evident in everything she did. Loser wasn't even the same dog he'd been a month ago. That dog followed her around as if he worshiped the ground she walked on. And if he wasn't following her around he was plopped beside the baby carrier watching Joshua.

"Yep, boy, they're pretty special," Cort said, driving back up the road to his house after following Lilly and Joshua home. He'd insisted on making sure they got home safely and into the house. Lilly was worn out. It was nearly nine by the time they'd cleaned Ringo's wound, and he wanted to do everything he could to make sure she and Joshua were protected.

He hadn't been able to keep from giving Lilly a hug before he left her at her door. It had been a long day of fighting off the need, and when it came down to it he just had to give in. She actually looked as if she needed a hug.

Her look of surprise lingered. She had been wonderful taking care of the cut, making sure Cort didn't look at the dried blood, instead sending him to tend to Joshua.

He couldn't help the hug. Anyone as dedicated as she'd been deserved more than a hug, but he didn't have a medal, and he didn't think she'd appreciate a kiss.

Though a kiss was exactly what he'd wanted to give her, he didn't think he could survive it. So he'd hugged her, and told himself it was simply a friendly hug, that it didn't mean anything.

But he was beginning to understand that he was on sinking ground.

Because watching her in action—tending to his horse, loving his dog and mothering her son—cemented Cort's resolve that Lilly was indeed a woman who needed children. She was made to give love and tenderness.

But none of his arguments could compete with how right it felt when he held her in his arms. Nothing else had ever compared to that feeling.

Sunday morning dawned bright and sunny. Lilly had been up practically all night. Joshua wasn't sleeping worth a penny, as Granny Bunches would have said. He'd cried most of the time, even when she sat in the recliner with him. Rubbing his tummy hadn't helped. Giving him a tiny dose of oil in his water hadn't helped, either, along with a host of other remedies she knew of for his little cramped stomach. Nothing helped.

She'd paced the house with him on her shoulder and prayed for hours. Samantha had circled the house looking in every window as she made the rounds from room to room. When Joshua's cries became exceptionally loud, she would smush her nose to the window and grunt. Lilly understood the sentiment well. Joshua's little tears had ceased finally, about the time the sun rose over the hill. Lilly's tears, though, had just gotten started.

Raising a baby alone was scary.

What did she know?

She'd thought about calling Norma Sue, but felt silly not being able to take care of a normal case of baby colic. She sniffed, running a shirtsleeve across her eyes.

She'd decided she was going to be on Norma's doorstep within the next few minutes if Joshua hadn't finally found relief and gone to sleep.

Lilly laid Joshua in his bed, closed the door and went to take a shower. She could see how easy it would be to get depressed when someone had had as little shut-eye as she'd been getting. She used to wonder why God made people need sleep. There were too many things she wanted to do in a day, sleep being the least of those things. She'd learned to live on little more than five hours a night. And liked it that way.

Now she daydreamed about sleep. She was a walking zombie.

Lilly had calculated the amount of rest she'd gotten in the past four days and it had been about three, maybe four hours a day. And those had been sporadic catnaps caught between Joshua's eating, sleeping and crying. So much for the traditional dinner she'd thought about cooking.

She relaxed her head against the shower tile and let the hot water soothe her muscles. She'd promised the ladies that she would take Joshua to church for the first time today and stay afterward for dinner in the small fellowship hall at the back of the building. She was so tempted to stay home and try to get a few moments of shut-eye. He was sleeping right now. The temptation to stay home was strong.

But she'd promised. She knew the ladies would be upset if they realized what a hard time she was having and that she hadn't asked for help. And she knew she could do this.

Yes, she could do this, she told herself again an hour later. It was ten-thirty. Sunday school started at ten o'clock...so she'd missed that, but she could make it to the morning service. She had prepared a bean casserole, and carried it out to the truck, and now she was gathering up all the stuff she would need for the morning. It felt as if she was moving away for a week! Or a month, she thought as she walked outside manhandling the playpen.

Opening the tailgate, she lifted the medium-sized thingamajig—oh, her mind was losing it. She couldn't even remember something as simple as *playpen* because she was so worn out. She had become a mumbling mess with lack of sleep. She would have laughed at herself—if she hadn't been so stinking tired. She was actually being worse than Esther Mae with word flubs. And that was sad.

Slamming the tailgate shut, she went back inside, and gathered the formula bottles she'd prepared. She also grabbed the diaper bag, making certain it had baby wipes and cream and a couple of changes of clothes.

Oh, and toys.

Oh…diapers! She'd almost forgotten the diapers!

She carried her load out to the truck, then headed back inside. She couldn't believe she'd forgotten to pack diapers.

Samantha had been trotting back and forth between each trip like a mother hen. Her frayed tail was wagging and her ears were perked and white smoke blew from her nostrils in the cold morning air. She waited at the back door and patiently peeked through the screen. Lilly knew if she'd really wanted to, the little burro would have opened the door with her talented lips and followed her inside.

Thankfully Leroy had realized Samantha needed to stay outside. Using cookie power, he'd trained her to wait beside the door for her treat. Stopping in the kitchen, Lilly grabbed her special donkey treat as she made the final trip, carrying Joshua and his baby carrier outside.

The expectant burro snapped up the banana Laffy Taffy and Lilly paused to watch the fuzzy girl smack away on the sweet treasure.

Their mutual love of the yellow candy stemmed from the many times in her childhood when Lilly would share her candy with Samantha as she listened to Lilly chatter about anything and everything.

They both had saddlebags to prove their love for the chewy treat.

Lilly really had to limit her own intake of the appealing taffy because of the baby weight she was struggling to lose.

Oh yeah, the dumpy, lumpy, leftover baby fat that clung to her short, stubby thighs. But that was another story.

Being tired certainly didn't bring out her sunny disposition, she thought a few moments later, driving down the dirt road. What had happened to her? Good question. She was just too tired to figure it out. It was taking all the energy she had to keep her eyes open and her focus on the road. Finding herself would just have to wait until after church, dinner, Joshua's feeding and the chores she still had to do around the farm after she arrived back home in the late afternoon.

Lilly hoped she didn't fall asleep during the service.

Her first Sunday back in church, it wouldn't do to fall asleep on the pew. She chuckled when a picture of her limp, snoring form sprawled on the back pew popped into her furry brain. Fuzzy brain…well, maybe she'd meant furry because her brain was a bit past foxy-fuzzy. Oh, man…her brain was just plain fried. Pure and simple.

## Chapter Fifteen

Cort stepped up onto the porch of the country church, took his hat off and sucked in a deep cold breath. Clint Matlock had stopped by the house and invited him to church and lunch. At first Cort had told him he had things to do—which he did, but nothing was pressing. Since Ringo was still healing, he had no competitions pending. He had time on his hands and he should use that time to get back to attending church each week.

Besides, Cort liked Clint. They were around the same age, give or take a few years, and they had hit it off standing in the yard, each of them with a boot propped up on the rear bumper, their arms resting on the tailgate. Clint had apologized for not coming out sooner to invite him, but explained that he'd been in court for a couple of weeks, helping prosecute some rustlers who had stolen from him a few months back. The case had taken a long time to come to trial because the same rustlers were charged in other cases, as well, and Clint had been tangled up pretty heavily in all of the messy proceedings.

Impressed by Clint's sincere invitation, Cort had promised to visit the church. It had been a while since he'd set foot inside a church building, and he had to admit he was nervous. But he was also determined to get his walk with the Lord back on a strong path.

Hesitating outside the door, he scanned the long narrow parking lot. Lilly's truck, parked at the back near a small outer building, caught his attention. It took him a second to realize that Lilly was still in the truck, or at least he thought it was her. The door was open and she was on her knees in the seat with her back to the door. From where he was standing it looked as if she was pulling on something with every ounce of strength she had. Setting his Stetson back on his head, he headed in her direction. He'd wondered if she went to this church, but he hadn't expected that she'd be the first person he encountered. His conscience pricked him about their last meeting. He'd been avoiding her again. He wasn't proud of it, but he was flat-out running scared.

She was in the seat. Since she was scrunched up, her dress flowed from beneath her coat over her hips and hung over her shoes. The hem jiggled every time she tugged at the seat belt that restrained the baby carrier.

"Click-in, click-out…yeah, right," she was grumbling as he placed a hand on the door frame. He held back a chuckle when she expelled an exasperated breath, then tugged again. "Come on!"

"My, my, are we in a bad mood?"

She screamed, spinning around so fast she bumped

her head on the rearview mirror. Her expression was comical infuriation. "Oh, it's you! You scared me."

"Are you okay?"

Slumping in the seat, she gently rubbed her temple. "When my heart stops banging against my ribs I'll let you know. You sure know how to snare a girl."

Cort filtered what she'd said. "Excuse me?"

"I mean scare a girl. Satan is trying mighty hard to make me turn this truck around and head home. But," she said, smiling and holding up her hand in a stop motion, "I'm not buying it. I've worked too hard just to get to the parking lot. I'm not turning back now when I have the church in my sights. Do you know how much stuff you have to pack just for a trip to town when you have a baby? I'm telling you, after all the trouble it took to get here…before I'd hang 'em up and head home, I'd sit in this parking lot just to snow—show the old man that I'm not letting him get me down."

Cort smiled. "I bet you would. Can I try and free Joshua's carrier for you?"

Lilly's smile broadened, lighting her eyes with warmth. "Joshua and I would greatly appreciate that. I don't know if you've noticed, but I'm trapped, too. I caught my skirt in the…the thingamajig." She waved her hand at the seat-belt clasp. "The clasp. I'm a little tired. As you can tell."

Cort took his Bible from under his arm and set it on the truck's hood. He knew he was treading on thin ice, liking the light in her eyes, but today he was going to try again to just be a neighbor and a friend.

He leaned across Lilly, pressed the buckle release

hard and pulled. Nothing happened. The soft smell of something sweet wrapped around him and it was all he could do not to turn toward Lilly and breathe deeply. "You ever had trouble with this before?"

He'd thought about her every day. Every hour.

"No, I don't know what I did. I was in a hurry trying to goad, I mean, load all the things I would need for Joshua during church and I don't know…somehow I caught my skirt and jammed everything."

He turned his head and looked into her eyes. They were mere inches apart. He could just lean in and kiss her. She took his breath away.

*Stop it, Cort.*

He fumbled with the clasp and pushed the thought from his mind. He concentrated, pressed hard and yanked. The clasp relaxed, freeing the carrier. And him. "There it goes. You're good to go now. I think it just jammed when you pushed it in, and you needed a little more muscle than you have to release it." He stepped back and held a hand out to her as she slipped off the seat.

"I'll carry him," he said when she turned to reach for Joshua. She nodded and moved out of his way while he lifted the carrier out of the truck, watching not to bump it on the sides of the door. He didn't want to disturb Joshua's contentment.

"Thank you. If you'll hold him for a sec, I'll grab the rest of his stuff." She stretched into the cab and pulled out a huge yellow striped bag with a big green frog sitting at the bottom corner. As she slung it over her shoulder, it looked bigger than she was. "There, all set," she said, holding out her hands for the carrier.

Cort shook his head. "I told you I'll carry Joshua. This thing is bigger than you."

She chuckled. "I have muscles from carrying Samantha's feed."

They'd started walking toward the church and Lilly held up her arm to show her pea-sized muscle hidden beneath her coat. Cort grinned, then stepped up onto the porch and paused outside the door. He could hear music inside. They were late, but he needed to say something first.

"Lilly, I'm sorry I didn't take care of all those chores for you. I told you I'd carry her feed. From now on there's no need for you to carry anything that heavy. I don't mind helping you, and I'm sorry I haven't come by more often. I keep telling you that and I haven't done it yet. But starting now, things are going to change. I'm coming down this afternoon to help you."

"Thank you very much for your offer, Cort. But I can manage."

"Anybody ever tell you it's okay to need help every once in a while?"

"Cort, you moved here and immediately started being harassed by my donkey, then you had to put up with me having my baby, and then my donkey harassed you some more. The last thing you need is for me to keep calling you to my rescue."

He cut in on Lilly's runaway explanation. "Lilly, I didn't mind my part in the baby delivery. I keep telling you, and you don't seem to understand I was privileged to be able to help you in that situation. I'd hate to think what would have happened if I hadn't been there. Again, blowing up at you the other day wasn't right, especially since you were coming to my rescue with Ringo. Even after I was rude—"

"No," she interrupted.

How was he going to get through to her?

"I thought after the other night we were past all of this."

"Past what?"

"I thought we were friends." Friends? Was that what they were? Had they finally made it to friends? "But I guess not."

The door to the sanctuary opened, halting all conversation as a prune-faced older man stared at them with condemning eyes. Only then did Cort realize that the music had stopped and the entire congregation had turned to see what the ruckus was all about.

"Oops," Lilly quipped.

Yep, that about said it all. Cort wanted to crawl into the shrubbery and disappear. His first visit to the church and he'd disturbed the entire proceedings.

"Well, don't stand there gawkin'. Come on in."

Cort couldn't help a double take at the *happy* greeter as he motioned them inside. Sure, Cort couldn't blame the man for his sour appearance, but *really*…the man looked as if he bit lemons in two for a living. And he was the greeter. Somebody needed to do a rethink on that one.

"Sorry, Mr. Thornton," Lilly whispered, stepping inside and patting the man on the coat sleeve.

Carrying Joshua, Cort followed her inside. Lilly started down the aisle looking for a vacant pew and he followed, more than likely looking a little sour himself.

"Glad you two could join us." The booming voice drew Cort's attention to the jovial man standing in the pulpit. "Lilly, while you three get settled why don't you go ahead and introduce your guest to those who may not yet have had the opportunity to meet him?"

Lilly screeched to a halt. "Oh, hi, everyone." She gave a little wave and ducked her head slightly. "This is Cort Wells. He recently bought Leroy's place."

Cort looked around the room, relieved to see smiling faces. Many he remembered from the dinner theater. He nodded his head. If he hadn't been holding Joshua he might have turned and walked out. If there was one thing he wasn't used to it was being the center of attention. And this would qualify hands down. Lilly didn't act as if she liked it too much, either. She'd said she was a loner. Maybe he should stay by her side. Give her a little support.

"We didn't mean to disturb the services," he said.

"Nonsense," the pastor said. "We're happy you wanted to join us this morning. We are especially privileged to have the man who watches over Lilly and Joshua in our midst. Everyone stand and greet Cort and Lilly as we sing 'When We All Get to Heaven.' Oh, and don't forget to say hello to Joshua."

Lilly's eyes were twinkling when she looked up at him. "Smile, Cort, and say hello," she said with a wink just as they were engulfed.

Cowboys came from everywhere, and a few women. Cort was swarmed by hugs and handshakes, a few rowdy slaps on the back and congratulations.

In the midst of it all Clint Matlock stuck his hand out. "Glad you made it, Cort. Lilly, too. And the baby. I hope y'all are planning on staying for lunch."

"Thanks, I thought I would. I—I'm glad to be here," Cort stammered as the full force of Clint's welcome hit him. Everyone moved back to their seats, and Cort slid in next to Lilly. Joshua was on her other side and didn't give him a buffer.

Did everyone here think he and Lilly were a couple? Clint thought so. He'd said *y'all,* as in the three of you. Reaching up, Cort inserted two fingers between his throat and his shirt and tie to loosen it. He didn't need Mule Hollow to put them together. A couple of friends, yes. He was having a hard enough time keeping his mind from wishing Lilly and Joshua could be his. The last thing he needed was an entire town, already caught up in matchmaking fever, to put their sights on them.

His resolve to do the right thing might not hold up under too strong an assault. Lilly was hard enough to resist on her own. Throw in Mother Nature and crazy Samantha's antics and he was sinking fast.

The last thing he needed was Mule Hollow getting in on the act.

# Chapter Sixteen

Lilly found a spot near the back of the room and waited for Cort to bring in the playpen. Lacy was holding Joshua, swinging him in her arms from side to side as if she was doing the twist.

"So, how's the romance going?"

Leave it to Lacy to cut to the chase. Lilly met Lacy's electric blue eyes—eyes zinging with mirth.

Honestly, Lilly didn't know how to answer the question. How was the romance going? Did they have one brewing? Did she want one to brew? She tore her gaze from Lacy's and watched Cort moving toward them, plowing through the group like a freight train barreling down the track. Oh, he was something. He could send her pulse racing like…well, like that freight train he resembled at the moment. He could also infuriate her. But he could melt her with a smile. As for romance…he didn't know she existed. She was simply the neighbor down the road he thought needed a helping hand. "There's no—"

Lacy cut her off, handing over Joshua. "Nope. Don't even deny it. Take the baby and enjoy some time with the man. You can try to deny it all day long, Lilly, but God has a plan. And I'm here to tell you that it's walking straight toward you carrying your baby's playpen. I think the luck of the Tipps ladies has turned for the better."

Lilly cradled Joshua next to her heart, watching Lacy stride away toward the food tables. Passing Cort, she slapped him on the back.

"Mighty nice of you to help out, Cort," she sang out, and kept on going.

"Did I miss something?" he asked, setting the playpen down beside Lilly.

"When it comes to Lacy Brown, we're all missing something. That girl has more zip and zing than anybody I know. She makes a tired gal like me feel like a worn-out dish towel." She also made a tired girl think. Or dream. Lilly pushed away the silly thoughts and swiped at her curly hair with the back of her hand.

Cort's hand touched hers as he reached to touch the stray curl dangling in her eye. Lilly swallowed and met his eyes as he gently pushed the piece to the side. His fingertips brushed her temple, then traced down the side of her face to cup her jaw. "Believe me, Lilly. You don't remotely resemble an old dish towel."

The touch of his fingertips froze Lilly's breath in her lungs, and his eyes reached into that dark corner of her heart that she'd been guarding so ferociously. What did she do now? Her sluggish mind was just playing tricks on her. Mean tricks.

As quickly as his touch appeared, it vanished. He

withdrew his hand, tucking his fingertips into his jeans pocket. An unreadable expression flickered across his face. And then it was as if nothing had just passed between them.

"Thank you for the compliment. I think." She forced her voice to sound nonchalant. He couldn't know that he'd just rocked her world. Flipped it like a pancake—a pancake that wasn't ready to be flipped.

He was grinning that half smile of his that she had come to know, kind of a Dennis Quaid half grin that carved a vertical groove from his cheek to his jawline along the right side of his face. It was a look that would melt hearts.

"It was definitely a compliment. Here, sit down before you fall down." He pulled out a chair, gently grasped her arm and helped her sit while she continued to hold Joshua. Her entire being was tuned to him as he went about setting up the playpen.

*Get a grip, Lilly! You're made of tougher stuff than this.*

And she was. She reeled in her emotions and focused on instructing Cort on how to open and set up the playpen.

"Are you getting any sleep?" he asked when he finally finished and held out his arms for Joshua.

"What happened to the real Cort Wells, the one who was afraid to hold a baby?"

His eyes darkened and he frowned. "Good try at changing the subject. You need help. And I'm here. Now, hand him over and you rest. Me and Joshua are becoming fast buddies."

Lilly relinquished Joshua to him. "I'm very glad you're here. I didn't mean to sound like I wasn't." His expression was one of complete concentration as he carefully accepted Joshua. Once he held him, he simply stood looking at him. Lilly's eyes teared up, watching his face change from deep concern to a gentle softening. She wondered what he was thinking. What was going on behind those beautiful dark blue eyes of his? So many times she'd thought about how he'd looked holding her son that night in her living room. It seemed so long ago.

When he shifted his gaze from Joshua, his eyes were bright. Lilly's heart skipped and held. Cort Wells, the man everyone had labeled a grinch, was truly touched while he held her Joshua. Tears…his eyes were bright with tears.

"I knew what you meant," he said quietly. "I'll just lay him down in here." He started to bend, then stopped. "Do you think I need to put a blanket down?"

It was all Lilly could do to hold back the emotions engulfing her. She was in a tidal wave being swept into deep water. She struggled to form coherent words. "Yes. Here, I have it in the bag." Grabbing the bag, she pulled out the thin frog-covered yellow blanket. Jumping to her feet, she hastily spread it on the bottom of the small pen and watched Cort gently start to deposit her child onto the soft nest.

He was bent over the crib holding Joshua inches from the blanket when he turned his head and looked up at her.

"On his stomach or his back?"

Lilly's heart rolled over and gave up the ghost. "His back, please. He'll look kind of like I did on our first meeting in your barn."

Cort chuckled, then placed Joshua onto his back, pulling the blanket over his little body. Before he straightened he gently ran his fingers over Joshua's hair.

It was all Lilly could do not to make a fool of herself by jumping up and hugging Cort.

"So do they eat all the time?"

Lilly looked about the room as folks piled their plates full. Roy Don had a plate that looked like the leaning tower of *potbellies* as he strode by, beelining for a chair so he could dig in to the massive feast.

"Not really. They try to have a church fellowship every month. As you can tell, if they did it every week there wouldn't be a lot of room in this building, because everyone would have gained a hundred pounds!" She leaned in and whispered, wrinkling her nose, "I really don't think people eat this much at home."

Cort hoped not. Pulling himself away from the urge to lean in closer to Lilly, he tilted his chair back on two legs and surveyed the group. "It's nice. I never attended many fellowships where I used to go to church."

"This is actually only my second time."

"Really? I figured you'd be right in the middle of all this."

"Nope." She glanced around, then looked at him. "I told you I'm a loner by nature. I come to church, sing in the choir, then go home. The gals are all trying to force me to mingle."

"Are you serious?" Cort didn't see her as a complete loner. Maybe that explained her reason for continuing to live all alone out where she lived. It made him all the more curious about her past. "I remember Lacy saying something about trying to get you to participate more."

"Mmm-hmm. It's a good thing, too, because I talk to myself sometimes. And that's bad." She yawned. "I'm really afraid I might conk out before this ends."

Cort stood. "Come on, let's go get us a pile of food. That might wake you up." He held out his hand and helped her up.

She glanced over at Joshua, who was snoring away. "Look at him. Just as content as can be now that I'm somewhere I can't catch a nap."

"It's because I held him."

Lilly looked up at him and frowned. "Yeah, right."

He laughed. "You hurt my feelings. You don't think I have a way with babies?"

"You didn't even know how to hold one until I forced Joshua on you."

"I'm a fast learner."

He placed his hand between her shoulder blades and gently propelled her ahead of him. They took their place in line behind Sam from the diner, and Cort tried not to think of how much he was enjoying spending time with Lilly. He tried not to analyze anything. Just to enjoy the day.

"How's that ornery old Samantha doing?" Sam asked.

"That was some sight—the two of you flying down the street on fire."

"Sam, you know I've been riding since before I could walk. And you know I've ridden all kinds of different-tempered animals."

"I know that. But bein' how you were pregnant and all, I figured them talents of yours should be set aside for later." He looked at Cort. "Ain't it right that you can't ever know what an animal will do?"

"That's about right."

Lilly looked from one to the other, her eyes wide with rebuttal. Cort had come to know that look. On their first meeting he'd thought she was an outspoken person, but he'd learned she sometimes held back. Now there was no hiding the fact she was itching to say something. It was clearly marked across her pretty face and by the way that pert nose of hers crinkled between her eyes.

Cort had come to the realization that some of his earlier assumptions about Lilly were wrong.

She wasn't one-dimensional. She wasn't boring. And she wasn't the negligent person he'd originally believed her to be.

Lilly Tipps had layers.

"Why did you want to be alone?" Lilly lifted an eyebrow and the corners of her mouth in a half grin at Cort's expression of surprise at her bluntness. He'd asked if she'd like to walk for a minute while the ladies were playing with Joshua. The cold air had helped clear the fog from her brain as they slowly circled the church grounds. She'd managed earlier to corral her feelings and had convinced herself that, being as tired as she was, she was simply overwrought emotionally and that was why her heart kept acting so weird when she looked at Cort. Now she wasn't too sure what was what, as Cort studied her for a moment. Finally he shook his head and his blue eyes softened, causing her heart to dip.

"Anyone ever tell you that you're pushy?" he asked.

She laughed, and a zing of energy rippled through her tired body. "Sorry, you have to remember that I was raised by a herd of grandmothers. To say that they were blunt would be an understatement. I have to hold myself back sometimes, because it rubbed off a bit too much on me. Believe me, though, I'm mild in comparison."

"I'd have hated to be a man around all that. How many grandmothers raised you?" Cort picked up a stick and pushed at a fallen leaf. Lilly watched, thinking about the granddads she'd never known. It always brought on a sense of loss. Pushing it from her mind, she smoothed the skirt of her dress and looked out across the church lawn.

"Up until I was twelve I lived with three grandmothers," she said, smiling at the memory of her crazy life. "Then Great-Granny Shu-Shu died at the ripe old age of one hundred. Granny Gab died six years later—she was eighty-one. Then Granny Bunches—who was really my great-aunt, but I always called her Granny—died three years ago. She was ninety." She sighed. "They would have been shocked and in love with Joshua."

She felt Cort's eyes on her and glanced over at him. She saw compassion in his expression.

"I'm sorry for your loss," he said, his tone subdued.

"But that must have been a great thing knowing that many people who loved you."

"It was so wonderful. And *never* boring. My grandmothers were characters."

"What about your grandfathers? You said your grandmothers had no need for men." He quirked an eyebrow.

She quirked one right back at him. "Hey, you said *I* was pushy."

He gave a waggish grin and held up his hands. "I can ask questions, too."

Lilly laughed. "Okay, for the guy who delivered my baby I guess I can tell you my family history. No, there are no grandfathers. They came, they left."

"All that bluntness run them off?"

Lilly knew he was joking, but she had always wondered if that was indeed what had happened. "Maybe."

"All of them? Every last one?" Cort's eyebrows drew together in disbelief. It was a common expression when the luck of the Tipps women was discussed.

"Granny Shu-Shu's husband left for war three years after they were married, and *chose* not to come home. He chose to abandon Granny Shu-Shu and his baby daughters, Gabriella and Beatrice. Granny Gab, my mother's mother—her husband left when he found out she was pregnant. Seems I'm not the only one who forgot to ask about children. They were married five months, and that totally ruined Granny Gab on men. My mother was raised to distrust all men and have no use of them. When my mom died, well, that was it for Granny Gab.

She hated men all my life. Granny Bunches—that was Beatrice—never married. She said she trusted that there was a good man out there for her. She just couldn't distress Gabby anymore by chancing to look."

"How about your marriage?"

Lilly plunked her fist on her hip. "You don't give up, do you?"

He shrugged. "I'm a curious guy. I want to know about my friend."

Lilly started walking again and Cort fell into step beside her. "Like I said, mine lasted just over a month. But it wasn't totally due to my mouth. I think I told you that like Granny Gab I didn't discuss children with my husband. I didn't find out until I told him I was pregnant that he didn't want any." She blinked and looked away from Cort. She didn't want him to see any weakness in her eyes. She'd shed her last tear over Jeff Turner. He was a no-good loser. Exactly the kind of man she'd been warned about all her life. "I think he was just looking for a way to get out of something he'd realized he didn't want. It had only been a month, but he wasn't around much."

A few minutes passed and Cort hadn't said any platitudes. When she looked back at him, he was watching her. He stopped in the middle of the road and turned toward her.

"He was a fool," he said, meeting her eyes dead-on.

Lilly's heart picked up its pace. "I think so. I'd take Joshua over his daddy any day. Truth be told, it took me a few months to move on, but I'm fine now." And she was. "Jeff's the loser in all of this. I'm really trying to trust God and move forward." She'd been thinking the past few days about how she wasn't going to be like her grannies. True, she'd spouted off some granny euphemisms about how men were not good for much, but she didn't believe that. God had created her especially for someone. And unlike Granny Bunches, she hoped to find him someday.

She wasn't telling anyone that she was looking, though. The way this town had gone matchmaking crazy, she didn't want anybody getting ideas about fixing her up. When the right man came along God would be leading the way, and He wouldn't need any help in the matchmaking business. That's what had happened with Lacy and Clint. Their marriage was coming up in February and God had done a great job bringing Lacy cross-country to plow their cars into each other—and to fall in love.

God was the ultimate matchmaker. And she was going to trust Him.

Looking at Cort and feeling the way her heart was thundering, she wondered if she dared imagine he was already here. That he was the one.

Cort reached out and lifted her chin. "I know he was a fool for leaving Joshua," he said. "But I wasn't talking about the baby. He was a fool for leaving you."

The cold air wrapped around them, and Lilly didn't think she ever wanted to move away from the inviting warmth that radiated from Cort. His eyes searched her face like a caress and his touch against her skin was like a dream. No one had ever looked at her the way Cort did. She blinked back a tear and Cort stepped closer, wiping the tear from her cheek.

"Why are you crying, Lilly?"

She couldn't help it. Why was she crying? Was it because she was tired? Or was it because Cort was giving her a glimpse of what she'd been missing all this time? When he took her in his arms, she thought she would break.

"All men aren't fools." His breath was warm against her ear as he pulled Lilly deeper into his arms. "I know you've had a hard go of things, being on your own all this time. But the grannies were wrong. You were meant to be loved."

Lilly lifted her face to his, her heart pounding in her chest. Could it be?

"Lilly." He set her away from him. "The right man is out there for you, and I believe God's going to send him to you, and you're going to have more little Joshuas to love."

Lilly blinked. She'd thought for a moment he… Lilly sucked in a deep chilling breath of air and wiped the last tear from her eyes. She'd almost made a fool of herself. He'd said they were friends. *Friends?* Of course, comforted friends.

She gave him a smile. It certainly wouldn't do for him to think she'd almost told him she loved him.

Where had that come from anyway? Sure, she'd had thoughts. Infatuations. Who wouldn't toward the man who'd come to her rescue? Who held her baby with tears in his eyes?

"I'm cold," she said, turning back toward the fellow-ship hall. "It's time to go in." Past time.

"You have a beautiful son, Lilly."

Lilly looked at Cort. They had come back inside and had made the rounds chatting with several tables of folks who had settled in for domino challenges. It hadn't taken long for them to end up back at the playpen watching a tuckered-out Joshua sleep. Norma Sue said that everyone had held him and played with him until he'd closed his little eyes and conked out on them.

Studying Cort, Lilly couldn't help but feel a surge of sadness. She'd started out the day totally worn out, wanting to hole up at her house and not go to church and dinner. But she'd had about the nicest day she could remember in ages. She now had a second wind and it was due in large part to Cort. He was a nice guy, but just a friend. Cort was not that much older than her. The most important thing was that he really liked Joshua.

She'd let her thoughts go crazy outside, but now everything was fine. She tucked all the displaced bits of infatuation away and chalked them up to weary emotions. The sadness was probably due to hormones, she thought. That was it. She'd heard they could act crazy after the birth of a baby. He liked her son. And that was all that counted.

Joshua chose that moment to open his eyes and let out a wail. Lilly stood and reached for him. "Whoa, baby!" she exclaimed. "Somebody needs a new diaper. Looks like duty calls."

"I'll go get us a plate of dessert while you take care of

that." Cort made a face when he got a whiff of Joshua. "Whew! Son, you have been a busy boy." Reaching over, he ran two fingers over Joshua's cheek, laughing when Joshua smiled and tried to grab the moving fingers sliding past his mouth. "Looks like he's hungry, too."

"He's always hungry." Lilly watched Cort walk off. Her crazy thoughts were churning again. He was a sweet guy. He made her want to talk, which was nice. She really hadn't had anyone to talk to in a long time, other than Samantha and Joshua. She looked around the room. Lacy, Clint and Hank were laughing at something Esther Mae had said over at the table where the two couples were hard at a game of chicken-foot dominoes. Adela and Sam were chatting with Sherri and J.P. while they all played the game at a table together. Looking farther across the room, she saw many women she'd become friends with, many people with whom she could drive into town and hold a conversation, but the thing was, she was more apt to immerse herself in her books and hide away at home.

She had been forcing herself to get out more in the past three months. And for Joshua's sake she would continue to try to let herself be more outgoing. It was true—she'd been hidden out there at the end of Morning Glory Road all her life. But having a conversation with just anyone wasn't easy for her, never had been. Until she'd met Cort Wells in the middle of his cold barn.

There hadn't been one moment that she'd had a hard time talking with him.

It hit her then that actually she looked forward to having conversations with her neighbor.

That was why her emotions were so crazy. He was her friend.

Her friend who liked her son and thought her ex-husband was a fool.

Her friend who thought she'd find love.

Just not with him.

# Chapter Seventeen

After lunch Norma Sue produced a volleyball and instructed a group of guys on setting up the netting. It was a pretty exciting moment for the church to realize they were actually having a church social *and* volleyball. Even if it was forty-five degrees outside.

"Why," Esther Mae huffed, "it's almost like the old days when we had children running wild around here and Norma Sue yelling for everyone to line up so she could divide up the teams. Y'all better watch out, 'cause when she comes out of the bathroom wearing those pedal pushers that touch the rim of her boots it's gonna be an all-out war. You might not know it, but that little ball of butter used to be a volleyball-playing machine."

Lilly and Cort were almost rolling on the floor laughing with the others when Norma Sue walked out in a pair of blue capris and flat-soled roping boots! She was grinning from ear to ear when she came to a halt in front of all of them, slammed her hands onto her rounded hips and shot a dour look at Esther.

"I know you all've been laughin' about me 'cause of something Esther Mae spouted off. That's okay, 'cause I'll meet you outside—" she jerked her head to the side toward the net "—and teach you that this old lady can still serve a volleyball up with a mean overhand."

"That's more than I can do," one of the young cowboys mumbled. "I've never played this game in my life."

"You're on my team, then." Reaching down, Norma grabbed his arm and tugged him up. "You, too, Cort Wells."

Cort frowned, and Lilly thought if he could have dug a hole and crawled into it he would have. He started shaking his head, but Norma was having none of it. She had one stunned cowboy standing beside her and it was obvious she planned on having another.

The funniest thing of all was that most of the guys were wearing jeans and boots. Many of them had changed into old blue jeans and T-shirts, but there were a few like Cort who still wore their good boots, starched jeans, long-sleeved Western dress shirts—and their belts and big buckles. They were definitely not dressed for volleyball.

Did Norma care? Not one bit.

Before it was all said and done, Lilly watched her, looking like an army sergeant, directing a failing squad trying to go AOL…no, that wasn't it.

AMUCK? Nope, that wasn't it either.

AWOL? Maybe that was it.

What were those initials they used in the military? Her declining brain couldn't come up with the correct letters, but she knew whatever they were they meant AWAY.

The guys were trying to get *away* very quickly from playing out in the cold.

But in the end Norma had them all having a great time. Even dressed in their Sunday-go-to-meetin' clothes, as Applegate Thornton put it.

You could bet he wasn't out there getting red faced and stirred up.

Then again, Lilly didn't care. She was watching Cort and trying to reestablish boundaries that she'd almost let her heart cross. She was glad to have him as her friend.

And for now that was good enough.

"That doesn't sound right," Cort said. They were getting ready to leave the church and head home. It had been an unusual day.

Walking over to the window of Lilly's truck, he listened to the engine grind as she tried to start it.

He'd helped her load everything into the ancient truck, said a reluctant goodbye, then stepped back and waited for her to start the cold engine. He couldn't remember the last time he'd had so much fun. Between enjoying being around Lilly and being goaded into behaving like a teenager by Norma Sue, he'd relaxed and found himself thanking the good Lord for leading him to Mule Hollow.

Of course, he wasn't allowing himself to have any misguided feelings along the lines of pushing past a growing friendship with his incredible neighbor. He'd had to rein in his runaway feelings when he'd held her in his arms. Her tears had had him crazy with feelings of protection. But he reminded himself that enjoying a woman's company didn't mean he was thinking about getting married. No matter how strong the feelings of wanting to protect and care for her were.

He couldn't help smiling as Lilly, wrinkled nose and all, leaned her head to one side, her sparkling eyes on him. Eyes that were far too weary.

"I'm too tired to think about this," she said with a sigh.

Cort knew it was true. For a while during the day she'd seemed to get a second wind with all the laughing and kidding that had gone on during the volleyball game. But he could tell she was worn out. The full-time care of having a new baby was showing. That was where the tears had come from when they'd taken their walk. He couldn't let himself think anything other than that. He reached for the door handle and opened the truck. "Come on. Out of the truck. I'm taking you and Joshua home."

"But what about the truck?" she protested even as he was taking her arm and helping her down from the tall seat.

"I'll come back and take care of it in the morning."

"But—"

"No buts, Lilly. It has been a long a day and nobody is going to hurt that truck tonight. The most important thing is you need some rest."

Looking up at him, she stood still for a second, then reached for Joshua. "You're right and I really need to get home. I've got a lot to take care of before the night rolls in."

Cort took her by the arms, turned her toward his truck and gave her a gentle push. "You go there, and I'll bring Joshua and the diaper bag. And I'll do your chores." He was taken by surprise when she turned around and wrapped her arms around his waist.

"Thank you," she said, giving him a quick squeeze then hurrying to his truck.

Cort couldn't move. He stood watching as she opened the door and climbed into the front seat. His heart was banging against his chest, and his senses were reeling from the soft scent of her. When she looked back at him with a quizzical expression, he realized he hadn't moved from where she'd left him stunned and silent. He'd almost crossed the line of friendship earlier when she'd started to cry. It had taken everything he had to focus on what was best for Lilly.

And it had taken a simple hug of gratitude to undo all his hard work.


It was six o'clock when they pulled into Lilly's driveway. She'd rested her head against the seat and immediately fallen asleep. She'd even slept through the bumps in the dirt road. As he brought his truck to a halt next to the tidy house, he couldn't help the feeling of longing that swept over him when he glanced at mother and child sleeping contentedly.

He hated to wake her. "Lilly," he said softly, gently touching her shoulder. Her soft curls had fallen in her face. He pushed them away from her eyes and tucked them behind her ear. "Hey, sleepyhead, it's time to wake up."

She was opening her eyes when he heard the noise. Lilly heard it, too. Her eyes widened and they both jerked their doors open at the same time.

Samantha was in trouble.

The squealing sound wasn't like the awful sound she'd made the first night of their acquaintance. It was more of a whimper. A raspy, honking whimper.

Cort rounded the corner of the barn first, halting when he saw Samantha's head rammed through a spot in the stall gate that had no room for a head the size of Samantha's. How she had accomplished the impossible, Cort would never know. Lilly gasped as she stopped beside him. Her hand came to rest on his arm. Instinctively he covered it with his hand in a comforting and calming effort. They didn't need to overexcite Samantha. Cort had seen horses break their necks in less dire situations.

"Samantha, what have you done?" Lilly said. Her voice was soothingly calm and caused Samantha to focus on her.

Cort let Lilly take a step toward Samantha. He could tell that Lilly understood calm was needed. Reaching out to the burro, Lilly placed her hand on Samantha's head and gently ran a hand down her face. Samantha blinked up at her and tried to nibble at her sleeve.

"We're going to get you out of there, sweet potato. You just need to listen to me and not get excited." Cort watched Lilly and Samantha; it was obvious they had a connection that had come from years of friendship. Cort knew horses, and he knew there was a level of trust that a rider and a horse had to have in order for them to work well together. Cort saw that trust flood into Samantha's eyes when Lilly spoke. He'd known that voice of hers was like magic the first time he'd heard it—now he knew for certain it was. Samantha closed her eyes and stood calmly as he and Lilly wiggled and twisted and pushed her big hairy head all different ways trying to free her from the metal bars.

Working close beside Lilly had Cort wishing he could stand in the barn all night with her. Of course, this wouldn't do, because they had a baby waiting patiently in the truck.

Each of them took turns checking on Joshua during the hour that they worked with Samantha. "I know if she got her head in, then there's a way to get it out." He pushed his hat back on his head and rubbed his chin while he studied the situation. Samantha watched him with steady eyes and pawed her foot. "She's never done this before?"

Lilly rubbed the burro's ear. "She's done a lot of things, but never this. She got stuck in the storeroom once when the door closed behind her *after* she broke in. She had her tail hung in the tailgate of my truck. Oh, and had her topknot of mane caught in the slats of the hay bin." Lilly tousled the wiry patch of long hair that hung down between Samantha's eyes. Samantha rolled her eyes up and looked longingly at Lilly, then spread her lips and showed her big pearly whites.

Cort chuckled. "I really do think this donkey is

human. And for some reason, I think she knows exactly what she's doing."

Lilly glanced up at him. "She might. She's a con artist. Aren't you, Samantha?"

Looking down at Lilly and the smile she flashed at him, he had to corral the overriding need to draw her near.

"Alfalfa!" she exclaimed, sounding as if she'd just sneezed. Slapping him on the shoulder, she said, "We need alfalfa."

"What's on your mind?"

"Give me a second."

She trotted down to the closet door at the back of the barn, then reached up and released the latch that was almost at the top of the door. It wasn't hard to understand why it was up so high. He was going to have to raise his latches higher to keep pesky Samantha out.

A few seconds later Lilly emerged with a bucket of cubes.

Samantha's ears immediately stood at attention. She slapped her tail from side to side and eyed the bucket as Lilly came to a halt in front of her.

"I bet she can get out of there if she wants to."

Cort nodded his head. "Yup, I think you're right. At first I didn't want to startle her, because I thought she would hurt herself. But she's smarter than any horse I've ever known."

Lilly took a cube and held it out to Samantha. She tried to take it in her mouth, but Lilly moved away. Samantha's eyeballs rolled toward Lilly, then back to the alfalfa cube, shot over to Cort then back to Lilly.

She wiggled like a puppy getting a T-bone steak. Cort chuckled. The burro did love her alfalfa.

"Set that bucket down right there," Cort said. Turning away, he walked over to Lilly and took her hand. "Let's go out and see what happens."

"Exactly what I was thinking." Lilly left the bucket on the ground and let him lead the way out of the barn. Once they were out of Samantha's sight, they raced like a couple of kids to the opposite end of the barn and peeked around the corner. Samantha still had her eyes on the bucket, and as they watched she stretched her neck out so that the top of her head sank into her neck—and she slid her head right out from between the bars.

Lilly had already unlatched the gate, so Samantha just gave it a nudge with her nose, then trotted right over to bury her head in the bucket.

"Why, the little sneaky piglet," Lilly gasped.

"I wouldn't have believed it if I hadn't seen it," Cort said in a loud whisper against Lilly's ear. He'd almost missed Samantha's great escape because he'd been too busy studying Lilly's profile. He did a hasty step away from her when she turned her head toward him. It was that step back that saved him. Another second and he'd have placed a kiss on the tip of her perfectly upturned, cute-as-a-button nose. It was getting hard to stop actions that seemed natural. He decided right then and there that when he got home he was going to have a powwow with the good Lord. There were some things that a man couldn't handle on his own and it was time to hit his knees and pray for discernment.

* * *

Cort moved around Lilly's kitchen like a man with a mission. After being tricked by Samantha, Lilly had insisted on fixing Cort dinner. But he wouldn't hear of it and instead had talked her into allowing him to prepare her dinner. She had never before had a man cook for her. She stifled a yawn and hoped she would get to enjoy the masterpiece he was concocting and didn't wind up falling asleep with her face in the plate. It had been a long day, but one of the best in her life. She'd been daydreaming about sleep ever since Joshua's birth, but right now she wanted to do nothing except sit there and enjoy watching Cort. She prayed that the yawns would go away and God would give her a second, no, make that a third wind. Maybe He would allow her to have a moment with this wonderful man. Cort's sweetness was emerging, and she was enamored with it.

"Ketchup?" the wonderful man asked. The smile he gave her was half silly as he slapped a hand towel over his shoulder then headed toward the refrigerator, his eyebrow lifted in question.

"You're getting warm," she teased. Shifting Joshua in her arms, she straightened the bottle so he could get the last of the formula into his growing little tummy.

Cort yanked the fridge door a mite too hard and one of Joshua's formula bottles flew out of the holder on the door straight at him like a fastball.

"Whoa, where'd that come from?" he said, catching it just before it hit the floor.

"I'm prepared. When Joshua wakes at night I'm bumping into walls, so I was afraid to try to mix formula with my mind—let me rephrase that—I was afraid to mix formula *without* my mind. I know I forget words when I'm tired—I don't want to think about what else I might be forgetting."

Cort found the ketchup. He chuckled, turning toward her. Lilly liked his laugh. It was low and gruff, and sent a shiver of delight coursing through her, making her want to do something really funny just to hear it again.

"I'm sure Josh thanks you." Cort dumped a good half cup of ketchup into the dish that Lilly had yet to put a name to, then cracked four eggs on the edge of the skillet, dropping them in one at a time. When he'd finished he took a wire whisk and went to town beating the mixture. She began to think it was some kind of omelet, scrambled. It looked awful, but smelled great.

She'd been thinking about her truck. It couldn't have picked a worse time to conk out on her. "Do you think my truck will be running tomorrow? Joshua has a doctor's appointment in the afternoon."

Cort brought two plates to the table with the scrambled egg mixture and toast. "What time?"

"It's not until three o'clock."

"I'll check it out first thing in the morning after I've exercised my horses. If it's just the battery and I can jump it with battery cables, then you'll be ready to go. If not, then I'll take you to the appointment and pick up the parts I'll need to fix it while you and Joshua are seeing the doctor."

"Oh, no, I couldn't ask you to do that," Lilly exclaimed. His hand on hers halted her protest.

"Lilly, you didn't ask. I offered. When are you going to just let me help because I want to? Besides, as tired as you are, you don't need to be driving all that way alone. It's okay to have a little support."

Lilly's heart melted a little more. He could help her all he wanted.

## Chapter Eighteen

Cort unhooked the battery cables from Lilly's truck.
Once he'd opened the hood of the old truck, it had
been obvious that aside from the fact that she probably
needed a new vehicle, the battery had seen better days.
He couldn't even jump-start it. He didn't know anything
about Lilly's financial situation. He didn't know if she
drove the old truck because she had to or because she
wanted to. He didn't like the idea of her and Joshua
being on the road alone in unreliable transportation.

"Loser, load up," he called out. Loser lay beneath the
oak tree next to the church. Tail dragging, the lazy beast
plodded over to the truck and hopped in. Cort watched
with amusement.

"Perk up, boy, we're going over to Lilly's, and I *know*
you want to see her." Yesterday had been a good day.
No, it had been a great day. No amount of denial could
change the fact that he enjoyed Lilly's company. He
knew it was bad, but he'd been happy when he realized
her battery was in such bad shape, and he'd get to escort

her to Ranger. Lilly and Joshua. Thinking about the little boy put a smile on his face. He'd come a long way since the night Lilly had practically forced him to hold the baby. As if she'd sensed how scared he was, but understood how much he wanted to cuddle the little fella. Now he couldn't wait to have any excuse to be near Joshua and Lilly. His heart was getting involved, and it terrified him.

Basically, he was in a mess. He'd spent time in prayer and in searching his Bible that morning looking for some kind of peace about what God wanted from him. But God answered prayers in His time and Cort had come away empty-handed.

So he'd come up with a plan of his own while waiting on the Lord's plan to reveal itself. Obviously he'd been put there to watch over Lilly and Joshua, so he would. He'd help out when they needed him. He'd look out for their well-being. God had actually given him a gift. He could be like an uncle to Joshua. All he had to do was remember that anything more than friendship with Lilly would not be in the best interests of Lilly and Joshua.

Lilly had said she'd made a mistake in choosing her first husband. Sweet Lilly, sheltered by her grannies. Her ex-husband had, in Cort's mind, taken advantage of her limited experience. If Cort's purpose was to be there to help protect them, so be it. The next bozo that came to fix Lilly's roof or anything else was going to have to pass through him to get to her.

Unless Cort thought his intentions were honorable.

Then it would be in Lilly's best interests for Cort to step out of the way.

He started his truck and backed out of the drive as he glanced heavenward. God would give him the strength to do what he needed to do. He'd struggled since Ramona left. He'd become less and less inclined to seek after God, to really rely on Him. His anger at all that had happened had put a gulf between them. Last night he'd taken a step toward reconnecting with God. He'd felt God's presence beside him and Lilly as they stood together in the churchyard. It had been God who'd enabled him to focus on being Lilly's friend.

He'd understood while looking into her sad eyes that God was with him. Because if he'd been relying on his strength alone he'd have said things to her yesterday that would only have messed up her life later on.

No matter how confused his life seemed, Cort knew and believed that God had a plan. He just had to keep treading water until he found solid ground.

Samantha was sitting on the side of the road between his and Lilly's house as Cort drove down the long, lonesome dirt road. She looked like a big dog relaxing on its haunches beneath the branches of an oak tree. A long blade of hay stuck from her mouth and she chewed it slowly, watching as Cort eased his truck up beside her.

Loser leaped through the open window and thudded to the ground at Samantha's feet like a bag of rocks.

Samantha looked down her broad nose at him sprawled out before her and continued chewing on the stalk of hay as if nothing unusual had just happened.

Cort propped his arm on the door and watched the

pair. They had a connection. He wasn't sure where it would lead, but just seeing Samantha perk up Loser was a kick in the pants. As he watched, Loser rolled over, picked himself up off the ground and, lifting his head, sniffed at the hairy chin of the burro before circling her in wary discovery. When he got too close Samantha bumped him with her nose and kept on chomping. Cort laughed. They were quite a pair.

Putting the truck in gear, he left Loser to walk the rest of the way to Lilly's. Exercise would do the lazy pooch some good. And maybe he'd learn to be civil to Samantha.

It was a nice day for a drive. The weather was cold but the sun was out. Cort liked this temperature. In the summers he had to rise before dawn so he could have his stables completely ridden before noon, just so the heat wouldn't overcome him. This was a time of year the horses loved, and he could get more out of them when they were happy. Today was a breezy, perfect day. A perfect day for a ride into town with Lilly.

Lilly was waiting when he pulled up to the house. She had on tan pants and a green shirt that brought out the gold flecks in her eyes. Her hair was loose, touching the collar of her coat, and it swayed with the breeze as she walked toward him carrying Joshua in the heavy car seat. Cort hopped from the truck to help.

"Hey, cowboy," she said as he took the carrier out of her hands. "Do you think I'm too weak to carry that?"

He smiled. She thought she was Mighty Mouse. "Nope, just don't want you carrying it while I'm around.

Did you get any sleep? You look good." He was rewarded with a pretty blush.

"As a matter of fact, I did. When he woke the first time I cheated and gave him a little baby rice with his formula like Esther Mae told me to do. He loved it. He slept the rest of the night. I think the poor boy was starving. Of course, when I woke up this morning I was scared to death that something was wrong. But he was just as happy as a clam when I charged into his room."

"Well, that sounds promising."

Lilly beamed, her eyes brighter with the extra rest. "Now, I just hope the doctor doesn't get mad at me."

Cort clicked Joshua into the backseat. When he turned and closed the door Lilly was standing beside him. He had to fight the urge to hug her. She smelled so good, like fresh soap and baby powder. He opened the passenger's door and forced himself to merely hold out his hand for hers. She looked at his hand, then back at his face.

When she lifted her hand and placed it in his, their eyes met and held for the briefest moment. In that second he wished…but it could never be right, so he pressed the wish away.

"You know," she said, looking away and climbing into the cab, "your cooking for me last night was a first. And all this helping me into the truck—I wonder if any of my grannies ever had a man do this sort of thing for them?"

Cort shrugged. "My mother taught me to open

doors for ladies. She would have skinned me alive if I hadn't."

A tiny smile quirked the corners of her mouth. Cort closed the door, jogged around to his side of the truck and climbed in. Lilly was an unusual woman brought up by unusual women. Her story intrigued him as much as she did. He couldn't imagine how a man could walk out on a woman carrying his child, how he could marry her and not treat her right. How he could do any of those things when that woman was Lilly was especially bizarre.

"You have everything you need?" he asked, determined more than ever to show Lilly she was special and deserved to be treated that way. Friends could do that.

"I'm wonderful. Thanks. Oh, Cort, look!" she exclaimed, pointing toward the road. Samantha was moseying up the drive with Loser trailing right behind her. They had the slow rhythm of lumbering elephants. It was pathetic.

"Loser has come to visit!" Lilly exclaimed, opening the truck door. She hopped out and jogged over to the dejected animals, giving each of them a hug.

Cort laughed, watching Loser wiggle like crazy. Why, the tangled heap of depression practically had his tongue hanging out. No, he *did* have his tongue hanging out lapping at Lilly's face, making her laugh out loud while dodging his wet kiss. When he tried to put his paws on her, Cort decided it was time he corralled his pet.

By the time he made it to her side Loser had knocked her to the ground.

"What do you feed this animal?" she squealed,

pushing at the dog, laughing so hard she was making little progress at keeping the excited mutt at bay.

"Obviously not the right thing, according to his manners. Loser! No."

Reaching down, he took Lilly's hand and pulled her off the ground. Her eyes were twinkling and she didn't seem upset by the dust that clung to her. Instead she slapped her hands on her pant legs as dust rose in a plume about her.

"Loser sure knows how to mess a girl up."

He wanted to tell her that nothing could mess her up, but he couldn't say that. "He's a goofball," he said instead, then reached to pluck a piece of grass off her forehead. "Missed a piece." His fingers found their way back to the curl that dangled over her eye. She swallowed hard, looked away and took a step back.

Cort's survival instinct held him firmly to the ground she'd retreated from, and he stuffed his fingertips into the edge of his jeans pockets. "We'd better hit the road or we'll be late."

She nodded. "My grannies would be shamed by my struggles to be on time lately. But I had to say hi to Loser. He's my buddy and I haven't seen him much. Unlike Samantha, he doesn't come visiting. I smile every time I remember how nervous he was on the wild ride to town to deliver Joshua. I think he was worse than an expectant father."

Cort led the way back to the truck, remembering not only Loser but the entire night. "He was pretty bad. But at least he didn't faint."

That got him a huge grin. "Ah, don't beat yourself up

about that. It was cute and terrifying at the same time. I doubt anyone had more excitement during a delivery than me. My gosh. What a night."

"Yeah, what a night."

They stood there grinning at each other, sharing a moment that connected them forever. Cort was the first to clear his throat and move back toward the truck. "I guess we better go."

"Yeah. Can't have the baby being late for his appointment."

Determined to stay focused, he loaded up and headed toward Ranger. Despite the friction bouncing between them, a shallow ease nestled about them as the miles ticked by. Cort liked the straightforward way that Lilly had of talking to him. She was funny and smart. They were about halfway to Ranger when he asked her how she supported herself. He knew the small operation she had going on at her farm wouldn't be able to do it. He was being nosy, but at this point he didn't care. His curiosity was getting the better of him.

"Besides leasing some of my land to my neighbor on the far side of me, and my pitifully small cattle operation, I keep the books for some of the ranchers around here and put together cattle sales catalogs for a man out of Ranger and another fella out of San Angelo. It keeps me busy."

"Sounds like it. Do you enjoy what you do?"

She smiled, looking toward Joshua, who was wide awake and infatuated with the ceiling of the truck. "Most of the time."

"I know what you mean."

She turned toward him and Cort glanced her way. She had a curious expectant expression.

"I figured you loved what you do," she said. "I mean those are beautiful horses you have at your ranch. And you go to all those competitions. You see all those exciting places."

Cort glanced at her again. Did he hear longing in her voice? "Going to all those places alone isn't what it's cut out to be."

He studied the road, thinking. "I enjoy the training. But…I don't know. I guess I'm getting older. I'd rather stay home and let someone else hit the circuit rather than spend another night in a hotel room by myself."

Lilly probably thought he was some bleeding heart now. He realized it was true, though. After Ramona left him, he'd thrown himself into his work. But being on the road reminded him of everything he'd lost. Not that Ramona had enjoyed going with him. She hadn't, and when she did go, it was because of who she was going to get to rub elbows with. Famous people sank huge amounts of money into the horse industry. Ramona had loved the social aspect. She'd never really gone just to spend time with him.

He should have taken that as a hint that all was not right in his supposedly happy home.

"I'd love to go," Lilly said, surprising him. "I mean, not with you. I mean…well, what I'm trying to say is that I've been on the farm all my life. Being raised out there with my grannies was a very secluded upbringing. Granny Bunches used to always tell me that I should sell the farm when they were all dead and gone and head out to see the country. Of course, Mule Hollow is all I've ever known. And I love it…."

Her voice trailed off and Cort found himself studying her again. She was looking out the window, a frown creasing her face.

He wondered what it would be like to show her his world. To see his life through new eyes. Lilly's eyes.

It was a dangerous thing to wonder about.

"He weighs eleven pounds, and the doctor said it was all right for me to mix a bit of cereal in with his formula if he's been that sleepless." Lilly hadn't stopped talking since she'd come out of the doctor's office. "Thank goodness he's an older man, because I don't think the younger doctors would ever agree to such a thing." She was so excited to think about getting some sleep and to realize that her giving Joshua the cereal early wasn't bad. She couldn't contain her excitement.

Not to mention the fact that she was enjoying spending time with Cort.

They were sitting at a restaurant near the doctor's office. Lilly hadn't been out to eat in a real restaurant in ages. Cort had insisted on taking her to this nice steak house when she'd suggested a hamburger place out on the highway on their way home.

Cort seemed to get joy from making her feel special. He'd opened every door for her, carried Joshua and even held her elbow as she sat in the chair he'd pulled out for her. What a man. Not that there weren't men out there who did those things. There just had never been one who did them for her. Of course, she'd dated all of three people in her life.

Not that this was a date…oh, no, she knew better than that. Cort was just her neighbor. No matter how nice he'd been last night and today she couldn't forget that he'd made himself quite clear at the church on not being the right man for her. He wasn't interested in dating her. He was just being a nice neighbor.

She was on dangerous ground letting herself acknowledge everything about Cort that made her heart go thump.

Last night as she watched him drive away she'd wondered about his past. His wife had hurt him. He must have loved her very much to close himself off now and hide behind that grim expression—which had been fading more and more. Why, he actually cooed at Joshua as he'd taken him out of the car earlier. She wondered about that, too. The way he appeared to want to play with Joshua, to open up to the baby, but instead seemed to fight letting himself have free rein. It hit Lilly that Joshua would be very good for Cort. The plan she'd been toying with didn't seem quite so far-fetched anymore. Actually, it might be the best thing for Cort. And she did want to help him. He had been so good to her and her child. Even if he didn't think he was the right man for her…

She smiled, turning the plan over in her mind. Yes, her son needed a father figure, and Cort had been there for them during the delivery and lived right down the road. It was as if God had placed him there—not to help them as she'd first thought, but for them to help him.

Yes, that just might be it. God worked in very mysterious ways.

Cort ordered a steak, medium rare, and balked when she ordered hers well-done with a bottle of ketchup on the side.

"I know," she said, laughing. "I'm a Texas girl, so what am I doing eating a well-done steak?"

"You live in cattle country. You know you can't get the true taste of the meat when you burn it up like that," he teased.

"Can't help it. I eat ketchup on everything. You put it in my eggs the other night, so I know you like it, too. And I want my steak cooked. That's the flavor I like."

"The flavor of shoe leather."

"That's a matter of opinion. It's all about the texture."

"Yeah, but…okay, we'll agree to disagree about the texture of our steaks. What do you say?"

Lilly chuckled. "I say sounds like a plan to me."

When the waiter brought their plates twenty minutes later Lilly and Cort had laughed and disagreed on all manner of food preparation. Cort liked cold spinach out of the can, Lilly didn't touch the green stuff—despite the never-ending effort on the part of the grannies to stuff the nasty plant into all manner of food. Cort liked peanut butter on an apple, Lilly liked banana and peanut butter squashed together in a sandwich. Cort said he couldn't look at the stuff because it looked nasty all squashed together, much less eat it. To each his own, Lilly thought. She knew he was missing out on one of life's premier foods.

They agreed on one thing: banana Laffy Taffy.

"If I had to choose one food to have on a deserted island with me it would be banana taffy," Lilly commented as the waiter set her steak down in front of her.

Cort laughed. "I love the stuff, but I might have to choose something else in that situation."

"Have it your way, but we only live once."

Cort just shook his head and began preparing his steak.

"Why, you sneak," she said as he opened the ketchup and bathed his steak in it. Looking up through a loose strand of black hair, he grinned sheepishly.

"I said nothin' about the ketchup. We were talking about the texture."

Lilly laughed. She couldn't remember the last time she'd had so much fun. Cort was a great guy.

Yep, she was certain the grannies would have changed their view of men if they'd known Cort.

At this point, Lilly really didn't care what the grannies thought.

## Chapter Nineteen

Lilly sat beside the window and gazed out across the lawn and into the pasture that stretched as far as she could see. Samantha was ambling about munching stalks of grass peeking up through the cold earth. The little dear had stuck close to the house for the past few days, always coming to the living-room window and looking in at her as she and Joshua sat in the rocking chair.

Lilly enjoyed rocking Joshua and staring out the window. As she sang lullabies to him she imagined spending time with him there in the yard, seeing the seasons pass as she held her child. It was a wonderful feeling…this feeling of not being alone anymore. Of having someone to love, to watch over. She'd also taken up reading her Bible to him. With Joshua's birth, a new sense of meaning had taken over when she realized she was responsible to God to raise her baby in a manner that God would approve.

Joshua was sleeping contentedly, and Lilly had risen early to have quiet time with the Lord. Her Bible lay open in her lap. The verses she'd read filled her with hope.

Oh, there was so much to learn. Sure, her grandmothers—at least, Granny Bunches—had taken her to church and shown her that God loved her. But she had realized long ago that Granny Shu-Shu and Granny Gab had had a tilted view of the world in general, including God.

It wasn't as if they hadn't known the Lord, but they hadn't walked with Him. Granny Bunches, in her soft sweet way, had never condemned the views of her mother and sister, but she had tried to show Lilly another way. A loving way. Lilly had prayed this morning that God would help her to focus on the teachings in the Bible and the loving things Granny Bunches had shown her, instead of the negative thoughts and ways that the grannies Shu-Shu and Gab had drilled into her day after day.

Just like the traditions she wanted to start setting in place in Joshua's life, she had come to the understanding that bringing him up in the knowledge and love of God was most important of all.

Sitting there in her quiet living room, with the soft rays of sunshine filtering through lace curtains that were ages old, Lilly felt something change in her heart.

Instead of the grannies' way, Lilly understood that it was time for her to find her own way.

And she wanted that to be God's way.

The air was brisk as Cort urged Ringo into a slow trot. The big horse was feeling frisky today. Beneath him Cort could feel the animal straining to move more quickly, anxious to feel the freedom that came with the release of pent-up energy. Cort gave the familiar cluck with his mouth, and the big horse expanded into a lope around the round pen. Cort tried to concentrate on the exercise at hand, but his mind was not on the horse.

It was on Lilly.

For days he'd let his guard down, tried to pretend that she could remain just a friend. But he was fooling himself. He had been from the first moment he'd looked at her. Lilly was a woman with whom a man could build a future. She was outspoken, but tender. She'd had her heart broken and her dreams dismissed, but she'd managed to hold on to her optimism.

She was a wonderful mother. Every time she and Joshua were near him, he had to fight the want that filled him. He loved—no, he wouldn't go there. He couldn't allow himself to acknowledge the feelings that had set up camp in his soul.

They'd sat together at church again. Her sitting next to him, as Pastor Lewis talked about God's plan for the family, seemed almost like a cruel joke. But he knew the messages were meant for the single men in the congregation who were vested in finding a wife and growing a family. Pastor Lewis was laying the groundwork for Christian men to become Christian husbands and fathers. Mule Hollow wanted to grow and become a thriving small community, and the majority of those wanting this plan to succeed were men seeking God's will for their lives.

Lilly would one day belong with one of them.

And Cort would just have to pray for grace to be able to watch her find the love she deserved.

"Hey, Loser," Lilly called, hating the name. The sulking dog saw her coming up the drive, lifted his scraggly head, then hopped from the porch and wiggled all the way to meet her.

"We've got to give you a new name." He lapped up the attention with every fiber of his hairy body. Cort had told her more than once that Loser had started living after he'd met her and Samantha.

The idea gave Lilly a warm fuzzy feeling. But it was time to do what she'd come to do, so she sucked in a fortifying breath and said another prayer, then looked around.

"Where's Cort?" she asked, supporting the sling that held Joshua against her as she scratched Loser between the eyes. He looked up at her with a big foolish grin on his face, but didn't answer. So she had to rely on her ears and the clanking noise coming from the barn.

She found Cort on the ground under a tractor. His long legs stuck out from beneath the large machine.

"Hey, neighbor, got a problem?" she asked, stooping so that she could peer under at what he was doing.

His hands were covered in grease, and when he looked at her she could see there was a streak of black running across one cheek. His eyes brightened when he saw her. And Lilly's heart faltered, then picked up a quicker pace. Even the two mile walk from her house hadn't caused her heart to pound as it was doing now.

This erratic beating was a feeling she'd come to understand only Cort's presence could produce.

"Nothing I can't handle," he said, scooting from beneath the tractor to face her.

They were only inches apart, and Lilly, without thinking, reached to pull a cobweb from just above Cort's ear. Her fingers froze on contact with his silky hair.

Cort's gaze locked with hers and she yanked her hand back, feeling at odds with their closeness. Wanting it, yet fearing it.

Only after she was stroking Joshua's hair could she speak. "I came to ask you something." Her voice wobbled.

With a power she didn't know she possessed, she forced down the fear overcoming her from the inside out and looked at Cort. He hadn't moved. He sat in exactly the same position as when she'd reached out and touched him. His eyes drilled into hers. The intensity threatened her willpower and almost loosened the unknown, unexplored feelings she was struggling frantically to file away until later.

Later, when she was alone, when it might be safe to really look inside her heart.

Not being able to take the proximity any longer, she crossed the room to sit on a hay bale.

The day was cold, but the sun had been shining during her brisk walk and had kept her warm. Now, in the shadow of the barn, the chill swept over her and she pulled the blanket more securely around Joshua. She knew the baby sling that strapped him to her surrounded him with her body heat. He was as cozy as a bug in a rug, as her Granny Gab would've said. But she needed something to occupy her hands, and fidgeting with the blanket fulfilled that need. When she looked up, Cort was on his feet wiping his hands and face with a rag. He had his back to her, giving her a moment to take a deep breath.

This was crazy!

*Calm down, Lilly. This is what God has been leading you to do!* "I've been thinking. And, well, you see...I was wondering. No, I was wanting to ask you—" As she faltered he turned toward her, his sweet face full of bewilderment.

*This is right. Ask him.* "I've been reading my Bible. And I was reading about when Hannah gave her baby Samuel back to the Lord, she actually said she lent him back to the Lord because the Lord had blessed her with him. I want to honor the Lord for blessing me with Joshua by promising the Lord that I'll raise him up in a godly home."

Cort raised an eyebrow, but didn't smile. "I think that's a great thing to do."

He had finished wiping his hands, and he came to lean against the stall railing a few feet away from Lilly. He tucked his fingers inside the top of his pocket and studied her.

He looked so strong and handsome. Lilly tugged at the collar of her coat and tried not to think about how his arms felt around her, or how safe she felt in them.

"Parenthood is serious business. Raising children

God's way is the greatest, most rewarding thing a parent can do."

Cort paused, and Lilly wondered at the sadness that flickered in his expressive eyes. Had he wanted to do the same thing for his children? Children he now understood he would never father? Lilly's heart ached. Cort would have made a wonderful father. Of this she was certain. This gave her courage to continue. If he denied her request, then at least she'd asked.

"I want to make this promise to the Lord in the sanctuary and I also wanted to ask you something. I know this is a lot of responsibility…that maybe with your business and your life you might want to say no. And I would understand. Really." *Out with it, Lilly!* "Would you be Joshua's guardian, godparent…if something were to happen to me?"

Cort's head swung up from where he'd been studying his boots. His expression was blank. His jaw dropped.

Good or bad, she couldn't tell.

"I mean, you did rescue us both. You are the reason he's okay." The light that had flickered in his eyes died, and Lilly fought to get it back when he didn't answer as he studied Joshua, a sad quirk turning the edge of his mouth down.

"And you would be such a good father to him…if, if something were to happen to me." There, she'd said it all.

Cort met her gaze and for a long moment neither of them moved. Or breathed.

"Nothing's going to happen to you, Lilly."

"I don't know that." Now that she'd spoken the words

she knew the importance of them. Knew she was right. Knew in her heart he was the one to fill the spot, should something go wrong and God called her home.

"Even if something did happen there are plenty of others who would be happy to raise Joshua. I'm sure Lacy and Clint would love to be his godparents. They'd be better than an old single guy like me."

"They would be wonderful. I know that. But you have a bond with him. And you are not old."

"Lacy has a bond. She delivered him."

Lilly reached out and laid her hand on his forearm. His muscles tensed beneath her fingers. "But you got him there. You came through the night and carried us to safety. You're the one God sent to take care of us."

Cort thought for a long moment and Lilly's heart sank. She knew he didn't want her, but she'd hoped that he would want Joshua.

"I'll be his godparent."

Lilly didn't know if she should be happy or sad at the tone of his voice. But then again, she'd known getting him to say yes would be like splitting logs with a rubber ax.

"I would be honored to take the responsibility that goes with the request."

Okay, so that sounded better. A tremor raced up the base of her spine and Lilly stood on shaking legs. "Thank you."

Tears of relief suddenly stung her eyes, and before she could help it, one slipped from the corner, trailing down her cheek. She dashed it away with her hand and turned to go. Her emotions seemed to be sitting on her shoulder these days. Thing was, she really didn't understand what was wrong. She couldn't blame her wobbly emotions on lack of sleep anymore.

Cort's hand on her shoulder stopped her.

"Lilly, don't cry. Nothing's going to happen to you." Cort gently turned her toward him and wrapped his arms around her, tenderly cupping Joshua between them. She melted.

*Home.*

The word swelled in her heart. Suddenly she knew the truth. She'd tried to deny it. Tried to overcome it. But in her heart of hearts she knew in the circle of Cort's arms she'd found her place.

"And with the rib, which the Lord God had taken from man, made He a woman, and brought her unto the man."

The familiar verse from second Genesis sprang out at her, surrounded her and she knew…

She knew she'd found the man God had intended her for.

Cort tightened his arms around Lilly and cherished the feeling of her and her child next to him. Waves of regret washed over him for a lost past and a future he could never have. But he could give her what she asked, knowing that he would do anything needed to make her life and Joshua's easier.

He didn't want to see her cry. Looking down, he tilted her chin toward him and looked into the shining gold of her eyes. When her lip trembled and her eyes misted, he kissed her.

He'd meant only to hold her, to console her, but his

heart got in the way, and the need to acknowledge his love for her overwhelmed him.

He did love her. He'd loved her from the first moment he'd seen her lying on the floor of his barn with that unbelievable bright smile spread across her lovely face. She had an undaunted spirit. One even a lasso couldn't hinder.

*But she can't be yours.*

The cruel truth hissed through him. It took everything he had to pull away from her. She had accepted the kiss with warmth and returned it with a sweetness that broke his heart.

"This," he said as he rammed a hand through his hair and tried not to heed the questions in her eyes, "isn't a good idea. It wouldn't work."

"Why not?" she asked. Her voice was soft. A whisper. Her eyes were dark with emotion. "I know I'm not your wife. But—"

"It hasn't a thing to do with Ramona. That's over. It's about you. You and Joshua. You need more than I can give you. You *deserve* more."

Lilly straightened. "I think you don't give yourself enough credit. And I know you don't give me enough."

"It's not about giving myself credit. It's about you having the family that I know God has in store for you."

Lilly's eyes flashed. "How do you know what God has in store for me? Who are you to say it isn't with you?" She stopped, and the silence stretched between.

Cort didn't want to hurt her, but he knew this was

for the best. Now he wasn't certain if agreeing to be Joshua's guardian had been the right choice. When she remarried, there would be a man in Josh's life. They wouldn't need him anymore.

"God has a husband out there for you and a father for Joshua. But it isn't me, Lilly. I have nothing to offer you. So the best thing would be for us to forget this ever happened."

The fire that flashed through Lilly's eyes took him by surprise. And his mouth dropped when she stepped away from him, plopped her hand on her narrow hip, cupped Joshua with the other hand and glared sassily up at him. "Well, cowboy, you can forget it if you want to, but *I* don't want to."

And with that she turned and flounced away, curls bouncing. With Loser trailing behind her.

## Chapter Twenty

The town was in an uproar. The ladies had gotten together and planned Lacy's wedding down to the last pink imported Shasta daisy.

Bless her soon-to-be-husband's big heart, Clint had given in to them plain and simply because he loved Lacy. Loved her with a love that Lilly could only wish to find. A love that she, in her own misguided way, had thought she'd found. But she'd been wrong.

Cort hadn't come after her.

Today Adela was watching Joshua while Lilly had a day out with Lacy. Lilly wanted her son to know the love of Adela, Norma Sue and Esther Mae. She wanted to encourage their bonding. Because of this she had agreed to the plan to get her out of the house and help with the final stages of Lacy's wedding.

Standing in the back of the church watching Lacy and Ashby Templeton discuss flowers, Lilly bowed her head and prayed that God would sustain her, that He would give her the strength she needed to do what He wanted her to do. It was a hard prayer to pray. Given the nature of her outspoken personality, she wanted to demand that Cort acknowledge that he loved her.

She needed Cort. Him and Joshua. And God. What a blessing that circle of love could be. But she didn't allow herself to demand such a thing because she didn't know if it was true.

Why would she even think that? Cort had never told her anything remotely close to admitting he loved her. Yes, he'd shown her care and friendship and kindness. But love? No. He'd flat-out told her that he wasn't the man for her. They'd hardly had anything remotely close to a romantic relationship. Sure, they'd shared one kiss. One tender big kiss. And then he'd run for the hills! Really, Lilly didn't understand why in the world she'd expected him to feel more. Who was she kidding?

Watching Lacy as she talked, Lilly smiled, despite the misery she felt inside. The crazy girl wouldn't stop babbling. It was as if she knew something was wrong, but she hadn't asked. She'd simply drawn Lilly into the final plans for her wedding with a great smile and a host of enthusiasm. Of course, this was Lacy, and she'd efficiently involved everyone. A Valentine's Day wedding in Mule Hollow was appropriate.

Molly had been writing articles about Mule Hollow every so often in her column for the paper in Houston and there were a few other big papers that were picking up the stories. Why, even a New York paper had picked up on them. They were a big hit with Molly's readership. The very first wedding for the town that had conducted a national "wives needed" ad campaign was big news…

at least to the growing army of faithful readers. The fact that the campaign had actually produced a marriage within the first six months was huge. It made women realize that this wasn't just a publicity stunt. It made them actually see that they could have a future in Mule Hollow.

"Lilly," Lacy said, plopping down in the pew beside her. Ashby settled into the one in front of them. "What do you think about pink baby roses and pink—"

"Sounds like a scene from *Steel Magnolias*," Lilly said, cringing.

"I loved that movie," Lacy gushed. "Julia Roberts walking down the aisle with an ocean of pink around her—it was great. Why, the first time I saw that movie, I knew if I ever got married I wanted that same sea of flowers around me." She was nodding her head and looking about the church. "Yep, yep, yep…I can just see it."

Ashby's gaze met Lilly's and they both burst out laughing. If there was one thing Lacy Brown loved it was pink. She studied them both as they subsided into a fit of giggles.

"I'm telling you, it'll be beautiful. Remember, it's Valentine's Day. Pink or red is the only way to go. And as you know, I'm a pink kinda girl."

Lilly straightened her face, keeping her eyes off Ashby lest they start chuckling again. "Lacy, it's your wedding, and if you want the walls pink, it would be fine with me. It's going to be beautiful no matter what. And you're right—pink on Valentine's will be perfect.

But please tell me you aren't having Clint wear pink, are you?"

Lacy smiled. "He loves me, but that would be pushing things a bit. Gray and black mix quite nicely with pink. I'm not wearing pink, so I couldn't ask him to."

"You didn't really think about asking him such a thing, did you?" Ashby asked, not certain when to take Lacy seriously and when not to.

"No. I didn't even think about it. Clint's a cowboy. Besides, he already wore pink once because of me. And he didn't like it one bit."

Lilly smiled, remembering the story of Clint getting an entire bucket of hot pink paint dumped on his head the day Lacy was painting her salon. The story was one she didn't think he would ever live down. But he'd handled it good-naturedly. He'd said it didn't matter what happened to him as long as he got Lacy in the end.

Lilly's heart twisted, thinking about Cort. She felt the same way about him. Anything was worth it, if she could have his love at the end of the day.

If only she could figure a way.

*Leave it in God's hands, Lilly.*

Sometimes it was easier to think something than to actually do it. She had to remind herself that God had big hands.

And that those big hands would take care of her no matter what.

After they'd finished at the church Ashby left them to take care of ordering the flowers. She had a contact in Hollywood—her former home—who was shipping the flowers out to Mule Hollow by Friday morning. Actually she was shipping herself out with them. And if Ashby had her way she was going to stay and run her Internet flower business from Mule Hollow. It was going to be one more opportunity for the little town. E-commerce was making possible several things that ten years ago wouldn't have been imaginable. Ashby's mail-order dress business was running as smoothly from Mule Hollow as it had from Hollywood. The dresses she'd helped everyone order for the wedding were gorgeous.

Lilly and Lacy then hopped into Lacy's 1958 pink Cadillac convertible, with the top up and the heater on, and headed for the community center, where the reception was going to be held. With the wedding only a week away, the decorating was already in progress. Today they were going to help put up white and pink netting along with fairy lights.

The scenery was whizzing past the Caddy's windows as Lilly relaxed in the deep seat.

"I just love to drive," Lacy said, sitting up straight, watching the road as she maneuvered the huge car down the blacktop. "I especially like to ride with the top down. Do you mind if I put it down?"

Lilly shot an unbelieving glance at Lacy. "It's forty-five degrees outside."

"Have you ever ridden in a convertible with the top down on a forty-degree day?" She glanced at Lilly with an excited grin and a raised eyebrow.

"Well, no. But it's cold."

"Girl, you need to live a little. Before we go to the

community center, we are going for a ride. Because you need to tell me what ails you."

Lacy slammed on the brakes and the Caddy skidded to a halt. Before Lilly could overcome the shock of the sudden stop she watched in horror as Lacy pressed a button and the Caddy's top kicked into gear. The cold of the day whipped into the car just as Lacy stomped on the accelerator. Flattened to the seat from the speed, Lilly felt her curls rise and start dancing above her head as if they were alive. The brisk cold stung her cheeks and the chilly air sucked a laugh right out of her. Lacy was laughing, too.

Lacy turned up the heat, and suddenly Lilly had the best of both worlds. She was warm, her feet were toasty and her hands, too, but the cold air on her face, blowing through her hair, sent a thrill of joy pulsing through her.

"I told you it was great," Lacy yelled over the wind as she whipped the car onto another farm road heading away from town.

"I love it. I could get used to this. Is this car for sale?" Lilly called out, knowing full well that Lacy would never part with her beloved car.

"Nope, nope, never. But I know where you could get one just like it."

Lilly considered it. She did need a new car, but she needed a family car. One she could feel safe in on the road with Joshua. "I guess I'd better pass. But I'm going to be asking for a ride in this one more often. Now that you have me hooked."

"That I can do." Lacy slowed the Caddy and pulled

the car over next to a deserted one-picnic-table rest area. "Okay, so now that I have you loosened up, tell me how things are going. God has really put you on my mind lately."

Lilly could hear the sincerity in Lacy's voice and she could see it in her eyes. In the short time she'd known Lacy her enthusiasm and love for God had inspired Lilly. She was bold for Christ and humble in her accomplishments for Him. Lilly knew she wanted to be like Lacy… in her own way. No one could be like Lacy—she was truly one of a kind. But Lilly could learn from her and she could trust her.

Sitting there in the cold air, Lilly felt comfortable enough to let Lacy inside her heart. "I married Jeff because I was lonely and to disprove the legacy my grannies tried to pass down to me. I made a bad choice." Lilly studied the landscape, the barren pastures waiting for spring. "It was a huge mistake. After he left me, after I started coming back to church, after I met you, I realized that I hadn't waited on the Lord. I tried to hate Jeff. But I couldn't. Jeff didn't know the Lord. He didn't care or understand that marriage is a commitment made before God. I let my wanting a husband get ahead of waiting on the one God had in mind for me. Do you think I'm right about that?"

Lacy paused for a few moments. "I can't say what God's mind was then. I'm sure He wanted you to do what you could to make the marriage work once you had committed to Jeff. But he left and it's over. You understand the concept—one man, one woman for as long as the two shall live."

Lilly nodded. "Yes."

Lacy reached over and placed a cold hand on Lilly's. "Do you still want a husband?"

"Yes. Yes, I do. Despite my grandmothers, I want to have a family. I look at Joshua and every negative thing my grannies said about marriage, about men, all of it just disappears into thin air. I want a husband. And I want more children. But I don't want just any husband. I want Cort."

Lacy smiled. "I thought so! I told you I thought he was your future."

"But Lacy, he doesn't want to marry me, for reasons I'm not at liberty to talk about."

"Do you love him?"

Lilly looked at her hands. "Yes, yes I do."

"Do you trust God?"

Lilly looked at Lacy. Her blond hair looked like whipped cream after a pie-smashing contest, but the wisdom that shone from her blue eyes reached far into Lilly's heart. "I want to trust Him."

"I was reading a verse this morning. 'Commit thy way unto the Lord; trust also in Him; and He shall bring it to pass.' I believe that was Psalm 37:4." Lacy thought for a second. "Nope, it was 37:5 because verse four is, I remember now, 'Delight thyself also in the Lord; and He shall give thee the desires of thine heart.'"

Lacy searched Lilly's eyes with hers as Lilly pondered the verses. Commit her way unto the Lord. That was what had been on her mind lately. She hadn't done that—at least, she hadn't tried to do that until recently. And she hadn't totally committed to it until she'd looked into the face of Joshua. "I want my child to know that his mother loves the Lord. My delight would be that he grow to know the Lord. That he join me in heaven one day. That he grow up to be a man of God. And I would like him to have the guidance of a father in his life."

"Are you prepared to wait on the Lord?"

The question shocked Lilly. She had been all set to go after Cort. To convince him that he was the man for her. But was she prepared to wait on the Lord? Was she once more trying to rush the plan that God had for her life? Lilly sat up straight and gawked at Lacy. "How in the world did you get to be so smart?"

Lacy laughed. "Oh, Lilly, it isn't me. God prepared my heart for this conversation. I prayed this morning that whatever it was that was bothering you, He would speak through me. That He would just kick me to the curb and use my big mouth to speak to you."

Lilly lowered her head and stared at her hands folded in her lap. "Yes, I'm prepared to wait on the Lord. Only He could have known what I needed to hear."

Lacy squeezed Lilly's shoulder. "God wants what's best for you and Joshua, Lilly. But whatever is going on may not be about you. It could be about Cort. Give it time and pray. God has a plan. And I have faith that whatever it is, it's gonna be wonderful. And it's gonna outshine anything you could imagine."

"But what if He doesn't give me Cort? How can I go on?"

"God's grace is sufficient to sustain you through anything. He promises that. He doesn't say His grace *might* be sufficient. He says His grace *is* sufficient. Things in this life hurt. You've already learned that. Life isn't fair. Satan is alive and well and striking out at every turn. But I know that when my dad left me and my mom, when he turned his back on us, it hurt so much. But God carried me through. He was faithful and I've used that pain to counsel many other people with similar problems because I understood what they were going through. He will carry you, Lilly. He will carry you every step of the way if you need Him to. But I know you. I saw in you a spirit, the first time I saw you singing in the church choir. Like this town, you have a spirit that wants to soar for God. You just have to trust Him. Act out on that trust and pass on His grace as the opportunity arises. You're going to be all right, Lilly Tipps."

Lilly reached over and hugged Lacy. "Thank you, Lacy. God blessed me the day you became my friend."

Lacy gave her a hard squeeze. "Girl, I can't even begin to list all the blessings He's given me. But you are one of them. And that Clint Matlock, bless his sweet soul, is the icing on my cake. And I wasn't even looking for him when God put him in my path." She released Lilly, put the car in gear, then gunned the engine, smiling big-time at the loud sound.

Lilly sucked in a breath and held on as they shot out onto the blacktop heading back toward town.

"You get ready, Lilly," Lacy called out like a cheer-leader. "Because our God is an *awesome* God and there is truly no telling what's going to happen next for you and Joshua. No telling at all."

Lilly couldn't help but smile.

Even when a bug hit her between the eyes.

# *Chapter Twenty-One*

Cort put the screwdriver back into his toolbox, then closed the door to the feed room and tried out the freshly relocated bolt near the top of the door. No way would Samantha get into the feed room now. He felt a bit guilty for having changed the lock. What would Samantha think, after having been allowed in the room all her life, to now being ousted?

She was just a donkey. A little pesky burro. But she seemed like more. He had grown attached to the old girl. Just as he'd grown attached to Lilly. And Joshua.

Loser was sitting at his feet. He wasn't lying at his feet—he was actually sitting there. At attention. Why, the dog even wagged his tail every once in a while. And if Cort even got near his truck, the crazy animal would run and leap into the truck bed and look expectantly at him. Loser wanted to go, but not just anywhere. Loser wanted to see Samantha. Cort felt the same way about Lilly. He wanted to get in his truck every time he passed by and drive over to see what was going on at the end of the dirt road.

But he couldn't do it. He'd kissed Lilly. Then he'd told her he wasn't the man for her. He'd turned the sweet woman away when, in his heart, he'd wanted nothing more than to hang on to her with both hands and never let her go.

He'd misled her.

And he'd hurt her.

But there was nothing he could do about it. He was learning the hard way that life wasn't fair, and it definitely didn't care how many times it struck him down.

When Ramona left he'd not been able to blame her. She wanted children. She'd always wanted them, and no matter how much it had hurt Cort to watch her leave, he'd understood deep inside that he had to let her go. It was for her best interests. Letting Lilly go was for her best interests, also. He just couldn't believe that God would lead him all the way out into the middle of nowhere just to dangle Lilly in front of him. But then, he hadn't understood much the Lord had been up to lately.

He looked over at the now almost smiling Loser.

"Well, I'm glad one of us is happy. I feel like God's put me on a merry-go-round. Only, there isn't anything merry about it. It's just one stinking heartache after another."

Loser tilted his head and barked, then ran over to the truck that sat at the end of the barn. He wiggled his body like a dust mop being beaten against a rug. The closer Cort got to the truck the wilder and more erratic his wiggling became.

"I'm not going over there, Loser. That's the last place I need to be." He looked at his watch and saw that it was nearing three o'clock. He had promised Clint he'd help him and a bunch of the other cowboys set up a few more tables for the wedding that was to take place on Saturday.

# *Chapter Twenty-Two*

"Lacy Brown, get away from that door."

Lacy ignored Norma Sue and continued to peek through the heavy door of the church. "It's packed!"

Lilly chuckled. Despite her heavy heart she was determined to enjoy Lacy's wedding. And so was Lacy. Lilly stood on tiptoes and peeked over Lacy's head. The little sanctuary was filled with all kinds of cowboys and a good many women. Some of them she recognized as having come to the dinner theater.

"You see anybody out there making eyes at each other?" Esther Mae asked, bumping into Lacy and then Lilly as she tried to get an eyeball to the crack in the door.

"Esther, watch it," Norma snapped. "Your big feet are steppin' on Lacy's dress." Lilly was glad Adela was playing the piano loudly, so it would drown out all the chattering.

"Norma, Norma, Norma, calm down," Lacy said with a laugh. "Look out there. Look how beautiful and happy Clint's mother looks. I'm so glad she came to the wedding and that she and Clint are getting to know each other again."

Lilly could see Clint's mother in the second row beside Lacy's mother. It was hard to believe, looking at her, that she'd run off with a man from the circus when Clint was just a boy. But she'd recently become a Christian and asked for Clint's forgiveness. Now here she was about to witness her son's marriage. God was incredible. He'd restored a family after years of separation. It did her heart good to know God's faithfulness.

Lilly thought of Joshua, and of Cort. Would God bring them all together as a family? Lilly had been praying for the Lord's will to be done in her life. And yet the moment Cort had walked into the church her stomach had started churning and her pulse had increased. Cort Wells made her happy even from a distance.

"Oh, and look at Molly taking all those pictures," Lacy hissed in an excited whisper, reeling in Lilly's runaway thoughts. "There's Cort sitting by Sheriff Brady. Lilly, just wait till he sees you in that dress. Oh, Molly just took their picture."

Lilly glanced down at the ice-pink dress she wore. She still couldn't believe she was one of Lacy's bridesmaids. Of course, Lacy was different. She'd wanted Norma Sue, Esther Mae and Adela to also be her bridesmaids, but they'd refused, declaring they were way too old. In the end she had her roommate, Sherri, as her maid of honor and Lilly as her bridesmaid.

Esther Mae and Norma Sue were watching Joshua for her.

"Okay, ladies," Ashby said from behind them. Everyone spun around, bumping elbows as they lined up in front of her. She was the acting wedding planner, and she looked the part in her elegant suit and silky straight hair.

"My, my, but all of you look like you've had your hands in the candy jar. What's going on?"

"We're just people watching," Norma Sue said, jiggling Joshua in her arms.

"Well, it's about time for you to march down the aisle."

Lilly was more nervous than Lacy. When the wedding march started Lilly was in place only because Ashby set her there and gave her a tiny nudge that it was time for her to get things rolling. She wanted to roll, all right. Right out the door.

Everyone in the church turned, watching her, but her feet wouldn't move.

"Go," Ashby whispered from behind the door. Sucking in a deep breath that immediately stuck in her lungs, Lilly stepped out.

Cort was sitting in the second row from the back, and his eyes caught hers. She was finally able to breathe again when she reached the front of the church and took her appointed spot.

In her mind's eye she could see Cort, standing where Clint stood waiting for his bride.

And Lilly wanted it to be her.

She so wanted it to be her.

*Please, Lord, give me peace. Help me be satisfied with Your plan for my life.*

\* \* \*

Cort had watched Lilly walk slowly down the aisle. Her curls were swept up on top of her head in a pleasing mass of disarray that exposed her smooth neck. Her barely pink dress contrasted with the warmth of her eyes. When their eyes met she'd looked away, toward the front of the church. Cort hadn't been able to tear his gaze away, following her every step.

And he noticed his weren't the only eyes that appreciated the picture of beauty Lilly made as she took her place at the front of the church. Cort was sitting near the back, and out of the corner of his eye he could see Bob Jacobs. He stood tall and straight in his tuxedo. He was, Cort felt sure, what a woman would find handsome in a man. And he watched every move Lilly made.

Sherri passed him on her way to stand in the maid-of-honor spot and Cort didn't even notice, he was so caught up in thinking about Lilly and Bob. One second Lilly stood there alone, then Sherri took her place beside her. Sherri was beautiful, too. Her normally crazy Rod Stewart hair was curled softly about her face, taking away the radical look she was known for and exposing a more vulnerable woman. But Cort had eyes only for Lilly. She was everything he wanted.

And there lay his problem. Nothing about it had changed since the first night he'd met her. He needed that kick in the head, and he needed it badly.

When he finally focused on the wedding, Lacy and Clint were beaming at each other as Pastor Lewis asked each of them if they'd take the other in sickness and in health, for richer or for poorer, in good times and in bad times. When Lacy reached out and cupped Clint's jaw as she said "I do," Cort's eyes again sought out Lilly.

There were tears in her eyes and a sad smile on her lips.

His heart ached. He wanted the best for Lilly. She deserved it.

It didn't matter that all he really wanted to do was walk to the front of that church, take her in his arms and ask her to be his. All that mattered was that Lilly get the family she deserved.

*Trust me.*

The words of the Lord came to Cort as he watched Lilly's lip tremble. Why was she near tears? His chest tightened and his fist knotted tightly.

Lilly needed whatever the Lord had in store for her. Once more he reminded himself of this. *Trust me.* Wasn't that what he'd felt God telling him this morning when he'd opened his Bible looking for answers? All day he'd meditated on the words. Was he trusting God? Did he believe that God had a plan?

Did he?

The answer was yes.

But watching Lilly, lovely Lilly, with her eyes glistening with tears and her lip trembling as she watched two people unite in marriage, he faltered. How was he to know if he should try for a future with Lilly or stay out of her way and simply be her friend?

Until he understood what God wanted from him he would stay out of her way. He would simply be there as her friend when she and Joshua needed him.

It felt wrong.

Every day it felt more wrong than the day before. Still, it remained the right thing to do.

Lilly stood on the front walk of the community center and studied the array of cars parked along Main Street. There had to be three hundred people here tonight. The inside of the building was bulging at the bricks with full capacity. Leave it to Lacy to make her reception a memorable one. Who but Lacy Brown would have a karaoke party for a reception? *An all-love-song karaoke bash!*

Bash was right. There were all kinds of love songs being butchered inside. While it was fun and hilarious at the same time, Lilly had needed to escape, to catch her breath and contain her nerves. Being near Cort—and yet his seeming so distant—hurt. He'd stayed across the room from her all night, talking with Roy Don and Hank.

Adela had taken Joshua home with her, saying she would leave the partying for the young adults. She was spending time with the youngster of Mule Hollow.

Now Lilly was torn between going to pick him up and heading home or going back inside. Cort continued to make it quite clear that he wasn't the one for her, that she needed a younger man who could give her children.

For the past week she'd tried to heed Lacy's advice and wait on the Lord. But it was so hard.

There was no way she could go over to Cort's without a good reason, as if she were throwing herself at him. No way would she ever do that again.

Lilly bit her lip thinking of the wedding. It had been

wonderful, yet her emotions were bouncing around and the least little thing was making her want to cry.

And love songs were the pits!

Sure, if you were in love they were perfect! But for someone whose love life was crashing around her feet, listening to off-key renditions really hurt.

She wasn't in the best of moods, and it seemed as if God wasn't listening.

"Hey, Lilly, you are a definite knockout tonight."

Lilly glanced over at Bob as he walked out onto the front walk to stand beside her. His dimples were huge and his grin was sparkling in the fairy lights that hung along the porch.

"Thanks, Bob. It was Lacy who was the knockout." Lilly pushed away her mood and smiled at her new friend.

"Aren't you cold?" He rubbed his hands together, cocked his head to the side and eyed her suspiciously. "Something wrong?"

"No and no. No, I'm not cold, and no, nothing is wrong. I just needed a break from all the love songs."

Bob nodded and relaxed against the railing, turning so he could face her. "I know what you mean. That ceremony really made me think about the future. I'm ready for the Lord to send me a wife to settle down with on my own little piece of land."

"I'm sure God's going to send you a great wife. You're a wonderful guy."

It was starting to get cold to Lilly now and she suddenly felt awkward. "I guess I'd better go inside. The chill is setting in through my coat."

"Yeah, and I think Lacy is going to throw her flower thing in a few minutes. You might catch it."

"I'm not even going to try."

"Why not? You might be the next bride in Mule Hollow. Any man would be lucky to have you as a wife."

Lilly felt the sting of tears returning to the back of her eyes and she fought them off. "Any woman would be blessed to have you as a husband. Maybe you'd better get busy and pick one out."

Bob held the door open for her, grinning down at her as she walked back into the warm room. As she passed by him he leaned close and whispered in her ear. "Maybe *you* should get busy picking, too."

Lilly paused in the doorway and looked up into his smiling face. Was he flirting with her? When he winked, she blinked, feeling heat rising up her collar. They were just friends. Right? She hadn't done anything to make him think she was interested…had she?

"Some guys don't know what it is that they need."

Lilly didn't know what to say. She moved past him into the crowded room, pausing when he reached for her coat.

"I'll take this for you, Lilly. That way, you can go find Cort."

What? She swung around and met his twinkling eyes.

He tugged playfully at a ringlet dangling near her ear, then spoke so softly only she could hear. "Lilly, anybody can see you're in love with the guy. I was just teasing you because you're so cute when you're blushing. Now, give me your coat and go catch that bouquet of flowers when Lacy throws it."

# Chapter Twenty-Three

"Nope, never did see anything quite like it," Applegate Thornton said, scratching his gray hair. His wrinkled face was scrunched up in a corkscrew grimace and frankly, Cort had never seen anything quite like *it* before.

It was six-thirty in the morning and Cort had come to Pete's feed store for, of all things, alfalfa. Samantha had stolen all of his, and Pete had informed him at the wedding that he'd finally gotten in a fresh supply. Since Cort hadn't been able to sleep, he'd decided to get a head start on the day by coming out first thing and picking it up.

He hadn't thought there would be a line.

Applegate Thornton and Stanley Orr had their morning checkers match over at Sam's Diner every daybreak until after nine. Once a week they came to Pete's for a new bag of sesame seeds. This morning Cort found himself behind them as Pete weighed and bagged the seeds, and then they weighed and balanced everything that had happened at the wedding reception Saturday night. Obviously a lot had happened after Cort left, having listened to about all the love singing he could stomach for one evening.

Not that he didn't appreciate love. He did. But when a fella was in over his head, with weights on his ankles, the last thing he wanted to hear was the fifty greatest love songs sung by fifty not-so-great crooners. But that hadn't been what sent him packing. It hadn't even been when Applegate had decided to try his hand at singing a Beatles favorite.

Cort had left when he'd seen Bob whispering in Lilly's ear and watching the pretty shade of pink she turned and the adoring way she stared into the cowboy's eyes.

Needless to say, Cort hadn't slept a wink, and he hadn't slept well last night, either. His mood was about as dark as the night he'd barely made it through. And standing in line at the feed store wasn't improving his attitude one bit.

"Did you hear what I said?" Applegate leaned toward him, as if Cort was the one who couldn't hear, and repeated himself, louder this time. "I said, never did see anything quite like it."

"He heard ya the first time, App. He ain't hard a-hearin'. I am. And I heard ya the first time. You ignoring him, son?"

Cort stared from one man to the next. "I heard him the first time."

"Then you were ignorin' me." Applegate's expression grew dark, his bushy eyebrows met in the middle and his skin wrinkled up around his nose as his lips drooped.

"No, sir, I was not ignoring you."

"Did ya hear that, Stan—says he wasn't ignoring me. Pete, did ya hear that?"

Cort prayed for patience and tried to step to the counter, but the older man slapped him on his back and chuckled.

"I saw you sneak off before Lacy threw that boo-kay of flowers. You shoulda stayed. Your girlfriend was standing there, not looking too happy…. Did you think she was looking happy, Stan?"

"Nope, she looked like she wanted to be home long 'fore they threw that flower ball. Can't say I blame her. Poor thang."

Cort shifted from one boot to the other. He didn't want to hear any more about Lilly. She'd probably caught the bouquet and would be the next bride in Mule Hollow. She and Bob would make a great couple. They'd have a houseful of kids.

"Tell him what happened, App." Pete said, trying to get App to tell, or move, probably so the line would thin out and he could get back to warming his feet over by the stove Cort saw in the corner.

Cort scooted his hat back from his eyes and studied the older man. "Mr. Applegate, what was so bad about Saturday night?" He'd decided it was better to ask and get it over with rather than wait.

"Okay, so there your girlfriend stood all quiet like with all them other outsiders. Them women were huddled up in the corner like a bunch of running backs going out for a pass. Lacy chucked the flowers, and I'm telling you they were heading straight for your girlfriend—"

"She isn't my girlfriend," Cort interrupted—to the wind, because Applegate kept right on going.

"We were all holding our breath that Lilly was going to raise her hands, so the ball of flowers wouldn't give her a black eye or anything, and all of a sudden like Michael Jordan getting hang time, football and basketball collided, along with a couple of them women. Right there in the building. This ole gal rose into the air in a dive that lasted all of ten minutes in slow motion. Yes, sir, that gal hung in the air with one arm out ahead of her and she snatched that bunch of flowers right before they hit Lilly. Onliest problem was, another of them gals was hangin' ten coming from the other direction."

Applegate rubbed his chin with two fingers and studied Cort. "Yup, Lilly just stood there. What'd you do to her? Seems to me a woman would have lifted a hand to catch a boo-kay if she wanted to get married."

"Yep, I think you're probably right about that, sir."

"Well, son, I'll tell you it was a good thing she didn't catch the flowers. That gal that did went down under a herd of brawlers. I think everybody came up with a petal."

"I don't know about coming up with a petal, but I know they were wearin' them in their hair," added Stanley.

"All I can say in their defense is that the cowboys didn't act much better when Clint threw that pink hatband. Yep, Lacy designed that thang all special like with them words proclamating 'I'm next' stitched across it. Yep, quite unusual, but there's a few black eyes this morning over that little piece of elastic. And onliest one fella wearing it around his hat." Applegate popped a few seeds into his mouth. Cort figured he'd grown tired of waiting till he got over to Sam's to chomp on the little fellas.

"In their defense," rambled Stanley—he was on a roll, too—"there were a few ladies that remained out of the scramble. Those nice teachers living over at Adela's didn't get into it—matter of fact, none of the ladies already living here got into the fight. They was real ladies about the whole thang and let them that wanted to brawl have at it. Can't say I blame 'em. It ain't like that boo-kay-catchin' thang is ever accurate."

Cort had about lost patience, and stepped up to the counter. Pete grabbed his pen from behind his ear and took his order while Stanley and Applegate eased up behind him.

"What you need all that alfalfa for?"

Cort looked to his right at Applegate. "For my stock."

"Leroy always ordered a ton of that stuff, too. Said his jack—"

"Donkey." Cort cut in on Stanley. "Samantha prefers burro or donkey to the biblically correct name."

Stanley scratched his head. "That's exactly what Leroy used to say about that donkey. She been letting your stock loose?"

"Yep."

"She's a stinker. Leroy used to get mad enough to

spit nails at that little donkey," Applegate said, setting his bag of seeds down.

That wasn't a good sign for Cort. He figured this was going to be another long story, and he really needed to go.

"Said to us many times that he raised that donkey to sell as a nursemaid to livestock, and he'd have sold her many times over just to get her out of his hair. But he couldn't do it, seeins how that sweet, lonesome Lilly needed something to love. And she shore nuff did love that Samantha. Ain't that right, Stanley?"

Cort's heart started thumping hard in his chest just thinking about Lilly needing something to love. He felt bad standing in the feed store listening to gossip about her and was glad when Pete came out with his order and they could go outside and load it into the back of his truck.

The two older men followed them.

Cort didn't hang around and encourage any more talk about Lilly. It was exactly as he'd thought. Lilly needed a large family to make up for all the years of loneliness she'd endured growing up. No matter how cute Samantha was, Lilly needed more than a donkey to love. She needed children and a husband who would love her the way she deserved.

Lilly stepped from the barn and ran a hand through her hair. It was a beautiful day. A robin ate feed off the ground near the door, promising that spring was soon approaching. Lilly stretched her arms above her head and arched her back to ease the strain of having unloaded the forty-pound sacks of feed from her pickup to the feed room. It felt good to be getting back in shape, but she'd very nearly overdone it today.

Walking to the gate, she propped one booted foot on the bottom rung and leaned her arms on the top rung as she watched her cattle grazing in the distance. The baby monitor was sitting on the hood of her truck to alert her when Joshua awakened from his afternoon nap. It was a good day. It would be a perfect day if...

Tears pricked her eyes, then she lowered her head in prayer. It was the only way she could find peace from the heartache plaguing her. From the what-ifs. There was no solution unless God stepped in and changed either her heart or Cort's. She'd realized the night of the reception when she'd watched Cort leave minutes after she and Bob had come in from the cold that she might not get her wish.

Her heart hadn't been into the rest of the evening. It was as if it had walked out with Cort. Even when the fight broke out over the bouquet she hadn't felt much. Let them fight over who would be the next wife of Mule Hollow. Unless God changed Cort's heart, she would never marry again.

But she knew she had a calling and she was blessed to have it. Raising a child to love the Lord was the most important thing she could do. Her highest calling. The world needed more godly men. She had begun diligently seeking God's wisdom and guidance in building her personal relationship with Him. She wanted her heart to be fully prepared to guide Joshua as he grew. If God chose to bless her with a godly husband, then He would.

She had peace, along with a few tears at times, but still she had peace knowing she was on the path God wanted her to be on.

If it was to be, then it would be. God was in control. Her insides were still turned upside down, though.

*Thank You, Lord, for blessing me so. For giving me a son, good friends who shared Your love with me and have pulled me into their fold. I am truly blessed. I thank You for giving me such a wonderful place to raise Joshua and such wonderful godly people to look up to as I endeavor to do Your will in this calling. Thank You, Father. I pray all these things asking that Your will be done. Amen.*

Lilly laid her head on her crossed arms and relaxed, watching the cattle mill around in the distance. They worried about nothing. Their food was provided, their welfare taken care of, by her, their caretaker. Lilly knew Joshua's and her welfare was being taken care of by the best caretaker there was.

Looking at her watch, she started walking toward the front of her driveway. Bob was supposed to be showing up any minute to start the new single-pole gate he was welding for her. It was an easy fix for her Samantha problem. With the gate in place Samantha could continue to have the run of the place without being able to get out on the dirt road. Thus she'd be unable to go down to Cort's and cause any more problems.

She, on the other hand, needed to see Cort. She was dedicating Joshua to the Lord on Sunday, and also wanted to announce that Cort was Joshua's godparent.

She needed to make certain he still wanted the responsibility and that he would be at the service with her.

She hadn't considered how uncomfortable standing up there with him would be.

She hadn't really thought about a lot of things when she'd asked Cort to be Joshua's guardian. In the event that something did happen to her, it was crucial that Joshua be comfortable in the new environment with his guardian. With Cort. That meant Lilly might have to be around Cort more than she could—no, she could handle anything. Cort was her friend. Nothing more. And she could handle this. With God's help she could.

That is, if Cort still wanted Joshua.

Cort was in the barn when he heard Loser go bonkers. Samantha was on the premises. Coming out of the barn, Cort saw her back end as she disappeared inside his house.

"Samantha!" Cort yelled, not certain why he even attempted to call out to her. It was as if she was deaf by choice. Loser was barking inside and Cort could hear crashing in the few seconds it took him to get to the back door. One look inside and he was ready to…well, he wasn't ready to shoot her or anything, but he was ready to sell her. Even if she didn't belong to him.

His temper was short anyway and the disastrous donkey tearing up his kitchen was the last thing he needed.

Yanking open the door, he stormed into the kitchen just in time to witness Samantha knocking the toaster to the floor as she wrapped her chubby lips around the bread bag and squeezed. The bag popped and bread blew out the end. Several pieces hit Loser on the head, causing him to jump, and run into Samantha's legs as the donkey spun toward the door—knocking his coffeemaker off the counter as she swung her bread-bag-filled mouth around.

The moment Samantha saw him, he figured she knew she was in big trouble.

Lilly was expecting Bob when she saw Cort's truck making slow progress toward her. Tied to the tailgate was Samantha. One look at Cort's scowling face told her Samantha had been up to no good. Again.

"Get in," he snapped, coming to a halt beside her. Lilly didn't ask questions. She could tell by the contrite look on Samantha's long face that he probably had good reason to be upset.

"I'm afraid to ask what happened," she said, slamming the door. Loser bounded into her lap with a joyous yelp and immediately tried to lick her to death.

"Loser, down, boy!" she exclaimed as Cort gave the truck gas. "Don't you pet this dog?" she squealed, trying to get a handle on the excited pooch.

Cort only grunted and kept on driving. Well, she wasn't thrilled to see him, either. Except she did have to ask him the guardian question.

He brought the truck to a halt beside the barn and wasted no time getting out. Lilly followed, allowing Loser to hop to the ground after her. When she rounded the end of the truck Cort was untying Samantha from the tailgate.

Lilly heard Joshua cry from the baby monitor. Time to get his bottle. "I'll be right back and you can tell me what happened."

Another grunt. Jogging to the house, Lilly grabbed a bottle from the fridge, placed it in the microwave, then dashed down the hall to get her baby.

When she exited the house a few minutes later with Joshua in her arms, happily smacking away on his bottle, she could hear Cort clanging around in the barn.

"What is that man doing?"

He was in fact busy fixing the wooden gate that used to work but had broken years ago. She hadn't needed the barn to be closed off and yes, if the gate worked, then Samantha would be limited to exiting into the pasture versus the yard.

But Samantha *liked* being in the yard.

"I should have fixed this weeks ago," he mumbled.

He was muttering again. Lilly hid a smile. He was so adorably cute when frustrated. An instant replay flashed through her memory of the first night in his barn when he'd been so mad at having lassoed a pregnant woman. That night standing in her cold barn, she'd wished for a man, any man. But God had sent her Cort. Not just any man, but the right man for her.

His blue eyes were screaming exasperation, flashing brilliantly in the clear February sunlight. She loved this man.

Yep, no mistaking it. She loved him.

"Do you have a hammer?"

She wanted to throw her arms around his neck and tell him how much he meant to her. She wanted to scare him to death if that was what it took to make him realize he was what she wanted.

"In fact, I do," she said instead as a giggle bubbled out of her. "And hello to you, too."

He looked up from the rusted hinge he was trying to pry loose from the gate and had the decency to look embarrassed by his rude behavior.

"Hello," he said politely, his gaze darting to Joshua. "He's growing."

"Babies do have a tendency to do that. Quickly."

He frowned, his eyes lingering on her baby before rising to her. Lilly's pulse picked up.

"Yeah, they grow up fast. So I'm told."

Lilly's heart swelled with sympathy for him. He so wanted children. She knew he loved Joshua, but... *please, Father, let him love me, too.* "Follow me, and I'll show you where the hammer is. Sorry I haven't fixed the fence. What did she do this time?" She could barely keep her voice steady.

"Instead of breaking and entering, she entered and broke my kitchen."

"Oh, no!" Lilly stopped and turned toward him. "I'm really sorry. I'll come help clean everything up and then I'll replace anything she broke."

"It's no big deal."

Lilly started toward the tack room, sidestepping when Loser scrambled past her. *What in the world!* Looking over her shoulder, she saw the dog skid to a stop beside Samantha, who was leaning against the door watching everything with big wide eyes. Her long ears twitched and her fuzzy tail swished in a rhythmic motion that reminded Lilly of a cat about to pounce on an unsuspecting mouse.

The little stinker was not in the least repentant about her activities. Well, that was about to change, because Cort was fixing the gate and Bob was going to weld her another gate at the entrance to her drive. That should curb Samantha's wanderings.

The small tack room was dark as Lilly stepped into it. "The light switch is that string there," she said, lifting her chin upward, indicating where Cort should reach up and pull.

He followed her into the cramped space and grabbed the string just as Lilly heard a familiar sound.

The creaking of the tack-room door as it slammed, shutting them inside.

"What!" Cort spun around as the mellow light illuminated the four walls and the sturdy wooden door.

Lilly didn't think much of it at first. The wind had blown it shut. But there was no wind.

Cort immediately twisted the handle and pushed, but it didn't budge. He put his broad shoulder to the door and put all his strength into it. Still the door held fast.

"Has this happened before?"

"No."

From beyond the door they could hear Loser barking, and then from just outside the door they heard the very familiar *Eee-haw* of Samantha.

*"Samantha!"*

# Chapter Twenty-Four

They coaxed, they begged, but nothing would budge the portly scalawag from her post in front of the door.

After Cort had pushed until there was no pushing left in him, Lilly handed Joshua over and peeked out the crack between the door and the wall. If she maneuvered herself just so, she could look over and see Samantha quietly lounging against the door munching on a piece of straw. Loser had settled down beside her with his chin resting on his crossed front paws.

"I'm telling you, it's as if they're at a sit-in, like protests people organize. You know, where the people sit down and won't budge until their requirements are met, and they get what they want." Lilly turned toward Cort, very aware of his nearness. Her heart clunked against her stomach at the picture he made as he ignored her every word. He was totally, beautifully lost in making faces at a contented Joshua.

So much for being desperate to escape, as he'd first acted.

Why, she'd have sworn he was terrified at the thought of being trapped in a small space with her.

After the first shock of their situation she was actually happy at the prospect.

Really, what could be better than being trapped with the two people she loved most in the world? Nothing. It was an answer to prayer—

*Oh, my goodness!*

She swallowed the yelp of happiness that almost escaped her and thanked the good Lord for this odd turn of events.

Cort's hat was pushed back from his forehead and his black hair peeked out from beneath it in a messy fringe. He really needed a haircut, but what else was new? He'd needed a haircut for a month and she'd grown used to the longer length. She'd grown used to everything about him. The way he smiled at her when he first saw her and the way he stuck his fingertips into the front pockets of his jeans. The way he strode across a room or an expanse as if he were on a mission. The way he laughed…oh, the way he laughed. It never ceased to bless her heart to hear the sound of his deep gravelly chuckle.

"I guess we just sit and wait," she said, ramming a hand through her hair. "Samantha has to move sometime. And if she doesn't, Bob is supposed to be here any moment."

Cort placed Joshua against his chest, letting the baby's head rest on his shoulder. He'd become so comfortable with Joshua.

"Bob? Are you dating him?" Cort glanced up from Joshua inquisitively.

"No. Bob's my friend. He's coming to build a fence down at the road."

"The two of you seemed to be close at the reception. I thought maybe—"

"We're friends, Cort," Lilly said firmly, then pushed away from the door and walked toward him. Her pulse pounded in her ears. Maybe the small space was the reason she thought she'd heard a hint of jealousy in his voice. She stopped just a step away from him.

"I was going to come and ask you again…I mean, we never did completely get the matter of your being Joshua's guardian settled."

"I told you I would. But nothing's going to happen to you."

"We don't know that. God doesn't promise us tomorrow. And as a good mother I have to look out for Joshua even in the event that I should be taken home to be with God."

"Why do you want me? Just because I helped deliver Joshua doesn't mean I'd be the best one to raise him."

"Yes, you helped deliver him and that gives you a bond with him. And with me. But I know you would raise him to love the Lord and to put God first. To always strive to walk with God. Those are the most important reasons." Lilly's voice broke. She willed away the tears stinging the back of her eyes. She wanted to be strong. She didn't want Cort's pity.

"How do you know that I would do that?" The question was just a hoarse whisper. His blue eyes were bright with bridled emotions. Emotions, Lilly knew, he'd tried to bury. Hopes he'd tried to tame.

She couldn't help herself—she touched his arm. The

one wrapped around her sweet baby. So secure. So reassuring.

"Cort, you had something terrible happen to you. You had your dreams stripped away because of something completely out of your control." She sniffed. "But you didn't turn away from God. You held on to Him. Even in your pain."

"But I was angry."

"Anger is a normal reaction. God expects and understands anger. I read yesterday the passage where it says be angry and sin not. I respect so much that you came to a quiet place to be still and to know what God had in store for you. Even in your anger you did what you needed to do to be in God's will."

*Please give me the right words, Lord.*

A tear slipped down her cheek. "He led you to me."

"Lilly, I can't—"

She placed three fingers on his lips. She had to say this. "The other reasons I want you to be Joshua's guardian are because you love him already and because you need him as much as he is going to need you. I'm—I'm not asking you to love me. I understand, in a weird way, that…" Her heart was breaking. Maybe she was reading God's will wrong. Maybe Cort was here only to be by Joshua's side. Maybe she was meant to be alone. Maybe the Tipps women had a destiny that was always going to stay the same. She hugged herself and stepped away from Cort.

Cort's heart was tearing apart. The look of hope and love in Lilly's expression wrapped around him, tearing at his resolve.

"Lilly, I can't give you more children." Didn't she understand that? "In the terms of the grannies, I'm worthless."

Lilly's eyes flashed. "My grannies, except for Granny Bunches, let bitterness color their world. Over time bitterness can warp people's thoughts, so much so that they can't see straight. So that they choose their own fate. I see that very clearly now. I don't want my life ruled by what the grannies told me. I want God's truths to color my world. In His terms you are priceless. And you are priceless…to me."

Cort took a step toward Lilly. He loved her. He'd been kidding himself. He couldn't let Lilly go without a fight. She was more precious to him than jewels. And Joshua…looking into Joshua's innocent face, Cort knew he wanted to be this child's daddy. He wanted to be the one to teach Joshua to tie his shoes. He wanted to hold Joshua's hand when they walked down to the pond to catch his first fish. He wanted to teach Joshua to ride a horse and he wanted Joshua to call him Dad. He wanted to be more than his guardian…. Lilly said he was priceless to God and to her. Could God have given him such a gift?

Looking into Lilly's beautiful face, knowing how special her spirit was, he felt hope flare inside him. He wanted to be the one who came home to Lilly at night. He wanted to love her for all of his days.

His pulse was tap-dancing against his temple. "I can't give you more children." He had to warn her again. She deserved so much more.

"I only want the children God intends me to have."

Lilly took a step toward him. Her eyes were bright and steady. "I love you, Cort. Could you love me?"

The break in her voice and the sudden questions in her eyes broke all his defenses. Did she think she was unlovable?

No hesitations now—Cort saw why God had brought him here. "I love you, Lilly. I've loved you from the beginning." He wrapped his free arm around her and pulled her close. She came willingly, and his world was right. As he held her and Joshua, his heart surged with emotion. "Lilly, I can't give you more children, but I promise you that I'll love you and Joshua with all my heart for as long as God will let me. And if you want to adopt more children, then we will."

Tears glistened in Lilly's eyes as Cort bent and touched his lips to hers. She wrapped her arms around his neck and he knew he was home. He was with the woman God had intended for him all along. He was blessed.

*Thank You, God.*

God had given him back his dream.

Lilly surrounded by children surfaced in his mind.

*Trust me.*

And he did. They were kissing when the tack-room door squeaked open. Cort and Lilly rested their foreheads together and turned to see Samantha with her big lips wrapped around the door handle like a kid with a lollipop stuck in its mouth. Loser sat on his haunches, his tail wiggling back and forth, his eyes expectant.

Cort kissed Lilly's ear. "I think that donkey had this planned all along."

Lilly touched Cort's face, for the first time allowing the sensation to fill her fully. "I think you might be right."

"Lilly, will you marry me?"

She kissed Joshua's cheek, then kissed Cort soundly on the lips. "I thought you'd never ask. Yes. Yes. And yes."

Samantha pawed the earth, drawing their attention as she lifted her chin, rolled back her lips, exposed her big pearly whites and let an earsplitting *Eee-haw* explode.

Loser yelped his agreement, nipped at Samantha's knee, then took off running with Samantha trotting after him.

Cort and Lilly burst into laughter.

"You do know we have to give Loser a new name?" Lilly said, gazing up into Cort's eyes.

Cort let her love wash over him, renewing him. "Oh, yeah. There are no losers around here anymore."

And then he kissed her.

## *Epilogue*



Lilly scanned the crowd outside the church, her gaze finding Cort holding Joshua close, like a pro. They were surrounded by a throng of well-wishers led by Norma Sue, Esther Mae and Adela. Lilly's heart swelled with pride at seeing *her guys* together.

The wedding had been over for an hour and she still couldn't believe she was Mrs. Cort Wells. Who'd a-thunk it? Lilly Tipps married—to the right man this time! "Well grannies, it looks like our luck has finally changed," she whispered to herself, knowing without doubt that Cort's love was forever hers.

"Talking to yourself already?"

Lilly turned to find her maid of honor grinning at her. "Hey, Lacy, you caught me chatting to the grannies about my new husband. Surely they're smiling right now."

"I'm sure they are. I know I am. I'm so happy for you. It's so cool how God brought the two of you together."

"Not too many women can boast that her hero rode to

her rescue on the back of a little donkey with a grumpy dog in tow." Lilly laughed, thinking back to the night Joshua was born.

Lacy laughed, too. "I don't think Joshua is going to believe us when we tell him the tale of his birth."

"Just think, Lacy. It's like I waited all these years and then Cort showed up just at the right time."

"God's time," Lacy added. "His timing is always perfect."

Lilly's heart skipped as Cort came striding up to stand beside her. Lacy immediately snatched Joshua away and started making faces at him as he gazed at her frilly blond hair with wide eyes.

"What's perfect?" Cort asked, giving Lilly a lingering kiss.

"This," she said, spreading her arms wide to encompass the gathering of friends. "I feel like I'm in a fairy tale." Her eyes brimmed with tears of happiness. "I love you so much, Cort. I never dreamed this could really happen to me." He put his arms around her and drew her against him in a solid embrace that she never wanted to end.

"I was thinking the same thing," he said. "I never dreamed my life could be so blessed. You make me the happiest man alive, Lilly. Are you ready to load up and head out?"

"I am so ready. Are you sure Samantha and Lucky will be okay while we're gone?"

"Yes, they'll be fine. Bob will check on them every day. Now that Samantha is back on her old stomping grounds, she's as happy as a clam. And Loser—I mean

Lucky—is like a new dog. He's so happy to have a friend that he won't even notice we're gone. I still can't believe you wanted to combine our honeymoon with a horse show."

Lilly touched his cheek. "Why not? I'm looking forward to seeing your world, and Oklahoma seems like a good place to start. Besides, I'm getting to meet all of your family. Just think, Cort, we're a family."

"Family," he said, tracing the outline of her face with his fingertips. "I do like the sound of that, Mrs. Wells."

"Yep, kind of a weird family," Lacy chimed in, holding Joshua high in the air as she looked up at his cherubic face. "Samantha, Lucky, Lilly, Cort and baby makes five. That's right, you cute little fella, I have the feeling that you're going to have one unusual upbringing."

Lilly laughed at that bit of insight and leaned her head against Cort's shoulder, loving the way she felt wrapped in her husband's strong arms. "One thing's for certain," she said, tilting her head and meeting his laughing eyes. "Our life won't be boring."

Cort smiled that smile of his that touched Lilly all the way to the tips of her tingling toes. "As long as it's with you, Lilly, it sounds perfect to me."

\* \* \* \* \*

Dear Reader,

I hope you enjoyed reading Lilly and Cort's story. The idea for this book started building in my mind the day I went to a friend's home to dye her horse black... yes, I dyed a horse black from the tip of his ears to the tops of his hooves! While there, I encountered the *real* Samantha. She was a bumpy little burro full of mischief and fun, and the moment I watched her in action, I knew I was going to create a story around a character similar to her. My sons were small back then and loved dogs and donkeys, among other animals, so I created Samantha and Loser specifically to make them laugh. Each night at bedtime I would read the scenes involving the pesky critters, and their laughter still warms my heart when I think about it.

I hope God blesses you in a special way today and that I was able to be a part of that with the telling of this story in some small way. Until next time I pray that through all of life you hold fast to the Lord. You can contact me at P.O. Box 1125, Madisonville, Texas 77864, and please visit my website, www.debraclopton.com.

In Christ's Love,

Debra Clopton

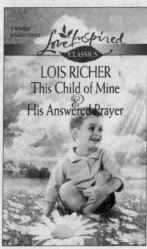
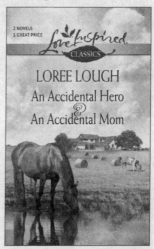

# REQUEST YOUR FREE BOOKS!

## 2 FREE INSPIRATIONAL NOVELS
## PLUS 2
## FREE
## MYSTERY GIFTS

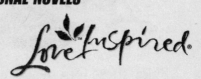

LIREG11

*When David Foster comes across an unconscious woman on his friends' doorstep, she evokes his natural born instinct to take care of her.*

*Read on for a sneak peek of A BABY BY EASTER by Lois Richer, available April, only from Love Inspired.*

"You could marry Davy, Susannah. He would look after you. He looks after me." Darla's bright voice dropped. "He had a girlfriend. They were going to get married, but she didn't want me. She wanted Davy to send me away."

David almost groaned. How had his sister found out? He'd been so careful—

"I'm sure your brother is very nice, Darla. And I'm glad he's taking care of you. But I don't want to marry him. I don't want to marry anyone," Susannah said. "I only came to Connie's to see if I could stay here for a while."

"But Davy needs someone to love him. Somebody else but me." Darla's face crumpled, the way it always did before she lost her temper. David was about to step forward when Susannah reached out and hugged his sister.

"Thank you for offering, Darla. You're very generous. I think your brother is lucky to have you love him." Susannah brushed the bangs from Darla's sad face. "If I end up staying with Connie, I promise I'll see you lots. We could go to that playground you talked about."

Susannah's foster sister Connie breezed into the room. "I'm so glad to see you, Suze. But you're ill." She leaned back to study the circles of red now dotting Susannah's cheeks. "You're very pale. I think you need to see a doctor."

"I'm pregnant." The words burst out of Susannah in a rush. Then she lifted her head and looked David straight in the eye, as if awaiting his condemnation.

But it wasn't condemnation David felt. It was hurt. He'd prayed so long, so hard, for a family, a wife, a child. And he'd lost all chance of that—not once, but twice.

How could God deny him the longing of his heart, yet give this ill woman a child she was in no way prepared to care for?

*Although David has given up on his dream of having a family, will he offer to help Susannah in her time of need? Find out in A BABY BY EASTER, available April, only from Love Inspired.*

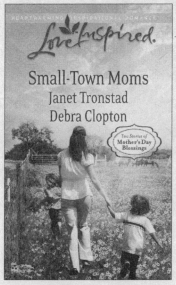